the
Caretaker

the Caretaker

APRIL C. ROYER

No Agenda Publishing, LLC
P.O. Box 565, Ooltewah, TN 37363
NoAgendaPublishing.com

The Caretaker

The Book of the Caretaker
Book 1

No Agenda Publishing, LLC
P.O. Box 565, Ooltewah, TN 37363
NoAgendaPublishing.com

This is a work of fiction. Names, characters, places and incidents either are the product of the author's imagination or are used fictitiously, and any resemblance to actual persons living or dead, events or locales is entirely coincidental.

Summary: Morgan is called at just sixteen to serve her country of humans and dragons as its Caretaker, using her magic to nurture, heal, and protect as they face an enemy empowered by dark magic. To serve them, she must survive. To save them, she must fight.

ISBN 978-1-7320058-0-8 (Hardback Edition)
ISBN 978-1-7320058-1-5 (Paperback Edition)
ISBN 978-1-7320058-2-2 (Electronic Edition)

Library of Congress Control Number 2018901840

Cover and interior page design: MLargent Creative
Cover calligraphy constructed from an alphabet by Arthur Baker

Follow the author

AprilCRoyer.com

First Edition
10 9 8 7 6 5 4 3 2 1

FOR MORGAN

Thank you for inspiring me to create a world
worthy of your beautiful heart and formidable spirit.

I am blessed to be your mother,
and honored to be your friend.

Acknowledgments

The Book of the Caretaker Series has been a work in progress for many years, and I am profoundly thankful to all who read, listened, critiqued, and encouraged. Since the first days of stumbling my way into Chemerie, I have been blessed with many special people who have supported me at every step.

Special thanks are owed to the Morgans, MoRo and MoPo, for the hours of listening to me read the story aloud. Your emotional investment in the characters, and the eager interest you brought each time you curled up on the sofa to hear the newest parts of the story, were the most amazing motivation and encouragement I could have hoped for. I am forever grateful.

Kathy Ingle, for unyielding support and encouragement at every turn, and for accepting my love for winks, smirks, and semicolons.

Michael Pugh, for going along with me when I lost my way and for not saying, "I told you so" when I came to my senses.

Stephanie Royer, for being an amazing sister-in-law, for fighting for Daniel, and for our shared love of the semicolon. I expect that same ferocity as we attack the rest of the series.

Libby Farrelly, for your constant support as one of the first readers of the first (and very rough) draft, all the way to being among the last editing and critique group. You are an amazing friend!

My husband, Adam, for his patience with my tendency to get lost in the stories in my head, and for tireless encouragement to keep working toward publication even when life did its best to derail the process, again and again.

Michael Largent, for always going above and beyond every request and for his unending patience in working with a strong-willed debut author. You truly are a blessing.

Pronunciation Guide

THE WORLDS OF THE CARETAKER

Alerian . . . . ä·LAIR·ē·un   Chemerie . . . . . KIM·er·ē
Arshek . . . . äR·shek   Erion . . . . AIR·ē·on
Berios . . . . BER·ē·ōs   Perian . . . . PEER·ē·un

MAIN CHARACTERS

Alec . . . . AL·lek   Irika . . . . AIR·rik·ä
Brya . . . . BREE·yä   Josef . . . . JOH·sef
Burke . . . . Burk   Kisik . . . . KIS·sik
Christina . . . . . Kris·TEEN·ä   Kyan . . . . KEE·yuhn
Daniel . . . . DAN·yuhl   Maric . . . . MAIR·rik
Emma . . . . EM·muh   Morgan . . . . . . MOHR·guhn
GranMay . . . . . gran·mey   Nikolas . . . . NIK·oh·lahs
Harrick . . . . . . HAIR·rik   Willow . . . . WIL·loh

DRAGONS

Asira . . . . ä·SEAR·ä   Manook . . . . . . mä·NUUK
Balia . . . . BÄL·ya   Menkar . . . . MEN·kär
Brit . . . . brit   Nulian . . . . NOO·lē·un
Drieden . . . . DRĪ·den   Sirzi . . . . SIERT·zē
Falin . . . . FÄ·lin   Tagien . . . . TÄ·jin
Gerzin . . . . GAIRT·zen   Yatu . . . . YÄ·too
Hirk . . . . hərk   Zetia . . . . ZET·ē·ä
Hytha . . . . HĪ·thä   Zirath . . . . zeer·RÔTH
Lirpa . . . . LEER·pä

The Quickening

MORGAN SPRINTED past the barn, leapt onto the back porch, burst through the door, and slid to a stop against the kitchen table.

"Daniel! Where are they?" Her brother cursed wildly as he wiped sweet tea off his guitar and himself. "GranMay and Father, are they here?"

"No, they're at the store. Why? Wha—, What happened?" he said as he saw the nasty scratches covering her left side.

"I wish I knew," she said as she paced the kitchen while wringing her hands. "I was having a great run, then … I woke up in a ditch. Now, my head is pounding, my hands are stinging like I played with bees, and … I'm really amped."

"Yeah, I see that," he said as he handed her a bottle of water. She downed half of it as she looked out the window over the backyard and barn.

"I told you they aren't here. What are you looking for?"

"I don't know! I ran back here as fast as I could. It was like something was telling me to hurry, to get back here, like something was wrong. Did anything happen?"

"Nothing, except you flying through the door babbling like a tweaker," he said with a smirk as he watched her pace. "Did you try an energy drink again?"

She rolled her eyes and turned the water bottle up again to finish it as she headed for the stairs. She paused on the third step and backed up as she turned and scanned the house with focus on the library.

"What?" Daniel asked as he glanced between her and his effort to wipe off his shirt.

"What is that?"

"What?"

"The humming … the weird humming music. Don't you hear it?"

"No, I really don't," he said as he frowned and moved toward her.

"Ugh, this is ridiculous," she said as she squinted and rubbed her temples. "I'm gonna go shower. Ask GranMay to come up when she gets back, OK?"

"Sure."

She started up the stairs, but stumbled with a curse as the humming shifted to a thunderous song of a thousand deep voices singing in harmony. It was beautiful but so painful she could hardly breathe. When she stood to take the next step, her head spun, and she pitched backward.

Daniel caught her just in time and eased her to the hallway floor. She flinched at the sting his touch caused and swatted his hands away. He tried to tell her something as he glanced back toward the kitchen, but she could hear nothing beyond the percussive music.

As the painful sensations reached her shoulders they shifted to a fierce burn that intensified as they progressed. Fiery pain exploded through her entire body the instant the two paths met in the center of her chest. Her body trembled and sweat soaked her clothes as she rolled to her side and curled into a tense ball.

All of her focus went to drawing the next breath and staying conscious until her father scooped her up like a small child. He carried her into the library to lay her on a small sofa. Her grandmother settled beside her and reached out to cradle her face. Morgan tensed, then gasped as their skin touched.

She held her grandmother's calm, confident eyes as a soothing sensation washed over her, quieting the deafening music, and quenching the fiery pain. Her body relaxed, and she took a deep, shaky breath as her grandmother smiled and swept tears from her cheeks.

"You know, don't you, GranMay?" she said with a hoarse, weak voice as she fought to stay awake. "You know what's happening to me, don't you?

"Yes, my girl, I do," GranMay said with a smile. "Your Quickening has begun, my dear. It is quite early, and intense, but the sensations are unmistakable. It is time for you to know who you truly are."

HOURS LATER, Morgan woke to her father and brother whispering across the room.

"Hey," Daniel said as he smiled and moved her way. "How do you feel?"

"Dazed and confused," she said with a sigh as she sat up.

"So, perfectly normal then," he said with a smile as their father knelt beside her.

"May I?" her father asked as he offered his hand. She slid her hand into his and shivered as tingles moved up her arm. As he caressed her palm with his thumbs, a faint opalescent shimmer was visible for a fraction of a second before vanishing again.

"What are you doing? What is that?" she said as she and Daniel both leaned in to get a closer look. Her father smiled as she flinched from a sharper tingle, then lifted her in a crushing hug. "Father, seriously! What is going on?"

"Oh, my girl, I know you are confused. But I assure you we have good reason to be so very happy," her father said as he kissed her forehead. "This is a very special day for all of us. It is time for you to receive the gift of your Mothers'. Please have a seat, and we will begin answering some of your questions."

She gave Daniel a lifted eyebrow as she sat down to watch GranMay remove something wrapped in a blue-gray silky material from a locked cabinet. GranMay shifted the fabric away to reveal a thick book with no title or markings on its rough leathery cover. Morgan rubbed her tingling hands and shivered as GranMay brought the book closer.

"What is it?" she asked as GranMay offered her the huge book.

The instant her fingers touched the book she gripped it tight and took in a sharp breath. Her skin heated, and the tingling in her hands became a sharp prickle as she pulled it into her lap. The feelings of urgency she had felt growing for a week became fierce and focused—she must read!

When she started to open it, her father placed his hand across hers and met her glare with soft eyes.

"Not yet, my dear," he said as he caressed her hands to coax them off the book. "You are not quite ready. We only wanted you to feel the power of the Book so you could better accept the truths we are about to explain."

GranMay tried to remove the book from her lap, but she held it firm. As GranMay laid a hand to her arm, the anxiety fell away, and she let go. She wiped her sweaty face on her sleeve and returned to rubbing her palms while forcing deep breaths. GranMay placed the book and its wrapping on the coffee table and sat down beside her.

"How can a book make me feel like that? And how can you ease both pain and anxiety just by touching me?" Before GranMay could answer, she turned to her father and added, "Did you say Mother left this to me?" Her father smiled and looked to GranMay.

"He said it is the gift of your Mothers', plural," GranMay said as she brushed her fingers across the cover of the book. "This is the Book of the Caretaker." Intricate markings of silver lines appeared across the Book at her touch, then faded when she lifted her hand away.

"It is a history of the women who have served as Caretaker to the dragons of Chemerie. You are destined to be a Caretaker, as were your mother, I, and all of our mothers before us. What you just felt was the magic within you responding to the magic of the Book."

Morgan stared at the Book of the Caretaker for many seconds then reached out to touch it and swallow hard as she felt the strange sensations again.

"Everything you just said should sound insane, but … I know it's not. I mean, I should be freaking out after all of this, but … " She managed a small smile as she looked up at her grandmother. "Somehow, I'm good. You just said magic and dragons, and I feel the truth in them as if … as if I've always known they exist. I don't really get it … but I want to."

When she turned to her father she found him struggling to hold back tears. That sight unnerved her more than anything else thus far. He smiled then nodded to GranMay as a single tear trailed down his cheek. GranMay's grip on her hand made her return her focus to her.

"For centuries the women of our family have served the dragons of Chemerie as Caretaker, acting as midwife, nursemaid, mentor, and friend. The magic you carry will guide you and allow you to fulfill this role. You must learn about the role and choose to accept the duty of your own will." GranMay paused as she glanced at the others, then held her eyes with a stern expression. "When you choose to accept the duty, as I am confident you will, you will take your mother's place in Chemerie, and she will return here to be with your father and me."

The room was silent as Morgan pulled her hands away and tensed. "Are you seriously saying our mother is alive?" With a nod from GranMay, she stood and moved across the room. She rested her shaking hands on the windowsill for a minute before turning back to them.

"I don't want to believe it because that means you have

both lied to us every time we have discussed her, and been wholly convincing every time. I don't want to think that you would do that to us." A pause to breathe let her see the truth of it etched on their faces. "Our whole lives you have lectured us on integrity, honor, and trust while lying with every breath!" She stepped closer to hold her father's eyes. "You let me believe my mother died giving life to me!" She felt tears filling her eyes and left the room before they could fall.

"Morgan, wait … " her father called. She paused on the stairs but did not go back.

"Let her be, Nikolas. The anger must lessen for the truth to take hold. She must come to terms with this herself," GranMay said.

"May, she is only sixteen. Can she really do this?"

"She must," GranMay said.

Morgan took the stairs two at the time and closed herself in her room as her emotions exploded.

"HEY, CAN I come in?" Daniel called from Morgan's bedroom door. He had the good sense to leave her be for two hours before checking in.

"Yeah."

He offered a glass of tea as he joined her on the window seat. She drained half the glass then gave it back.

"You OK?"

"Magic, dragons, our mother alive … it's just ridiculous," she said as she gazed at the mountains around their house with unfocused eyes. "Yet, I know it's true."

"Ridiculous, true, and awesome," he said as he kicked her legs with a smirk. "Oh, hey, you don't know the best part.

You will be happy to know that you have been blessed with my company in this adventure! While you are the Caretaker, I am your primary protector, and I'll be with you through whatever mess you find yourself in."

"Sweet! I can blame you for anything I do wrong," she said as she kicked him back. "You clearly know all about this, so tell me where we're headed. I've never heard of Chemerie."

"I'm not surprised. It's a bit of a trip." His grin broadened as he said, "Chemerie is a country on a planet called Erion. We get there by way of your magic somehow."

"Good grief!" she said rubbing her face hard. "Dragons, magic, and now space travel! This is insane!" They both laughed for a moment but went quiet as they heard mumbled voices from downstairs.

"Morgan, you have to forgive Father and GranMay for the lie about Mother's death. Just think about it for a second. You know a child could never understand, accept, or protect the secrets of Chemerie. There was no other way for them to deal with this until your Quickening. And, it's always been done this way."

"Understanding they had to doesn't make it hurt less. It kills me to know they lied like that. And, what's worse, I feel like a complete idiot because I never suspected. I never saw it in their eyes or heard it in their words." She stared out the window a moment as she sighed then looked at him again. "You fooled me too, big brother. You didn't learn about this today, did you?"

"No, I found out the semester I dropped out of college and came home. I became so stressed out I couldn't concentrate; thought I was losing it. But then the anxiety eased as soon as

I got home. Father explained enough for me to understand and embrace the connection to you. Surely you noticed."

"Hmm, let's see … you left for college an annoying big brother interested only in his music and his motorcycles. And now you are sitting on my window seat looking at me with honest concern. Yeah, I noticed."

Another wave of Quickening made her cringe and shiver. She took a few deep breaths as she rubbed her palms to ease the sharp tingling in them.

"Does rubbing them help?" Daniel said as he slid closer to take one of her hands.

The instant his hand touched hers, she was hit by intense worry. Her breath caught in her throat as she realized the emotion she felt was not hers … it was Daniel's. It was in that moment that she accepted the reality of her magic and the amazing new path her life was about to take.

"GRANMAY, FATHER, I'm sorr— "

"You are forgiven. Now come give me a hug," GranMay said with open arms as Morgan entered the kitchen with Daniel. She moved into the familiar safety of GranMay's embrace and sighed as she relaxed against her.

"So, will we get to meet Mother before the exchange happens?"

"Yes, Christina will be the one to complete your Quickening and training in Chemerie before she returns here."

"Why don't we all just live there together as a family?"

Her father pulled her to sit in his lap and hugged her as he answered.

"This method was put in place to ensure the survival of

the Caretaker line. If we were to all live there, a well-executed attack could kill us all. You must understand, my dear, while we serve the country of Chemerie, there are many others that inhabit Erion. Some of those inhabitants would see the people of Chemerie fall and have our dragon brethren enslaved. Our family has accepted the hardship of separation to ensure the survival of our brethren in Chemerie."

By the time he finished talking she was near tears because she felt his pride and passion through his touch. She smiled at him and then at GranMay as she considered his words and quelled the tears.

"This duty is one our family has given its life to for hundreds of years. You both know I could never refuse it. I'm ready to learn."

EVERYONE ATE DINNER then gathered in the library.

"GranMay, I get why I have to live apart from Mother. But, I don't see why I'd leave the safety of Earth before having a daughter. Why would I risk ending the line before I get married and have children?"

"Your logic has a flaw. You see, only the union of a Son of Chemerie and a daughter of the Caretaker line will transfer the gift to the child," GranMay said.

"You are a Son of Chemerie?" Morgan asked her father.

"Of course, we are all children of Chemerie and Erion. I came here to raise and protect you and your brother just after your birth. GranMay taught me to fit in here on Earth. You will serve, and in time, you will marry. Then, when you have a daughter, your husband will come here with her and her siblings," he said.

Daniel broke in to say, "But, I'll stay there with you. My job is to support and protect you, so you can do your job."

She nodded then paced the room as she thought. She laid a hand to her stomach as it started to ache.

"It is a hard truth you have just come to," GranMay said. "It is that truth which makes the decision to accept the duty so difficult."

"To give up my children and my husband … it's unimaginable now. It will be near impossible when I'm holding a newborn daughter in my arms. GranMay, how did you ever do that?"

GranMay did not answer and dropped her eyes to her hands folded in her lap.

"She did her duty, and her brethren honor her for it," her father said as he reached over and took GranMay's hand.

"I'm sorry, GranMay," Morgan said. GranMay smiled and nodded, but her father still had a slight scowl.

"Your magic will afford you a profound love and trust for your husband," he said. "It is an honor for him to serve you and his country in this way." He softened his tone and added, "Knowing that he will be here to protect and love your children will make it easier for you to let go."

She held her tongue and just nodded.

"You will not have to endure the pain alone," her father said as he moved to her. "Daniel will help you through it. And, you will have built a relationship with the dragons that is as deep as that of mother and child. They will all support you."

She nodded again then dropped her head against his chest. GranMay moved to them and lifted her chin.

"When your daughter reaches her Quickening, she will join you in Chemerie. The magic you share will allow you to bond with her in ways no other human can conceive. Then, when she is ready to fulfill her role, you will be reunited with your husband and parents here on Earth."

GranMay reached up to wipe the hint of a tear from Morgan's eye and moved her hair behind her ear before adding, "When your own granddaughter is born, you will care for her from infancy to Quickening. Your connection to her will be enhanced by the magic you share." She cupped her face between her hands and said, "It is a powerful and precious bond, I assure you." Morgan took a deep breath as she felt a strong rush of love accompany GranMay's words.

"I agree, but now I will have to say goodbye to you for years."

"Yes, I will stay here with your father."

Morgan kissed her cheek and held her tight for a moment before leaning back to ask, "You said my Quickening came early. Do you know why?"

"No, I do not, my dear. I have never known it to happen so early. I will admit that it worries me."

Mother and the Queen

THE NEXT DAY, Morgan sat on the window seat of her bedroom flush and trembling from another intense round of Quickening sensations when GranMay came to ease her pain.

"The images flicker when the tingling is the worst," she said as she studied her palms, "But I still can't make it out." "They will be visible when you are on Erion in the presence of all the magic there. Once your Quickening is complete, they will be visible anytime you are near another source of our magic. In fact, it does not have to be a great deal of magic at all. The traces of magic present within any child of Chemerie will reveal them," GranMay said as she folded her hands in her lap.

"Then yours…Show me, let me see yours!"

"Absolutely not!" GranMay said as she laughed and hid

her hands. "I want you to feel the wonder of seeing your own when you return home."

Morgan stared at her for a second, then said, "Pride."

"What do you mean, my dear?"

"I just felt your pride when you said 'home' even though we weren't touching. That's how you've always known how to comfort me. You could feel what I was feeling."

"That is impressive. Your Quickening is moving along well indeed. At this rate, you will soon be able to hear my thoughts as well," GranMay said.

"What?! You've been able to hear my thoughts my whole life? About everything and everyone?"

"I have only listened when appropriate. I never eavesdropped if I did not think you needed help. And no, I did not interfere in your relationships." She quieted as she added, "Except when warranted, of course."

With that last comment, Morgan received a hint of mischievousness from her grinning grandmother and responded with a look of complete annoyance.

AFTER MANY DAYS of difficult Quickening, Morgan was allowed to open the Book of the Caretaker.

"What language is this, GranMay?" she said as Daniel leaned over her shoulder to inspect the strange symbols covering the pages.

"Looks like hieroglyphics to me," Daniel said. "Translating that should be fun." She smiled as she scanned and turned the pages. "Can you read it?"

She nodded but continued to focus on her reading without looking up.

"It is a phonetic representation of the language of the dragon written in an ancient script. The magic within her allows her to read it, just as it allows her to understand their language when spoken," GranMay said.

Morgan tucked her feet under her and snuggled into the sofa with the Book. She read only a few moments before Daniel nudged her.

"Care to share with the less fortunate?"

"Sorry," she said. She started reading aloud but stopped at his loud laughter.

"I assume that is dragon-tongue. It sounds cool, but I have no idea what you just said," he said. "English please."

"I didn't even realize I wasn't speaking English. Weird! I'll just give you the highlights then. It's written as a diary, but most of what I have read is a dry history of events and facts. There is not much personal stuff or detailed descriptions." She continued to read the rather vague record and pieced together a picture of the world they were about to join.

"It sounds like Erion is a much younger planet than Earth and not yet damaged by pollution. With that clean environment, the physical aging of people there is much slower than we're used to. While Chemerians grow to adult size in about the same time as people here, they live much longer. By the look of the numbers I've found, it looks like living past a hundred and fifty is common."

"That's awesome. But it does mean we're going to have a hard time judging age. Every adult we meet will seem younger than they really are," Daniel said.

"Yep, and it says Chemerians' intellectual growth is faster

too. That explains our graduating with honors two years early."

"That and the strict study time," Daniel said with a wink at GranMay.

She read for a long time and was flipping pages with a frown when Daniel cleared his throat.

"Sorry, but this is annoying," she said. "The Book stresses the necessity of the Caretaker's magic within Chemerie, but there's no description of the magic's origin or of how the human-dragon relationship was initiated."

"You said it's like a diary. Is there a family tree?"

"Not mapped out, but I've tried to follow it back a ways. One weird thing is I've found only two instances of a Caretaker having more than one daughter. In one instance, the second daughter was born after her mother returned to Earth and did not carry the gift of magic. One Caretaker suggests it was the absence of the dragon's magic during the pregnancy, and another thought it to be a limit of the magic itself in passing to only one child.

"The second instance was a brief comment about the birth of twin girls. It is just a few lines here early in the Book," she said as she found the page. "It just reports their birth, it doesn't say if one or both received magic and there is little about their term of service."

"Get to the dragons, girl. What are they like?"

"Well, they aren't described. It refers to them by name, tells about many who were of particular importance because of their actions or strong connections with a Caretaker, and refers to the dragons' leaders called the Council of Elders. As for appearance, I can tell you there are many different scale colors mentioned with reference to richer coloring in the older dragons."

"What about size? How big do they get?"

"No idea. Sounds like they grow fast their first few years, but I haven't found anything about how large they get or how long they live," she said. "I would say they get pretty big if humans ride them though."

"Ride them! Cool! That has got to be incredible. I still haven't wrapped my head around actual living dragons. And now we're talkin' about flying with them."

GranMay and their father were exchanging grins and glances as they played chess and listened in. Morgan knew it pointless to ask for more information from either. They wanted them to be surprised.

After a few more minutes of reading and page-flipping, she popped up and slapped Daniel's leg.

"Sweet! You will be able to talk to the dragons too. They understand English!"

"Awesome!"

"Oh," she said as she kept flipping pages.

"What?"

"They only speak dragon-tongue aloud, so their responses to you will be limited to nods and simple gestures like that. Only the Caretakers can communicate with them in a meaningful way."

"How meaningful? Are they intelligent like humans?" Both GranMay and Nikolas gave him a sharp look before dropping their eyes back to the game board. "Yikes, struck a nerve with that one," he added in a whisper.

"I see why. They're very intelligent. They actually pass

ancestral knowledge via their DNA, so a hatchling carries all the knowledge of its ancestors. As they get older they can use more and more of it. That explains the level of respect the Caretakers seem to have for the Elder dragons." She looked to GranMay and asked, "Is that true of the other Chemerians? Do the rulers of Chemerie respect them that way too?" GranMay nodded without lifting her eyes from the game, then said, "Checkmate, my dear Nikolas." Morgan and Daniel both laughed at the surprised expression on their father's face. Morgan did not fail to notice how GranMay had avoided her question.

She watched Daniel replace their father with a challenging smile to GranMay, then refocused on the Book in her lap.

"What?" she said, sitting upright. "You have got to be kidding! That's the biggest bunch of horse sh— " She bit her tongue as she closed the Book with a snap, then gave GranMay a sharp glare before leaving the library.

SHE WAS STILL fuming after taking an extra-long run. Daniel was waiting for her outside their barn.

"So, what made you lose it?"

"My MATE!"

"Your what?"

"Exactly! It seems I do not have a choice in who I marry. The magic has already chosen my 'magical mate' for me."

"Oh!" Daniel said. "Well, has it always been done that way?"

She nodded as she walked around him letting her muscles cool and her heart rate fall.

"Then it can't be too bad. Father and GranMay seem to

have loved their spouses. We never saw them together, but we've seen it in their eyes and heard it in their voices when they tell stories about them."

"Don't act like this wouldn't tick you off! Neither of us is about being told who to love!"

"You're right. I would be ticked if it were another person choosing for me. But, that's not what you said," he said, stepping in front of her to get her focus. "You're talking about the magic that is inside you being involved in your decision. It's part of you. So why wouldn't it be part of your feelings about who you marry?"

She paced a moment longer before stopping with a sigh. "So, you think I would have chosen the same man without the magic's involvement, and that the magic will simply make the connection to him stronger."

"I think that's how you need to look at it. Otherwise, you're gonna to be out here runnin' for a couple more days."

She smirked then clasped her hands under her chin and batted her eyes as she used a syrupy southern drawl to say, "Oh, my wise protector. Your wisdom has eased my spirit. How can I ever repay you?"

Daniel took off after her as she cackled and tried to dodge him. She was soon hurled into their pond with a huge splash. They commenced a grand wrestling match that left them soaked, muddy, and laughing.

SHE GRADUATED from high school the next week and said goodbye to her friends. Her story was that she was going to a private university overseas on a swimming scholarship. This way no one would be suspicious when she disappeared.

Thankfully, she had never had a serious boyfriend. She had never made time and had never met anyone who interested her that much.

Her part-time job at a horse ranch was harder for her to leave. Her employer hated to see her go because she had been able to work with many horses that had reputations of being unmanageable. The horses were her friends, and she loved them as much as any she had at school.

As she walked away from the barn for the last time all of the horses whinnied and pawed the ground. Her heart ached as she left them behind.

While she walked home, her thoughts lingered on Gran-May and her father. Her magic did nothing to lessen her heartache as she fought to accept living without them.

THAT NIGHT she curled up with GranMay and the Book of the Caretaker in the library. Soon after starting to read, she found herself singing a song in the dragon language.

"The Book is teaching you much more than the words written on the pages. It allows you access to the more profound abilities the magic provides." With that cryptic comment, GranMay kissed her forehead and left her alone.

She returned to reading and again found herself singing. This time she heard another voice joining in. A rush of comforting sensations washed over her and her eyes grew heavy.

An image soon formed in her mind. It was a blurry image of a woman sitting on the steps of a stone gazebo. As the image cleared, she realized the woman was singing along with her.

When GranMay returned to the library, she found her

staring across the room with tears streaming down her face.

"Yes, my dear. That was your mother singing with you. It is almost time for you to go to her."

THE NEXT MORNING Morgan found Daniel in the barn practicing a rapid series of powerful movements with a handsome metal sword. He had been working hard on his fighting skills and now moved with a fluidity and grace she would never have thought possible.

"Your face is tellin' me we're about to be off on this grand adventure," he said with a smile.

"Yeah, it's time. My Quickening sensations chilled out a few days ago, then last night, everything amped up again. I can feel the pull like an ache," she said as she watched her palm glow slightly as her thumb swept over it. "I don't know if I'm ever gonna feel ready to be a Caretaker of dragons. But, it's time to find out."

"Well, I'm ready if you are," he said as he twirled the sword with a smirk.

She tried but failed to match his smile as he placed the sword into the silk-lined box.

"Father's?"

"Yep, from his days as a Knight." "The metal is gorgeous. What is it?"

"Not sure, it's mined on Erion. Father says it's never been nicked or needed to be polished. Just wipe off the funk and go shank the next guy."

"I'm so struggling to see you as a Knight. Sir Daniel!" she said with a small laugh as she glanced back toward their house to wave at their father. Daniel laughed a little too but was quiet as she met his eyes again.

"Listen, I'm usually a big kid with you, but I need you to know that I take this very seriously, and have no intention of letting you down. They called you way early. And, yeah, that's probably gonna get you some doubters over there. But not me. I won't treat you like a kid. I'm hoping you'll trust me enough to confide in me and let me help you navigate this bizarre new life. I may not talk as formal as Father, and expect to seem like a massive redneck in Chemerie, but I will protect you, little sister."

"I know," she said as she laid a hand to his chest and smiled. "I can see how serious you are, and I've felt it more every day since my magic awoke. I can definitely feel it right now." She took her hand off of him and massaged it to relive the tingle as she glanced back toward the house again. "Knowing I'll have you with me is the only thing keeping me from falling apart right now. I just can't imagine not having them."

He put an arm around her shoulders to squeeze her against him and ushered her toward the house.

"Let's get goin' girl. I'm ready to see some dragons and meet our mother!"

THEY RETURNED to the house to find their father and GranMay bearing presents.

Daniel opened his to find a magnificent sword and scabbard much like that of their father's. He also received a handsome black uniform with deep purple accents including a beautifully embroidered dragon on the back.

Morgan's gift was an intricately carved amulet made

of the same metal as the swords. The image was that of a dragon with wings partially extended as it clutched a large egg-shaped blue stone with all four feet. The dragon was framed by a hexagon that had small round diamonds at each corner. She also received a uniform with a longer coat and more elaborate embellishments that made it distinctively feminine. There were small dragons on each arm and a large one that wrapped around her waist, up her back, and ended with the head hanging over one shoulder. Each also received a pair of sturdy black boots to complete the ensemble.

The family all ate a huge breakfast that started with excited discussion. As they finished, the room was quiet.

"All right now, I will have no more of this moping around," GranMay said as she handed them each a simple leather messenger bag. "Go shower, then pack a small number of your clothing items. Soon you will not need them, but having them will make the adjustment easier. You may not take anything else, such as toiletries, trinkets, or any of those electronic gadgets."

"Wait, what?" Daniel said with wide eyes.

"Are you serious?" Morgan said.

"I get why I can't take my motorcycle, but...my music? My guitar?"

"Son, I explained that there is no electricity there," their father said with a smirk. "You will have ample opportunity to use your musical talents with the finely crafted instruments made by your Chemerian brethren."

When they both started to speak again, GranMay lifted her head and both shushed.

"Go on now," she said.

"Yes ma'am," they said as they stood. They were quiet until out of earshot then resumed their complaints to each other as they climbed the stairs.

ONCE OVER THE SHOCK, they did as they were told and reported back downstairs looking very sharp. While putting on the uniforms both had noticed the bright green gems sewn into the coats as the dragon's eyes. They were the exact color of their own eyes, a trait that had gotten both of them marked attention. She looked him up and down and raised an eyebrow.

"You look like a Knight already. It suits you."

He actually blushed a bit as he leaned in to examine her amulet closer.

"And that definitely suits you."

They followed their father and GranMay to the library to watch as he locked the door and she unlocked the book cabinet. She turned to Morgan and smiled.

"The Book of the Caretaker belongs with the youngest in the Caretaker line. You have learned much from this already, and you will learn much more as you continue to consult it during your many years of service to our country. When you are ready, you will add your own part of history to it." She slipped it into Morgan's bag and touched her cheek before turning to nod to their father. "Alright, Nikolas, it's time we show them the way home."

Their father locked the book cabinet then pulled it to the side. GranMay stepped forward and pulled a brick out, revealing a hidden plate with a carving matching Morgan's amulet. When their grandmother laid her hand to it, they heard a click. Their father stepped forward to lean into the wall and reveal both a door and a hidden stairway.

Morgan and Daniel exchanged grins then followed their father down the curving stone staircase and into a circular chamber lit with a series of candles around the walls. A single line of dragon language circled the room interrupted only by a large light blue stone. Morgan was turning in a circle reading it when she noticed the light of the candles being reflected as dancing light onto the ceiling and walls.

"Morgan, check out the floor," Daniel said.

"Well, that's just…awesome," she said as she stared at the pool of shimmering undulating dark purple liquid. An intricately carved ring of the same metal as her amulet encircled it.

"Alright then, both of you step onto the portal pool and move to the middle please," GranMay said.

"Onto the pool? Don't you mean jump into the pool?" Daniel asked as he eyed the ominous dark liquid.

"No love, I mean step onto the surface of the purple pool in front of you. You will not fall through. Not yet anyway," GranMay said with a smirk.

Morgan and Daniel exchanged a wary glance then stepped together onto the pool. Both let out a breath of relief as they found the surface to be squishy yet rigid enough to hold their weight.

GranMay walked over to the stone embedded into the wall and stood below it.

"The words and harmony which will activate the portal gate are written on the wall. It starts here. You will sing it aloud in a moment. When you do so you will feel many strange sensations and a bright light will eclipse your vision. You must continue repeating the verse until you arrive in Chemerie. Take a moment to memorize it, please."

After two turns she nodded, "I'm ready, GranMay."

GranMay smiled as she stepped forward to wrap her in a hug.

"Yes, I believe you are indeed, my girl." She kissed and hugged both her grandchildren then said, "May the magic keep you until we meet again. I love you both with all I am." She turned as she wiped away tears.

Their father embraced Daniel with a pause to look him hard in the eyes and pat his cheek then moved to Morgan where he laid his forehead to hers.

"Farewell, my sweet girl. I love you. Be well, and enjoy your wonderful new life." He lifted her into his arms and hugged her fiercely for only a few seconds before kissing her forehead and moving to stand beside GranMay outside the portal circle.

"Daniel, stand behind Morgan, then reach around her to take her hands palm-to-palm. Lace your fingers and do not let go during the transport no matter what you feel," their father said.

Morgan had shared the pain in both GranMay and her father as she held them and now wiped many tears from her face. She grasped Daniel's hands as she said, "You ready, big brother?"

"Yep, lead the way, little sister," he replied as he gave her hands an encouraging squeeze.

She took a deep calming breath and began to say the words of the verse aloud in dragon-tongue.

"All that I am, and will ever be, I now offer to my brethren, both man and dragon. I devote my spirit, and the gift of magic within me, to serve my country as a Caretaker of Chemerie."

Again, and again, she repeated the chant. The harmony became more natural, and the song more fluid with each repetition. Daniel was soon humming along with her.

The purple pool began to glow, as did the stone in her amulet. It soon grew so bright it forced her to close her eyes. Next, a tightening or squeezing feeling began to creep up her legs. They both tensed as the strange pressure moved up their bodies.

As the liquid neared their necks, she heard her mother's voice join hers in the chant. She relaxed back against Daniel's chest and felt him relax as well.

Just before the liquid covered their faces, the pool beneath them turned to weightless vapor, and they dropped into a free fall with the bright light consuming them.

THEIR FREE-FALL lasted only a few seconds before their feet found solid ground again, making both stumble. The second they touched down, she gasped and pulled her stinging hands from his. She began to tremble and was struggling to breathe as she dropped to one knee.

"What's wrong? What can I do?" he said as he knelt beside her.

She tried to give an encouraging smile, but managed only a grimace as she caught her breath enough to talk.

"It's the magic. There is so much here. It's like my bones are on fire again... just give me a minute."

Both flinched as the sound of a deep rumbling hum filled the air and rattled their bones. They looked up to find themselves surrounded by beautiful dragons, all of whom were humming a melodic tune.

Within seconds her trembling stopped and the pain faded. As the dragons' song quieted, she stood with Daniel steadying her.

"Are you OK now?"

"Yeah, their song helped. Oh man, Daniel, I can feel their magic. It's different from mine or GranMay's," she said as she gazed at the many dragons around her. She took in the features of the cobalt blue dragon standing nearest her. Her mesmerized inspection was broken only when the dragon bowed to her.

"Welcome to Chemerie, my Lady. I speak for all of the dragons of Chemerie when I say we are most honored to have you accept the duty of Caretaker," the dragon said in a deep melodic voice.

All of the dragons bowed their heads and hummed a deep rich tone that transferred a sensation of respect and love to her. She shivered at the feel of their magic and smiled as she looked back at Daniel.

"What did it say?" he asked. She translated for him, then they both bowed to the dragon who had spoken.

"Thank you for helping with my pain and for the welcome. I promise to do everything I can to serve you as well as my Mothers before me."

As she turned to study the many beautiful dragons, she felt something new. She focused on the feeling then turned to look at the sky.

"What is it?" Daniel said as he followed her gaze.

"Mother."

"Can you see her?" he asked as he squinted and scanned the horizon.

"No, but I can feel her magic. She's getting closer."

The dragons around her exchanged glances, but Morgan didn't notice. Her eyes were locked on the approaching group of dragons carrying her mother. She and Daniel watched as three dragons approached and circled high above them.

"Look at the size of the dragon she's on. I never imagined they could be that big," Daniel said. "They're so big and powerful yet so graceful, amazing."

The huge green dragon carrying their mother landed and moved forward as many of the smaller ones cleared a path. It raised a front foot to allow their mother to move from the large saddle onto its palm. The massive creature lie down and settled her on its front leg before giving Morgan and Daniel a slow bow of its head.

They both bowed in return, but neither took their eyes off their mother. Two large men who had accompanied their mother moved forward to stand to either side of her. Both had easy smiles as they bowed.

"She is truly beautiful, isn't she?" Morgan whispered. "Yeah, she is. I can see both GranMay and you in her face."

"Welcome home, my children, please come let me see you," their mother said. They moved to stand in front of her, staring and taking in every detail. She wore an amulet identical to Morgan's and a beautiful dress of a light flowing material.

The two men to her sides offered a hand as the dragon

lifted its leg. Their mother took their hands as she stood and continued to hold them as they moved closer.

Morgan felt tremendous joy as her mother opened her arms to her. She moved into them without hesitation to be overwhelmed by love through the magic they shared. Tears flowed unchecked as her mother held her for a long moment then leaned back with a smile.

"Look at your palms, my Daughter. See the markings of the magic you hold."

Morgan gazed at the intricate and brilliantly colored images of dragons on her hands. They were nearly three-dimensional in appearance and perfect in every detail. Her left palm had a dark red infant, still curled within the confines of its shell, twitching and shimmying around as if ready to hatch. Her right hand had a cobalt blue adult centered in her palm with its tail trailing down her wrist. The adult dragon on her hand bowed to her and gave its wings a little flourish. She twitched and smiled at the tickle it caused.

Daniel had been looking over her shoulder and whispered, "Utterly awesome! Can you feel them moving?"

She nodded as she used a finger to gently stroke the hatchling on her left hand. It reacted to her touch as if alive.

Their mother shifted and opened her arms to Daniel. As he slid into her embrace, Morgan felt another surge of love from her mother. It was not as intense as when she was touching her, but it was still profound. Their mother held him for a long moment before releasing him with a kiss to his cheek.

With a nod to her dragon mount, their mother took the hands of the two men beside her and moved into the dragon's waiting palm. With gentle grace, the dragon lifted her back into the saddle at the base of its neck and stood.

"Come, my children, let us go to the castle and get you settled in. I would like to introduce you to a few of your brethren. Morgan, you must address the dragons directly and request permission to ride them. Be sure to introduce and speak for Daniel as well."

Their mother's mount left the ground with graceful strokes of its massive wings. Its movement was smooth and never jostled her. The two men had mounted their dragons and followed close behind her.

When they were away, Morgan turned to the large cobalt dragon that had spoken earlier and bowed.

"Can I have your permission to ride on your back to the castle, Sir?"

The dragon made an odd rumbling noise deep in its throat, which was mimicked by the rest of the dragons.

"What's that sound? Are they growling or laughing?" Daniel said.

"I have no idea," she said as they looked around. A sharp note from the dragon she had spoken to brought silence again. "My name is Balia. I am a female, my Lady. And I would be honored to carry you to the castle."

"Oh, I'm sorry if I offended you."

"There is no need for apology, my Lady. I am in no way offended. Please come and touch my body so your magic can show you my nature," Balia said as she dropped her head.

Morgan moved to the side of her head and neck. When she placed her hands on the beautiful cobalt scales of the dragon's hide, she was hit with a rush of sensations that caused her to gasp and flinch back. Daniel moved to her while scowling at the dragon.

"What happened?"

"Uhm, it's hard to explain, it was like I felt the essence of her character … no, more like her spirit. It was feminine, maternal, and intelligent. I also felt respect, but I don't understand why when she doesn't know me," she said as they moved back to face Balia from a few yards away.

"We respect you for the commitment you have made, Lady Morgan. We respect Sir Daniel for the same reason," Balia said with a deep hum as she lifted her head.

Morgan translated for Daniel and both said, "Thank you."

"My Lady, you should address Menkar, the large red male dragon behind you, to carry Sir Daniel. For female dragons do not like to carry males if we can avoid it," Balia said with a wink.

She did as Balia suggested and Menkar agreed to carry Daniel with a deep rumbling hum. Morgan noted that his voice was less melodic and rather harsh in comparison to that of Balia.

Next was the task of getting aboard. When she looked up at Balia, the dragon placed her right front foot, palm up, in front of her, then nodded. Once she sat down, Balia moved her up to let her slide into the saddle with ease.

Daniel had a bit more trouble. Menkar was neither gentle nor patient. Daniel had just grabbed hold of the saddle when the foot was pulled away.

"Please wrap your hands and feet in the loops on the saddle and harness for security, my Lady," Balia said. Morgan did so and relayed the information to Daniel just in time.

Menkar leapt into the air and made hard strokes to gain altitude fast, almost dislodging Daniel in the process. Balia shook her head and grumbled, "Males!"

Balia took flight with grace, just as their mother's mount had done. Morgan never felt the sensation of losing her balance. As they climbed higher, Morgan tensed. Balia began to hum a tune that transferred a calming sensation to her. With that, she was able to relax and begin looking around. The first thing she noticed was that all of the dragons who had been around the portal were now all around them, acting as a guard.

Focusing beyond them, she took in the landscape of the young world of Erion. It was stunning, as beautiful as she could imagine possible. The clear waters of the rivers and lakes, the lushness of the plant life, and the clarity of the skies all seemed unreal. She took in a long, deep breath of clean air and felt the peaceful, reassuring sensation that she had just come home.

As she scanned the world below her, she saw many small homes built of stone, but only a few people. Those she spotted were working in fields or tending a variety of livestock. They waved to the dragons as they passed over, and received light roars of greeting in return.

Morgan wondered what the population of Chemerie was when she still saw few people in the streets as they approached the more developed area around the castle. She had her answer the instant they cleared the high castle wall. A great roar of cheering made her jump and tuck closer to the saddle's front bolster.

"The people of Chemerie welcome you, my Lady," Balia

said.

Balia swooped low over the crowds and asked Morgan to wave to her brethren. Menkar circled once behind Balia then broke off toward the back of the castle with Daniel.

Morgan was dumbfounded. She could not believe that in the period of less than two weeks she had gone from high school student, who in no way drew attention to herself, to someone hundreds of people were cheering for in welcome. Not to mention she was riding on the back of a living dragon!

She waved as Balia circled, and her heart filled with pride. It took only a few seconds to realize it was pride felt by her mother, who was watching from a high balcony of the castle. As her mother laid her palms together, Morgan heard her voice as if she was sitting beside her.

"Balia, Mother wants you to make one more loop around and then take me to her chambers, please."

They soon landed on a huge lawn and moved up beside the large terrace. She slid from the dragon's palm down to the terrace floor beside a beaming Daniel.

"Can you believe this place? It's ser— "

"One sec," she said as she turned around to bow to Balia. "Thank you very much for the ride Balia. It was very nice of you."

"It was an honor to fly with you, my Princess," Balia said as she bowed.

Morgan watched Balia glide away with a smile that faded as she considered the dragon's words. "My Princess?"

"Princess? What are you talking about?" Daniel said.

"That's what she just ..." she said as she turned. When she spotted their mother standing behind him, she went mute. Daniel turned when he saw her expression.

They stared at their mother, who now wore a magnificent crown and plush cobalt and black robe with elaborate silver cording and embroidery.

"Come, my children, the people of Chemerie want to greet their Prince and Princess," their mother said.

"No Way!" she said as she took a step back into Daniel. She was shaking her head as she looked to him. "This was definitely not in the Book!"

Their mother smiled and laughed as her escort led her into her chambers. Daniel sobered first, and gave Morgan a light push in the small of her back to get her started. He kept his hand there for support, or to keep her from bolting. Either was a good choice.

Their mother led them through her chambers, down a wide hallway, and out onto the large front balcony of the castle. Morgan required a stronger push from Daniel to make it through the last set of doors.

The crowd exploded in cheers when the three of them reached the railing. Hundreds of people were cheering, and nearly that many dragons were roaring along with them. Morgan took Daniel's hand with her trembling one.

"Sweet Mercy!" she whispered.

"Couldn't agree more."

Their mother, known formally as Queen Christina, introduced them. When she introduced Morgan, she did not only say, "Princess Morgan" but added, "and your future Queen." With that last bit, Morgan's knees wobbled. Thankfully, Daniel was ready to keep her from hitting the floor.

3

The Transfer

"HOW AM I SUPPOSED to be Queen? To a country and culture that I don't know? Caretaker! Caretaker they said, servant to a race of dragons. That, I signed up for. But this? This is … un-freaking-believable!" She stopped her pacing and sat down on the huge plush bed to rub her face hard. "I swear to you, there was nothing in the Book that even hinted at this!"

She dropped her head and massaged her neck as Daniel sat down beside her and nudged her shoulder.

"That's not really surprising. And it's not hard to get why Father and GranMay failed to mention it," he said with a laugh as he nudged her again. "Can you imagine if they dropped this bomb at the dinner table?"

She tried to laugh but managed only a sigh.

"C'mon," he said, putting an arm around her shoulders to

jostle her. "It's crazy. But, also, completely amazing! We just flew with dragons! And, we have our mother, at last. We get a chance to know her."

"Yeah, but, for how long?" she said as she looked up to meet his eyes, "You know she's sick. You saw how weak she was, how she needed help to stand, and a hand to steady her. That's why my Quickening came so early."

His face fell as he moved to stare out a window for a long moment, then gave her a confident and supportive smile.

"We'll do everything we can to make sure Father and GranMay get to see her before she …" He swallowed hard as his face tightened. "You need to start training as soon as possible."

"I will," she said as she joined him to look over the city courtyard. "And, maybe we're wrong, and she's not that sick."

"Didn't you feel it when you touched her? Are you lying to me to make me feel better?" he said with a scowl.

"No, I did not feel it! I was overwhelmed by love from her. When her dragon helped her stand, the sense hit me. I have no idea if it was a normal deduction, or if I did get something through the magic. And, no, I was not lying to you!"

She turned away from him to face the window. He sighed and rubbed his eyes before gently gripping her shoulders to turn her back around.

"I'm sorry. Truth is, I don't have your gifts, and I'm gonna be jealous sometimes. I know my role in this and I don't mind standing behind you as you lead. But … just promise me you will never hide something from me to protect my feelings. I need to know we have that between us."

"You're my big brother before anything else. No magic, or titles, or duties will change that. I know a lot's going to change for us here, but we'll always be honest with each other. Agreed?"

"Agreed! And thank you."

She started dragging him out into the hallway as she said, "Let's go find Mother. If training isn't the plan for the morning, then we need another way to relieve some stress."

They were led into their mother's chambers by a formal and polite chambermaid.

"The Princess and Prince to see you, my Queen. Can I bring you anything?"

"No, Neesa, thank you," their mother said.

She was sitting at a small table with the two men who seemed to shadow her and another older man. Morgan felt annoyance from someone and struggled to hold her face placid as her mother stood and moved toward them. They both received hugs and a kiss to the cheek. Daniel kept his arm around her as they talked.

"Will I be training this morning?"

"No, you and Daniel should spend some time settling in. Your training will begin after lunch. I will see you both then." She gave both a warm smile then turned around to face the three men again.

Morgan and Daniel turned for the door and took a few paces before she swayed and grabbed his arm. She looked back at her mother who was now being lifted from the floor and helped into a chair by the three men. Daniel saw what had happened too and steadied her as he pulled her the rest of the way out the door. Neither said a word until they reached her room again and closed the door.

"Am I right that you just felt her pain when she collapsed?"

"Yeah. But, the pain I can handle much better than the grief I felt for a few seconds. I think she's keeping it all from me somehow and couldn't when she fell," she said as she held her arms tight around her middle and gazed out the window.

"Are you still hurting?"

"Yeah, but it's not bad. I really want to exercise. Will you ask the Knights down the hall what our options are?"

"Sure. And, I'll give you the minute alone you actually want too," he said with a smirk as he left.

AFTER CONSIDERING THE OPTIONS, they decided to take a swim. They put on shorts and t-shirts they had brought from Earth and grabbed some towels from a chambermaid.

They walked through gorgeous gardens before they reached a large clear lake fed by a waterfall. Sheer cliffs encircled much of the lake with a white sand beach facing the gardens.

Both stopped when they saw that the lake was occupied. It was surrounded by young dragons of various colors and sizes, with the largest being the size of a horse.

"They are beautiful, aren't they?" she said.

"You should have this time to yourself. I'll check out the Guard training grounds. See you later," Daniel said before heading back into the gardens.

As she continued toward the lake, the younglings moved closer. She was aware that she was ignorant of the customs of this world, and decided to err on the side of politeness by bowing to the group.

"Would any of you mind if I share the lake with you and go for a swim?"

Many voices replied at once, making her jump as they hurried closer with sweet croons. She relaxed and laughed as their excitement filled her. Several were shooting nervous glances at the water.

"Excuse me," she said to the largest youngling near her. "Is there something wrong with the water, or something in it that you're concerned about?"

"Oh no, my Lady. It is quite safe. We all heard you were coming for a swim, and wanted to see you. And perhaps meet you. We were looking at the water with concern because none of us knows how to swim yet. We are a bit afraid of the water."

"Well, I don't know much about dragons yet. But, I would bet that with those webbed feet of yours, you could move a lot of water with each stroke. Can the adult dragons swim very well?"

"Oh yes, my Lady. They love it, and swim often," he said with a little hop and wing flutter. "It also serves to keep their scales clean. And that is important to most any dragon."

"Well, I need to go on in for a good workout. But, when I'm done, I'd love to visit for a bit." She smiled and jumped again as all the dragon younglings around her crooned and clambered around with excitement again.

As she eased into the water, she turned to smile back at them. The dragon she spoke with hopped in and out of the shallow water as she waded out into the deeper area.

Less than ten seconds after she dove in and disappeared

under the water, she heard a huge splash in front of her. A second later, a warm palm lifted her to about six feet above the surface.

She sat up, and peered into the alert face of Balia.

"What's the matter, Balia?"

"You could drown, my Princess. I can not let that happen!"

She laughed at first, then sobered as she felt the tension in the dragon through the contact.

"I appreciate your concern, but you don't need to worry about me drowning in this lake. Seriously. I'm an excellent swimmer. I'm used to swimming a mile or more every day. It's one way I relax and stay in shape."

Balia's expression did not change and she made no move to return her to the water.

"If you're that worried, you could stay in the lake with me while I swim. You'll be close enough to snatch me right up if something happens."

Balia considered this for a moment then lowered her back into the water.

"Yes, my Lady, but please, do stay on the surface."

She broke into a steady freestyle across the lake and was tickled to find Balia swimming upside down below her to watch her every move.

After she swam two lengths of the lake, she heard more splashing and raised her head to see many of the little dragons braving the water up to their bellies.

The one she had been conversing with teetered on his hind feet then took a mighty lunge into the water toward her. He flailed his wings, making great splashes with little progress as he bobbed below the surface and came up sputtering.

She started toward him as fast as she could go. Balia poked her head up and supported Morgan with her foot as she watched the flailing youngling.

"Falin, tuck your wings, you silly boy," Balia said. "You are not a water dragon. Simply use your feet to pull your body through the water and your tail for direction. You can learn to use your wings when you are older."

The little dragon did as he was told and dropped from the surface. Morgan held her breath until he burst from the water right in front of her. He was talking so fast she could not understand a single word but smiled as his happiness washed over her.

Balia reached over and dunked him back under with a quick nudge on his head. He came up sputtering, but quieter.

"Speak sensibly or hold your tongue, Falin," Balia said. The young dragon gave her a weary look before speaking again.

"I can swim now, my Lady, can I please swim with you?"

"Sure! Tell ya what, I'll race you! First to the falls. Go!"

She dove from Balia's hand and stroked hard toward the falls as she kept an eye on Falin. He struggled to get past her, then celebrated his accomplishment with acrobatic flips and flops on the surface.

A while later, she plopped down on the bank and lay back to soak up the sun as her heart rate slowed. She took deep breaths, enjoying the clean air and all the lovely fragrances from the garden.

"Is it time to visit, my Lady?"

She opened her eyes to find many little dragon heads studying her.

"Absolutely," she said as she sat up. "So, what would you

like to know about me?"

"When are you to mate and have your daughter?" Falin asked.

"Oh, uhm, well … I have a lot to learn to be able to serve as your Caretaker before I worry about that."

Falin made a sweet crooning hum and touched her arm with his snout. She shivered at the magical touch and touched his snout in return. Others piped up with simpler questions about her and Daniel for a few minutes.

"Could I touch some of you and practice using my magic?"

Their answer came in the form of chirping and shifting around, each of them trying to be the first.

Touching them taught her so much about the magic they shared. It became quick and easy to tell their gender. She could feel strong emotions from all of them. From the larger of the group, she was able to get a sense of their personality. He could sense characteristics such as brave or timid, mischievous or well-mannered. From Falin, she received a strong sense of bravery, respect, and a huge desire to please and protect her.

She also learned about their features and how they change. Their scale colors were muted in comparison to those she had seen on the major dragons and they weren't as muscular. She ran her hand over the outstretched wings of Falin with awed amazement. The structure and function of the amazing creatures around her left her speechless for many minutes as she took in every detail.

After saying farewell, she watched from the edge of the garden as Falin urged his friends to join him in the deeper water. He was not acting as to boast or brag. His focus was only to help the others.

"How was it?" Daniel said as he jogged up to her.

"They're amazing creatures," she said as she looked up to track the flight of two very large dragons passing over them. "To be so massive, and strong, with powerful magic, and yet … they're kind, gentle, and compassionate toward people."

"I'm still trying to believe this whole place is real. Seriously, it's like Camelot on crack with a bad-ass Guinevere leading the charge."

They both laughed as they headed for the castle.

THEY WERE MET on the garden terrace by a nervous chambermaid who curtsied and took Morgan's arm to usher her inside.

"My Princess, you need to prepare for your Quickening Ceremony. There is not much time left. Please come, and we will assist you."

She soon had six women giving her instructions and helping her through bathing, drying, powdering, weaving her hair into a magnificent braid, and finally wrapping her in a formal dress.

Her only one point of major concern was the application of the corset. She was sure every rib she had was cracked and suspected one of the maids was on steroids.

An hour later, she was staring at the unknown woman in her mirror. Daniel appeared at her shoulder looking handsome in his formal attire. He stared at her with an odd look of surprise that shifted to one of pride.

"It seems my baby sister has become a beautiful Princess."

She smiled and felt her cheeks flush as a Knight of the

Guard cleared his throat at the door.

"Queen Christina requests that you join her and your guests in Kindred Hall. This way, please," the guard said as he bowed and swept an arm toward the Hall.

Daniel offered her his arm, and she latched on.

They followed the guard to a balcony that overlooked a massive Hall. A curving staircase dropped from one side of the balcony to the deep blue stone floor below. The Hall was lined with many columns of a bright white stone with veins of the same blue running through them. Magnificent draperies hung from the many tall windows, and elaborate chandeliers shone throughout. One end of the Hall was a set of massive doors that allowed for Elder dragons to enter easily.

The gathered crowd held more dragons than people, and every head was pointed their way. Morgan's insides clenched as every dragon bowed, and the people dropped to one knee.

A gentle hand fell onto her shoulder and a warm rush of love from her mother accompanied it. She turned with a smile as she heard her mother's voice through their magical connection.

"It is time to complete the Quickening of your magic, and for you to receive the knowledge of your Mothers and your dragon brethren."

Her mother took her hand and, with her escort at her side supporting her, they descended the stairs with Daniel following behind. Once they reached the floor and moved toward the center of the Hall, the largest of the dragons moved forward.

Their mother turned to Daniel and took him into a strong embrace. She held him for a long moment then kissed both of his cheeks before releasing him. She smiled into his face with eyes full of tears.

"I love you, my dear boy. You look so much like Nikolas, very handsome, of course. I feel your love and devotion to protect Morgan, and I am proud beyond words. I cannot adequately express how important your role will be, but have no doubt you will handle it with conviction. You are, after all, your father's son." She kissed his cheeks again and stepped back as she said, "The ceremony is for Morgan alone. Please step back to join your uncles behind the circle of dragons."

At first Daniel looked perplexed, as did Morgan, at the word "uncles." A gentle pat on his shoulder by the handsome gentleman who had been supporting their mother answered their question. The two men who had been near her at all times were her mother's protectors and, therefore, her brothers.

Both of her uncles bowed to her and her mother, as did Daniel, and they backed away. Morgan moved to the center of the floor then waited there while her mother moved to lay a hand to the same Elder dragon who had been her mount that morning. The great dragon hummed a long deep note as it laid its head along the side of her mother's body. Her mother took many deep breaths then moved to stand with her again.

Her skin began to warm and tingle as the circle of huge Elder dragons closed in.

"Man, that's a lot of magic!" she thought as she shivered. She smiled when she noticed her mother smirk, having heard her thought.

"Seek my thoughts with your magic," her mother said.

She raised an eyebrow at first, then straightened her face and concentrated on that idea. To her amazement, she soon heard her mother's words through their magic.

"We will now use the magic of the dragons to transfer the knowledge of your Caretaker ancestors, as well as some from the dragons' ancestral knowledge. Do not be afraid of the power you feel. Surrender yourself to it and let it fill you.

"The Caretaker is given only what she needs to fulfill her role and guide Chemerie. The extent of the knowledge transferred will depend on the amount of magic within you, and the discretion of the Elder dragons within our circle. They will examine your spirit and only allow so much knowledge as they deem appropriate. You must open yourself to them and allow them to see the true nature of your spirit and your capabilities. Are you ready?"

She nodded then glanced around at the many dragons looming overhead as her mother raised her hands with palms facing toward her.

"Take a deep breath to calm yourself, then place your palms against mine. When they touch the transfer will begin."

Morgan took two deep breaths for good measure before laying her hands against her mother's.

Her entire body was filled with sharp, painful tingling for many seconds before those sensations faded to be replaced by a floating sensation. The dragons' song was a percussive rhythm buffeting her body as intense magic flowed at a very fast rate. Her eyes grew heavy and closed. As the intensity of the dragons' song increased, a squeezing sensation accompanied it.

"Relax and let them in; they will not hurt you, trust their love," her mother said.

She forced her body and mind to relax as she took deep breaths. As her instinctive resistance dropped away, a sudden rush of emotions, thoughts, images and sounds bombarded her senses.

As she concentrated on offering no resistance to the transfer, the tingling returned and climbed to a painful level. Her mother laced their fingers and tightened her grip as the pain tripled, making her gasp.

She gritted her teeth to hold in a scream for many seconds as fiery shocks tore through her. As the dragons' song quieted, the pain faded, leaving her floating once more in the warmth of her mother's love.

SHE WOKE within a huge dragon palm. All of the dragons were humming a gentle melody that transferred calmness. The room was aglow with the luminous green eyes of all the dragons and her mother. The dragon markings on her and her mother's palms, as well as the stones in their amulets, were also glowing brightly.

She was still a little woozy and jumped when a new voice filled her head as a strong jolt of fear and frustration washed over her.

"Is she all right? Why did she fall? What the heck is going on? I am about t—"

"Daniel, I'm fine. Relax, big brother."

He calmed a bit, then she received a flash of bewilderment as he realized he had heard her in his mind and not with his ears.

She smiled as she lay still a few more seconds to enjoy the feeling of her new magic. The power within her was electrifying, and she felt the presence of the knowledge she had been given as a fortifying confidence.

While she could not access all of the knowledge transferred to her yet, she now had a far better understanding of her capabilities. She also understood the urgent need that brought her to Chemerie almost ten years early.

4

The Hatchling

MORGAN MET HER MOTHER'S EYES, holding them as she stood, then turned to Daniel.

"Daniel, we have to go. Say goodbye to Mother…then head outside to Menkar and those waiting to accompany us. I will explain more in flight."

Daniel's face was hard as he nodded and moved to their mother where she now sat on her mount's foreleg. He held her trembling form for many seconds, then kissed her cheeks and forehead before leaving.

Morgan took her mother's hands again and struggled to control her emotions as she looked into her eyes. Through their contact, she felt the profound pain and fatigue her mother had hidden before. As the desire to help entered her thoughts, her magic acted.

Her mother took in a quick breath as healing magic passed to her. Tears filled her eyes as she smiled.

"Thank you, my Caretaker."

"Thank you for the gift of Caretaker. I am very thankful to have met and bonded with you. Knowing your spirit is precious to me. Please tell Father and GranMay that I love them, and I am ready for this duty. You can rest knowing that I will serve the dragons and people of Chemerie as honorably as I possibly can."

She wrapped her in a tight embrace and supported her weight as she relished the love and magical connection they shared.

"Trust in the magic you hold and in the pure spirits of your Chemerian brethren. I love you, my strong and beautiful Daughter. May the magic keep you until our spirits touch again. Farewell." She kissed Morgan's forehead, then stepped back to bow her head. Morgan returned the bow, then hurried toward Balia as she fought tears.

ONCE SHE WAS SETTLED into the saddle, Balia and Menkar lifted off together. They headed toward the high mountain range to the northeast of the castle with great speed. An escort of a dozen large major dragons carrying Knights surrounded them.

"Mother won't live much longer," she said as she connected to Daniel. *"She's going to Father and GranMay tonight. We will never see her again."*

She gave him a moment before glancing his way. He nodded, so she continued.

"Mother has been too weak to serve the dragons for months.

Eggs have only a small window of time within which they can be Quickened, and hatchlings depend on the magical connection with the Caretaker to survive the first few months. Many have died, and more are very near it. The dragons moved their brooding females, and the very young, to their hidden Ancestral Lair. We're headed there now, so I can try to help them."

He nodded again and turned back to gaze over Menkar's head. She could feel his sorrow and apprehension. Behind these fresh emotions, she felt devotion to her and dedication to his duty. They were both quiet for the next half hour as they struggled to accept their mother's imminent death.

"My Caretaker, we will travel through a lake and water-filled tunnel system to reach the Lair," Balia said. *"You must strap in well and lay your body tight to the saddle behind the bolster. Take a very deep breath just before we break the surface and close your eyes. The force of the water at the speed we will travel will be considerable, my Lady."*

Morgan relayed the message to Daniel, and they readied themselves. The group of dragons dropped over the lake and approached a massive waterfall. Just before reaching it, Balia and Menkar folded their wings to drop and cut through the surface of the water with grace.

It was all she could do to hang on through many twists and turns. Just as she was about to run out of breath, Balia shot upward and broke the surface again.

They were now inside a gigantic cavern deep within the mountains. There were many large tunnel mouths around the walls. Some were near floor level, but most were high above. Light filtered through many natural cracks in the ceiling.

The cavern was filled with many female dragons. Morgan reached out with her magic to take in their feelings. There was a mixture of worry for their young, excitement at her arrival, and sorrow for the early loss of her mother.

When she dismounted Balia and stood by her head, the group of dragons bowed as one and hummed their welcoming salutation. Annoyance from many of them washed over her as Daniel moved to stand beside her.

"May I speak with the Eldest dragon, please?" she said as she shifted closer to Daniel. A massive copper-colored female, the largest Morgan had yet seen, moved to the front.

"I am Zetia. I am the Eldest Female and overseer of the Lair, my Lady," the great dragon said as she bowed her head.

Morgan focused for many seconds and reached out with her magic to Zetia's consciousness. Instead of a sensation like spreading her arms, it was more like a direct reach to her spirit.

"I realize it is against your traditions, but I am hoping that you will let my brother stay with me." Zetia was silent as she glanced at Balia and several other dragons. *"My mother will die soon, and I will be the only living female of the Caretaker line. While I can feel the weight of that responsibility, he can't. I need for him to watch and learn, to understand the importance of my role in Chemerie. It will strengthen his connection to me and his dedication to his role as my protector."*

Zetia nodded and transferred her decision to the rest of the dragons.

"Could you take us to those who need my help the most?" she asked aloud in English.

Zetia held out a foot for them to mount and waited for

them to settle on her shoulders before leaping into the air with strong strokes of her massive wings. She landed on a ledge then crouched low to move through a large tunnel. They soon entered another large cavern where Zetia soared to land smoothly at the far end. As Morgan and Daniel dismounted, Zetia indicated three small hatchlings huddled together on a bed of straw against the far wall.

"Those are the weakest of the hatchlings, my Lady," Zetia said as she made a sad noise deep in her throat.

"Just me for now," Morgan said to Daniel as she moved toward the group of little dragons.

She stopped a few feet from them and concentrated on the ancient knowledge she now carried.

"Teach me what I need to understand about the bonding of Caretaker and hatchling," she said to herself, to her magic. Within seconds the knowledge came to her in a rush of images, sounds, and emotions.

She knelt before the smallest and frailest of the group and placed her hands together palms touching. Her hands tingled and grew warm with the surging magic. The dragons of her markings stirred on her palms as she reached out to place them on either side of the small dragon's head.

"I am Caretaker Morgan, and I am here to serve you. Please trust me and let me share magic with you."

She continued repeating these words as she concentrated on the spirit of the little dragon. Finally, she heard a small voice return her calls.

"Will you leave me like the other?"

"I will give you all I have as long as I can. Only death will pull me away."

The young dragon made a very weak crooning sound then opened its mind and spirit to her.

When she felt fear and a sense of abandonment from the little one, she passed her love and devotion. The hatchling opened her eyes and blinked slowly.

"I will share with you, Caretaker Morgan. I see your spirit is pure. I choose to trust you," it said in a raspy whisper.

"Thank you, my precious new friend."

As she focused on the dragon's spirit and her desire to help, her magic flowed through her. She pushed the healing magic to the little one for a few minutes before she felt the hatchling's will to live return and its body growing stronger.

DANIEL WAS MESMERIZED as he watched both Morgan's eyes and the little dragon's eyes begin to glow. After a few minutes, the small dragon stood on its own and moved to snuggle against her chest, tucking its head under her chin and wrapping its tail around her torso. Morgan wrapped her arms around it and sang in the dragon language for nearly half an hour before repeating the entire process with the next youngling.

It was amazing to watch as she revitalized the little dragons. As each was healed, it clung to her, crooning. Nearly two hours passed as she worked. When she finished, she failed an attempt to stand. Daniel started toward her but stopped as she settled down on the bed of straw.

He sat down a few feet from them and watched her sleep with the younglings snuggled against her. Completely amazed, and a little saddened, he accepted the reality that his little baby sister was a very different person as of that day.

AFTER NEARLY an hour of snuggling, Morgan checked each of the small dragons in turn, then shifted them to get up.

"Daniel," she said as she rustled his hair.

"Yeah?" He sat up groggy, then his eyes widened. "Did I just …"

"Sort of," she said with a smile as she sat down beside him. "I can focus the magic enough now that I'll be able to hear your responses through the connections I form to your consciousness. We'll be able to use it to talk in private."

"So, can I reach out to you on my own, without you initiating it?"

"I think I'll hear you if you're concentrating hard or if you're upset. But, I don't think you'll ever be able to hear my thoughts if I don't want you to."

"I doubt you will ever do anything you don't want to again," he said with a glance at the pile of sleeping little dragons. "That was incredible. How did it feel?"

"Completely amazing. Seriously, I can't even begin to describe how awesome it was to feel their bodies and spirits grow stronger, and … to feel their emotions during all of it." She stared at her palms as she swallowed hard. "I feel so different. It's like I'm still me, just amplified … so much more alive." She glanced at him and smirked as her cheeks flushed a bit. "I know that sounds crazy."

"Nah, not really," he said as he stood up and offered her a hand. "I mean, we are talking about magic and dragons. It's hardly a stretch to think it would feel pretty freaking awesome."

He laughed as he brushed dirt off her dress.

"My clothes will do, but we really need to find you something to wear other than a formal ball gown," he said as he placed his coat around her shoulders.

"That would be nice," she said as she fought with the bodice. "And you can bet I'll be burning this evil corset as soon as possible." Her smile faded fast as she turned and stared toward the far wall of the cavern. "It'll have to wait. I need to go to the eggs now. I can feel that there are at least two in trouble."

They walked for a couple hundred yards down a steeply dropping tunnel before it opened to a room full of small pools fed by natural hot springs. The room was hot and humid and contained three small clutches of dragon eggs.

She walked around the clutches as she focused to call forward the knowledge she needed to complete their Quickening. As it came forward, she knelt and placed her hands together until they grew hot again. Next, she opened her hands and held them palm up in front of her.

Her eyes and dragon markings began to glow, casting a soft blue light over the cavern as she sang a beautiful song in the dragon language. At the right moment, she picked up one of the eggs. With the egg resting on only her left hand, the one with the design of a dragon in the shell, she sang another full verse of the song.

Next, she placed her right hand bearing the design of the full-grown dragon against the opposite side of the egg and continued the song. She held the egg in this position for a few minutes before shifting it to only the right hand where she held it for the last few verses.

When she finished, she kissed the egg and caressed it before placing it back with its clutch. She repeated the

Quickening process with five more eggs before she stood and moved back toward Daniel.

"It's an incredible and fulfilling process, but it does take a bit out of me. I feel like I just ran a marathon." She raised her hand to rub her eyes and swayed. Daniel caught her and lowered her to the ground to lean back against him.

"You haven't eaten in too long, and you need sleep. Which would you like first?"

He didn't get an answer. She had fallen fast asleep in his arms.

He looked at his little sister and smiled as his chest ached. He took her hand in his and squeezed it as he focused as hard as he could.

I love you, my sister, and I dedicate all that I am to helping you fulfill your role of Caretaker. I will gladly give my life to save yours.

He had not expected a response, but saw a tear roll down her cheek as a comforting tingle moved through his hand. The tingle increased as the adult dragon on her palm shifted around with a flourish of his wings.

A while later, a large minor female dragon crept into the cavern with a bow of her head to Daniel. She offered her palm to him, then lifted them both to her back. She carried them back to the cavern where the hatchlings were housed.

Zetia was waiting with many others. When Daniel had dismounted, Zetia ushered him to a corner where they had piled a large amount of straw and covered it with a piece of old cloth. At first he was annoyed, but quickly realized this was a place of dragons, and was not likely to have accommodations for humans. They had provided the best they could.

He bowed his head in thanks and laid Morgan on the bed. He adjusted his coat to cover her well and rolled the cloth up to cover her feet. When he stepped away, the three hatchlings she had bonded with moved onto the bed and snuggled against her again. She gave a sweet sigh at their touch and smiled as she wriggled deeper into the warm embrace.

HUNGER AND DISCOMFORT woke Morgan the next morning.

"Balia, would you mind returning to the castle to bring clothes and food for me and Daniel? I really don't want to leave yet, but we are getting hungry and gross."

Balia chuckled in amusement and gestured to the large pack on her saddle harness. Morgan detached the pack and found within it a change of clothes for both her and Daniel along with enough food for two to three days.

"She realized exactly what I would do and had the bag prepared before the transfer even happened," she said in a wavering voice as Daniel stepped to her side. He kissed her head as he gripped her around the shoulders and urged her back to sit down.

They ate some bread, fruit and cheese and washed it down with water and wine. He gave her the bottle of water and set the wine down on his opposite side. She raised an eyebrow and nudged his arm.

"I don't imagine magic and inebriation go very well together," he said with a wink.

She laughed as she stood and moved to Zetia's head.

"I would like to bathe. Would you allow me to use the hot springs of the egg room?"

She was given permission with a warning to be careful of the high temperatures. They had a bit of a political dilemma when Daniel wanted to take a bath. Tradition did not allow men in the Lair at all, and the idea of his being left in the egg room unattended brought low growls and hisses from many of the dragons.

"Don't worry about it. I'm OK," he said.

"No offense, but you smell, and it is not OK," Morgan said as she looked back to Zetia. "Lady Zetia, he is but one man. It offends me that you would question his honor, but let me ask one question. Do you expect he could do any harm to the eggs while under the watchful gaze of their mothers?"

Zetia gave a short snort of irritation and conceded. Daniel took a fast bath while being watched closely by three minor dragons. He returned with red cheeks and a sour expression, but smelled much better.

The rest of that day and the next flew by as she worked to bond with various hatchlings and initiate the Quickening of many more eggs. When all of the needs were taken care of, she addressed Zetia again.

"Will you be moving the group back to the dragon chambers of the castle now, my Lady?"

Zetia looked over the crowd of dragons as she hesitated to answer. Morgan did not wait for long before connecting to her alone again.

"Lady Zetia, I understand that it was a great heartbreak when my mother got sick and could no longer serve you properly. I also understand that you see me as a child, and question my ability to serve and to lead. I can only promise to give you my best, and will not be offended if you choose to stay here. I will make

arrangements to come here often with appropriate supplies. I have a great deal to learn about my life in Chemerie, but I want you to know that nothing will come before serving as Caretaker to our dragon brethren."

Zetia bowed and hummed.

"You honor us with your devotion and respect, my Lady. I prefer the group stay here in safety and stability for now. Thank you."

Morgan bowed and turned to leave. Before she reached Balia she was struck with intense fear and disappointment.

She moved back toward the group of dragons and let the magic guide her to the strong feelings of sorrow. The source was the fist hatchling she had bonded with, the one who had been closest to death. The young female hatchling looked to her with teary eyes.

"You said only death would pull you away. Are you dying too?"

"No, little one," she said as she dropped to her knees and scooped the precious dragon into her arms. She held her tight as she stood and turned to Zetia.

"She needs me, my Lady. May I take her with me to the castle?"

Zetia had come to her side when she lifted the youngling and now dropped her head to touch her snout to that of the hatchling as she crooned.

"You saved my daughter's life after most had considered her beyond hope. Her place is with you, my Lady. She will become your most devoted protector."

Morgan smiled into the eyes of the hatchling and passed love and devotion. The young dragon crooned and tucked her head under her chin.

"Thank you, Zetia. Your trust means more than I can say."

She walked back to where Daniel, Balia, and Menkar waited. When Daniel reached out a hand to stroke the hatchling, it scurried away around her back.

"Please don't be afraid of him little one. He is my brother and my protector. He would never hurt you."

The hatchling moved to put her head on top of Morgan's shoulder and peered at Daniel. Morgan took Daniel's hand palm-to-palm and connected to both him and the hatchling.

"Open your hearts to each other and see what you find," she told them.

A few seconds later, the hatchling moved down her arm, onto his, and rubbed her snout against his cheek with a sweet croon before hurrying back.

"I guess she liked what she saw," Morgan said with a laugh as she stroked the hatchling.

"And what is the beautiful young Lady's name?" he asked with a smile as he brushed the little one's cheek with the back of his fingers.

"I think the closest English pronunciation would be Lirpa."

Daniel gave a deep bow and said, "Very nice to meet you, Lady Lirpa." Lirpa bowed her head in return then tucked against Morgan's neck with a croon.

5

A Great Loss

MORGAN AND DANIEL arrived back at the castle after night had fallen. They were greeted by their uncles who introduced themselves as Josef and Maric. The group gathered in a small private dining room where a fantastic meal of goose, various vegetables, and decadent sweets awaited them.

As they ate, Josef and Maric gave them a better understanding of their roles. They learned that Daniel was not only Morgan's personal protector, he was also an Admiral of the Guard of Chemerie. He would act as the primary liaison between Morgan and the Admiralty until she was married, and a new King was crowned. Over the next few months, he would be taken through intense Knighthood training in which he would learn to fight both on land and aboard dragons.

That training began the next morning. Each day he rose

before dawn and worked with Josef and Maric in a mixture of physical training and philosophical discussion of the strategies of war utilizing the skills of dragons. He returned to his room each night well after dark, where he collapsed with exhaustion.

She spent her time during these weeks studying the history and customs of Chemerie. She would soon be crowned as Queen and was determined not to enter the role ignorant of those she was to serve.

MORGAN MARVELED at the rate at which Lirpa was growing. The dragon ate three times her weight in food each day and had doubled her size. Lirpa did not appreciate her increased girth and still pounced on her and scurried over her back; a habit that usually sent her stumbling to one side or toppling over altogether.

Despite her size, Lirpa never scratched her. Upon further investigation, she found that the young dragon could retract the claws back into her palms like a common house cat on Earth, using only enough of each claw to secure herself. This was a habit that flustered Morgan's tailor and chambermaids as they often had her coats and shirts returned to them with massive rips and tears.

She asked them to design a long coat made of a sturdy material that would hold up under the dragon's weight because she knew she would continue to allow young hatchlings to climb over her if they desired the comfort of her touch. The women made a magnificent knee-length cloak with four amply sized pockets for an egg or a newly hatched dragon on the inside. The outside was covered with strong braided cables in a beautiful pattern that provided the larger hatchlings with an easy foothold.

Morgan tried it out with Lirpa, who gave an approving series of croons and chirps.

"She asks that I thank you on behalf of all the dragons of Chemerie." The two ladies bowed and left the room blushing and smiling. The next week Morgan found two similar cloaks of different colors hanging in her closet.

Another fascinating characteristic of Lirpa's growth was her intelligence. Her comprehension of the things around her grew each day without any marked effort. She was approximately six months old and already had the intelligence level of a very capable adult human.

While Lirpa was born with a great amount of knowledge of dragons and magic, she was naïve of the ways of people. She became excited when faced with a major point of difference between the dragon's view and the people's view of a situation. Her most questioned matter was that of clothing.

"It seems pointless to cover oneself. A dragon is quite proud of their advancing color and girth," Lirpa said as she watched her dress one day.

"For us, it is not a question of being proud or ashamed. Our customs simp—"

"But, are not all females formed equally and are not all males formed equally? What is being hidden if all are made the same?"

"There are many reasons. A practical reason is the protection the clothes provide. Our skin is not as tough as your hide."

"What are the other reasons?"

"Propriety mostly, the fact is that humans prefer to wear clothes. It is a point of custom which is not likely to change," she said with finality. Lirpa nodded, but was not satisfied. Morgan knew the discussion would come up again and hoped it to be when she was much older.

ONE MORNING Morgan strolled out onto her terrace to find a glum-looking Daniel sitting alone in the garden below her room.

"What has you looking so down this beautiful morning?"

He turned his head to smile up at her. *"I'm fine. Just anxious I guess. Nothing to worry about."*

She felt sadness and longing in him.

"You're missing your life on Earth, aren't you?"

"Yeah, I guess I am. I do love our life here. I just miss letting go, you know? We spend so much time being proper and studying to fulfill our roles ... I'm getting very antsy. Don't you feel that way too?"

"Absolutely! I am somehow reminded how important it is for me to be safe every day. It's making me crazy."

"I never realized how much of a release riding the stallions at the ranch or my dirt bike were for me. The wild and out-of-control feeling was great. I am suffocating being so safe and proper!"

"I'll be right there. I have an idea."

Minutes later she was smiling up at her brother as he strapped his legs into Menkar's saddle.

"Morgan, I have ridden dragons many times now. It's not the same. It's very cool, but it's not the same reckless feeling I was referring to."

"So, you feel the dragons are too calm, too sedate, to

satisfy that need?"

"Well, yeah. They are very concerned about being safe and controlling their movements. I am grateful for their care, and it is amazing to fly for sure. But the energy is not the same as riding a wild stallion who has been in the barn too long and is ready to run till he drops. But, it will be nice; thank you."

She turned her back to him as a wicked grin lit her face. She connected to Menkar knowing he had heard their conversation.

"My friend, will you give him a sample of how you like to fly when you are bored and need a taste of being out-of-control? He needs a serious jolt to cheer him up. Just don't snap his neck or drop him, please."

"Ready when you are, Menkar," Daniel called out. "Let's go for a ni— Whoa!"

Morgan laughed as she watched Daniel get flattened on his back when Menkar bolted from the ground. They flew at incredible speeds and turned a series of acrobatic loops and spins as they headed out toward the mountains.

The exhilaration coming from both made her laugh aloud as she sat down on the lawn to watch and wait for them. After a while the smile slipped.

"Are we going to let the males have all the fun or go chase them and beat them at their own game?" Balia said as she landed behind Morgan.

Morgan whooped as she sprang to her feet and dodged Balia's offered foot to vault up her foreleg and land in the saddle.

"Nice mount, my Lady. Now strap in please," Balia said

as she chuckled.

Many of the Knights, Squires, and dragon keepers hanging around heard her whoop and noticed her unorthodox method of mounting the dragon. Most gathered around as she strapped her legs in, fastened an extra safety belt on at Balia's insistence, and wrapped her hands in the wrist loops.

"Let's go, my friend!" A second later she was squealing as Balia bolted into the air.

She had never felt so alive as when she laid flat to Balia's neck and connected. Her magic allowed her to anticipate every move as if she were flying herself. It was the most awesome feeling of oneness and power she could imagine.

Balia caught up with Menkar as he swooped low over the lake and Morgan connected to all three at once.

"How about a race? First to the Ancestral Lair without getting more than a tail's length above the tallest trees wins!"

Both dragons roared in agreement, and Balia pulled a fast, tight loop then shot forward past the younger dragon. She rose and fell with the tree line then shot straight up as they neared the first mountain ridge. She soared straight up along the cliff face only to fold her wings as she neared the crest and drop like a rock back down the other side of the sheer ridge.

Morgan whooped and screamed with joy as they flew. Soon she noticed they had pulled far ahead of Menkar.

"Balia, we may damage their pride if we beat them by this much. Maybe we should let them catch up a bit. But still win of course!"

Balia turned a slow loop and dropped in right behind Menkar where she nipped at his tail. He whipped his tail at her and put on a great burst of speed as she chuckled.

The major female let the younger and smaller male get a little ahead as they approached the waterfall then shot past him just before dropping into the lake. Morgan and Balia came out of the water in the main hall of the Lair a few seconds before Daniel and Menkar. Menkar nudged Balia hard, and she nipped at him playfully in return.

Morgan and Daniel laughed as they untied their legs and slid down the dragon's legs to the ground. They both sprawled on the stone floor and breathed hard through continued giggling.

"That was without question the coolest thing I have ever done. You rock, Menkar!" Daniel said.

Morgan noticed Menkar did not reply and froze when she felt why. She gripped Daniel's wrist to quiet him as she tilted her head back and looked up to see the huge head of Zetia looming over them. *"Uh oh!"*

"Good day, Lady Zetia. I apologize if we disturbed you," she said as she sat up.

Zetia looked at Balia who dropped her head and moved back a few steps. Morgan got to her feet and bowed to the Eldest Female dragon as her neck flushed.

"What did she say to you, my friend?" she asked Balia while holding Zetia's gaze.

When Balia did not answer she moved to stroke her head. Without turning her head from Balia, she spoke to Zetia through the connection to keep her words private.

"I hope you have not reprimanded my friend for giving me such a wonderful experience. She saw my unhappiness and anxiety at being held too still and relieved that with a simple fast flight. She

has done nothing wrong, Lady Zetia."

"She has a duty to protect you, young Caretaker, as do we all!" Zetia said in a loud booming voice. "She risked your life greatly for no reason. I find that very wrong indeed!"

"Her reason was friendship! She showed compassion for me and that I find no fault in! As my friend, she sees that I will give all I am to serve my brethren, but understands that I must live my life as well. I am glad she loves me as a friend and not only as her Caretaker. Her love for me is based as much on who I am as it is on how I can serve her!"

She turned and vaulted back into the saddle aboard Balia, and Daniel boarded Menkar. She glanced at the many shocked dragons standing around the hall and looked back to Zetia as she forced a deeper breath.

"Lady Zetia, before I go, may I ask if all are well here? Do any of my brethren need my assistance?"

Zetia paused a long time as she scanned the many dragons now gathered around her.

"I apologize to you, my Caretaker. You, of course, have the right to live your life as you wish. I would ask that you stay and visit with your brethren here. They were very happy to feel your approach," Zetia said as she bowed her head and started to leave the cavern.

"Please wait," Morgan called as she focused to calm herself. She slid back to the floor and walked forward to drop to one knee and bow her head before Zetia.

"Please forgive me, my Elder. I am still struggling with the limits I have to live under here, but … that is no excuse for being so disrespectful. I am truly sorry, Lady Zetia." She waited for a reply from the great noble dragon as she struggled to control her emotions. She was near tears by the time Zetia dropped her head and touched her shoulder.

"I love and respect you for your beautiful spirit and not only because you carry the magic my kind depend on. I am truly sorry if you thought otherwise, my Princess."

Morgan stroked her and felt honest love and devotion through the contact.

"Thank you, Lady Zetia. That means … so very much. I would love to visit with my brethren for a while, but I must return to the castle tonight. I didn't tell anyone of my intention to go so far and they'll miss me soon. I really don't want to disappoint or anger anyone else today."

SHE STAYED and visited with the younglings and hatchlings as well as with the older females who were there to care for them. The hatchlings soon figured out what her cloak was for, which led to her being covered with them at once as each chirped and scurried about. She knelt to steady herself and laughed as they played. Their affection and friendship was just the medicine her heart needed. It soon made her frustration disappear altogether.

"May we go home now, my Caretaker? Are you here to take us to the castle?" one youngling asked.

"No, little one, I have only come for a short visit. I will come back for a long visit soon if you would like that." Most of them chirped with contentment at her returning, but some remained sad at not accompanying her then.

"Lady Zetia, I am having a hot water pool made ready in the hatching area of the castle's dragon chambers. I hope it will serve to give the hatchlings the same comfort with water they have after

being born here. Is there anything more I can do to make you feel confident in returning the group to the castle?"

"We will come home soon, my Princess, but not yet. The pool sounds very nice and we thank you for your thoughtfulness."

Morgan felt the tension in Zetia and waited a bit before speaking again.

"I am not so naïve that I don't realize your delay is due to your lack of confidence in me. What must I do to convince you?"

Zetia looked away to watch a group of younglings playing tag with Daniel for a moment before she answered.

"I do not mean to hurt you, my Princess. Please consider my position. You did not receive proper training and I can take no risk in this matter. I trust your spirit, but I am unsure of your ability to control your magic as yet."

Morgan knew there was more behind Zetia's refusal to return because she felt a hint of deceit as she spoke. She gave the younglings a last round of hugs, and boarded Balia.

"I very much hope to prove myself worthy soon, so you can bring our family back together," she said as she bowed once more.

Zetia returned the bow and answered, *"I do not doubt your ability, only your experience. There are two among us who will lay their clutches soon, and I do not wish to move them now. I will consider the matter again when their eggs are ready to be Quickened."*

Morgan's heart ached as she had to wave goodbye to the many younglings and minor dragons, especially when one of the smallest flew toward her and turned back only at the call of his mother.

She drifted between sad and mad all the way home and

did not speak of her conversation with Zetia to Daniel or Balia. She wandered the castle and grounds most of the night as she considered her readiness to be Queen.

MORGAN AND DANIEL were soon questioned about the vaulting move by several of the Guard. They asked her to confirm that the major and minor dragons were accepting of their learning and using this method as opposed to the formal method of being lifted in their palm. She found none who were not curious of the method and willing to allow it. In truth, it was easier for them and faster.

She and Daniel illustrated the move then sat on the lawn and laughed as various Knights and dragons attempted it.

"I'm sure you've noticed that the females have learned the skill faster than the males, both dragon and human."

Daniel narrowed his eyes as he turned his head to her.

"I think Menkar and I need a rematch with some new rules and a new course."

"Yeah? You think you two have a shot at beating us, do ya?"

"Sure do, little missy!"

"Bring it, old man!"

She connected to their dragon companions as they raced toward them and made sure they were interested in another crazy ride. Balia was hesitant at first, but conceded as Daniel and Menkar both started badgering her for being scared to lose.

The Knights watched as their exuberant Prince and Princess vaulted into their saddles while badgering one another in loud voices. A large crowd of Knights and Squires had gathered by the time they bolted into the air as if off to war.

They rode the two massive dragons for half an hour, each smiling and hooting with joy the entire time. When they landed on the lawn and collapsed onto the grass breathing hard, they were soon surrounded by many Knights and Squires, including Josef and Maric.

"Oh mercy. I think we're about to get grounded."

Daniel let out a cackle that he failed to hide with a cough. They both sobered and sat up as they saw their uncles' intense eyes. The two men held stern expressions for only a few seconds before smiling and offering hands to pull them to their feet.

"That looked incredibly fun," said Maric, the younger brother.

"But incredibly insane as well," added Josef, the elder brother and ever-present voice of reason.

"Totally jealous, both of them," Morgan said as she smirked at Daniel.

"Insanely fun is more like it!" Daniel said with a huge smile.

They laughed together as they were bombarded with questions from the group around them about how it felt. Neither was surprised to find that flying like that was unheard of given the strict propriety the Chemerians lived under.

"If both the dragon and rider enjoy it, why shouldn't they share such an awesome experience? We have plenty of harness straps, I would think," she said.

"My Princess, will you ask if any other dragons would be interested? Because many of us are for certain," blurted one of the youngest Knights.

She smiled at the eager young woman then closed her

eyes to focus as she opened her connection to all the dragons around the field.

"My dragon brethren, if you would be interested in carrying a rider through a wild flight like we just had, give a little roar, please."

Many of the Knights and Squires jumped as the whole group of dragons roared at once.

"There's your answer, my friends. They like having fun as much as we do."

She saw bewilderment on everyone's face at the same instant she felt that emotion from Balia.

"What is it? Did I do something wrong by asking them?" she asked Balia.

"No, my Lady. I am just quite surprised to see you connect to so many spirits at once. That is a wonderful skill you have developed, my Caretaker."

"Thank you, my friend. So, how about a more relaxed flight as we watch our friends have their first crazy rides together?"

MORGAN AND BALIA flew along with Daniel and Menkar in wide slow circles around the castle as they watched their friends shoot past them whooping and roaring in delight. The dragons enjoyed sharing their skill of flying. It was a way of bonding with their human brethren, and that, they cherished.

Joy and laughter from a group of minor dragons and Squires practicing the vaulting move together got her attention. Two Knights were helping them, and Morgan got a strong urge to join the lesson.

Before she could ask Balia to head that way, she felt the joy of children and younglings coming from another group at the far end of the field near the lake. It was that group she chose to join.

As they landed, a female Squire and all those she was helping either bowed or dropped to one knee. She bowed in return and smiled.

"Good day, my friends. Can I join the fun?"

She could feel that the Squire was nervous, but the young woman did not show it.

"You are of course welcome, Princess Morgan. I hope I have not offended you by working with the younglings."

"Not at all. I came to join you because I felt their joy and wanted to thank you for spending time with them like this. I'd like to help if you don't mind the company."

"We are honored, my Lady," the Squire said.

Morgan smiled and patted her shoulder before kneeling in front of a small boy of about four who was petting Falin.

"And what is your name, young man?"

"I am David, my Princess."

"Have you tried the vaulting move yet?"

"No, my Lady, I was just asking if my dragon brother would mind if I tried," the boy said. She was surprised at his perfect speech and manners, but reminded herself where she was.

"What do you think, Falin, are you ready to give it a try?"

Falin gave a quick nod with an eager snort and proffered his leg as he braced himself. She was a little concerned. The boy was small, and so was Falin, despite his huge heart. The youngling had grown a great deal since she met him, but he was still barely twice her size.

She stood close to Falin's back as the little boy backed up to run toward them. He vaulted and threw his leg up, but did not quite make it high enough. Falin felt his mishap and shifted to place himself under the boy.

"That was fantastic, young man," she said to the boy, "And you are a wonderful friend, Falin." Both beamed as they took a proud walk around the field.

She helped many other pairs, then took a seat on the soft grass against Balia's side. The smallest of the younglings and children played around them while they watched the Squire work with the largest among the group. Balia allowed both the dragon and human younglings to crawl over her and crooned to them.

"May I ask your name?" Morgan said to the Squire.

"I am Squire Willow, my Princess."

"You have a very good sense of the younglings, Squire Willow. Are you comfortable with the majors as well?"

Willow glanced toward Balia, then looked down as she stroked the youngling beside her.

"I enjoy interacting with the dragons any time I can, but I have never worked with nor ridden a major, my Lady. Actually, I have … " Willow's answer died in her throat when she saw Balia rise.

Balia proffered her leg and nodded to Willow.

"Balia says it's time that changed. Please, show us all your vaulting skill, and honor Balia with your first ride aboard a major."

Willow hesitated as she gazed into Balia's eyes. A little girl of about eight shoved her toward Balia to get her started. Willow's face broke into a huge grin as she took off for Balia, vaulting into the saddle with ease.

"Strap in, please," Morgan said.

"I am ready, Lady Balia. And thank you very much," Willow said.

Balia lifted into the air and soared easily around the valley for a while before making a few sharper moves, but nothing too crazy. After their ride, Willow dismounted by sliding down the shoulder and leg of the dragon as Morgan had done. She moved to Balia's head and bowed low before thanking her again.

"She says you are welcome and thanks you for working with the younglings so kindly," Morgan told Willow as she moved to stand before her. "Would you consider splitting your time between your Knighthood studies and helping me with the younglings in my care? I know I could get it approved by the Admiralty and would be grateful."

"It would be an honor to assist you, my Princess," Willow said with a bow. "Thank you very much."

Little David tapped Morgan's leg and bowed when she turned to him.

"My Uncle calls me to dinner, my Lady. Thank you for helping us today. It was an honor to spend time with you."

She rustled his hair as she said, "It was wonderful to meet you, David. I hope to visit more soon."

Her face flushed as she watched him run across the field. When he reached his uncle, he bounced with excitement while pointing back to her. The Knight bowed to her, and she waved back. When she started to open a connection and speak to him, her head spun and her hands tingled.

The turn to board Balia made her wobble. Willow and

some of the children were watching as Balia scooped her into her palm.

"I'm fine. Just forgot to eat lunch today," she said with a smile to the children before looking to Willow. "Please come see me tomorrow, and we'll talk more. Goodnight, everyone."

"Are you well, my Princess?" Balia asked with concern as they lifted gracefully into the air.

"I feel fine now. I felt weird before, but I have no idea what it was. It felt similar to the symptoms of Quickening."

DANIEL WORKED with the Admiralty of the Guard to plan ways the new level of aggressive flight could be utilized in times of battle. He seemed much more content since he had established a relationship with a few of the large male dragons and went on wild rides often.

Morgan worked with Willow and the younglings most every day. Willow looked young to Morgan but was actually a bit older than she was. She doted over the younglings every day when she was released from classes. Morgan had told her she would not allow her time with the younglings to interfere with her education and wasn't surprised to hear her classwork had improved since she found such a wonderful motivation.

They discussed plans to make the hatching rooms more hospitable for the brooding females. Morgan had steam generators and a hot waterfall placed in the large room nearest the poolroom for the comfort of the largest brooding females who could not fit into the smaller room. She had asked to expand the poolroom's size, but after consideration of the construction of the building, it was deemed impossible.

DANIEL ALMOST SKEWERED MARIC as Falin burst through a door roaring. They both hurried to follow as they saw his panic.

When they reached the poolroom, they found Morgan pale, trembling, and unconscious at the edge of the pool where several younglings sang the dragons' healing song as they snuggled against her.

"She just collapsed and was moaning and clutching as if she had been stabbed in the chest. But there are no wounds," Willow said as she shifted to let Daniel take her place.

"Her magic allows her to feel the pain of others. She received pain that is too strong for her. It must be great pain from many," Maric said as he took one of her hands and raised his other to him. Daniel copied his actions and gripped both of their hands. "Open your mind to her, so she may draw from our strength. Focus on your love for her as hard as you can."

As they closed their eyes and concentrated, Daniel heard the young dragons change the cadence of their song and increase the intensity. His hand started to tingle against hers. Moments later, she finally opened her eyes.

As he lifted her to a sitting position, tears poured down her face. She was still clenched and trembling with pain as she tried to stand.

"The breeding group at the Ancestral Lair has been attacked by other dragons. Many have been killed, and many more are too wounded to escape. The battle continues, and it is weighted heavily against our brethren. Maric, gather the Guard. Hurry, please."

Falin shot from the room to spread the news before she

even finished her statement. Maric dashed out of the room as Daniel lifted her in his arms and carried her back up to Kindred Hall.

"Put me down. I need to carry myself." She connected to the dragons she could reach and found many of the largest had left at once while others met the Knights in the court-yard.

They soon reached the courtyard where the Knights were mounting upwards of twenty great dragons and awaiting their Admirals, now Josef, Maric, and Daniel, to mount and lead them out. The dragons clawed the ground and snorted, anxious to be off.

Morgan felt intense worry from Daniel as he pulled her to face him.

"You are so weak, yet you're the only one who can heal the injured. We both know that taking you into a battle and risking your life is unacceptable. Promise me that you will be reasonable if you go with us."

"I am going!" She pushed feelings of conviction with her words, and he nodded.

He helped her to the waiting palm of Balia then boarded Menkar. With them settled, Josef gave the signal and the group lifted off, falling into a tight formation surrounding Balia and Morgan.

"Let me help with the pain, my Caretaker," Balia said. Morgan lay down against her neck. Through the great dragon, she grew stronger and was able to block most of the pain.

She focused to reach out with her magic farther ahead. When they approached the mountains near enough to see the waterfall, she connected to Zetia. The Elder dragon's words came in fractured phrases but she understood enough.

"Admirals, they were attacked from above. The enemy dragons dropped huge boulders and blasted through a weak point in the highest of the tunnels. Enemy dragons and other horrible beasts called Marocks flooded the main chamber. Split your Guard and attack from both entrances. Balia has given the location of the upper entrance to your mounts. I will go through the upper entrance in hopes of reaching the hatchlings and eggs the soonest."

"No, Morgan," Daniel said, *"I couldn't keep you from coming, but I'm not letting you go in there until it's safe. You won't serve the dragons by getting yourself hurt or killed. Now stay back and wait for my call, please."* She glared at him for many seconds before nodding.

Minutes later, she and Balia set down about a mile from the entrance that had been blasted through the upper wall of the chamber. They watched as half of the Knights of the Guard flooded through it.

In order to hear Daniel's call, she had to open her connection. That meant that she felt the emotion of every Knight and dragon in the battle. Her heart wrenched with the rage and fear each felt. She trembled from the pain shooting through her. Even the help of Balia could not block it when they were so close to the Lair.

The pain worsened as she started receiving flashes of what those fighting were seeing. Connections formed and broke, one after another. She connected with a Chemerian major dragon just as she bit into the neck of a huge male enemy dragon. A second of triumph was followed by unimaginable pain. The connection was lost as the dragon died.

Next, a Knight of the Guard leapt from the back of her mount to drive her sword into the back of a huge Marock approaching Josef from behind.

The connections formed and broke without her control. The worst was viewing through the eyes of a hatchling she had bonded with as it watched an enemy dragon slay its mother. She shared the hatchling's rage as he launched himself at the enemy dragon, then welcomed death herself as she felt the hatchling die in the jaws of the enemy dragon.

The battle was absolute chaos, a hailstorm of teeth, talons, swords and blood. She used Balia's strength to pull her mind away from the group enough to stop the images. It worked for a moment, but the frantic calls of two minor female dragons defending the egg room broke through. They were fighting a large group of Marocks with all their might, but were outnumbered.

"Let's go, now!" she screamed to Balia. "The Marocks will crush the eggs!"

Balia did not stir, but Morgan could hear her trying to warn the dragons within the Lair of the call from the egg room.

"Your safety must be protected if there is to be any survival of our kind. Losing any of my kindred is pain beyond reason, but the loss of you could mean the loss of us all," Balia said.

"I know you are right, but this is not who I am. I cannot just sit here and feel them die!" She slid from Balia's back and sprinted for the dense woods.

Balia failed to grab her and roared as she lifted off. Morgan heard only the pained screams of death and calls for help from those in the battle as she ran her top speed through the rough brush.

DANIEL OPENED his eyes as Menkar burst from the water inside the main cavern. The roaring and screeching of the dragons fighting all around him was deafening, and he had only sight with which to judge his actions.

"Let's try our new moves in these tight quarters, my friend," Daniel yelled as he patted Menkar hard on the neck. Menkar let out an angry roar and dove for an enemy dragon carrying a rider and lance. As they approached, the enemy dragon rolled to bare teeth and talons at him.

Menkar swooped and flipped over the enemy dragon's head as he bit its neck and placed Daniel in striking distance of the rider. Daniel swung his sword and opened the rider's neck then shifted off the saddle to avoid the slashing talons of the enemy dragon.

Menkar made a quick roll himself and gouged the drag-on's hide with his fore and hind claws as he repositioned his bite to crush the dragon's neck. He released the dragon as it died and roared as he put on a burst of speed for a tangle of dragons on the floor to the right.

He did not slow and slammed into an enemy dragon that had just tackled a female Chemerian dragon. He and the female overpowered the enemy then exchanged quick croons before both were off again.

Daniel saw a pair of Chemerian Knights standing as guard around a group of youngling dragons. They were holding off a group of hairy beasts that roared much like the dragons.

He and Menkar joined the ground effort. Daniel let his fighting skills flow as everything around him became a blur of movement.

Time seemed to stand still as a deafening roar and chilling screams filled his head. He turned to see the Knight behind him crushed in the snapping jaws of a major enemy dragon. His blood ran cold as the beast turned for him. A second before it reached him, a huge tail sent him flying across the cavern.

He lifted his spinning head to see Zetia attack the huge enemy dragon as a group of Marocks and enemy soldiers ran toward the younglings. He started running back at them when Morgan's voice filled his head.

"Daniel, get a group to the egg room fast. I am coming."

He focused to answer her without success then redirected his steps as he called to Josef and Menkar.

MORGAN BROKE the connection to Daniel to block his argument as she ran for the Lair. Logic had left her. Only passion carried her now.

She ran less than five minutes more before she was grabbed and lifted into the air by a huge hairy beast with the strength of ten men. She recognized the thing from the battle images as a Marock.

The beast sniffed her hair and neck then licked her face. She kicked and punched to get away, but received only a harsh blow to the face for her efforts. The Marock gave a bark-like laugh as it threw her over a shoulder and continued to walk toward the entrance to the cavern.

She held her pounding head as she fought to focus and

soon felt Balia circling above the tree canopy.

"Please wait, my friend. Please don't hurt yourself in reaching me!"

She opened her mind to Daniel but couldn't focus. Desperate to keep Balia from crashing through the tree canopy, she opened to the entire Guard and explained her situation.

The smell of the beast was horrid. It was a mixture of wet dog and dung. As it walked, it used its free arm as a third leg reminding her of gorillas. A vicious gorilla with pointed ears, long hair, and longer legs would describe this nasty creature well.

As they neared the cavern she became dizzy and nauseated. The amount of emotional and visual information she was receiving became a heavy blanket falling over her mind. To prevent passing out, she thought only of closing her mind. A veil of magic rose around her mind, and the sensations stopped. Her mind was quiet.

A moment later, the beast carrying her stopped, sniffed the air, and started backing up in a crouch. When she opened her connection again to reach for Balia, a jolting flash of tingling hit her and her body grew hot. That shock of magic allowed the emotions of the hundreds fighting in the Lair to pass her fragile new guard. The pain and anguish overwhelmed her in seconds.

A KNIGHT of the Guard lie hidden in the underbrush. He had been startled minutes earlier when Morgan's voice entered his head, calling for help.

He was very still as he heard the Marock approach his hiding spot on the trail. Just as he had hoped, the beast did not smell him and took no notice as it passed. Once the beast was out of earshot, he climbed a tree near the path. He had asked his dragon mount, Broon, to wait near the mouth of the cavern for three minutes as he ran ahead. The dragon was then to begin walking along the path in the direction they had heard the Caretaker's call.

While moving across a limb over the path, he felt a shock move through him, as if he had been hit over the head. He dropped and clung to the limb as his head spun and his whole body tingled. The sensation lasted a few seconds then stopped as abruptly as it had hit him. He gathered himself and hung upside down over the path by his knees.

In one hand he held a short and very sharp knife. He heard the Marock stop a short way up the path and begin to back-track. He hung silent in the darkness as the beast drew closer then reached out and delivered a quick and deadly blow to the side of its neck. The beast dropped to the path in a heap, spilling the limp form of the Caretaker out to the side.

The Knight dropped to the ground and knelt beside the young woman. When he rolled her over and saw her face for the first time, he froze.

"So beautiful," he said as he reached out to move a strand of hair from across her face. When his finger grazed her skin he jumped from a sharp shock that left his hand tingling. Broon crooned as he approached and put out his palm.

"Are you sure you can carry both of us?"

The dragon nodded and snorted, so he lifted the Care-taker, careful not to touch her skin again. Broon wrapped his neck around them and nudged them into his palm.

With the Knight and the Caretaker aboard, the minor

dragon moved back toward the next meadow where Balia paced and growled. Once within reach, she sniffed and crooned over Morgan.

"I believe she is only unconscious, Lady Balia," the Knight said.

Broon dropped to the ground as Balia offered her palm. The Knight had never ridden a major dragon, much less a female, and knew this offer was only made to him because he would need to hold onto the Caretaker during the flight.

Balia took to the air with grace and roared as she flew to the newly formed entrance to the dragon Lair. She landed at its edge then dropped into the cavern and swooped to the floor below. The battle had been won by the Chemerian forces, but many were lost or near death.

Balia again offered her palm to assist the Knight in dismounting with the Caretaker. As he stepped off her palm he heard other dragons land nearby then the approach of frantic footfalls. He glanced up as he laid the Caretaker on the floor to find his youngest Admiral running toward him and moved back at once. Daniel dropped to his knees beside her, took one of her hands, then held up his other palm toward the Knight.

"We need to wake her. Many need her help. Please, take her other hand and mine. It will form a healing circle."

The Knight knelt and grasped the Caretaker's hand, gritting his teeth to the sharp sensations of her magic, then took Daniel's.

"Open your mind and heart. Think of nothing but the respect and devotion you hold for the Caretaker. Will you add your strength please, Balia?" Balia laid her snout against

Morgan's belly and began to hum.

The Knight did as he was told and focused on feelings of respect. He could feel nothing except the intense tingle in his arm from the contact to the Caretaker.

His mind suddenly filled with the image of her face, and his heart lifted again. With this thought, he felt his and the Caretaker's hands grow hot and her grip tightened around his hand. An unimaginable rush of emotion took his breath as the tingle from his hand exploded all through his body. He watched his Caretaker wake as the strong sensation consumed him.

MORGAN SAT UP as the Knight slumped over across her legs. She looked at Daniel and connected to learn what happened in the battle and how she came to be here. Through the connection she felt his pain and noticed a deep gash in his side. She took both of his hands to send healing energy. Once his wound was closed enough to stop bleeding, she let him lift her and turned to the other Knights around them.

"Someone watch over this brave Knight, please. He is only unconscious. Please let me know if that changes."

She opened herself to the cavern and network of caves around it as she struggled to not let the feelings overwhelm her again. Forcing slow deep breaths, she connected with each living human and dragon to assess their needs.

"The egg room," she shouted as she turned and ran toward Balia.

She vaulted up to the saddle, and they shot from the ground. Daniel and Menkar were close behind with four other dragons and Knights trailing them as well.

She slid from Balia's back at the small tunnel entrance and sprinted on as she focused on the fading spirit ahead of her. When she reached the egg room, she dropped to her knees and put her hands to the minor female's head. She began to sing the dragons' healing song as she pushed her healing magic. It took almost ten minutes, but she was able to stabilize her, leaving only minor surface wounds.

She crawled over to inspect the eggs the dragon clutched to her belly and almost vomited. Tears streamed down her face when she saw that all but one of the clutch had been smashed, killing the infants within. She picked up the lone surviving egg and placed it in one of the padded pockets of her cloak.

As she searched through the dozen scattered around the room, she found only three others that survived. She stored the eggs in her cloak and searched to find the next dragon in need. Her heart ached as she realized it was Zetia herself.

They found her back in the main chamber. When Morgan reached out to lay her hands on Zetia's snout, the dragon moved away.

"No, treat all others then return to me. I have lived a long life and will not take years from the younglings," she said through blood-filled lungs. Morgan's entire body ached as she turned away, but she knew argument with Zetia was futile and disrespectful.

She worked for hours healing those she could. The Knights and dragons brought the wounded into the main chamber and helped where they could as she went to work on them. She became so focused that she had to be touched to become aware of someone calling her.

After hours of work, Daniel took her by the shoulders and lifted her to her feet. He led her to a pile of straw and forced water and food on her. As she ate, her eyes fell on Zetia's great form lying against the far wall. She reached out to her but felt nothing in return; she was gone.

Tears filled her eyes as the devastating loss of so many dragon spirits hit her. Grief shifted to anger, and she pulled herself back together to return to her work.

When she had done all she could, she returned to the brave Knight who had risked his life to save hers. She sat by his head and lifted it into her lap. When she placed her hand on his cheek to wake him, she flinched back to stare at her tingling hand. Her markings were aglow as if she had touched a dragon. She moved her hand away and stared at the handsome man as Daniel knelt beside her.

"Are you ready to go? You've done all you can here and we need to take the survivors back to the castle."

She kept her gaze on the Knight's face as she answered.

"I'm not leaving until he is stronger, and I can wake him without pain. You can send the rest of the party on to the castle, but we will wait."

Daniel hesitated a few seconds, then joined Josef and Maric in organizing the return to the castle.

"WAKE UP, brave Knight. I want to thank you properly."

The Knight took a deep breath as a comforting warmth drew him to fall back to sleep, then struggled to open his eyes and focus. When he did so his breath caught in his throat. He was gazing up into the beautiful face and slightly glowing eyes of the Caretaker.

Her smile jolted him to his senses and he stood, then bowed.

"It is my honor to serve you, my Caretaker. I apologize for my weakness. I have never experienced a healing circle before and was not quite prepared for it."

He was mortified when he felt his cheeks flush. He scanned the cavern and noticed that it was now empty except for the Caretaker, two Admirals, three dragons, and himself.

"How may I serve you, my Lady?"

Morgan nodded to Daniel. He helped her stand, then moved to the Knight.

"What's your name, Sir?" Daniel asked.

"I am Sir Alec."

"Sir Alec, you saved the life of your future Queen. You did so by honor and not by order. For that, I offer you the post of your choice within the Guard. Do you know what your choice would be, or would you like some time to consider it?"

Alec's gaze swept to Morgan, where it lingered for a couple of seconds before returning to Daniel's.

"I would choose to serve the Caretaker in the position that she feels most profitable to her, Admiral."

"Alright, I will talk with her when she has rested," Daniel said as he shook Sir Alec's hand. His smile faded as he gripped the man's hand and stepped closer.

"I thank you personally for saving my sister. I can't really express just how grateful I am."

He stepped back and bowed to Alec then looked to Morgan. She used the arm he offered to steady herself as she looked at Alec.

"Thank you, Sir Alec. Both for the rescue, and for your help in waking me."

"It is an honor to serve you, my Caretaker," Alec said as he bowed while holding her eyes.

"My brother will fly with me. Menkar will carry you home."

THE FLIGHT back to the castle was a silent one. Morgan lay along Balia's neck and connected to her. They both shared their despair over the loss of so many dragon spirits.

"I am sorry I ran from you."

"I understand. We all understand how deeply a Caretaker feels the emotions and pain of those around her. It is I who apologize for not being prepared to stop you."

"You should not have to stop me. You would not need to if I had more control over my magic. Zetia was right to not trust me yet."

"Do not say that, my friend. Every spirit you saved today is testament to how capable you are. None questions your ability or your place as our Queen and Caretaker. We are very proud of all you have accomplished since joining us so young."

Morgan passed her gratitude through their connection, but said nothing before falling asleep.

DANIEL WALKED with Morgan to her quarters, where she was greeted by the best thing she could imagine. All around her room and balcony were young dragons of all ages. The group began to hum and sing in the dragon language. She took a deep breath as their love filled her.

She felt a nudge on her hand and turned to see Falin carrying Lirpa. Both were looking up at her with worried eyes.

She knelt and hugged Falin with one arm while gathering Lirpa up into the other. She kissed and nuzzled Lirpa, then put her on the bed so she could remove her cloak.

"Will you take these to the egg room where the brooding females await them, please?"

"I certainly will, my Caretaker. Goodnight," Daniel said as he kissed her head and turned to leave.

"Thank you for not chastising me for my stupidity in running off alone."

"I had not even considered it. Get some sleep, my brave little sister," he said with a smile.

She slipped off her filthy top layer of clothes and lay down on her bed amongst the dragons as their songs filled the room. As the smallest joined her on the bed and snuggled up close to her body, her tension faded and she drifted off to sleep.

6

Lord Harrick

THE NEXT MORNING, Morgan woke to find Falin and Lirpa still sleeping beside her. She moved from between them and went onto her terrace. With a deep breath, she opened herself to all the dragons she could reach to check their health. Feelings of both grief and thankfulness washed over her as she did so.

A moment later, she found pain, fear, and exhaustion in a youngling who had his guard up between them. Her bare feet slapped the marble floor as she ran through the castle toward the dragon chambers. She almost flattened a house-maid on the way and apologized in magic without stopping.

She had been so focused on the youngling's spirit, she had not noticed it was not alone until she reached the doorway and halted. The dragon youngling was lying at the edge of the warm pool of the hatching chamber with his head resting in the lap of Sir Alec. Blood was seeping into the pool from wounds all over his small body.

She watched as Alec stroked the dragon and hummed a comforting tune in his deep voice. Beside him lay a length of chain with a broken cuff bracket and some tools.

"Thank you for comforting him, Sir Alec."

He did not act surprised to hear her voice and smiled as he spoke to the dragon.

"Look, my friend. Your Caretaker has come to you, just as I told you she would."

She knelt near the little dragon and examined the wounds he carried. She stroked his head as she spoke with Alec alone.

"Has he been here long?"

Alec shook his head as he continued his hum to the dragon.

"You can answer me through thought while I hold the connection. Tell me what you know, please."

"He just arrived moments ago. I was about to come get you. I only wanted to help him calm a bit before leaving him. I am sorry to delay telling you, but I could not leave the bindings on him another second."

"Do not apologize for being a loving friend."

He gave a small smile and started to shift the youngling's head from his lap.

"Please stay." An odd look crossed his face, so she added, *"Your presence is obviously comforting to him."*

He settled back in with a nod and continued to comfort the dragon.

"Where did he come from. Why was he not here last night?"

"I have a guess, but you will need to ask him, my Lady."

The youngling looked up at her, lifting his head only a

couple of inches from Alec's lap.

"It is very nice to see you again, my Caretaker. Please, can you help my friends who were taken away?"

"We will certainly try. But first, may I heal your wounds?"

The youngling nodded and shifted to hang his head across Alec's thigh. She scooted closer to place her hands to the sides of his head. She pushed healing to close his wounds then let her magic flow freely to strengthen him. When she finished, the youngling took in a deep breath and gave a sweet sigh.

"I am sorry to add to your pain, but I have to ask if you will show me what you saw. Do you feel up to it?"

The youngling tensed at first, then relaxed and shifted closer to her as he nodded.

"I will show you, my Caretaker. It will help to save my friends."

She glanced at Alec as she caressed the youngling's head in her lap.

"He is going to share his experiences from yesterday with me. Will you please stay while I do this? I'm not really sure how this will affect me. I like to think of myself as a strong person, but the power of the magic has overwhelmed me a few times already."

He nodded, then watched as she placed her hands on the sides of the dragon's head again. The eyes of both the dragon and Caretaker began to glow. After a quiet moment, she began to flinch as if stung. Many muffled groans escaped her, and a lone tear slid down her cheek. Her facial expressions showed anger, fear, and pain.

When she released the dragon's head she leaned forward to lift it further into her lap and wrapped her arms around the trembling creature. She held it for many minutes as she hummed the tune Alec had been humming. He joined her and caressed the little one's back until Falin and many other younglings arrived to comfort him.

When she stood and swayed a bit, Alec caught her waist. He did not seem to notice the sharp breath that touch had caused as he let go and knelt to move the tools and bindings to a shelf.

"I need to speak with the Admiralty," she said as she started toward the stairs. "Many more of our dragon young-lings have been taken."

She swayed again as she reached the stairs and flinched as he laid his warm coat over her shoulders and gripped her upper arms with it to steady her again.

"Please take this," he said as he coaxed her into the coat. She didn't fight as she realized her camisole and tights were soaked and clinging to her.

They walked to the study where the Admiralty of the Guard was gathered in a heated discussion of the previous day's attack.

"… and we do not even know how they found the Lair!" Maric was saying.

"I do," she said as she stepped into the room.

The group stood and fell silent as Daniel moved to her.

"What happened?" he said as he steadied her and threw a sharp glance at Alec.

"I'm fine. Please, just get me to my seat," she said only to him as she pushed him to get him started. To the rest of the room she said, "Everyone, please sit. I need to tell you what I've learned from an injured youngling who just returned to the castle."

Josef gave Alec a nod of dismissal, and he turned to leave.

"Sir Alec, stay please," she said with authority as she moved her eyes between those of her uncles and brother. "You will be part of this mission by my request and I want you to know all the information available."

Alec turned, bowed to her, and moved to the end of the long table to stand behind a senior Knight. Josef looked perplexed but gave no argument.

She drank some cool water and took a few deep breaths as she spoke to Daniel.

"Have you been told about Lord Harrick, the evil Son of Arshek who has a castle in the mountains far to the east?"

"Yes, of course, I understand it was his militia that attacked the Lair."

The group went quiet as she raised her head.

"Lord Harrick has taken a number of hatchlings and at least one large youngling alive." She continued despite the many gasps and looks of rage spread through the room. "He does not mean to just enslave or kill our dragon brethren. He means to breed them to one another, and with his own, in order to increase the size of his fleet."

She paused to let that sink in before continuing to the far worse news.

"The factor which makes this an even more dangerous situation for all of us, is that Lord Harrick has some amount of our Chemerian magic within him."

The room began to rumble with hushed curses, and many gave her looks of disbelief.

"I have never heard of this. My Princess, are you quite sure?" Josef said in a quiet voice.

"Yes, I am quite sure! Lord Harrick's lineage was part of the knowledge passed to me. I will explain all of the details later, but right now we need to discuss our intentions." Her tone had brought silence from the group again, and no one spoke for many seconds.

"We must strike with all our might to crush him once and for all," Maric said as he slammed his fist on the table.

"No brother, we will not ask our dragon brethren to enter into such a battle so soon. We would surely lose more of them to the evil of Lord Harrick," Josef said.

Rumblings broke out through the table as many began to argue the points of a large assault.

Morgan gave Daniel a pointed look, and he knocked hard on the table as he stood.

"Our plan should be based on as much fact as possible. I suggest we learn all we can from our Caretaker before any idea is considered," he said. This time his tone brought silence before he sat back down and nodded to her. She scanned the eyes of the many men and women at the table before she spoke again.

"Some of the abilities of the Caretaker line are within Lord Harrick despite his being male and of Arshek. I do not know how much of the magic remains because many generations have passed since the crossing of the bloodlines. But I believe that is how he found the Lair. Once the dragons returned there, he felt their presence via the magic.

"He may not have even known he was capable of detecting our brethren before then. Our dragons have been too far away from him to have felt their presence.

"Now, however, being in the presence of the younglings,

he will undoubtedly experiment with them in an attempt to use this magic. If successful, he could gain a great deal of information from them. I hope to never need to force my way into a dragon's mind, but it can be done if one is strong enough and willing to cause them severe pain."

She paused, having to swallow hard at the thought.

"My friends, I do not have to tell you how much damage could be done to our land if the information held within our dragons is taken by Harrick. I am not talking about what they have witnessed themselves in their short lifetime; the true fear is him accessing the ancestral knowledge that lies in each of them."

She stood and looked into the eyes of Daniel, Josef, and Maric in turn as she continued.

"It is my wish that a tactical group of Knights attempt to rescue the younglings tonight. Waiting is not an option. The longer Lord Harrick is around them, the more likely it is he will learn to force his way into their minds. We cannot let that happen."

AN HOUR LATER, Daniel knocked on her bedroom door. Before he managed to strike the door the second time, he heard, *"Come in, brother, and quietly please."*

He walked to her place on the terrace and knelt beside her chair. The youngling dragon that had been abducted lie asleep beside her with its tail wrapped around her leg and its large head across her torso.

"He just fell asleep for the first time since his escape," she said with a sad smile.

He nodded as he stroked the dragon's head.

"What's his name?"

"Yatu. His sadness is profound. He lost his entire living family in the attack and feels a tremendous amount of guilt for escaping without the others."

"It's time for the Guard unit to leave," Daniel said without looking at her.

"And you're torn. You are my protector, but also serve the dragons as I do."

He nodded with a deeper scowl.

"You have to go, Daniel. This is more important than anything right now. Besides, I am quite safe. Have you not noticed that the major dragons have taken to keeping watch over me in shifts since my return yesterday?" she said as she gestured at the terrace railing.

He moved to look over it and found a male major dragon lying just below her terrace in the garden, having made a large flowerbed his own. The dragon nodded in respect, and he returned the notion.

She could feel his anxiety level dropping and smirked.

"Good hunting."

He smiled and laughed as he started for the door, but stopped and knelt beside her with a sigh.

"Are you sure you want Sir Alec to come with us tonight? When he joined me in the healing circle with you it felt diff—"

"I know that he is the right person to be there to comfort the dragons in my absence. That is what matters, and that is why he is going," she said as she gave him a sharp look.

"Alrighty then," he said with a scowl as he stood.

"Wait," she said as she grabbed his arm. *"I'm sorry."* She rubbed her eyes as he knelt again. *"Look, I know what you're*

getting at, and you could be right. I'm just not ready to think about that yet."

"I'm not suggesting you marry the man tomorrow. I just wonder if we should protect him until you know."

"That would be unfair to him, don't you think?" she said as she continued to caress Yatu.

Daniel joined her in comforting the little one as he sighed.

"You're right. He is a Knight of the Guard. That's who he is. To ask him to step away from his duty would be wrong. Besides, I don't know if I could respect him if he did."

He moved to kiss her on the head and turned to leave.

"We're off then. I'll see you soon, bearing gifts I hope."

He had closed her bedroom door and reached the end of the hall when she connected again.

"Of course, keeping an eye on him wouldn't hurt."

He grinned and chuckled as he walked on.

A GROUP OF SIX KNIGHTS aboard major dragons took off from the courtyard and turned east. They flew to the foot of the mountain range that conceals the Ancestral Lair, and the dragons dropped to land in a meadow near the lake's edge. The Knights dismounted and put on all their gear in silence. They would make the rest of the journey on foot.

They made quick work of reaching the top of the mountain. While resting at the crest until dusk, they studied the valley beyond, finding a spot of light on a ridge to the north.

"Probably a Marock lookout. I imagine they are expecting us, after all," Josef said.

They scanned the area and saw no other light or movement. The group made their way down the back of the mountain and across the valley under cover of night. After crossing two more ridges they huddled close at the tree line of a wide river.

"This river runs into the lake that lies below Arshek castle. We can use it to approach but must get out well before it enters the lake," Maric said.

"Why can't we enter the lake?" Daniel asked.

"Well, I personally do not fancy getting eaten by a water dragon," Josef answered.

Daniel was perplexed, but went with the assumption that water dragons were very bad and he did not want to meet one if it could be avoided.

The men entered the swift-moving river in turn. Daniel mimicked Josef and Maric, keeping his feet downstream with his body below the surface and rising for breath as seldom as possible.

After twenty minutes, he saw Maric dive for the bottom of the river. He followed but the current rushed him past the others before he could grab hold of a rock at the bottom.

He looked all around and spotted a series of ropes extending up from the bottom of the riverbed. The string of lines stretched from one bank to the other and each had a buoy of some type at the top. While Daniel could not see what the buoy was made of he was sure it was a trap of some kind.

In desperate need of a breath, he started to inch his way to the edge of the river by grabbing onto rocks. This was a tedious task as most of the rocks he grabbed came loose when he pulled on them.

Once he was free of the current, he started to stand then froze when he saw light through the surface of the water. He was getting dizzy due to lack of oxygen but knew the Arshek patrol would kill him if he made a sound. With the desperate assumption that they were on a bridge or dock, he swam toward the lights and surfaced under them.

His assumption had been right. He was under an outpost occupied by three Marocks who were in no hurry to leave. Great! Now what?

He jumped, almost giving himself away as a hand covered his mouth, and something brushed against his legs. Next, a head rose from the water right beside him.

"What are you doing?" he mouthed at Alec.

"Helping you, Sir," Alec replied with a smirk.

Daniel gave him a doubtful look that asked, "How exactly?"

Alec smiled and brought up one hand holding a large snake, and the other a rope tied to his waist that led upriver. Daniel swallowed hard as he glared at the snake.

Alec mimed the plan. He would put the snake on the deck by the Marocks who would then panic. In their moment of distraction, Alec and Daniel would submerge and pull themselves upriver via the rope.

The plan worked well. Except for the part where the snake fell into the water just after they started upstream, and the Marocks commenced flinging rocks and other objects into the water in an effort to kill the snake. Whether it was fear of the snake catching up or fear of being bludgeoned to death, Daniel would never know, but he found a great deal of strength from somewhere and moved up that rope as if propelled by a motor.

Once back in the woods, the group moved past the yelling Marocks on the dock and up a ridge toward the enemy castle. They stopped in a thicket, well concealed and with a good view of the front of the castle.

The castle was built into the side of a tall rock face, carved from the mountain itself. The curved front dropped to the lake below. There were two main entrances with drawbridges on each side where the castle curved back to the ridge face.

"Well, here is where our knowledge of what to expect ends, my friends," Josef said. "It has been many years since any of our brethren have been this close to the castle of Arshek. We will need to split up and scout around it. Before we can act, we must determine where the guards are located, possible entry points, number and location of any dragon guards and, if we are lucky, where the dragons of Chemerie are being kept."

Daniel went with Maric and Alec, to move along the top of the ridge toward the back of the castle. Josef took the two other Knights, Cris and Victor, to descend toward one of the main entrances.

When Daniel's group reached the end of the ridge they could see the area behind the castle. Daniel's breath caught in his throat as he spotted a huge dragon hold. It was a metal cage the size of a coliseum with ten-foot walls around the base.

He was shocked to see that every dragon within it was bound in some way. Dozens of major and minor dragons were chained to the ground and each other. The younger ones had great metal bands wrapping their wings against their bodies.

He recognized the sinister-looking dragons from the battle the night before. They were very different from the

Chemerian dragons. These dragons had a sleeker build with more spikes along most of their neck and back as well as around a wide forehead crest.

The men watched as a group of guards entered the dragon hold from the base of the castle wall. They held a cage full of infants and eggs out in front of them and gestured to it with daggers when the large dragons moved toward them.

"They control them by threat of killing their young. Friggin' cowards!" Daniel said.

"Look, our brethren are in the corner by the far wall," Alec said as he pointed out a cage away from the majority of the dragons.

The Arshek guards made their way to the cage containing the Chemerian dragons. When they opened the door, the largest of the younglings moved to the front and took a protective fighting stance. Two men pointed long sharp spears at him as they moved to opposite sides and flanked him. One of them made a quick jab grazing the youngling's shoulder and the other threw a red powder into its face. The youngling shrieked in pain and swung his head around like mad.

With him distracted, each of the men grabbed a smaller dragon and retreated. Once the cage was secured again, they wrapped heavy leather straps around the snout and wings of the small dragons then carried them into the castle.

THE TWO SCOUT GROUPS met back at the thicket and shared information. The awful treatment of the dragons was to their advantage. With the Arshek dragons confined via chains, the Knights should be able to free the Chemerian dragons without having to fight them.

"The Arshek army barracks are on the opposite side of the castle than the hold. That is fortunate for us of course," Josef said as he sketched a basic map of the castle and surrounding structures. "The desolate housing complexes nearest the hold are occupied by laborers. I believe our route to the hold should be to approach from the woods that flank it to the north. We will avoid as many prying eyes as possible but will be faced with scaling the wall. After that, it is a matter of getting our dragons out as fast as possible. I am sure the Arshek dragons will alert the castle of our presence."

"We brought more than enough rope to scale the outer wall of the dragon hold and the openings between the bars looked wide enough that most of us should be able to squeeze through," Maric said. "The question to be answered now is how to free our brethren without the Arshek dragons alerting the guards too quickly."

"We could offer food up to the large dragons as a distraction. We saw many sheep in the area," Alec said.

"Good idea. Who among us are the best hunters?" Josef asked. Sir Alec and Sir Cris both grabbed bows and left at once.

"For this mission to be a success, we must save every Chemerian dragon. We have to wait until they are all in the cage. Perhaps when the guards are making another exchange," Daniel said. Everyone nodded then he added, "One more problem though. We can't hope to get the largest youngling I saw through the bars. And we can't exactly carry him through the castle and out the front door."

"Josef knew of the hold. He has a hope," Maric said. Daniel turned to see Josef putting together a serious looking metal apparatus.

"A bar spreader. It works well on standard weight bars. I have no idea what we will find down there however," Josef said.

"How will we handle it if he will still not fit through?"

"We will explain that he cannot allow Harrick to bond with him. We explain the danger to Chemerie. Our young brother will fight to the death before succumbing once he understands the situation."

"Can he refuse though? Morgan said they can be forced."

"If he understands the danger posed by going to Harrick, he will not go. He will give his life for his kind and country."

Daniel hung his head and muttered, "I hope it does not come to that."

THE PLAN WAS IN PLACE and the jobs delegated an hour later. Everyone moved to their positions and waited for over half an hour before the group of two men and two Marock guards entered the dragon hold again. As they neared the Chemerian dragon's cage, the largest youngling ushered his brethren away from the door again and stood in front of them.

Daniel stood atop Josef's shoulders to look over the wall as the two human guards dropped the two younglings back into the cage and slammed the door without reaching to take any others. He felt a second of relief until he realized the guards were gathering a large metal mesh sheet. They stretched it out and mimicked throwing it before turning back to the cage.

"They're going for the largest youngling and he doesn't know the risks. Signal the archers," Daniel said.

Josef's signal was quickly followed by two of the Arshek guards falling to the ground with arrows protruding from their chests. The remaining guards rushed toward the cage of the Chemerian dragons. Daniel helped Josef up, then both dropped into the hold. They ran full speed for the cage while drawing their swords.

Daniel yelled a quick, "Hey" to get the attention of the remaining Marock guard. It turned just in time for him to deliver a harsh thrust of his sword into the heart of the beast.

Josef flew past him and leapt onto the back of the last human guard just inside the cage door. The guard reared and stumbled back, slamming Josef against the side of the cage. Stunned, Josef dropped to the ground.

Daniel looked up to see the Arshek guard with a knife raised over Josef.

"No!" he screamed as he ran forward.

The Arshek guard stopped his swing and stumbled. Daniel reached him just as he fell dead with a small dagger sunk deep in his neck.

Daniel looked back to see Alec and Maric dropping into the hold. Alec had thrown the deadly dagger.

"We do not have long. The major dragons are almost done with the sheep we gave them," Alec said as they reached them.

As the others worked to load hatchlings and direct younglings, Daniel knelt in front of the largest youngling and explained the situation with Harrick. The youngling nodded and rushed from the cage toward the major dragons with a roar. He swooped and darted around the heads of the large dragons, keeping them occupied while the Knights got the rest of the younglings out of the hold.

When all except the largest youngling were out, Daniel called to him. The youngling broke toward him, but was caught by a vicious talon blow across his back that sent him crashing to the floor.

"Will he fit?"

"If he can make it, yes," Josef said as he worked to force the heavy bars further apart.

Daniel ran for the small cage where he snatched up the bucket of powder the guards had used. The Arshek majors lurched against their chains in effort to bite the youngling lying on the floor.

Daniel threw the powder up into the face of those snapping at the youngling. As the Arshek dragons snorted and roared in rage, some of the powder wafted back into his face.

His eyes were on fire and he could only see blurry outlines. Dropping to the ground, he groped around to find and lift the youngling over his shoulder. He tried to run but had to slow as his vision darkened. He stumbled and had just gotten to his feet again when Alec took his arm.

"This way, Sir."

Once over the wall, the group set out at a run toward the woods. Alec carried the youngling and guided Daniel. After falling twice, Daniel pushed Alec away as he tried to help him up again.

"Just go, save the youngling."

The Knight followed the order and took off toward the woods without him.

After running only a few more yards, he fell hard to the ground again and let out another string of curses.

"That was educational, my nephew," Maric said as he and Josef grabbed him by the back of his coat, hoisted him off the ground, and half-carried him at a full run into the woods.

They reached the river just as distant roars rose from the Arshek castle. Everyone jumped as mighty roars filled the skies, then exchanged smiles as they saw their own brethren.

Balia let out an agonized cry and moved to smell and nudge the unconscious youngling in Alec's arms.

"Is he still with us, Lady Balia?"

She nodded and crooned a pitiful sound.

"He is yours?"

She nodded, then nudged him toward her palm. The other Knights were mounting their dragons and trying to get all the other younglings settled. Balia clawed the ground for only a moment before nudging Daniel in the back.

"The injured youngling you saved is hers, my Admiral. She is anxious to get to the Caretaker, Sir."

Daniel touched her and said, "Go Balia, go to Morgan."

The One

"*MY CARETAKER, I am coming with an injured youngling. I will meet you near the garden, my Lady,*" Balia said.

"*I will be waiting,*" Morgan said as she ran to the terrace railing and leapt to the waiting palm of the major dragon watching over her.

She reached out with the connection again and found Alec aboard Balia, but could not detect the youngling. The worry she felt from both Balia and Alec made her heart ache as she paced the lawn near the gazebo. When she felt Balia approach and begin to descend, she ran forward to meet her.

Balia helped Alec and the youngling to the ground as soon as she touched down and laid them beside Morgan. Alec laid the youngling on the grass and Balia settled to touch her snout to her son's head. She continued to sing the dragons' healing song as she connected to Morgan through their magic.

"He is almost gone, my Caretaker. I want very much to see my little Manook live, but you must be careful. It will take a great deal of magic."

Morgan took the little one's head in her hands, and her eyes glowed bright. After a few minutes, she could feel herself getting weak and the youngling was still far from stable. She detached for a moment, breathing hard and trembling.

Needing more energy to pass to Manook, she laid one hand to Balia and one to Manook and focused again. Only a moment later, she had to let go and steady herself as her head spun.

"Please, my Caretaker, do not push too far. He would not wa—" Balia began.

"I will not stop until I have no more to give. I need to give more at a faster rate but … " She looked up at Alec and raised her hand to offer him her palm. "Will you help me?"

He looked at her palm for a second, then held her eyes as he knelt. They both took a deep breath just before he grasped her hand in his. As his fingers slid between hers, both shivered. They tightened their grip as sharp prickling and heat moved up past her wrist.

"Lay your other hand to Manook's head, please." She refocused to send healing magic to Manook. As Alec's hand touched the dragon to complete the healing circle, the magic flowed much faster.

She was sweating from the heat building within her, but did not release her hold to Alec. The wound along Manook's back sealed, but he was still not stable.

Her own heart was beating faster than she had ever felt it and her hands were growing cold. She pushed once more with focus on his heart and lungs.

ALEC OPENED HIS EYES to see Manook lift his head and rub against Balia's snout. He felt his Caretaker's grip loosen and reacted just in time to catch her as she fell limp across the youngling. He shifted around Manook to lay her back against him.

"Balia, is she alright? Has she pushed too far and risked herself?"

Balia dropped her head to touch Morgan's chest and began to hum again. After just one verse of her song, she lifted her head and nudged Alec's hand and then Morgan's. He took both of her hands, laced his fingers in hers, and squeezed their palms together.

The first few seconds he felt the same tingle and heat he had felt when touching her earlier, then everything changed. A shock like a lightning strike through his spine hit him as they took in deep gasps together.

"Take my energy, my Caretaker."

Remembering his experience weeks before, he let himself think of her beauty once again. He felt her hand twitch in his and his heart leapt. As he gazed at her face and let his heart speak what it felt, her chest began to rise and fall with shallow breaths. Ignoring how his body began to tremble and grow cold, he gripped her tighter still.

"All that I have is yours, my Caretaker; I will gladly die so you may live."

DANIEL WAS ABOARD MENKAR in the middle of the tight formation of dragons. He could see nothing and lay forward against the dragon's neck as they flew. The group landed on the lawn near the gardens rather than their normal spot in the castle courtyard.

A group of Knights were mumbling off to one side as Daniel shifted from Menkar's palm.

"What's going on?" he asked.

"Let us find out," Josef said as he took Daniel by the arm and led him forward. He halted his steps when he saw what had drawn their interest.

"It is Princess Morgan and Sir Alec. They are ..." Josef said.

"What? They're what?" Daniel said.

Josef cleared his throat and lowered his voice to say, "They are lying on the grass beside the youngling. Both are asleep, and they are, uh, entangled a bit and holding hands."

"Really?" Daniel said with a scowl.

IT TOOK A FEW HOURS for Morgan to wake. She found Daniel snoozing in a chair beside her bed. She hesitated to wake him as she noticed the lingering tingle in her hands. A slight shiver moved over her as she remembered the intense sensations touching Alec had caused. She took a minute to enjoy the memory before waking her big brother.

"Nice to see you made it back safe, big brother," she said as she moved to rustle Daniel's hair.

"I'm glad to hear you sounding so good. You had me worried," he said. "I couldn't wake you when we got back, and you've been out for hours. Are you sure you're OK?"

"Yes, I'm fine. I just pushed hard trying to heal the youngling. I guess I pushed a bit too far."

As she spoke, she moved to sit in the chair next to him and noticed he did not follow her progress with his head. He still stared at the spot she had been standing.

"What's wrong with your eyes?" she asked as she took his hands and started pushing healing energy. He removed her trembling hands from his and laid her palms to one another.

"No, you need to rest. I'm not in pain and can wait until you're stronger."

She climbed back into her chair and fought tears as she watched him staring across the room.

"Tell me what happened last night," she said.

"You first."

"What do you mean?"

"I would like to know why my little sister was found asleep in the arms of a certain young Knight."

Daniel broke the following silence with a laugh. "Man, I wish I could see your face right now."

"What are you talking about?"

"Only what the entire castle is talking about, I imagine. When we got here, we found you and Sir Alec entangled with one another, holding hands, asleep on the lawn beside the youngling." He paused then said, "Well? Please explain yourself so I can start squashing the rumors before they get out of hand."

"I have no idea how that happened. I must have passed out while he was helping me heal Manook. But we were on opposite sides of him and only holding one of each others' hands at that point."

"Really? Then I need to have a word with Sir Alec, right now," he said as he stood and turned toward the door. He stumbled on the rug, and she grabbed his arm to steady him and hold him still.

"Just wait, please. We need to talk to Balia first. I am just as annoyed as you, but she can show me the truth before we confront him."

She led him to the terrace railing as she asked Balia to join them. Balia soon landed beside her terrace and placed her head atop the railing.

"My friend, I need to know what happened in the garden last night. Will you share your memory with me?"

"Yes, of course," Balia said. Morgan connected to her and watched the night's events unfold from Balia's point of view.

She took in a quick breath as she watched their hands touch. Her hands and chest warmed as she watched him join Balia in saving her. He had begun to tremble and tears fell down his face, yet he never let go of her hands. He let her take all she needed from him, then fell unconscious beside her.

She saw the position of their bodies as they lay entwined and understood how a horrible misconception could be made. To her amazement, she found she did not care in the least.

She broke the connection and laid her head against Balia as she accepted the truth she could no longer deny. Sir Alec was indeed her magical mate. He would be her husband and the father of Chemerie's next Caretaker.

"Congratulations, my friend. He is a strong and devoted spirit," Balia said as she crooned and rubbed her snout to Morgan's side before lifting off.

Morgan watched her dear friend returning to the dragon quarters to be with her weak youngling before moving to sit beside Daniel on a lounge chair. He put his arm around her and pulled her to him when he felt her trembling.

"Tell me, please."

"You were right," she whispered through trembling lips as she reached out to take his hands. "Let me show you." When he had viewed the night's events, he squeezed her hands and wrapped her tight into his side with a kiss to her head.

"He's a good man, Morgan. One to be proud of. And he obviously cares deeply for the dragons … and for you it seems."

"How can he care so much when he doesn't know me?"

He smiled as he rubbed her arm and shoulder a few seconds then said, "The same way you care for him, little sister."

She dropped her head onto his shoulder as she admitted the truth in his words. Just seconds later, she let out a growled huff and stood to pace the terrace again.

"I am definitely not ready for this, Daniel. I have too much to deal with in becoming Queen and learning more about the magic to serve the dragons."

"Well, you can't expect him to disappear. You're going to have to deal with it somehow. I imagine your magic will make it hard to ignore him."

Her face filled with a wicked smirk as the perfect solution hit her. She was glad for the moment that Daniel could not see her face.

SHE STOOD on her terrace the next afternoon as Sir Alec was announced by her chambermaid.

"Thank you, Neesa," she said without turning. For a few

seconds, she closed her eyes and let herself enjoy the sensations of the strong connection she shared with this man.

"Are you well?"

"Yes, my Lady, quite well."

She turned and looked into the deep gray-green eyes of the man she knew to be her future husband. Again, she allowed herself a couple of seconds to take in his very handsome form before she continued.

"I have decided on your new post, Sir Alec."

She felt his apprehension and excitement, but he showed none of it as he stared into her eyes.

"I would like for you to oversee the new Guard unit which will be placed within the Ancestral Lair. This unit will function as a first line of defense against further attacks by Lord Harrick. You will be given the proper rank for this post, a large complement of Knights and dragons, and measures will be taken to make the Lair more agreeable to people." She paused here to enjoy the look of surprise on his face and the emotion that accompanied it. "Is this post acceptable to you?"

"It is an honorable post, and I accept with a grateful heart. I thank you, my Princess."

"Your Admirals have been informed of my decision, and they await your official acceptance. Good day, Sir Alec."

"Good day, my Princess, and thank you again," he said as he bowed without breaking eye contact with her. He held her eyes for three long seconds before turning to leave.

She let out the breath she had been holding during the long eye contact and laughed as she dropped into a chair while rubbing her trembling tingling hands.

8

Queen at Seventeen

THE WEEKS FOLLOWING the rescue of the abducted dragons flew by as Morgan worked to serve the hatchlings and younglings with Squire Willow's assistance. She spent hours bonding with the new hatchlings and made a point to connect with every dragon she could feel within Chemerie.

One afternoon about two weeks after their return, she was sitting on the lawn surrounded by younglings when she felt a strong surge of impatience behind her. She turned to see the emotion expressed on the faces of both Daniel and Josef.

"Alright, I will take time to meet with the Admiralty this afternoon."

"Thank you, my Princess," Josef said with a bow before turning to leave.

"Uncle Josef, wait, please." She smiled as she felt his surprise and stood to face him as he turned back to her. "You and Uncle Maric are our closest family, and I would like to drop the formality of titles when possible. I want to know you both. Family has always been the core support for me, and without Father or GranMay, I … "

Her words were lost as Josef stepped forward to lift her in a strong embrace.

"I love you, my niece. And I would love to know you more. I only wanted to show you the respect you deserve. Maric and I have struggled with what an appropriate distance is since you came to us so young. We wanted to give you and Daniel the independence you needed, yet we both long to know you and about your lives on Earth. I imagine it has changed a bit in the last twenty-five years."

"You know our mother and we yours," she said. "We have so much to share, and I look forward to spending more time together with your families. Will you all join us tonight for dinner?"

"I am sure I speak for us all when I say we would love to, my dear," Josef said. He turned to Daniel and paused with a broad smile. "We are also proud to watch the tenacity with which you watch over your sister. She will not always appreciate it, as Christina did not, but I am sure you will not let her arguments stop your efforts to protect her. Your love for her is profound, and it warms our hearts to see. I have watched you become a strong Admiral despite your youth, and now I hope to know you as a friend as well, my nephew." He embraced Daniel then left with a warm smile to both.

"I think opening ourselves to our family here will be good for us. We've kept ourselves closed for fear of seeming weak.

And probably because we fear the pain of losing yet another we care for. No one will ever replace Father and GranMay, but we need family. I need family." She sat back down to play with the younglings around her. "Father was right in saying I would love the dragons, but he was wrong to suggest it would replace the need for the love of my own family. I no longer need them, but I miss the comfort of their love so much it hurts. It hurts every day."

"I know. I feel it too."

MORGAN PAUSED OUTSIDE the Admiralty chambers to focus herself. She smiled as her skin warmed as if standing in the sun, and a light tingle crept up her back.

From so far away? I wonder if he feels anything.

Her question was answered when the door opened just before she grabbed the handle. Sir Alec smiled as he stepped back and bowed. She gave him a polite nod and moved past him to take her seat at the head of the table. She saw the smirk on Daniel's face and shot him a warning look while passing annoyance via her magic. Once all the Knights were seated, she leaned forward to begin.

"Many generations ago there were twin daughters born to a Caretaker, and both children carried the gift of magic. Unfortunately, the bond between the girls was broken by the competitive spirit they shared, and one left Chemerie before her Quickening.

"She broke all ties to Chemerie and was not seen again for many years. It was not until the week after her mother died, some twelve years later, that a letter arrived addressed to her twin, the current Caretaker. The letter said only, "You do not mourn alone. She was my mother, I loved her dearly, and I will miss feeling her spirit."

"When the messenger was questioned as to her whereabouts, the news shook our country. They learned the estranged twin was living in the Arshek castle at the side of the reigning Son of Arshek, Lord Bareth. It is still not known if she joined him by choice or by force, but the result was the same. It was through her that the blood of the Caretaker line and the Arshek line joined."

"How does the magic of the Arshek line differ from our own?" Daniel asked.

"Their magic is referred to as the Dark magic and ours the Pure magic within the oldest entries of the Book of the Caretaker. While the magic of Chemerie is strengthened by love, friendship, respect, and honor, the dark magic of Arshek is fed by hate, jealousy, and greed. Some of the knowledge I received from the dragons suggests that there is only one magic, the nature of which is determined by the purity of the spirit wielding it.

"Either way, the children that resulted from their joining were not as strong as their parents in either form of magic, yet all had powers, both male and female. Through the generations, different children of the line have exhibited various skills attributed to each magic's history. None have shown the ability to connect to the dragons of Chemerie, that we know of, until now."

"Did Harrick succeed in gaining access to the younglings' knowledge?" Josef asked.

"I've connected to the four hatchlings he tried to manipulate. The good news is he failed to achieve full bonding with any of them. However, I have no way to determine how much information he managed to gain from his feeble attempts."

"So, the conclusion is that Chemerie cannot afford even one dragon to fall into the hands of Harrick or any Son of Arshek again," Alec said.

"Exactly. Harrick may grow more efficient at using those skills now that he has felt them. While the older dragons understand the danger, and will not let themselves be bonded with, the younger hatchlings may be overwhelmed. We cannot ignore the fact he has great skill with his dark magic. If his attempts to coerce them with the Chemerian magic fail, he will undoubtedly turn to his more sinister techniques. We were lucky this time, my friends. I suggest we not expect such fortune again."

MORGAN LOOKED OUT over the castle courtyard and the beautiful city surrounding it as she thought of her first day in Chemerie when the news she was to be Queen rocked her to her core. It had been less than a year, yet seemed so far away now.

Her official coronation, the ceremony in which she would be crowned Queen of Chemerie, was set for that afternoon. It would have occurred weeks earlier, but had been put off and rescheduled for her seventeenth birthday due to the recent battle and aftermath. While the reason was awful, she was thankful for the delay. Now, she would accept the position with a true feeling of belonging and kinship to those she would serve.

"I know my duties and responsibilities well, and I have fallen in love with this country. I am ready, but are they ready for me?"

She laughed at herself then quieted as her eyes scanned

the people and dragons all around her. The future of Chemerie was at the front of her thoughts at all times now. The threat of Harrick's darkness and her responsibility to preserve the magical link between the people and the dragons of Chemerie haunted her day and night.

Her responsibility to preserve the Caretaker line was always at the edge of her thoughts. It was one thing to be Queen at seventeen, and another altogether to consider marriage and motherhood. Of course, meeting Alec had eased that worry a great deal.

As she thought of him, she watched a group of children and youngling dragons playing in the courtyard. She recognized some of them from the day she met Squire Willow, and returned their enthusiastic waves.

The adorable young David stopped mid-wave and looked to his left. He squealed, "Uncle!" and ran into the waiting arms of Alec.

"Well, at least I know what that weird feeling was now."

Alec listened to the fast chatter from David for a few seconds then smiled up at her. She smiled and gave a nod to which he bowed. Even from that distance, she felt a rush of warmth as he held her gaze a few seconds.

She continued to watch as he joined in on the kid's game of tag-n-toss with the younglings. He tripped on purpose to allow the kids and younglings to pile on top of him. Their laughter was contagious, and she found herself laughing out loud.

MORGAN STOOD in her chambers before her large mirror admiring her gorgeous gown. Her tailors and seamstresses were amazing. The cloud blue fabric rustled with the breeze while shimmering between multiple shades of blue as it moved. The wide scoop neck with silver threading complimented her amulet, and the fitting of the bodice was perfect.

"If you're ready, I have a birthday gift for you," Daniel called from outside her doorway.

"Awesome, where is it?" she asked as she turned.

She took three steps toward him, then froze with a gasp.

"Happy birthday, my girl!"

Her eyes filled with tears as she felt the spirit who wielded those words.

"Surprise!" Daniel said as he stepped into the room.

GranMay entered the room behind him, and Morgan flew into her arms. After a moment of holding the tight embrace, she pulled back and held up her hands. GranMay smiled as their fingers touched, then gasped as she pressed their palms together.

They connected in that deep, encompassing way Morgan had only felt with her mother. Neither was known to cry often, but neither of them could stop the tears from falling when the deep love they shared was enhanced by the power of their magic.

She shared all her major experiences since arriving in Chemerie and then sought from GranMay information about her parents. She flinched as profound loss hit her. GranMay grasped her hands to keep her from breaking the connection and pushed a burst of emotions.

"I understand. She died happy in the arms of her mate. I should mourn and miss her, but never feel sorry for her. She was proud to serve, grateful for the joys of her life."

"Insightful as always, my girl."

Morgan's eyes dropped to GranMay's chest and saw the amulet her mother had worn. She traced it with her finger, and GranMay pulled her into another wonderful hug. Daniel cleared his throat and smirked as he glanced at the door again. Her magic reached beyond the strong influence of GranMay's and she bolted for the door.

"Father!" she squealed as he lifted her into his arms and swung her around in a circle. Tears flowed again as she hugged him tight and took in his emotions.

"What are you two doing here?! I thought you were to stay on Earth?"

They exchanged mischievous grins and laughed.

"We figured we could be waiting quite a while for you to settle down enough to consider having a child. So, we decided to break the rules and come here to help in any way that we can until that time comes. A birthday surprise seemed fitting," her father said.

She hugged him tight for a long moment then turned on Daniel.

"Don't think that I don't see your hand in this. I have no idea how you convinced the dragons to contact them. Thank you, big brother." She kissed his cheek and hugged him tight.

IT WAS her dear GranMay who crowned her Queen, a joy she would never have hoped for. They stood before the city on the main balcony as dragons flew overhead in intricate patterns to honor her coronation.

As she knelt for GranMay to place the crown on her head, and for her father to drape the grand robe over her shoulders, she closed her eyes and opened her connection. She cherished having the key people in her life near at that moment. She felt GranMay, Father, Daniel, Josef, Maric, and twenty feet below her in the Guard formation, Alec.

She rose with a beaming smile and waved her thanks to the people and dragons of Chemerie for their trust and acceptance into their world. Closing her eyes, she focused to open her connection wide, touching all within her reach.

"Thank you for your trust, my friends. I will give you all that I have as your Queen and Caretaker." There were many gasps from the crowd as they heard her voice in their heads, and the cheering doubled in response.

As they walked toward Kindred Hall, GranMay took her arm and connected.

"How did you do that?"

"Do what?"

"How did you connect with so many at once, my dear?"

"I just focused, I suppose."

GranMay stopped her and looked at her as if seeing her for the first time.

"I have never known any other to be able to do that, Morgan. Your power is great, just as Christina said."

She was both confused and elated at the seriousness of GranMay's declaration. Her cheeks flushed as GranMay tucked her hand in the bend of her arm and led her toward Kindred Hall. Josef announced Morgan's father as King Nikolas and GranMay as Queen May, which brought joyous applause and cheers of, "Welcome Home!"

Though not at the front of the balcony yet, Morgan could see the majority of the elegant crowd gathered in the Hall. She scanned the many faces and smiled to those she knew as they caught her eye. Her eyes soon locked on those of Alec. She connected to him, trying to seem unshaken by his gaze.

"Hello, Sir Alec. I hope you are well."

He bowed as he replied without breaking eye contact.

"I am quite well, my Queen. I offer you sincere congratulations and my deepest thanks for your commitment to serve the people and dragons of Chemerie."

She met his formality with a curtsy and slow nod of her head.

"You are very kind, Sir Alec, thank you." Through the connection to him she could feel a slight tingle begin to warm her skin.

"Oh my, he is a handsome one, isn't he?"

"GranMay!" Morgan snapped aloud in reflex.

This got the attention of her father, who looked to Gran-May. After a few seconds, both turned together to look toward Alec. Morgan felt her face go scarlet. She gave Gran-May a frustrated look and turned to scan the crowd on the opposite side of the Hall.

Once GranMay and her father were focused on those around them again, she glanced back to where Alec stood. Her hands clenched, and her body tensed at the sight of a beautiful woman hugging him. She took an involuntary step forward when the woman rose to her tiptoes and kissed him on both cheeks. Her skin grew hot, and her hands stung as she watched the couple holding hands and smiling into each other's eyes as they talked.

She was startled from her glaring by a nudge from Daniel and her father's raised voice.

"Queen May and I thank you all for the warm welcome

home, my brethren. And now, it is with great pride that I give you Queen Morgan, Caretaker of Chemerie."

As she stepped forward to stand between Father and GranMay, everyone in the hall below dropped to one knee and spoke as one.

"You honor us all with your pledge of service. Our spirits soar with pride and thankfulness. With joyous hearts we hail Queen Morgan, Caretaker of Chemerie."

As the group rose, her father escorted her down the stairs. The staircase was lined with Knights of the Guard along both sides. As she passed, each one laid an arm across their chest and dropped to one knee with their head bent forward. Each whispered something as they knelt, but kept their words inaudible. As she reached the floor, every Knight around the room dropped as one in the same manner and gave the same muffled whisper together before rising.

Beautiful music began to play when she reached the main floor, then the crowd parted to clear a path to the center of the Hall. Her father led her forward then surprised her by releasing her hand and stepping back to stare at her with intense eyes. He crossed one arm across his chest just as all of the Knights had done and knelt before her.

"My spirit to your service, my Queen," he said in a strong, proud voice.

The sincerity of his words was reflected in his eyes as he rose. She was blushing and trembling a bit when he stepped forward and took her hand and waist. He kissed her forehead, winked just as the orchestra started a beautiful piece, then swept her into a waltz.

"I apologize for all the complaining about dance lessons," she

said. Her father laughed and added a few extra spins to tease her as they moved around the floor.

As the music shifted to the next piece, Daniel replaced her father. He wore a huge smile, and the pride she felt from him made her blush again. They did not speak. They just glided to the music. She was ready for a rest, but found Daniel replaced by Maric and then by Josef.

The piece she danced with Josef had a slow pace, which allowed her to glance around and still keep in step. She missed a step when her eyes caught sight of Alec dancing nearby.

"Sir Alec and his sister are very close, much like you and Daniel. It is nice to see siblings stay close as they grow up, isn't it?"

"It is indeed, my very perceptive Uncle," she said with red cheeks as they both laughed.

As the piece she danced with Josef came to an end, she started to move off the dance floor. She stopped as a warm tingle moved up her back and turned just as Alec spoke.

"May I have this dance, my Queen?"

"I could never refuse the man who saved my life."

She held his gaze as she stepped forward to slide her hand into his. The intensity of the warm tingle tripled when their hands touched, despite his gloves between them. It increased yet again as he placed his other hand on the small of her back.

"Oh Mercy!"

They began to move with the music as she focused to block the sensation.

"It is quite warm in here, my Queen. Would you care to take a walk on the garden terrace and cool off?"

She realized he was being considerate, yet struggled to answer. She questioned the propriety of it and was about to say no when GranMay entered her mind.

"It is quite acceptable, my dear. Go and get to know the man a bit."

She controlled her facial expression with great effort.

"Yes, that sounds like a great idea."

She moved ahead of him while she connected to GranMay.

"I can not believe you were eavesdropping. You swore you only listened in when I needed help?"

"I was sure you did, my dear."

She actually heard GranMay's chuckle and felt her amusement clearly before raising her guard.

"If you would rather be alone I ccr——"

"No. Please, walk with me. Sorry if I seemed weird. I was closing off my thoughts from others."

"You mean others can connect with you without your wanting it?"

"Only my GranMay. And she assures me she will only do so when she thinks I need help," she said with a smile.

They descended the terrace steps and entered the gardens at a slow relaxed pace, which gave her the opportunity to block the sensations a bit.

"Your Grandmother seems very nice," he said as she stopped to smell a winter rose. "I never knew her before, but her youngest brother, Sir Kisik, is my father."

The rose was crushed in her hand as her neck flushed.

"Come again?" she said as she shifted to face him.

"He raised me after my birth parents were killed. Technically he is my adoptive father, but I consider him my true father."

"Oh ... I'm sorry to hear of your birth parents," she said as she started walking again.

"No sympathy is necessary, my Queen. I never knew my birth parents and I was blessed with wonderful parents in Sir Kisik and Lady Cora. They treated me with the same love and respect they gave their blood children, Burke and Emma, and I never wanted for anything."

"I've been so busy with my duties, I have not considered that I have blood relatives here I have never met. Or perhaps I have met them and never knew they were my relatives. Mercy, I hope I haven't offended anyone."

"No one would be offended, my Queen. Everyone considers all Chemerians as family. It is not necessary to differentiate," he said. "I would be honored to introduce you to my siblings this evening. They are your blood family, and I know they are eager to meet you, my Lady."

"That would be nice. Thank you," she said as she struggled to keep a straight face.

They chatted about the successful establishment of his Guard unit at the Ancestral Lair, the young dragons in her care, and the dragons' progress in settling back into the dragon chambers of the castle.

Soon, she looked around to realize they had wandered through the gardens and were now standing at the very spot they had fallen unconscious atop one another. She thought of what they must have looked like and turned around as she felt her face blush. He touched her arm, so she faced him again.

"My Queen, I have informed all of the men of the Guard

of the correct interpretation of that evening. I assure you, not another word that suggests impropriety will be spoken of the matter."

She nodded and held his eyes as she took a deep breath and connected to him.

"So, what did you tell them, Sir Alec? What did you say really happened?"

He took a deep breath as the connection formed, held her eyes, and took a slow step toward her as he replied.

"I told them enough to quash the rumors, but admittedly left out some of the details, my Queen."

"I think that was wise, Sir Alec," she said with a smirk.

He held her gaze many more seconds, making her efforts to block the sensations from him difficult.

"May I ask a bold question of you, my Queen?"

"As long as it is not too bold, you may."

He paused, taking a slow deep breath.

"Would I be correct in assuming that the sensations I felt when my skin contacted yours were a normal part of the Caretaker magic?"

She broke the gaze with that question and turned away from him.

"The sensations you felt were most definitely a result of the magic, yes."

He didn't reply for a few seconds then stepped up very close behind her. Warm tingling spread over her back and she shivered as his warm breath fell over her neck.

"Yes, but was it normal, my Queen?" he said in a whisper.

"Oh, Sweet Mercy!" she thought as her heart pounded.

A flourish of wings behind them made him shift away and

turn. She let out the breath she had been holding and forced another before turning. They both knelt to offer hands to the crooning Yatu.

"Well, you are looking much better and flying very well, my friend," she said.

Yatu crooned again as he touched his snout to her cheek. He then climbed up on Alec's knee and rubbed against his chest. Alec started to hum and gently stroke his back. She felt the warmth of love between them and quietly slipped away.

When she reached the terrace steps, she turned to look back at Alec and the little dragon. After a minute of consideration, she followed her heart.

"Sir Alec, you would be wrong in your assumption. The sensations you felt were not normal at all."

"That is very good news, my Queen," he said with a handsome smile and a slight bow of his head.

"I agree, Sir Alec," she said as she matched his smile.

MORGAN MINGLED with the crowd and greeted as many people as she could. GranMay introduced her brother, Sir Kisik.

"It is very nice to finally meet you," she said. "I am sorry I have not been able to before tonight."

Kisik laughed as he took her hand and kissed it.

"As a former protector of the Queen, I understand completely that your duties come first, and I am glad for the opportunity to meet you this evening, my dear."

Morgan chatted with them a few minutes, then smiled as she felt a now familiar warm tingle creep up her spine. Gran-May gave her a curious look. She smirked as she relished having a small secret from her nosy grandmother.

Sir Kisik raised his hand to greet the three young people stepping up behind her and said, "My Queen, I believe you know my youngest lad, Sir Alec. May I also present my beautiful daughter, Emma, and my eldest son, Sir Burke."

"It is very nice to meet you both. I hope we can find time to get to know one another very soon," she said.

Emma moved forward and took her by the arm to spin her around and ushered her into the crowd.

"Well, there is no time like the present, Cousin," said the lively young woman with an infectious smile. Morgan noticed a concerned look in Alec's eye as they flew past him and Burke.

Emma was wonderful. She treated her like a sister rather than with the rigid formality she received from most Chemerians. She took her around and introduced her to many other young men and women near their age.

As they moved around the room, Emma explained the relations between all the people they spoke with. She was sure she would not remember any of it but she enjoyed the experience a great deal.

They took a seat on a small sofa and were promptly supplied with wine by a strolling waiter.

"May I speak candidly, Cousin?" Emma asked with a sheepish smile.

"Please do."

"You have my little brother tied up in knots. I have never seen him so nervous and distracted. Honestly, I am concerned. I love him dearly and do not want to see him hurt. You see, he believes that he may have a magical link with you. He has not told me directly mind you, but I read him easily. I would ask that you tell him quickly if that is not the case in order to lessen his disappointment."

"I will not hurt him, Cousin. He is not wrong. I have little doubt that he and I are meant to be together. But, I am not ready to deal with it just now. I have so much to learn in order to serve as Queen and Caretaker. I need to be comfortable in my role on my own before I consider marriage."

"Alec has a wonderful spirit. Perhaps you could just explain your concerns to him. I truly believe he would function better if you spoke with him about it. I was not joking when I said you have him completely out of sorts," Emma said with a laugh as she spotted Alec shooting them furtive glances across the dance floor. "Did you see the look on his face when I took you off earlier? He knows I am bold enough to speak my mind and is nervous as a goat in a dragon hold right now. Just look at him. He cannot stand not knowing what we are talking about." She gave him a sassy little wave to which he shook his head and resumed his conversation with Burke and another Knight.

Morgan was amazed at how comfortable she was with Emma. She felt as though she had known her forever and laughed comfortably as she watched her harassing Alec from across the room.

"Emma, I really do appreciate your concern for Alec, and for me, but I am serious when I say I am not ready to act on this yet. Please understand my position."

"I agree that the perfect time is whenever you feel ready. I do not mean to be pushy. I am just acting the big sister I suppose. Besides, it is quite entertaining seeing my formal little brother a bit off balance for once."

"Your little brother is sneaking up behind us, Cousin," Morgan said as she smiled.

Emma looked confused then smiled as she spotted Alec over Morgan's shoulder.

"How did you spot him so quick?" Emma whispered.

"I didn't. I felt him coming," she answered with a wink. She smiled at the shocked look on Emma's face as she stood and turned to face Alec and Burke before they said a word.

Burke darted ahead of Alec and asked her to dance. Again, she noted the look of annoyance on Alec's face as she was swept past him. She and Burke laughed as they watched Emma scurrying through the crowd to get away from Alec.

"Those two still act like little kids when they get around each other," Burke said.

"So, is David your son or Emma's?"

"He is my first born, my Queen. He has not stopped talking of his day working with you. I thank you for the loving impression you have made on him," he said as his eyes twinkled.

They chatted about his kids and his wife for a bit before she fell silent to focus through a complicated series of steps to a fast-paced melody. As the piece ended, he kissed her hand and bowed to her formally.

"Thank you for the honor, my Cousin and Queen."

"Just 'Cousin' will do, Sir Burke."

He smiled as she hugged him.

"Then you must drop the 'Sir', my Cousin," he added as they left the dance floor arm in arm.

They approached a harassed looking Alec. She smiled at him until he relaxed and smiled too. She was just about to ask him to dance when Burke spoke.

"Alec, is it not about time we head back to our post at the Lair?"

Alec nodded and bowed to her as he held her gaze once again.

"It was a pleasure celebrating with you, my Queen. Goodnight and farewell."

"Goodnight and farewell, Sir Alec. And to you, Cousin. May the magic keep you," she said with a nod to each.

Alec and Burke headed for the main doors to the courtyard, and she headed up the staircase. When she reached the top, she turned back to spot Alec again.

"*Sir Alec,*" she said. She waited for him to meet her eyes. "*I believe you still owe me half of a dance. I will consider it a debt unpaid and expect payment with interest the next time we meet.*"

He smiled a very handsome smile as he bowed his head to her.

"*I look forward to the settlement of that debt, my Queen.*"

She could swear she heard the deep resonance of his voice even through their magical connection. With a nod and a sly smile, she turned to head toward her chambers. As she exited Kindred Hall, she focused on the sensation she received from his presence and found it did not disappear until she was halfway down the hallway.

When she reached her chambers, she found GranMay settling in.

"You are now Queen, my dear. Your chambers are now those of the Queen," GranMay said.

"As the elder Queen of the castle, you should have those."

"I am not the reigning Queen and have no intention of

acting as such. My role here is simply as your grandmother. You are the Queen, and you must learn to accept the honors of that graciously, my girl."

After a loving hug goodnight, she continued down the hall to the grand chambers that occupied the entire end of that wing of the castle. When she opened the doors, she noticed many differences in its decor from the day she arrived in Chemerie. The grand chambers had been redecorated with new furnishings, tapestries, and linens all around. A new wardrobe had been placed in her closet and fresh flowers were in every room.

She took in her new quarters a few moments, then changed into a comfortable pair of pajamas and settled herself on the plush cushions of the window seat in her bedroom.

The view was gorgeous, even at night. She took in the gardens, lawn, lake and mountains to each side. She thought of the similarity of the view to that from her bedroom on Earth, then laughed as the silhouette of two major dragons crossed the moon above her.

"Thank you," she said to Daniel.

"For what?"

"I'm calm, fully relaxed for the first time since coming here. Thank you for my birthday gift."

"You don't need their help. But, I knew having them would comfort you. You should thank Balia for her efforts to convince the Elder dragons."

"I will find her tomorrow. She is too far from the castle for me to connect right now."

"I'm glad to hear you've let yourself relax at last. Enjoy it, you deserve it. Goodnight, little sister."

EMMA CAUGHT UP with Alec as he was preparing to board Menkar in the courtyard.

"Our new Queen is really something quite remarkable. Isn't she, little brother?"

Alec looked at her with a raised eyebrow.

"What are you talking about, Emma?"

She moved in to kiss his cheek and hug him.

"She felt you coming before she saw you. That seems rather special, does it not?" she said into his ear.

Alec kissed her cheek and moved to vault aboard Menkar, then turned to her with a broad smile.

"I agree, my Sister. It is not normal at all."

ALEC AND BURKE landed in the main chamber of the Lair and removed the harnesses from Menkar and Broon.

"I have never known you to smile that long in your life. What has you so pleased, little brother?" Burke asked with a sly grin of his own.

Alec's smile broadened as he glanced around, checking that they were alone.

"I think I have finally met my magical partner. When I am near her, I grow warm all over, and the touch of her skin sends intense tingling sensations all through me. Is that similar to what you felt with Mira?"

"No, not at all."

Alec's face fell as he turned away, so Burke turned him back around.

"The connection you describe is stronger than any I have experienced, or even heard of. It is clear her strong magic makes the sensations far more intense. You have been greatly blessed, little brother."

"How did you know I was speaking of Queen Morgan?"

Burke burst out laughing, and it took him a few seconds to calm enough to answer.

"Maybe it was the fact that you could not take your eyes off of her all night, or how you got jealous when she danced with anyone else, even me. Alec, you did not hide it well, at least not from me and Emma. Our sister has been quite worried about you. I would not be surprised if she discussed the topic with Morgan this evening," Burke said through his laughter.

Alec rubbed his face and groaned at the thought.

9

Whispers

OVER THE NEXT few months, Morgan gained a much greater ability to control her magic. She gave special attention to controlling the physical sensations that accompany bonding with and healing the dragons and humans she served.

She had only healed a few major injuries in humans thus far and found it to involve a very different skill than the healing of dragons. When working with the dragons she had to direct her magic to work along with theirs. The magic within the humans of Chemerie was very subtle. Though coordinating was not required when healing them, the only source of magic to pull from was her own. Because of this, the healing of a simple broken arm could be very draining.

Her most recent focus had been her ability to connect with others from a distance far greater than her sight could offer. One afternoon she sat in the small stone gazebo of the snow-covered garden lawn with her legs crossed and her eyes closed. With her connection wide, she worked to focus on specific people throughout Chemerie to speak to them alone or to a select group.

After many discussions with GranMay, she now understood she had a far greater breadth and depth of magic than either GranMay or her mother. That fact was one she did not think about much because it brought far too many other questions along with it.

As she sat quietly and practiced her control, she found all of her family, focusing on each of them in turn to say, "hello" or "boo" where appropriate. Chancing a much farther reach, she focused to the east toward the Ancestral Lair some sixty miles away where she had stationed Alec. She had seen him only a few times over the months since they danced at her Coronation Ball and thought of him more and more between those meetings. She focused hard and was about to give up when she felt the familiar warmth of his spirit.

"Hello, Sir Alec. Are you well this beautiful winter day?"

"I am quite well, my Queen. It is very nice to hear your voice. I was not expecting a visit from you today, are you near?"

"No, I am on the castle's garden lawn. I think you know the spot."

"I know it well, my Queen. Will you be there long?"

She did not really understand the point of the question until she focused hard again and realized he was getting closer. He was aboard Menkar, flying with his brother, Burke, who was aboard Broon.

"That was not very kind. You let me think more of my skills

than I should. I expect more from my Knights, Sir Alec."

"I sincerely apologize, my Queen. It was inappropriate of me t—"

"Relax, I was only joking, Sir Alec. You haven't offended me," she said through a laugh. *"How far out are you? Wait, don't tell me. Give me a minute."* She focused with all her might on Menkar and received quick flashes of what he saw. *"You are approaching from the southeast and are two or three miles from the castle, near the orchards, yes?"*

"My Queen, your skills have surpassed anything I have ever heard of. That was amazing, my Lady."

She actually blushed despite no one being there to see her face. Once her embarrassment lessened, she opened their connection to include Burke.

"I invite you both to dinner this evening. Emma already plans to join us, and I hope Mira and the boys will come as well. Will you be able to attend?"

"We will make it a priority, my Queen. Thank you for the invitation."

"Wonderful, I will see you both in two hours then."

She sprang to her feet and headed for the castle. As she neared the terrace stairs, Alec and Menkar swooped overhead. Menkar roared in greeting. She could feel the warm tingle rise on her skin as she locked eyes with Alec for a few seconds.

She waved to them as she passed her love to Menkar then resumed her quick pace toward her chambers. On her way, she passed Daniel who grabbed her hand to swing her in a wide circle.

"Where are you headed so fast?"

She released his hand, spun twice, and resumed her pace. "To prepare for dinner."

"But you have two hours!"

She turned a quick circle to flash a broad smile as she continued on.

"Ah! I assume we will have more dinner guests," he said with a laugh as he watched her go.

SHE WAS STANDING in the private dining room chatting with Josef when she felt a warm rush of emotion wash over her. Though she raised her guard, she could not help blushing so much Josef stopped mid-sentence.

"Are you feeling well, my dear?"

"Yes, just a little warm. I'll go cool off a bit." She passed reassurance as she touched his arm, then headed straight for the balcony. Many deep breaths of the cold night air calmed her and helped to lower her body temperature. She faced away from the room as she let her guard drop again.

"Hello again, Sir Alec," she said, still smiling over the courtyard below the balcony.

"Good evening, my Queen," he replied in his deep voice.

She turned with a teasing smile on her face as he answered.

Burke and his young son David were just behind him, so she focused on the little one wriggling to get down. When she knelt with open arms, David ran to her to be scooped up at once.

Burke smiled as he stepped around Alec and kissed her on both cheeks, "It is good to see you, Cousin."

"It is good to see you too, Burke," she said. *That was a little mean. You are agitating him on purpose, my Cousin,"* she added as she tickled David, making him wriggle and giggle.

Burke only smiled before taking David from her and throwing him high in the air to make him squeal.

"I hope you are all hungry. The cooks have a beautiful turkey waiting for us," she said as she walked to the door.

As she turned away, she heard a scuffle behind her and glanced at the reflection in the glass of the terrace doors. She smiled as she saw Alec shove Burke to the side with a warning look before moving ahead of him to enter after her.

During dinner she had to focus on keeping the sensations she received from Alec in check. She had become far more perceptive to the magic around her since she had seen him last and found their connection to be very affecting. Each time she let her mind wander while in discussion with someone, she would feel the tingling warmth rise again.

At one point she got irritated with it and shot Alec an ugly look as if he were doing something to her intentionally. He avoided her eyes the remainder of the meal.

She had felt a little sorry for him when her father asked to sit beside him at the table. The temptation to eavesdrop on their conversation was fierce, but she didn't. GranMay, however, was eyeing the two of them.

"You should be ashamed of yourself, GranMay."

"I am far too old for that, my dear," GranMay replied with a smirk.

Morgan and Emma talked for the majority of the meal. Emma was getting very morose about not having found her mate yet. She was ready to marry and have children. Morgan tried to comfort her and get her mind off of it by discussing other issues.

After dinner, everyone retired to the garden terrace, which had been cleared of snow and lined with cauldrons of hot coals to keep the small area a bit more comfortable. They enjoyed coffee or hot cocoa as they mingled. Morgan moved through the dinner party, chatting with her family and friends as she flanked Alec's movement with conscious effort.

She was eyeing him from behind the very tall Josef when her father gave her a sweet kiss on the cheek from behind and wrapped her in a hug when she turned.

"He seems to be a fine man, my dear. I enjoyed talking with him this evening, and Daniel told me of the bravery and devotion to duty he has exhibited."

"Uh-huh," was all she offered before kissing his cheek and darting away.

A bit later, she was standing away from the crowd humming to the sleeping David snuggled in her arms. Burke and Mira came and took the warm little one from her with kisses of goodnight.

Emma kissed her cheek as well then winked before disappearing inside. The party had begun to break up, and she turned to find herself standing with Alec who looked anxious. She focused to block the sensations from him as he moved closer to her.

"Have I said something to offend you, my Queen?"

"You did nothing consciously, Sir Alec. I am sorry for giving you that impression," she said as she looked over the glistening snow-covered garden.

She gestured to the garden, and both laughed as they watched three youngling dragons darting through the paths. It was a favorite game for the evenings when the paths were clear of people. It was a perfect racecourse with many sharp turns for them to practice their maneuvering. The rules were simple: no landing and no flying higher than the trees, first one to the lake wins. The gardeners often howled the next morning when they found many flowerbeds trampled by those who could not make a turn in time.

They stood quiet for a moment after the younglings left before he stepped a bit closer. "May we use the connection for privacy, my Queen?"

"Certainly, what's on your mind?" she said as she turned to him. She thought she knew where this was going, but found she was way off base.

"I am very concerned about the behavior of the dragons that have spent long periods of time in the Ancestral Lair, my Lady. I get the impression they are bothered by something. They are restless. Honestly, after seeing how the magic has developed within you, I am even more worried about the possible impact their proximity to Lord Harrick may be having on them."

She felt the anxiety within him grow as he spoke and had to raise her guard higher to block it.

"I doubt if Lord Harrick could do any harm to the major dragons. They know to protect their minds from the darkness when they are that close to him. Younglings may not be able to, which is why I requested that only mature major dragons accompany you to the Lair."

He nodded as he shifted to look over the garden again, but still had a wrinkle of worry between his eyebrows. She located Menkar hunting in the forest nearby.

"Could you please join Sir Alec and me on the garden lawn, my friend?"

"Yes, my Queen. However, if it is not urgent, I ask your patience while I finish my hunt. I will only be a few minutes."

"Take your time and fill your belly, my friend."

She had been looking out over the garden as she spoke to Menkar. She now turned back to find Alec looking at her with a soft expression.

"You contacted Menkar didn't you, my Lady?" She nodded. "Thank you, my Queen. This is the reason I have returned, and it has been troubling me a great deal."

She patted his shoulder as she walked past him.

"Shall we go to meet Menkar in our secret spot, Sir Alec?"

He chuckled as he followed close behind her.

THEY MOVED through the garden and arrived at the edge of the lawn, but did not venture any further just yct. All the garden paths had been cleared of snow, but the lawn area had not. She was wearing only dress slippers and did not fancy walking out into the foot-deep snow until necessary.

When Menkar landed and she hiked up her dress to begin walking toward him, Alec gently grasped her arm to stop her progress.

"Please, allow me, my Queen."

She had barely turned her head to ask his meaning when he swept her into his arms and carried her toward Menkar. She felt the warmth of their connection building despite the many layers of clothing between them.

Menkar offered her his front leg as a perch out of the snow, and she snuggled against his warm hide while stroking him. He grumbled as he looked back at her and she felt annoyance.

She laughed and removed her gloves to caress him and share magic freely. He relaxed as she soothed him and gave a deep rumbling croon.

"I have missed you, my Queen. How may I help you?"

"Have you had any trouble while in the area of the Lair, my friend? Have you felt the darkness at all?"

Menkar looked at Alec with an odd expression before saying, "It is not the darkness of Arshek, but it is troubling, my Caretaker."

"May I join with you so you can show me?"

"It is not something to see, but to hear and feel. I am not sure you want to, my Queen, it is quite unpleasant."

She pushed reassurance as she shifted to lay her hands to his head.

"Please show me all of it. Concentrate on it and let me experience it through you."

Alec watched the now familiar process in which both Morgan's and the dragon's eyes began to glow. With the deep cut of her dress, he could see that the blue stone in the center of her amulet glowed as well. He watched her face as she viewed what Menkar experienced and stepped closer as she cringed and shivered. The expression she wore was one of deep sorrow by the time she released the bonding and leaned her head against the dragon.

"Are they dreams or visions you are experiencing while awake?"

"They come at any hour. If you are asleep when they come, you will wake."

"Have you heard of this kind of phenomenon before? Is there anything I can do to help free you of this?"

Menkar crooned a deep and pitiful sound before he

answered, "There are ancient memories I have that record similar whispers. It is said that only the birth of new lives can free the spirits of those taken too soon."

Her head shot up and she gasped, making Alec flinch and shift closer to her.

"Menkar, are you telling me these are the sounds of the trapped spirits of our own dragon brethren?"

"Yes, my Queen."

"Was there something we could have done to have prevented their entrapment? Was there something I should have done?"

Menkar gave a deep rumble of anguish as he shifted his head away and nudged at the snow with his snout.

"There should have been a Connection Ceremony within the week after they were taken. We did not perform it because we were so concerned for recovering those younglings who were taken and for protecting the few who survived. I am uncertain if the Ceremony will work so long after their entrapment. A dragon older than I will have access to more of the knowledge. Perhaps speak with an Elder, my Queen."

She caressed him for a long moment as she passed her love and sympathy.

"Thank you for sharing this with me, Menkar. I will do my best to help free our friends."

Menkar nudged her and Alec before lifting off and heading to the dragon chambers to rest. She was watching him disappear into the dark night when Alec touched her arm.

Only when she saw his expression did she consider his having not understood a word of their conversation. She summarized everything she had seen and Menkar's explanation, then stood quiet as she wrapped her arms tight to herself.

"They were only whispers. Yet, they were the most agonizing and mournful sounds I have ever heard. They tear through your heart and rip at your spirit. To know those are the trapped spirits of our own brethren is …"

She was shivering, both from the disturbing memory and because she was standing in the snow. Alec saw the problem and offered to lift her, but she declined. They walked back to the terrace in silence, both deep in thought. When they reached the chairs on the terrace, she sat down, pulled herself into a tight ball, and stared into the gray night.

Alec didn't interrupt her thoughts. He moved a large heating pot close to her and settled into a chair beside hers. She was quiet for many minutes before closing her eyes and laying her hands together.

"In the event of great loss of life through violence, the spirits may linger in attempt to protect those that survive. These lost ones can only be released to eternal rest by the initiation of new life in equal number with the direction of the Songs of Connection." She opened her eyes and blinked to refocus on the world around her.

"Did you get that from, Menkar?"

"No, it was part of the ancient dragon knowledge passed to me at my Quickening. I focused on the need and brought it forward."

"So, does that mean an egg needs to hatch within the Lair while you sing a ritual song?"

She was thinking again and closed her eyes to seek connection to Balia. A moment later, she opened her eyes to meet his.

"Balia tells me that, in a dragon's eyes, life begins for the hatchling when the egg is Quickened. I think I will need to take the same number of eggs as there are spirits trapped. Then perform the Quickening ceremony on them while singing the Songs of Connection."

Alec looked at her with solemn eyes then dropped his gaze to his hands.

"I do not expect we have that many eggs at present. We lost over a dozen dragons and most of the eggs in the attack," he said.

"We lost seventeen dragon spirits that day, including those Quickened but not yet hatched. And you are correct. Currently, we have only nine eggs that have not been Quickened. However, Balia and Sirzi are due to lay a clutch in the next week or two. I will use the time until they arrive to learn as much as I can about the ceremony." He nodded and they both fell quiet for a few minutes.

"Alec," she said as she met his eyes. "Thank you for coming to me with this. It is this kind of care for the dragons which makes you so valuable to me at the Lair."

"I am very glad to hear that you value my service to you, my Queen," he said with a bow of his head.

He rose and politely offered her a hand. The instant their bare fingers touched they both flinched, then tightened their grip.

Their eyes were locked as he dropped down to one knee in front of her. As he moved, they adjusted their hands so they touched palm-to-palm. He watched her eyes for the slightest hint of admonition, she offered none.

She lowered her guard and took controlled deep breaths

as the sensations filled her. Their fingers laced, hands gripped tight, as both began to breathe faster. Intense sensations of warmth, tingling, and dizziness washed over her in waves that intensified so fast her head spun.

She closed the connection and raised her guard a bit to regain control. Her heart was already racing, but its pace doubled when she saw the emotions she was feeling mirrored in his eyes.

"No, my Queen, I would not think this normal at all," he said in a whisper.

He had not released her hand, and she made no move to make him. The sensations passing between them were intense, yet comforting.

"This will make a simple kiss seem boring, I imagine," she whispered as her eyes shifted to his lips with the thought.

"Oh, I think not, my Lady," he whispered as he leaned in to let his lips gently touch hers. When he leaned back just enough to pull his lips from hers, she tightened her grip on his hand. He moved his free hand up to caress her face and kissed her again. His touch to her cheek and neck added to the already incredible blast of sensation the kiss brought.

It was her first kiss and it was wonderful, an absolute dream … right up to the point where Daniel cleared his throat behind her.

Alec did not panic and go flying away from her. He simply moved back, released her hand, and stood at attention to his Admiral. She followed his lead and dealt with the situation with dignity and poise.

"Go Away, Daniel!"

"I will, but you will go with me. Now, little sister!" he said

as he glared at Alec with red cheeks.

She felt his anger and knew there was no changing his mind.

"At least give us a private minute to say goodnight," she said in a calmer tone as she stood and looked at him.

He nodded and turned away as he said, *"I will be generous and give you two, my Queen."* He walked ten feet away, then stopped to stand with his back to them.

"Sorry about that, he still insists on acting the big brother," she said as she moved to Alec's side.

"He has every right to be upset, my Queen. I should not have done that, I am sorry for dishonoring y—" She touched her finger to his lips which cut him off, despite their use of the connection.

"First of all, you did nothing that I did not want you to do, and you owe me no apology. Secondly, I would prefer you call me by my given name when we speak privately."

He nodded with a relaxed smile and held her gaze as he said, *"Yes, Lady Morgan."* She raised an eyebrow at him and he chuckled as he corrected himself to say, *"Yes, Morgan."* He gave her hand a light squeeze, sending tingles through them both, then stepped back and bowed.

"Goodnight, my Queen."

"Goodnight, Sir Alec."

She fell into step behind him, hoping to blow right past Daniel, but was stopped by a sharp bark of, "Wait!"

She felt her brother's anger boiling and cringed a bit when the harsh emotion struck her. He saw her reaction and took a minute to calm down before turning to face her again.

"Morgan, you've put me in a seriously weird spot here. I

would normally say something about how you barely know this man and can't trust him yet. But I realize you know him better than I do given your abilities. But I have to say something. I know the intensity of a kiss and how easily that can carry someone past their better judgment. I can only imagine what the intensity of the connection you have with him could lead you to. Actually, no, I don't want to imagine that at all. Which is why you need to show better discretion. If for no other reason than for the propriety of the position you hold!"

"I know you want to protect me from getting hurt, or from embarrassing myself. But please put our new situation in perspective. He is not just some guy I am dating Daniel. I have felt the magical connection I have with him. I know this is the man I am going to marry. Surely that puts a very different set of rules into play."

"Yeah, I know," he said as he rubbed his face with a sigh. "Rules I am completely ignorant of."

"There is also more to consider. I cannot ignore the fact that if I die before having a daughter the Caretaker line dies with me. That is the hard truth of my responsibility, and it is with me every day. I would not have married or considered having children this early had we stayed on Earth. But our lives are not those, and I am not that person any longer. I can't tell you if it is the magic or natural attraction, but I am ready to know him and move forward. I ask that you let me do so and support me in it."

She stepped to her worried brother to take his hand. He smiled as he received a rush of love through the contact and relaxed a bit.

"I can tell you something that will help you rest easier as I begin to see more of him," she said.

He glanced at her then mumbled, "Doubt it."

"My magic makes it impossible to fake the emotion of love to me. I can tell you that he is not faking. He loves me. He truly does … even now." A single tear ran down her face as she added, "And what is more amazing, I know that I love him as well."

Daniel held her tight as she fought crying.

"I'm sorry if I ruined it for you. I just freaked a little when I saw him kissing you. I wasn't ready for that yet."

She laughed against his shoulder.

"Neither was I," she said, "But it really was amazing, Daniel. It was just one short kiss, but our connection made it something else entirely."

He shuddered, pushed her back to hold her at arm's length, and gave her a very stern look.

"OK, I made it through that statement, somehow. But, from this second forward, you must promise to never tell me about the sensations you have when you touch him. Not ever! Agreed?"

Her face split into a wicked grin as she held up her palms to him and wiggled her fingers.

"Perhaps I should share them with you instead, my brother?"

She laughed aloud as he shivered and went very pale.

THE NEXT MORNING Morgan woke to find GranMay sitting on the foot of her bed with a devilish smile, looking as though she was about to pop. Morgan grumbled and rolled over with a move to escape from the opposite side of the bed.

"Do not make me sit on you and bond to get the information I seek!"

Morgan rolled back over, chuckling, and patted the bed next to her. GranMay snuggled in beside her and kissed her forehead.

"It was incredible GranMay. It took all the control I had to keep from passing out again. And that was just touching with one hand. Then he kissed me, and everything went completely crazy inside."

GranMay did not reply aloud, but Morgan felt her confusion and concern. She sat up and saw those emotions expressed on her face as well.

"What? Are you upset that I kissed him? I'm seventeen for goodness sake!"

GranMay shook her head, patted her on the shoulder, then pulled her back down to snuggle against her.

"No, no, dear, I am not upset, just confused. I have seen many examples of how your skills with the magic surpass any I have, or have even heard of, but this is still surprising. The sensations you are describing are far more intense than those one would expect from simple contact, bonding perhaps, but not a simple kiss. I know it is asking a lot, but will you share a bit of it with me so I can better judge the situation?"

Morgan hesitated, then offered her hand. She shared examples of when they were near but not touching, when they touched, and when they kissed.

"My goodness, Morgan. That was very different from my experiences and from your mother's. We both reached that level of intensity in connection with our husbands, but it was certainly not from a simple touch or kiss. And the way you can feel the sensations without even touching him astounds me. I don't understand it at all," she said with a wrinkle of concern on her brow.

Morgan chewed her bottom lip until GranMay touched her face.

"Daniel was right, I'm afraid. You must be careful to control yourself. I can see that level of intensity being quite hard to keep in check. Especially with someone as handsome as Alec."

Morgan smiled as GranMay said that last part and laughed.

"He is very pleasant to look at, isn't he? Perhaps now you understand why I gave him a post as far away as possible." They laughed a few seconds before she hurried from the bed. "The handsome devil is headed this way. Will you greet him while I dress, please?"

SHE ENTERED the sitting room off her bedroom a few minutes later to find GranMay and Alec holding one palm together. Putting guilt aside, she connected to Alec to listen in. She found that he was sharing events from his youth when living in the home of GranMay's brother, Sir Kisik. She backed out of the connection and felt herself blush with shame as she turned to leave.

"Could I have a word before I depart, my Queen? I had hoped to further discuss the situation at the Lair."

"Do you mind?" she asked GranMay as she turned to face them.

"Only the nosy part of me," GranMay said with a wink as

she moved to kiss her cheek.

Alec hurried to open the door for GranMay, then returned to Morgan in the sitting area. When she sat on the small sofa, he remained standing.

"I wanted to ask if you would like for me and some of my unit to return here in two weeks' time to help transport the eggs and serve as your escort to the Lair."

"Yes, that sounds appropriate. If the eggs have not come by that time, I will send a messenger with a later date for you to return."

"Very well, my Queen," he said with a nod. He held her eyes as he hesitated for a few seconds, then bowed and turned for the door.

"Alec," she said as she laid a hand on the seat beside her. "I think we need to talk, don't you?"

As he sat beside her, she turned to face him and held out her hand. When he took it in his, the rush of emotions made her take in a deep breath. She smiled, having noticed he had the same reaction. They sat quietly for a moment as they enjoyed the sensation of their connection.

"Morgan, I have never felt anything like this before."

"Well, I should hope not," she said with a smirk as she squeezed his hand.

He smiled in return, but his eyes grew serious.

"I was not referring to the physical sensations of our connection. I was referring to the way I feel when I am away from you."

She stared at him for a long moment before managing a reply.

"I have never been in love before either."

"Did you just say you love me?" he said as he touched her cheek. He leaned toward her until his face was very near hers then stopped. "I love you too, Morgan. More than I ever imagined possible."

She leaned in and kissed him. This time they were not interrupted.

The intense warmth and tingling built very fast, making their bodies flush. As she broke the kiss, both were sweating, and their hearts were racing. She sat back a little and shifted her hand so they touched with just their fingertips.

As she calmed herself, she passed healing energy to slow his heart rate. They held the other's eyes as they calmed and laughed without embarrassment.

"I want to explain something. I need time to learn more about my abilities and become fully confident in my position as Queen and Caretaker, before I will be ready for us to talk about any big steps. I did not choose to send you to command at the Lair only for your exceptional skills. While I had every confidence in you being a perfect choice for the post, I also liked the idea of keeping you at a comfortable distance from me. That has not changed, Alec. I need to take this slowly. Do you understand?"

"Yes, I do understand. And I will stay away as much as you need me to. It will be difficult, of course. You are hard to put out of my mind, my dear."

"Thank you for understanding."

As they looked into each other's eyes his face broke into a mischievous smile.

"I promise to be a respectful Knight in the company of others, my Lady. But, could I ask what the rules are, my dear?

I would not want to miss an opportunity, unknowingly."

"An opportunity for what, exactly?" she asked with a laugh and a raised eyebrow.

He grinned as he leaned in very close again to stop just shy of her lips as before. She did not hesitate to close the gap and kiss him again. This time it was he who broke the kiss after only a couple of seconds.

"I do apologize for my forward actions last night. I need you to know that I will never make a move to advance our level of familiarity again. I will leave it to you to decide when you are ready for more from me."

She saw and felt the sincerity in his words. With a small nod and smile, she leaned over to him and hovered within an inch of his lips until she felt his emotions rise, then kissed him with meaning.

They enjoyed a few minutes of privacy before she walked him to the door.

"How could you tell the dragons at the Lair were upset when you cannot talk to them?"

"They were restless and acting strange, I suppose."

She stopped him with a tug on his hand and waited for his eyes to meet hers.

"If you love me, you will trust me. Telling less to avoid the truth is a lie, and it hurts."

"You are right, and I am sorry," he said as he shifted closer to touch her cheek as he gripped her hand. *"I absolutely trust you and want you to trust me. The truth is that, as long as I can remember, I have been able to sense how a dragon is feeling. Only intense emotions, it is not really communication. I hesitated because I have never shared this with anyone. It has always been*

a private matter shared only with my dragon brethren. I feel sure that Burke and Emma may have noticed, but we have never discussed it."

She could do nothing but stare at him for many seconds.

"I have no knowledge of a Chemerian male being able to sense emotions in dragons. It has been many generations since even the men of the Caretaker line have carried magic strong enough to use that way. Have you ever heard of it?"

"No, never. That is why I have never discussed it with anyone."

She saw him watching her closely for signs of disapproval, so she focused to keep her face relaxed and her voice calm as they said goodbye.

SHE SWAM as fast as she could go. It had been over an hour in ice-cold water, hoping exercise would help her think, or not think. But still, there was no getting around the only realistic conclusion. There was substantial magic present within Alec. The problem was the only logical explanation for that to be true.

She was scared, mad, confused, and many other things she could not even define. So, she swam. She ignored all the arguments of her family about the stupidity of swimming outside in the winter, and she swam.

Focused exercise was always the one thing that would allow her to clear her mind. However, this time it was not working. She struggled up the bank and fell in a heap into the warm waiting palm of Balia, who tucked her into the bend of her neck to warm her.

As she sat in the warmth of Balia's embrace, trying to force Alec and his magic from her mind, Balia gave a deep rumbling croon that pushed happiness and love.

"It is time, my Queen. I will lay my clutch tonight, and they will be ready for Quickening in a few days. Sirzi believes her clutch will be here within two weeks as well."

"That is wonderful news, Balia. Congratulations, my dear! Are you excited?"

"It is not my first clutch, and it will be a long time before they hatch. But yes, it is a very happy feeling and I am a bit anxious. Will you come and share it with me, my friend?"

"I would be honored. Thank you for your friendship, Balia. You have no idea how precious you have been to me since I arrived here. I love you." She sat quietly a minute before she saw the added beauty of her friend's offer. "You saw my worry and offered this unusual gift to help me feel better. I appreciate the sentiment, but are you quite sure?"

"I have planned to invite you to join me for some time, my friend. Knowing my asking eases your sadness is an added pleasure."

Morgan lay forward across her snout as she crooned again. Her friend sang a beautiful tune as they each deepened their connection to share their love for one another.

LATER THAT NIGHT, Morgan sat with Balia as she lay in the hot poolroom of the dragon chambers. Balia was still a small major dragon, yet she already filled most of the room herself.

She let Morgan experience everything through a deep connection. Through it she felt the pain, the apprehension, and ultimately, pure joy when Balia nosed her five beautiful, healthy eggs into a neat pile.

They sat together for a long time as Balia sang to her eggs and nudged them so the stack was just right.

"It will not be all that long before you will have your first child and experience much of this for yourself," Balia said.

Morgan sighed and dropped her head as the worry came rushing back. Balia crooned and nudged her.

"Balia, I want to share something with you and I would ask that you keep it from all other dragons and people. Are you comfortable with that?"

"Of course. Not because you are my Queen and Caretaker, but because you are my friend."

"I believe Alec has magic within him, magic of his own, which is much stronger than the normal traces within all Chemerians."

"It is very unusual, but his magic is very weak."

"I know, but...wait, what? Balia, you knew about this? Why did you not tell me?"

"Because Alec is also a very good friend to the dragons, and he asked us not to. Of course, had you asked me of it directly, I would not have lied to you."

"Can you explain it to me then?"

"I have never received information from him, but he can sense if I am angry, sad, or happy. It is more than any but a Caretaker could sense for certain."

"I have concentrated on the idea of a man holding enough magic to use it, and have found nothing within the memories passed to me. I do not understand why this knowledge would not have been given to me."

"Either the information is not known to us, or it was determined that you should find the information on your own when the time was right. Sometimes giving too much information can be unkind to the Caretaker."

"Unkind? I think letting me fall in love with him and then find out he has magic within him is very unkind."

"Why does his having magic bother you so?"

"Because it is the same magic I carry! Our magic is supposed to only be present within the Caretaker bloodline."

"It may not have been present in males at this level for hundreds of years, but you have still not said why his having magic is a bad thing."

"Human Genetics! If he has the magic of Chemerie then he could be too close a blood relative of mine for us to safely have children."

"I do see the reason for your worry now. But please know that I have never known the magic to bring two mates together who were not suitable for one another in every way. You must have faith in the wisdom of the magic, my friend."

"I wish I knew who his parents were. Maybe then I could figure out his connection to the Caretaker line."

"Then you should bond with him. It is time you embraced his love for you. Once you have felt your magical link to his spirit, you will not question its validity again."

Morgan laughed and sighed.

"I can barely control the sensations of touching his hand. How could I possibly handle a bonding with him?"

"You will never be able to rest until you come to terms with this information. You may not find what you seek within the bonding, but it is the most logical first step. The bonding will show you his true spirit. In love, that is all that matters, my friend."

They sat for a while longer, enjoying the quiet comfort of each other's company.

"Why have I never met your mate, Balia? Why have you hidden his identity each time we have bonded?"

Balia's head dropped and she crooned a pitiful sound in her throat. Profound sadness and loss came from her and poured over Morgan.

"I am so sorry. I did not know you lost him."

"It is not the loss alone that hurts so deeply. My heart aches because his is one of the spirits trapped in the Lair." Morgan caressed her and pushed love as strong as she could for a moment.

"Balia, you are a wonderful friend to me by listening and offering support when I need you. Please, let me be that kind of friend to you as well. It hurts to know you have told me nothing of losing your mate. I want you to trust me with your pain, as I do you."

"I do, my friend. I have talked of it with no one, not even my mother. You are my dearest friend Morgan. I speak of it to you now because I feel your love for me, and I trust you completely." She nuzzled Morgan as she crooned, then laid her head at her side to sleep.

THREE WEEKS LATER, Morgan stood on the garden lawn watching a crew load bags packed with seventeen dragon eggs onto the backs of Balia and Sirzi. The male major dragons would carry only people. This was the result of the females refusing to allow a male to carry the eggs.

GranMay walked up to stand beside Morgan and put her arm around her waist.

"Are you going to tell me what has been bothering you before you go?" GranMay said.

"I will bond with Alec during this trip. There is something I must know, and that is the best way to find the answers I need."

"You know how greatly this will affect you. Are you sure you are ready to control the unusual intensity of your connection with him?"

Morgan looked at her with a stern expression then turned to gaze over the field again.

"No, I am not sure. But it's the unusual nature of our connection that I question. I must have the answer, so I must do this."

"Though I do not know your reason, I respect your conviction. I only suggest you be cautious. While bonding is meant to be wonderful, it can be very painful if allowed to proceed too fast. Perhaps begin by opening to him without touch. You may build a tolerance that way."

Morgan thanked her for the advice and hugged her good-bye before heading to Menkar.

"Will you pay me the honor of allowing me to fly with you to the Lair, Menkar?"

Menkar crooned while nudging her into his palm. He lifted her up to sit in front of Alec.

"Are you ready to depart, my Queen?" Alec said.

She nodded without comment. She had considered riding a different dragon to avoid conversation with him, but knew her riding with any other than the unit commander would draw suspicion.

They left the ground to join the formation of major dragons. Once in the air, and out of earshot of any of the others, Alec leaned forward to speak in her ear.

"I have missed you. Are you well?"

"I am fine. Thank you." She said nothing more for the entire trip to the Lair.

As they rose from the water in the main chamber of the Lair, she was hit with the agony and longing of the trapped spirits. She bent forward as the pain of it struck her and Alec grabbed her arms to support her. The warmth of his touch made her flinch and hurry to move down Menkar's foreleg.

She leaned against Menkar's snout as he hummed the dragons' healing song.

"Unload all of the eggs and lay them out in a large circle in the middle of the chamber, please," she said to Alec without looking his way.

When they finished, she stood before the group of Knights with a solemn face.

"The dragons will take all of you to wait outside the Lair. I must perform the ceremony alone, with only the dragons present." She had communicated this to the dragons on the flight in, and they were waiting for the Knights to re-board.

She connected to the dragons again, *"Please return here after you have dropped them off. I will need all of your strength, my friends."*

Every one of them bowed to her in answer. She turned back toward the circle of eggs and found that Alec had not moved to Menkar. He was standing near the chamber wall staring at her through angry eyes.

"I am sorry, but you too must go. I will find this hard enough without the added distraction of the minds of people. And you know very well you, in particular, are a marked distraction," she said with a small smile.

"I would request to stay, my Queen. It is my duty to protect you and leaving you alone in this Lair is not safe," he said as he continued to stare at her.

"Sir Alec, I have checked the Lair and there are no threats to me present. If you would like, you may ask the dragons to post half your men at each entrance. Either way, you will adhere to my wishes and leave the Lair, so I can best serve our dragon brethren!"

"Yes, my Queen," he said as he bowed. After one more angry glare, he marched past her to board Menkar.

Once all the men had left the Lair, and the male major dragons had returned, she moved to the center of the circle of eggs. The dragons moved to form a greater circle around them with their heads pointing inward toward her.

She turned a slow circle as she looked into the eyes of each dragon to connect. With her hands held in front of her, palms up, she began to sing the Song of Connection in dragon-tongue. The dragons joined in on the second verse, and the dragon markings on her palms began to glow and move around.

When they finished the song, they began again, such that it became a perpetual chant. With the beginning of the next repetition, she knelt and changed her chant to include verses from the Song of Quickening. She lifted the first egg in her left hand bearing the image of the dragon still curled in its egg. After two verses she placed her right hand, bearing the image of a full-grown dragon, on the opposite side of the egg. Two verses more and she shifted the egg to lie atop only her right hand.

As she finished the second verse with the egg in this position, and therefore completed its Quickening, she felt a rush of relief and joy. She looked up to see a misty image fly a circle above her then shoot up to disappear through the top of the chamber.

She repeated this process for sixteen more eggs. As she completed the Quickening of the last egg she heard a faint voice whisper from above her.

"We thank you, my Queen. We leave our young in your very capable hands. May the magic keep you, my Caretaker," said the ethereal voice.

She watched as the misty image held still and took form. It was that of Zetia. The ghostly dragon bowed to her before swirling and shooting up to join the others. As Zetia was freed and the song stopped, profound exhaustion hit Morgan. She lay down on the stone floor and smiled at Balia.

"Your mate is free, my friend. They are all free."

SHE WOKE lying atop Balia's front leg to the sound of pacing boots on stone. She did not open her eyes or move.

"How mad is he, my friend?" she asked Balia.

"He has found reason to snap at every man here and has gnawed his fingernails away on all fingers. I think it is more worry than anger, but it is too close to be certain."

She lay still for another minute, then sat up to connect to Alec as she caught his gaze.

"I had to do my duty, just as you have to do yours. When there is a conflict, my duty must come first. I hope you understand."

"Of course, my Queen. Can I get you anything to make you more comfortable, my Lady?"

She did not miss the formal address despite the privacy of

the connection, but did not let her temper rise to meet his. His anger was very small compared to his hurt and frustration with having to hide his feelings for her.

"No Alec, I am fine. But thank you for your concern," she said. He turned and was moving away when she added, *"Tomorrow I would like for us to take a large step in advancing our level of familiarity, if you would permit it."*

He actually tripped and nearly fell forward at those words, but did not turn to face her. He collected himself and continued into a small cave without responding. She chose to let him be.

Later that night, she was woken by a nudge and croon from Balia.

"Your Love has not slept, my friend. He paces the floor in the next chamber."

Morgan patted her friend then headed for Alec. She entered the small cavern silently to find him standing with his back to her.

"Is there something I can do for you, my Queen?" he said with his back still turned.

She was stunned to realize he had felt her presence, just as she could sense his.

"Yes, there is. You can forgive my coldness earlier and allow me to explain my feelings."

"There is nothing to forgive, my Lady. You were well within your station as Queen to use any tone necessary to lead the Knights of the Guard to obey your wishes. It is I who apologize for questioning your instructions."

He had still not turned to face her. She moved to him and placed her hands on his shoulders. Even through the material of his shirt, she could feel the warm sensations flowing between them. She studied his feelings and found he was not angry, he was hurt and scared. He stepped away from her touch and remained facing away from her.

"Will you not forgive me, Alec?"

He turned his solemn face to her and stood silent for a long moment.

"You ordered me to do something today that went against everything I am. I am a Knight of the Guard whose first priority is to assure the safety and well-being of our Queen. I am also a man who is very much in love with you and that means I want to protect you against any threat, pain, or unhappiness. Given those convictions, there is no reason I should have followed your orders today. My anger and disappointment are for my own actions, not yours."

"You followed your heart."

He had begun pacing as he spoke and now stopped and turned on her.

"Did you hear nothing I said? I left you alone in a chamber still red with the blood of our murdered brethren. How is that following my heart? I see it as betraying my heart altogether!"

"Alec, please sit and listen to me," she said while taking a seat on a small bed nearby.

He reluctantly moved to sit and left a great deal of room between them.

"You did what you did for the exact reason I did what I did. Your connection to the dragons helps you to see how crucial my role to serve them is. When you saw the conviction in my eyes, you knew it was the right thing to do. You put their happiness before the possibility of random danger. I see no fault in that. I do not question your loyalty to me as your Queen or as your partner."

"How can you forgive me when I cannot forgive myself?"

"Two reasons. One, I know you did the right thing and would have lost all respect for you had you not. And two, because you are my partner and I have to."

He gave a weak chuckle and lay back as he rubbed his face. They both relaxed a bit as the tension left him.

"It was very hard to hear you speak to me so coldly today. I know I have to accept living this double role, but I won't deny that it cut me deeply."

"I am sorry that I hurt you. And I do apologize for using such a cold tone with you. But, I cannot apologize for my insistence."

He rolled to his side to stare at her for a minute with passionate eyes.

"Your conviction to serve the dragons as fiercely as you do is why I fell in love with you so fast. It is just quite difficult when your duty conflicts with my need to protect you. I doubt that will ever change."

She looked down and stayed quiet for a few seconds before speaking without meeting his eye again.

"Is it too much to ask? Do you wish to stop serving as a Knight or ... to sever our relationship?"

He sat up in a flash with a deep scowl.

"Of course not! I will do neither until death takes me, and I will love you long after that!"

The wicked smirk that filled her face made him laugh along with her as he flopped back down.

She lay back and slid her hand into his. They both took deep breaths together as the calming warmth flowed between them.

"It would be quite hard to walk away from this. I suppose you will just have to put up with me," she said.

He squeezed her hand and sighed as he said. "I suppose so."

They both laughed until he rolled toward her and kissed her hand.

"So, what was that about advancing our level of familiarity?" he asked through his most wicked of smiles.

She nodded then stood up where she held her arms open wide, and her face serious.

"I have decided to allow an embrace." She was struggling not to laugh as he stood up.

"I think that sounds lovely, my dear," he said as he moved into her arms to wrap her in his.

He laid his cheek against her head and gently rubbed her back with one hand while the other held her snug against him. She relaxed into his strong embrace, warm and safe. Their connection was making her skin tingle lightly, and she was very relaxed.

He began to sway as he hummed.

"I still owe you a dance, my love. Will you join me?" he whispered.

He moved her arms up to wrap around his neck and wrapped his around her waist. He hummed the beautiful melody they had first danced to, and they moved together for a long time before finally saying goodnight.

MORGAN WOKE to Alec yelling orders to his unit. They were all running around, loading eggs and supplies onto the dragons. He took her hand and lifted her sharply to her feet.

"We must go, my Queen. A scout patrol found tracks of the Arshek dragons in a clearing near the entrance they blasted during the attack. The tracks are fresh, and there were at least two different dragons."

She did not argue as she boarded Menkar with him. Just as they were going to take off she cringed and turned her head toward the top of the massive chamber.

"They are here," she said as she felt the presence of very different dragon spirits full of anger and hate. She alerted all of the Chemerian dragons and agreed to the females' request to go now to keep the eggs safe.

"We must keep them from pursuing the females. We can not lose the eggs," she said to Alec. He nodded in agreement and directed his men. He had two of the force fly up to meet the enemy dragons when they entered and held the rest back on the cavern floor. She noticed he positioned Menkar to the back of the group to protect her.

There were only two of the enemy dragons, and they were no match for the large group of major dragons they found when they entered. After only a few clashes of talons and fangs, the two younger Arshek dragons turned tail and retreated.

"No! That was just a diversion. Their majors must be pursuing the females and the eggs. Go! Go!!" Alec yelled to his men and their mounts.

Morgan, Alec, and Menkar were the last to leave the Lair. Once they broke the surface of the lake outside the mountain ridge, she opened her connection wide and searched for Balia.

"NOOOOO!" Morgan screamed as she doubled over clutching her stomach from sharing the tremendous pain Balia was enduring. The brave dragon was standing her ground against two enemy major dragons to protect her clutch. She was already injured badly, but would not give in and let them take the eggs. Morgan gasped as she struggled to block Balia's pain.

"Hurry, Menkar, they are under attack. The females will die before giving up the eggs." Menkar put on a burst of speed that nearly unseated his riders.

When they arrived at the scene of the ambush, the Chemerian male dragons had slain or were forcing the retreat of all the attacking Arshek dragons. Menkar made a wide circle around the scene until the Arshek dragons were away, then shot down fast. As soon as he touched down, Morgan jumped to the ground and ran to Balia where she fell against her neck.

Balia was barely alive, curled around her clutch, taking shallow raspy breaths. She had massive gashes all over her body, and blood was pouring freely onto the ground. Morgan pushed hard with her connection and finally got a weak response from Balia.

"Protect my children so they may serve you, my Queen. Good-bye, my dear friend."

"NO! You are not leaving me!"

She placed her hands to the sides of Balia's head and focused her healing magic to push with all she had. Some of the wounds were healing, but not fast enough. Balia trembled a bit as she transferred the magic, but she could not connect to her again.

She did not stop. She could not stop. She pushed and pushed until she was soaked with sweat and trembling. After many moments of this, Alec and Burke took hold of her arms and pulled her back from Balia's lifeless body.

"You must stop, my Queen. You will kill yourself if you go too far," Alec said in a cracking voice.

"I will not let her go!" she screamed as she jerked away from them. A second later, she grabbed Alec's wrist and pulled him to her. "Help me, as we did before." She slid her hand into his and laced their fingers as she reached out toward Balia again. He caught her second hand, holding it and her fierce glare.

"I beg you, do not go too far, my Caretaker. We need you, my Queen!" He laid her hand to Balia as a tear slid down his face, then dropped his voice to say, "I need you. Please. If it is her time, let her go."

Tears streamed down her face as she used the added strength of their link to seek connection to Balia once more while pushing healing faster for another long moment. A roar of rage left her as she pulled her hand from Alec's and slammed her fists into Balia's side. A second later, she crumpled against her as sharp pain shot through every cell of her body. She panted with her forehead to Balia's side for a long moment then pushed back to stand and start moving around her large body.

Tears continued to slide down her face as she moved to Sirzi, who was being guarded by an anxious Menkar. He shifted from Sirzi's head to their clutch in an effort to protect both from any more harm. He stopped only when Morgan held up her hands to him.

"Lend me strength so I can try to help the others, my friend."

Sirzi had fought to protect her own clutch and was also badly injured. Morgan hesitated before laying her hands to Sirzi as she glanced past her at Balia's still form. She closed her eyes and swallowed hard, then pushed her healing magic once more. She was able to stabilize Sirzi and relieve her pain, before again rebuilding her strength to move on to others who needed her. For an hour, she moved among the remaining injured dragons and Knights until all who needed her were helped.

When she finished, she returned to Balia and placed her hands to her neck. She concentrated on the spirit of her dear friend in hopes she would hear her.

"I am so sorry, my friend; I am so sorry that I am too weak and inexperienced with the magic. I have failed you, my dear," she said as tears flooded her face again.

As she wept, she thought of the spirits trapped in the Lair. With her hands to Balia's head, she sang the Song of Connection to assure her spirit a rightful release. She was still crying hard with her head against Balia when Alec laid a hand on her shoulder.

"We must get back to the safety of the castle, my Caretaker."

She wiped her tears and cleared her throat, then faced him without moving her hands from Balia.

"Send the others ahead. We will do her burning. I will not leave her like this."

"The dragons wait to carry her home, so we may perform her burning with the company of her brethren, my Lady." She nodded and took his hand. He steadied her and supported her waist as they moved to board Menkar.

Once they were in flight, Alec asked Menkar to drop back away from the rest of the group, then wrapped his arms tightly around her.

"I am so sorry, my love. I know you loved her dearly. But you cannot blame yourself. You are very strong with the magic, but your skills were never meant to stop death altogether. Her injuries were too severe to be undone." She could only respond by pulling his arms tighter around her.

She listened to his words, but could not take them in. Her heart was crushed. Her magic had failed her.

Her pain and grief lessened as she relaxed into his embrace and let herself cry, knowing that he understood her pain and did not judge her weak.

After a few minutes of forcing herself to calm, she was able to regain control.

"Did the enemy take any of the eggs?"

"No, my dear. Two were crushed when Sirzi was tackled to the ground. The rest were all accounted for. Harrick did not get his prize."

THEY LANDED on the garden lawn with the rest of the party. Balia's body had been laid on the massive top ledge of the rock cliffs surrounding the castle lake. Morgan dismounted then looked up to the high peak to see a huge green dragon land near her friend.

The great Elder dragon let out a horrible roar of rage and anguish. Morgan's heart nearly imploded as she felt the pain of Balia's mother. The combination of her own pain and that of the Elder dragon buckled her knees.

She looked up from her position on the ground and saw

that the Elder dragon had taken flight, and many people were already working to cover Balia's body with bundles of hay soaked in aromatic oils. Balia's mother was joined by a massive red male. Together, they flew slow mournful circles high above Balia's body.

She could stand no more. She rose and walked to her chambers alone without a word to anyone. Moments after she reached her chambers and sprawled across the bed, GranMay joined her. She did not say a word. She simply laid a hand to her back to lend comfort through the magic.

"I cannot watch her body burn, GranMay."

"If you do not, you will fail her. It is of the greatest honor among our dragons to die in battle and have their bodies burned in the presence of the Caretaker."

"I have already failed her! She is dead because I am too ignorant and weak!"

"Morgan, you are the strongest of all your mothers before you, and I will not have you blaming yourself," GranMay said before pausing to calm herself. She caressed her back as she continued, "My dear, the magic has its limits. I do not believe that you could have done any more to save her had it happened after years of training. Our magic is wonderful. It helps us relieve the pain of many, and to hold off death in most cases. But in situations like this, where the damage is so severe, even our magic cannot prevent death. Our magic is meant to enhance the quality of our lives, not to prevent our lives from ending."

Morgan stood and looked out the window at the crowd gathering around the lake below the cliff bearing Balia's body.

"I will honor her, but I cannot be their strong Queen right now."

"You will be gliding high above the burning. No one will see you cry. Of course, they would not judge you if they did. They understand the profound connection between dragon and Caretaker."

She turned and headed for the bathroom.

"She was much more than a dragon I serve; she was my best friend."

AS DUSK FELL, the people and dragons of Chemerie gathered around the lake grew still and quiet. Morgan stood at the window of her bedroom. Though she should be outside already, she had not been able to move quite yet.

Her heart lifted when she felt Alec approaching. She met him at the door and flew at his chest. He stood stiff and barely returned her embrace. As she leaned back, she saw the reason. She had hugged him in plain view of the two Knights who were waiting to escort her.

She shifted back and looked into his eyes. He took her in his arms and kissed her head without hesitation. They held each other for a long moment before she looked up at him again.

"I need you with me. No more hiding."

He smiled and took her back into his embrace to hold her tight to his chest.

"I am very happy to hear those words, my dear. I feel as though I can breathe again." She smiled as his joy washed over her, and felt the sorrow in her heart lessen as his love filled her.

He took her hand and wrapped it in the bend of his arm as he led her down the hall. They exited the castle arm-in-arm and walked through the gathered crowd toward Menkar, who waited on the lawn to carry them.

They flew up to the cliff bearing Balia's body. She slid down to the ground and walked forward to accept the burning torch from a man whose face was wet with tears. She swallowed back her own tears and stepped to the mound of hay covering her friend.

"Thank you for being such a loyal friend. You have taught me so much and helped me learn to serve our brethren. I promise you I will learn more and grow in strength of magic. Then, perhaps I can prevent this type of early death in another of our brethren. I love you, Balia. Goodbye, my dear friend."

She threw the torch on the great mound of hay and remained as the fire grew in intensity. She waited for it to reach its fullest height, then ran to vault up to Menkar's back. Alec wrapped her tight as Menkar leapt and dropped very fast before turning sharply up to climb higher than she had yet gone. Her head throbbed as her ears struggled to adjust to the difference in air pressure before Menkar started circling, slowly dropping to hold about a hundred yards above the fire below.

Morgan flew, wrapped in Alec's arms, for the entire time the fire burned. At first she was overcome by the grief of the loss and wept. But she soon stopped crying altogether. She thought of how Balia had referred to Alec as "your Love" and not by his title.

She was so grateful for the wisdom of her friend. Balia had helped her accept that she did love Alec already and that it was time to let herself have that joy. With that comfort within her, she was able to focus on wonderful times she spent in Balia's company, and not only on the pain of her loss.

She doubted she would ever be able to release the guilt of not being capable of saving her friend, but now she had the strength to move on. She had promised Balia she would continue to grow and to learn, and that promise she would keep.

Connection

AFTER SAYING GOODNIGHT to Menkar, Morgan and Alec sat on the terrace in the quiet of the night. She was leaned back against his chest, wrapped in his arms. Neither of them flinched as they heard a throat clearing and turned to see their family smiling at them.

"Well, I see you two like breaking tradition about as much as Christina and me. We disappeared for a weekend as a way of announcing our engagement. Yours was at least a bit more subtle," Nikolas said as he and the others settled into chairs around them.

"Is it officially engagement as yet, or are we just in the dating phase?" GranMay said.

Morgan was about to answer when Alec spoke.

"Well, Queen May, I have not asked formally, but I do not think I am too forward in saying I have every intention of calling this beautiful and amazing woman my wife. I have been blessed by the magic and am a very grateful man," he said before pulling Morgan tighter to him and kissing her head. He realized his manners and looked toward her father to add, "with your permission, of course, King Nikolas."

"My permission you have," Nikolas said with a smile as he crooked a thumb at Daniel. "However, it is him you need to worry about, young man. Mistreat my daughter, and it is his wrath you will suffer."

"I would ask your permission as well, Admiral," Alec said with a bow of his head. Morgan thought that a bit much but said nothing.

"The magic you share makes the pretense of permission redundant, but I give it all the same," Daniel said.

"The bonding went well then, I take it?" GranMay asked.

Morgan tensed and felt Alec do the same.

"We did not have the opportunity to discuss nor act on that, GranMay."

"Oops, sorry, my dear. I had assumed that was the reason for your change of heart about keeping your partnership a secret for a while."

"No, I thank Balia for showing me the value of a loving partner. We talked many times of my dilemma, and she made many subtle moves to push me in the right direction. I needed his support today, and Balia's words allowed me to take it."

"Excuse me," Daniel blurted. "Is this 'bonding' something they should be doing before they're married?"

Everyone burst into laughter, except Alec, who was unsure of the answer himself. He chuckled along, but Morgan felt his apprehension. She squeezed his hands and passed reassurance, which made him shiver.

GranMay struggled to get her laughter under control as she saw Daniel's stress-ridden face.

"Bonding is focused sharing of magic, a connection deeper than any words could provide. You feel the very essence of the other's spirit. You can also share life experiences from any time in your conscious life with the other. It is an intense experience for certain. But, you needn't worry, Daniel. It only requires the touching of palms."

"All I really needed was that last part. Thank you."

Everyone laughed again as the family rose and left the new couple to their quiet night.

THEIR OFFICIAL ENGAGEMENT was announced to the city from the same balcony that she had been crowned Queen. Their wedding date would be on her eighteenth birthday, exactly one year from her coronation as Queen. This was much sooner than she had ever envisioned, but she knew it was right.

That afternoon they flew with Menkar to a secluded meadow high in the mountains. Menkar left them with a promise to stay near and return an hour after nightfall. The meadow was gorgeous. They were at the cusp of spring and green was starting to peek out from everywhere.

They spread out a large blanket with a picnic basket and ate as they talked about the whirlwind of activity they had been through since she arrived in Chemerie. After an hour of tense chatter, Alec shifted closer and held her eyes.

"Tell me why you considered having our first bonding at

the Lair under such odd conditions? That hardly seems the time or place for something so precious." She did not meet his eyes when he finished his question, so he turned her face to his with a finger under her chin. "I do not need your magic to tell that you are keeping something from me. Remember your words to me, if you love me, you must trust me."

"I do trust you. I am just afraid of the answer I was seeking. I'm not sure I want it anymore."

"Ask me any question and I will give you the answer if I have it."

"Do you know who your birth parents were?"

"No, I do not. They were killed in a ground battle with Lord Harrick's army. Many were killed, and I was so young they had no way of telling who had been my parents. Kisik took me home, named me, and his family has been mine ever since."

She nodded and turned to look across the meadow with a furrowed brow. He stroked her long hair and kissed her hand.

"Morgan, please trust me enough to say what is troubling you."

"Your ability to sense the emotions of dragons is a result of the magic within you. You carry a significant amount of our magic, my dear. It is more than any but a Caretaker has carried for many generations."

"But, how can that be?"

"That is the question, isn't it? My worry was that your blood relation to me is too close for us to responsibly have children together."

He lay back on the blanket and stared into the sky as he considered her words.

"You are hoping to find out who my parents are through the bonding, so you can then decide if we can marry. Why did we announce our engagement before we answered this question?"

"I did not plan the sequence of events, Alec."

"I am sorry if I sounded accusatory. This is just quite a shocking bit of news."

She could not help but chuckle at that understatement as she rubbed her face and focused to relax herself.

"Yes, I know. It has troubled me from the moment you told me about your ability. But the ambush and loss of Balia reminded me that I should trust the magic. She said it has never failed to make a proper match. So, I choose to trust, and am not sure I want the answer anymore," she said as she lay beside him and stroked his dark hair.

He lifted up on his elbow to look down at her. She was feeling a jumble of mixed emotions from him, and his eyes were just as unrevealing of his thoughts.

"I am tempted to agree because I want nothing more than to be your husband. But the truth is, we will not rest with our marriage if we do not solve this riddle. I suggest we do our best to find the answer and deal with it together." He lifted her hand and placed his palm to hers.

"Are you sure?" she said.

"Very."

"Alright then, but I need to explain something," she said as she sat up and faced him. He sat up and scooted up in front of her. "When we have touched thus far, the sensations have been strong and I have had to focus to maintain control." He smiled and she fought the urge. "Those were simple connections with light physical contact. Bonding is far more intense, and you need to know that it could hurt if I cannot control the pace of it."

"I understand and forgive you for any pain I feel," he said as he offered his hands to her. She looked at them, but did not take them.

"I'm serious, Alec. I'm worried that this will be more than I can handle."

"Can this actually kill you like the healings if you go too far?"

"In the healings, I am passing part of my life energy to the other and directing the magic. In bonding, both are sharing their energy. I believe it could only kill if one was very strong with magic and chose to take life from the other by force."

"Queen May says your abilities are the strongest she has ever seen. She has bonded to others safely, so surely you can as well."

"Your magic is my concern. It makes our connections much stronger than any GranMay or our Mothers before her have felt. While I have bonded with GranMay, my mother, and many dragons, the magical link we share will make this far more profound. GranMay suggested we practice deep connection from a distance and try to build a tolerance of sorts. Shall we try that first?"

"While that sounds very enjoyable, will it not deplete the energy you could be using to control the bonding?" She nodded. "Then I think we should go straight to the bonding. You can use your energy to move slowly into it. I have watched your skill develop in times of necessity and I am confident you will handle this as well. I trust your skill, my dear."

"Thank you." She held her face serious as she started to undo the buttons of her coat.

"What are you doing?" he said as he fought the urge to follow the progress of her hands.

She gave a wicked grin as she continued to unbutton her coat.

"GranMay lied to Daniel so he would not interfere."

She let him stare at her as she removed her coat and began undoing the buttons of her shirt before bursting out in laughter.

"Oh, my word. Your face is priceless. So much stress," she said as she calmed her laughter. "Relax dear, I'm going to be wearing a sleeveless shirt much like your undershirt. Take off only your top shirt, please."

"That was a little wicked," he mumbled as he removed his coat and shirt.

"The more our skin contacts, the more easily I can enter and, hopefully, maintain bonding. I will have my guard up at first, then begin dropping it. If you feel pain, please let me know."

He nodded, so she scooted closer and laid her palms to his cheeks, which made them both shiver and take deep breaths.

"Now, lay your arms along mine and your hands to my shoulders or neck."

He let his hands touch her wrists, then moved them up her arms at a slow pace without taking his eyes from hers. She shivered and swallowed hard as her entire body responded quickly. As his hands rested against her neck, he caressed her cheeks with his thumbs and smiled.

"You are glowing, my dear," he said. She raised an eyebrow. "Your eyes are glowing as they do when you connect with the dragons. You are a beautiful woman, and those eyes are an amazing addition."

She pulled his head toward her and dropped her chin to let their foreheads rest against one another. She smiled as she felt his disappointment. He had been hoping for a kiss.

At that point, she took a moment to deal with the rush of sensations now flowing through them. Once the sensations settled into a deep comforting tingle, she dropped her guard enough to connect. Both took a sharp breath and gripped a bit harder for a few seconds as the sensations amped up. Another moment was required to get that under control.

"I am going to start by deepening our connection. Once I feel I have that under control, I will begin to concentrate on your spirit to initiate bonding. You need to focus your mind on the essence of who I am, and I will join you when I am ready. Start searching deeper for my spirit when you hear me seeking yours. Alright?"

He did not answer for many seconds, then he lifted his head to meet her eyes.

"I love you, Morgan."

The emotional rush that accompanied his words made her eyes burn as she shifted to kiss his lips.

"And I love you, Alec."

They shifted to lay their foreheads together again as she began to drop her guard. Both were breathing hard, quivering, and breaking a light perspiration within seconds. As her guard dropped completely, the tingling reached a painful level, and their body temperatures were climbing fast.

Focusing only on his spirit, she pushed once more and gasped as the unique weightless sensation of deep bonding took her. The painful physical sensations vanished as bonding took hold and both relaxed against the other.

"Show me his spirit, show me his heart."

She reached out to his spirit and could feel the wonderful purity and power of it. It was strong, loving, honest, and beautiful. It gave her an intense feeling of safety and comfort as she let it wash over her. The feeling of oneness and completeness that filled her was amazing.

She had not felt the sensation of Alec touching her spirit, but could hear his voice as faint overlapping echoes. The effort of holding the bonding was making her weak, so she focused on their purpose.

"Show me his parents, show me his lineage."

A swirling wash of images and whispering voices filled her mind. The transfer was too fast to process, so she focused to offer no resistance.

When the dizzying transfer stopped, she let herself relax in the blissful state and reached out to touch his spirit again. She felt a resistance this time and was too weak to fight it.

When they dropped out of full bonding, the weightless sensation disappeared, and she was hit by intense trembling, tingling, and heat. She let him go as the pain hit and crumpled to the blanket. All she could do was hold her arms tight to her body until the pain eased and the shaking subsided.

When she opened her eyes, she found him unconscious. She leaned over him to lay her palms on his cheeks and focused to push healing energy.

A few seconds later, she was flying backward as he lurched upright. He stared with unfocused eyes into the night, breathing hard.

"Are you alright?" she asked as she moved to kneel beside him. He did not answer her. She put her hand to his cheek, then flinched as he grabbed her wrist and locked his eyes on hers. Intense anger and fear passed through the touch until he let go and stood up. He moved to put on his shirt, coat, and sword rigging without a word.

"Alec, please talk to me."

He glanced at her for only a second. When their eyes met she flinched from a strong sensation of sorrowful loss mingled with profound self-loathing.

"I will not be returning to Chemerie with you tonight, my Lady. You should take Menkar back before it gets too cold. I would like to be alone for a while. I have some things to think about," he said as he adjusted his rigging.

She shot to her feet and planted herself in front of him as her face flushed.

"I would like to know why you are lying to me and trying to send me away. Neither is acceptable no matter your reason, but I would like to hear it at least!"

He rubbed his face as he walked a few paces away where he stopped facing away from her.

"I now know exactly who I am. And now I understand that I cannot marry you. Our blood can never mix. We can not have children."

"How close is our blood relation? How many generations are there between us?" He did not answer as he paced the meadow in front of her.

"*Alec, ple—*"

"Please do not use your magic to connect to me anymore."

She gritted her teeth, fighting to respect his wishes.

He walked to the picnic basket and began stuffing his pockets with food items.

"Enough!" she shouted as she moved to grab his wrists. "Just stop and tell me what you learned that is so bad you are willing to leave me."

Again he failed to hold her eyes and pulled his hands out of her grip with a step back. He looked across the meadow for a moment then forced a deep breath before meeting her eyes.

"I am not a Son of Chemerie at all. I am a Son of Arshek. I am the blood son of Lord Harrick himself."

That statement quenched her temper for the moment and made her breath catch in her throat. She focused on his words, and the images she received that pertained to them came forward. She saw images of Harrick and a frail woman holding a baby. The next image was the woman kneeling by the baby in the woods, crying. The next was of a younger Kisik picking up the baby.

While she stood frozen with shock, he turned and started walking across the meadow. When she called out to him, he did not stop.

"So, your way of handling this is to run away from it? You are going to abandon me, your entire family, and all of your brethren who love and trust you?" she shouted across the meadow. He did not respond. "You coward!"

That made him turn on her, just as she had hoped. She marched toward him as she continued.

"I must be a complete fool. I actually believed you when you told me you would die before severing your partnership with me. I mean, here we are, with the first real test of your word, and you are running away like a scared rabbit."

His face was fire red as he stood stiff with clinched fists. But a few seconds later, his shoulders dropped, and he turned to leave again.

"If you truly care for me, you will fight for me! And if you will not, then I will! I will not let you leave without a fight. If you do manage to get away, I will follow."

She had felt Menkar flying overhead and the concerned dragon was now landing beside them.

"Menkar, I know you love him, my friend. But right now, I need you to help me save him. Please, do not let him leave this meadow."

Menkar nodded and moved to block Alec's path. Alec tried to get around him three times, then stopped and turned to face her.

"I am not going back to Chemerie. I am not going to marry you. I am leaving this meadow alone. Do not make me fight Menkar to do that."

Menkar snorted and pushed him toward her with his snout, making him stumble to the ground.

She felt the determination in Alec to leave and was sure she knew his intentions as well. She chose to risk angering him beyond forgiveness in an effort to save him from his own rage.

"Will you take him back by force if I ask it of you, Menkar?"

"It will hurt me greatly, but I trust you, my Queen. I will do what is best for him."

She spoke in a cold, authoritative voice aloud and in English, so both would hear and understand.

"Sir Alec, as a Knight of Chemerie you took an oath to serve its Queen and Caretaker until death. I am ordering you to accompany me back to the Castle of Chemerie. Menkar, if Sir Alec leaves this meadow against the direct order of his Queen, it will be considered an act of desertion against the Guard. Sir Alec, will you keep to your oath or be taken back to the castle by force?"

Alec stared at her in disbelief before his face flushed again.

"You would take me back under a false charge by force?" he yelled as he stepped closer to her. "You would ask that of Menkar, knowing he is my friend?"

She matched his tone and stepped right up to his face to reply.

"You would break your engagement to your Queen and Caretaker, knowing full well the magic will never provide another partner? You would do this without a fight, knowing that if you do so the Caretaker line will die with me?" She had to pause to check the waver in her voice. "Tell me, Alec, which of us commits the greater evil here?"

They stood toe-to-toe, staring and panting in anger, until Menkar startled them with a loud growl right beside their heads.

"Shall we go now? All of us?" the dragon said gruffly as he nudged Alec in the back, pushing him into her.

Alec understood Menkar without actually knowing his words. He stepped back from Morgan and turned to glare at him.

"No! I am not going back with you," Alec yelled at Menkar as he started backing up. The dragon growled low in his throat and dropped his head to Alec's height as he flanked him.

"You are to be detained to face the charge of desertion,

and are not being given a choice," Morgan said. "Your only choice is your accommodations during flight."

Menkar continued to flank Alec as he tried to get past him. Alec eyed him, judging his chances of making it to the dense woods.

"Little wounds I can heal, but do not hurt him badly, my friend. Take him with care," she said to Menkar.

Alec made a few quick moves that the dragon easily blocked, then sighed and looked at her as his shoulders slumped.

"Taking me by force gains you nothing. My reasoning is not going to change. I can never return to Chemerie. I do not belong there."

"I will not allow you to be killed or captured by Lord Harrick. Either is an unacceptable option to me."

"I was going of my own free will. I thought perhaps I should meet my father," he said in a flat voice.

"You hope to use your blood connection to get you in the door, with full intention of striking Harrick down at the first opportunity. The only flaw with your well thought out plan is the level of danger you face. I feel the self-loathing inside you, and I know how far you will let it push you!" She paced beside Menkar as she focused to bring her breathing and heart rate down to near normal before facing him again. With a heavy sigh, she moved to stand just in front of him, and held his angry stare with one of controlled authority.

"I do not think you will hear anything I have to say in your current state of mind. I insist we return to the castle and discuss this in the morning."

He eyed her and Menkar, then dropped his eyes to the

ground as he shuffled his feet. Menkar offered his palm to them, and she habitually got on first. With her perched on his front foot, Menkar could not catch Alec when he bolted for the woods.

Alec was out of sight in three seconds, which brought a string of curses from Morgan as she leapt to the ground and started to chase him. Menkar moved to stop her.

"My Queen, these woods are a very dangerous area at night. Please, let us track him from the air."

"There is no need for tracking, my friend. We know exactly where he is headed. Let me try to speak with him from the air once more. Then, I will ask that you take me home. You and the Senior Guard can return and apprehend him."

They found Alec running through the woods and soared over his head in wide circles. She connected to him, despite his wishes.

"Alec, the answer to your worry about contaminating the Care-taker line has already been answered by the magic. It would never have partnered you to me if there were any danger in the crossing. You must trust the magic, my dear. I trust it. I know you are my only magical partner. Losing you means losing everything to me. Don't you see? Without you, the Caretaker line dies. For that reason alone, I will fight to keep you. But I will fight till I die to keep you, because I love you. And I know you love me, despite your best effort this evening to make me think otherwise. You are a pure spirit of Chemerie and you belong with your Chemerian brethren."

"How can you ignore this, Morgan? I am the blood son of the most evil warlord to be seen in a hundred years. No amount of love for you will change that," he said as he continued to run hard and fast through the dense woods. *"We do not know his magic*

enough to know how it may manifest itself within me. You cannot look within me and be sure there is no darkness hidden there, can you? Can you tell me that I would never pass the darkness to my children? Admit that you do not know. Your ability is great, but you do not have the power to answer those questions. I will not chance it. I love you and Chemerie too much."

"You are letting fear blind you … and breaking my heart."

Her entire body ached as she asked Menkar to turn for home.

"Daniel, please gather our family. I have news I need to share with everyone at once."

"We've all been worried about you. Are you OK?"

"Not in the least. I'll explain when I get there."

ALEC STOPPED as Morgan finally flew off to the west. He sat with his head in his hands, alone in the middle of the woods, and wept until rage pushed him to the east again.

An hour later, he reached the top of the last mountain ridge and took a moment to consider his possibilities for approaching the castle. For a man on foot, and in a hurry, there were not many choices. He knew the areas around the river and lake were the easiest traveled by foot and provided a rather direct route.

With dawn breaking soon, he continued his quest as fast as he could run. Morgan's words filled his mind as he ran. He wanted to believe that his blood did not matter, but his heart could not be convinced. He ached as he thought of her harsh words, especially when she called him a coward and said he was breaking her heart.

He loved that woman more than anything. Living a long

life without her was not an option he cared for. Again, he came back to the conclusion that made his chest burn: he was now expendable.

MORGAN WAS in her sitting room surrounded by her family. She stood and moved where she could see everyone's face.

"Before I explain what has happened, I want everyone to know that my conviction to marry Alec stands, and I will not listen to any argument to the contrary."

She found no challenge in any of them but felt their anxiety grow. Having nothing to offer to calm them, she took a second to calm herself enough to continue.

"My choice to bond with Alec so soon was based on a need to know his lineage. I discovered some weeks ago that he contains a considerable amount of magic of his own." She stopped to let the grumblings of dismay die away, then continued, "When we bonded today, he was faced with the identity of his birth parents, in particular, his blood father."

She could not help but glance at Kisik and had to pause a few seconds when she anticipated the worry her next words would cause him.

"Alec is the blood son of Lord Harrick."

Again, she paused to give them a chance to accept the reality of her words.

"My only goal in seeking his parentage was to determine if we were too closely related to have children. That is now answered. There are over twelve generations of marriage separating us, making the relation inconsequential. In my eyes, there is no longer any reason for me to question my marriage to him. I trust the magic and therefore have faith in the pairing it has set for us.

"He, however, sees the situation quite differently, choosing to leave rather than risk contaminating the Caretaker line with that of Arshek. He sees himself expendable and is heading to confront and kill Harrick with no fear of death … because he welcomes it."

Emma let out a small gasp and sat down beside Kisik. Her pain and fear made Morgan pause as her throat tightened. She steeled herself as she met Kisik's eyes and held them for many seconds. The calm confidence she found within them was the empowerment she needed at that moment.

"I threatened him with his oath of Knighthood. I said his flight from me would be an act of desertion, yet he still fled. You all know his heart and know he would never have done that if he did not mean to never return. Therefore, I now ask that my Senior Guard uphold my threat and apprehend him before he reaches Arshek castle. What say you, gentlemen?"

Daniel stood first and was joined by her father, Maric, Josef, and Burke, who all laid an arm across their chests and bowed. She looked at the resolve in everyone's face and saw GranMay, Kisik, and Emma give her a nod as well. She looked to Daniel and held his gaze a moment.

"Please be discreet. The time will come that we share this with our brethren, but I would prefer to have him standing confidently at my side." Daniel nodded. "Menkar understands and is willing to take Alec by force. He is waiting for you in the garden. I will ask him to choose a like-minded partner to carry the others."

Morgan stood against the terrace railing and stared into the night. She closed her eyes as GranMay caressed her back, sighing as loving support washed over her. Emma came to support her as well.

"They will bring him home, and then we will speak with him together. When faced with the support of the entire family, not to mention my undeniable charm, he will see reason in the end," GranMay said. "The journey may be long and difficult, but you will have your partner just as the magic has arranged. Keep your faith in the wisdom of the magic."

Morgan nodded and let tears fall. She had been strong through all the confrontation with Alec and explanation to the family, but GranMay's words, echoing the words of Balia, tore down all of her defenses.

"MY FRIENDS, are you ready for this?" Daniel asked as he stood before Menkar and Broon. The great dragons' heads drooped as they nodded. "I know, it feels like a betrayal, but we are doing the right thing."

He had asked Josef to stay with Morgan. The remaining four of the Senior Guard boarded the two dragons and headed to Alec's last known location.

After an hour of searching, they found him floating down the river that leads to the lake outside Arshek castle.

"Menkar, try to take him fast and let's get out of here before we have company," Daniel yelled.

The great dragon nodded and dove toward the water to approach Alec from up-stream. Just before Menkar was close enough to grab him, Alec dove down out of his reach. Neither Menkar nor Broon could spot him before they had to rise to avoid detection by the Arshek guards stationed near the lake.

Just after passing the blockade, Menkar dropped into a steep dive, still stroking his wings to pick up speed.

"Look!" Daniel yelled to his father as he pointed at the lake.

Alec was attempting to swim the width of the lake to reach the castle. With the light of the breaking dawn, Daniel could see the outline of a massive water dragon headed straight for him.

Menkar reached the beast just in time to claw it across the head as it lunged at Alec. The beast let out a piercing shriek and curled under the black water. Daniel thought it had retreated until he saw a massive spade-ended tail rise from the water and crash down on Alec.

In just seconds, the tail wrapped his unconscious body and pulled him under. Menkar let out a great roar and dove.

"Bail!" Daniel yelled as he rushed to untie his and Nikolas' legs.

They jumped free as Menkar cut smoothly through the surface. The men searched for any sign of Alec as their bodies were buffeted by the dragons roaring and rolling beneath them.

More than a minute later, Menkar broke the surface with a great splash. He was holding the limp form of Alec across his head so he could keep him above the water level. As he moved toward Daniel and Nikolas he thrashed in circles and kept dropping back below the surface.

"He is wrapped," Nikolas yelled as he grabbed Alec and started for the shore.

Daniel dove and swam hard to grab the saddle harness on Menkar. He stabbed his dagger at the great tail of the water dragon. It took all his strength to hold on as they thrashed through the water.

After many stabs from Daniel and bites from Menkar, the water dragon gave up and disappeared into the dark water. Daniel held tight to Menkar as he swam to the edge of the lake, then hurried toward the others gathered around Alec.

Nikolas was trying to resuscitate him, but he was still not breathing, and his heart was still. Menkar joined Broon in humming the healing song, and Daniel took over the breathing for his father. After two minutes of effort, Daniel and Nikolas switched duties.

"One, two, three, four, five, breathe. One, two, three, four, five, breathe," he chanted. They worked for over five more minutes while the two dragons hummed their song of healing, to no avail.

"Menkar, Morgan said he has a lot of magic. Can we use it to help, like we did with her?"

Menkar and Broon nodded and shifted to touch their snouts to Alec as they continued humming their song. Daniel and Nikolas each took one of Alec's hands, then formed a circle with Maric and Burke. All closed their eyes and began to focus on their willingness and deep desire to share their life energy with Alec.

After another long minute of waiting, a light shock made them all jump, including Alec.

Horrible gurgling sounds came from him as he continued to jerk and heave. Nikolas rolled him to his side, so the water in his lungs could be coughed out. Alec sputtered and coughed for a moment before he relaxed to breathe in shallow, ragged breaths. He was blue, cold, and unconscious, but he was alive.

THE TWO DRAGONS flew faster than Daniel had yet witnessed. They were still far from the castle when he heard Morgan enter his mind.

"What happened? Were you not successful? I do not feel Alec with you."

"He is with us, but he is unconscious and weak after almost drowning. Menkar fought to rescue him from a huge water dragon. I thought he was gone, but our dragons were able to use his magic to save him."

Daniel finished his explanation and answered her many questions as they flew on. When they landed, she rushed forward to Menkar. She knelt and held Menkar's head with glowing eyes as the men dismounted and laid Alec on the grass.

The men were all quiet as they watched Morgan move to Menkar's belly and encourage him to roll to his side. The men all groaned as they saw the great gash along his underbelly; it was nearly the height of Morgan standing beside it.

Morgan spoke to Daniel as she went to work on the awful wound, *"Will you please take him to my chambers? I will be along after I am sure Menkar no longer needs me."*

Daniel passed the message to the others and stepped aside as Burke moved in to lift Alec. As Burke moved off, Daniel and Nikolas paused to watch Morgan with similar smiles.

"I dare anyone to question her devotion to her duty. Even with her fiancé injured, she focuses on the one who needs her most," Daniel said as Nikolas nodded. As they walked, Nikolas stopped and waited for Daniel to meet his gaze.

"You risked your life for Menkar today, knowing that beast could kill you easily. That action is among the bravest I have ever seen. I know you have questioned your station as an Admiral, having not served as long as others. Question it no more, my boy."

Nikolas hugged him, then moved on toward the castle. Daniel stayed in his place, staring after him as he swallowed back his emotions.

MORGAN AND HER FAMILY were gathered around her bed where Alec lay. She and GranMay sat on each side of him and joined their palms with each other and him to form a healing circle. The healing went fast, given the inclusion of two Caretakers. Alec's breathing became deeper and more regular, and his color returned to normal soon after.

They covered him with warm blankets and moved to the sitting area of the large room. Morgan sat and dropped her head to her hands.

"You should rest, my dear. You will need strength to face him when he wakes to find himself returned here by force," GranMay said.

"I know, but my mind will not calm."

Daniel took her hand and led her to the bed. He scooted Alec to one side and pushed her to lie down on the other side, under her own blanket, of course.

"Now rest, you'll know when he wakes up."

She sighed and rolled to look at Alec's handsome face. Her breathing paced his as she dropped her guard just enough to feel the familiar warmth of their connection. Slowly, she dozed off.

She woke a short while later to a feeling of warmth building in her chest. She opened her eyes to see Alec looking at her with intense eyes.

"I could not let you go. I had to stop you."

That did not have the desired effect. She had hoped her devotion to their relationship would break his icy front. Instead, he bolted from the bed away from her and ran right into the massive chest of Maric who had been standing guard beside him. He caught his balance and shifted to move around Maric.

"You will hold your place, Sir Alec," Daniel barked. Alec turned to face him as he marched forward. "You are not here by choice and do not have the option to leave. You have been brought here before your Queen to answer the charge of desertion from your duty as a Knight of Chemerie."

"I give no argument to the charge, Admiral. I accept whatever punishment the Queen sees appropriate."

The room was dead silent. Morgan stepped forward and replaced Daniel in front of him.

"You know very well that any formal action would become public knowledge. Do you want this shame to be known by the entire castle and for that shame to be reflected onto Kisik and your siblings?"

Alec glanced at Kisik and Emma standing behind her, then met her eyes again.

"No. I would have preferred they had never known themselves," he said. "You would not let me spare them. So what would you have me do, Queen Morgan?"

"I offer to stay the charge as long as you do not flee. It requires that you remain in this room without need for restraint, that you listen without argument, and open your mind to consider the words spoken to you. It is that or official charges and imprisonment. Which option do you choose?"

"I choose the option which brings the least dishonor to those who showed me kindness. I will not flee." His tone was cold and emotionless, as were his eyes.

She nodded, then moved to the sitting area where she took a seat. Alec and everyone else joined her, and the silence grew heavy.

One-by-one each member of the family reasoned with him. They spoke of the wisdom of the magic, of loyalty to country, of his responsibility to his engagement, and of his lack of any real connection to Lord Harrick based on the life he has lived.

He looked each in the eye as they spoke, even Emma, who had been crying. When everyone except Morgan had spoken, he still sat silent, his face blank.

She could feel only anger toward her and bitter self-loathing within him. He met and held her eyes as she stood and moved to stand in front of him.

"If, when I am finished, you feel nothing for me or your commitment to me, I will release you from it. However, I will not let you leave my company without showing you the one thing that confirms your kinship to Chemerie more than anything any of us could possibly say." She knelt and raised her hands toward his face.

"No!" he yelled as he pushed his chair back to dodge her.

She gave stern looks to her two uncles who flanked his

chair, then looked into his face again.

"I am not asking."

Maric and Josef held him in the chair by force as she placed her hands on his cheeks and pushed to connect. He fought her with all his might and, given his bit of magic, that was a considerable barrier.

Once she gained access to his mind, she showed him all she had learned from Menkar. She passed the full brunt of Menkar's devotion to him and his willingness to die to defend him. She let him feel every bit of the pain and rage the dragon felt as the great beast ripped at him.

"Morgan, Stop!" he roared through gritted teeth as he fought to get free. She swallowed hard and pushed on. Alec groaned as he was hit with the profound anguish Menkar felt when he thought he had failed to save him.

As a final jolt to convince him, she deepened their connection into full bonding, and shared the magical connection the dragon felt during the healing on the lake shore. She made sure that every ounce of the intensity was transferred before dropping the bonding, and letting herself fall back against GranMay, who knelt behind her.

SHE FELT THE EMOTIONS begin to shift within him and asked to be left alone with him as only sorrow and gratitude filled his heart. He lay in a trembling heap on the floor with his face buried in his hands. The words she started to speak froze in her throat as she felt a gentle push against her guard.

"Please call Menkar. I would like to speak to him," Alec said.

She stared at him for a few seconds, then looked away as she did as he asked.

"Your dear friend would like to speak to you. I have shared your experiences from today with him. Please come to him, Menkar."

Menkar landed in the garden beside Morgan's terrace a moment later, accompanied by Sirzi.

She watched as Alec stood and went to his friend. He leaned heavily into his neck, resting his head against his hide and wrapping his arm around his snout. He spoke in a quiet voice as he stroked him.

Morgan did not interrupt or attempt to listen in. She forced a much deeper breath as Menkar crooned and wrapped his neck around Alec. Menkar held Alec close to him for a moment, then nudged him toward her with a low hum in his throat. Alec reached toward Sirzi only to be nudged along by her as well.

Once inside, he picked up the chair he had knocked over and sat down across from her.

"Do you now see the truth in where you belong?"

"Yes. I understand what you meant to show me. Menkar's actions were moving, but it was the magic that changed my heart. The magic he and I carry is the same; I felt the oneness of it. It is that of Chemerie," he said as he looked into her eyes. He then looked back down at his hands.

"I want you to know that I meant what I said about releasing you from your commitment to me. If you have accepted that your rightful place is here with your Chemerian brethren, but are still concerned about marrying me, then I will not hold you to it. I would rather you be here where you belong than flee to escape your tie to me."

Alec looked into her eyes as his filled with tears. He moved to kneel in front of her chair, where he crossed one arm over his chest and bowed his head.

"My Queen, I was convinced that I was a threat to our country. A trap set by Lord Harrick to destroy the purity of our magic. You were determined to bring me home, and I was willing to die to prevent it. You saved me. You forced me to listen to what I refused to hear. Thank you for showing me my true place is here. I am so sorry for not trusting the magic, for not trusting your word. Please forgive me, my Queen."

She leaned forward, held out a hand, then waited silently until he took it in his. To control her emotions she had her guard raised high, but still felt the warmth and tingle in her hand.

"Of course I forgive you. I felt your pain and understood your reasoning," she said.

He stared at her hand in his as he let his official pose relax. His thumbs moved gently over her skin a moment before he leaned down to kiss it.

Her heart was aching as it pounded in her chest. He had spoken of his loyalty to country and asked forgiveness from his Queen. He had said nothing about their personal relationship. She held her breath as he looked up again.

"Morgan, I love you more than my own life. I would die with pride to protect you from harm. It is that conviction which drove me away tonight." He paused and swallowed hard before he continued, "But now, I know my magic is that of Chemerie, and I choose to trust it, as you do. It has partnered me to you, and I am very grateful. If you can forgive me, and will still have me as your husband, I wa—"

She flew into his arms and shared a crushing embrace for a long time while tears fell and magic flowed unchecked.

"I am so sorry for hurting you, my love. I am ashamed that I did not have the same conviction about our partnership that you have. My fear blinded me, as you said. Please forgive me, Morgan. Forgive me for doubting us."

She leaned back to look into his eyes as she caressed his face in her hands.

"You have not felt it as I have, or you would never have doubted it. When we bonded yesterday, did you seek my spirit or only your lineage?"

"I focused on the answer we sought. I thought of my lineage."

She slid her hands over his neck as she closed her eyes and tilted her head forward. He laid his forehead to hers and tightened his grip around her. They entered into full bonding in seconds.

She opened herself to him with no resistance or hesitance. The feeling of weightlessness the bonding brought was blissful. She drifted within his beautiful spirit as he sought hers, then gasped as his spirit touched hers at last.

The loving sensation of his spirit touching hers was punctuated by an intense jolt of energy that moved through both of them. As the sharpness of it faded, a lingering energy remained, and wove itself with the loving feelings that bound them. It was the most wonderful sensation that sent intense tingling throughout her body. She knew what it was before her ancient knowledge defined it. It was the link the Book of the Caretaker had spoken of, the magical link of spirits shared between mates. She mused over how she had dreaded those words when she first read them. If only she had understood the amazing truth behind them.

She held the bonding for as long as she could without losing consciousness, then released it with care. They were both flush and trembling as they opened their eyes and shifted only enough to focus on the other.

"I will never question our link again. I felt it as soon as I sought your spirit. I feel it even now."

"Me too. It is like a hint of the weightlessness stirring within my heart," she said.

"For me it is a heat deep within me that builds as I look at you and touch you," he said in his deep melodic voice. He pulled her slowly to him and again stopped just before touching her lips. She kissed him with a passion that caused the sensations of tingling and warmth to rise very fast again.

"Our magic is amazing," he said as he released the kiss and smiled.

"Yes, it is, my love," she said with a smirk. Alec lifted an eyebrow and she laughed.

"It seems the deep bonding to Menkar and Broon, coupled with your final acceptance of its existence, has allowed your magic to develop further. You initiated this connection, my love, not I."

He stared at her for a few seconds as he blushed, then pulled her to him again.

"My Queen, My Caretaker, My Morgan. I love you. My heart and spirit are yours forever."

THEY CUDDLED TOGETHER on the terrace and talked through their feelings. Each made sure the other understood what their thoughts and concerns had been and that they were now in complete agreement.

"I do not claim to understand how a son of the Arshek line could be meant for the Caretaker of Chemerie, but I am very thankful it has happened," he said as he traced and teased the dragons on her hands.

"It is proof that a man is defined not by who his parents are, but who he grows to be. You may have his blood, but you do not have his dark spirit, my love. Your spirit is pure and beautiful because of the life you have lived and the choices you have made."

They were quiet for a long time in each other's arms before she felt him growing anxious and nudged him to talk.

"I do have questions now. I wonder why I was left here. Was it by order of Harrick. Did he expect me to grow up loyal to him, and one day provide information about our country? Or, perhaps my mother was acting alone. I wonder who she was, if her spirit was black as well. Does Harrick even know I am alive? If so, does he know who I am and of my relationship to you?"

She stroked his hair and wondered to herself if he would rest without those answers.

MORGAN TOOK A LONG WALK alone in the gardens to clear her head a bit the next night. Things had been moving so fast for the last few days it was exhausting.

She walked for a long time then settled on the terrace to look up at the brilliant night sky and let her mind relax.

"May I join you, my dear?" GranMay said.

"Yes, please do," she said with a smile at the loving warmth she felt from her dear Grandmother. GranMay brought a

blanket for them and snuggled in.

"You handled everything this week with such strength. You have grown so much since receiving the knowledge of the Dragons and you have used it well, my dear."

"Having their knowledge within me is both wonderful and bizarre. It is amazing to be able to ask a question of myself and receive information from within my own mind that I was not conscious of having. And just as amazing is the fact that the information I am calling forward was once the thought or experience of a dragon. It's all just so amazing, GranMay. I still wonder if I am dreaming sometimes."

They snuggled together for a while longer then GranMay shifted to look at her.

"There is a great deal more information available to you that you have not embraced, my dear. You have forgotten the Book of the Caretaker."

"I read it all before I came here. It was quite vague and left out some pretty big points. What are you referring to?"

"Remember singing with your mother? Was that written on a page?"

Morgan thought about the feeling she experienced as she heard her mother's voice for the first time through the magic of the Book.

"You have had a great deal happening since you came here and have been a brilliant Queen and Caretaker. Your relationship with the dragons has served you well, but I worry that your only perspective of the magic, our country, and your role has been that of our dragon brethren. Please, take time to bond with the Book of the Caretaker, my girl. It still has much to teach you from the human perspective of your Mothers. And when you are ready, you

should add your contributions to it as well."

"Thank you. I am thankful to know that I can learn more of my Mothers' perspective, beyond what I received during my Quickening ceremony. Perhaps that will help me feel more confident."

GranMay chuckled and shook her head as she snuggled back in.

"No one who has seen what you have accomplished since coming here could ever believe you feel unsure of yourself. I am very proud of you, Morgan. You truly have surpassed your Mothers in many ways."

MORGAN SETTLED IN on the window seat of her chambers with the Book of the Caretaker. She laid her hands on the Book and thought of her mother. Her head filled with beautiful singing as glimpses of her mother's life started to move through her mind.

She saw her as an infant in GranMay's arms and as a young girl walking with her grandmother, Maric and Josef. She saw her as a woman of around twenty-six as she and her brothers stood on the portal between Earth and Erion. Next, a great happiness and joy filled her as she watched her parents marry in the castle garden.

As she focused on her own connection to her mother, she saw her mother, father, and a toddler Daniel huddled together on a bed while she slept in her mother's arms.

She flinched as the joy of that moment turned to intense heartache. Tears fell down her face as she watched Father, Daniel and herself disappear through the portal to return to Earth.

Her mother had stood strong and smiled until they had

disappeared. The instant she could no longer feel their spirits, she collapsed into the arms of Josef and Maric with racking sobs. Her brothers tried to comfort her, and many dragons began to sing a supportive song, but still her mother lay on the ground, tortured by the loss of her family.

Morgan removed her hands from the Book and rubbed them to ease the stinging. She sat crying as she thought of the inevitable day she would suffer the same loss. It was the one thing that had scared her most of everything she was expected to do. Yet, somehow, sharing her mother's experience made her feel more prepared to face that day.

She calmed herself and laid her hands back on the Book as she thought of her mother's life after their departure. She viewed a series of images, including quiet times caring for the dragons and intense battle scenes where the forces of Arshek had attempted to overtake Chemerie.

She stepped through her mother's life in Chemerie until two years before, where the record just stopped. She assumed she had become too ill to keep it up to date. As she put the Book away, she promised herself to make bonding with it a regular activity.

Fathers

MORGAN AND ALEC returned to the secluded meadow high in the mountains for some private time. Menkar stayed this time, napping in the warm sunshine.

Less than an hour after they arrived, Menkar jumped to his feet and roared while rushing toward them.

"Come to me!" he called.

Morgan's breath caught in her throat as she felt what he had. She had barely reached out for Alec when a group of massive Arshek dragons crashed into the meadow.

Menkar roared and charged. Two of the enemy dragons moved together to block, bite, and tackle him as the rest surrounded her and Alec. She started toward Menkar before being seized by Alec. He held her close against his back with one hand and brandished his sword in the other as he turned them in slow circles.

Menkar fought against the Arshek dragons holding him and received a number of small bites and talon cuts.

"Hold, my friend. Do not let yourself get hurt, please. You cannot defeat this many and we will need you to make our escape if the opportunity arises," she said.

She no sooner got those words out before all hope for escape left her. The space between the dragons was filled in by a full battalion of the Arshek Militia. The group included men and Marock soldiers wearing full battle gear.

Alec's grip on her tightened as a section of them shifted to open a path while the rest snapped to attention. A painful, cold blast made her raise her guard as high as possible.

"He is here," she said as she gripped Alec's arm.

A great shiver ran over her as Lord Harrick entered the circle of dragons. He was a tall, broad-shouldered man with long black hair and harsh bone structure. A sinister smirk filled his face as he walked forward.

"What should we do?" she said to Alec alone.

"Wait. Do not act. By all means, do not let them know who you are. Lie if necessary," Alec said without taking his eyes from Harrick's dark face.

Harrick circled them while Alec turned to keep himself between him and Morgan. Harrick stopped then stepped closer while looking only at Alec.

"You can drop your sword. I will not have you killed just now. You will come to Arshek Castle as … my guests," Harrick said in a deep and raspy voice. Both the Marocks and humans of the Arshek Militia laughed.

"I am afraid we will have to decline your invitation, Sir. But thank you all the same," Alec said, matching his sarcasm.

Harrick laughed a huge bark of a laugh as he continued to hold Alec's gaze. He took another step closer to them wearing the most evil smirk Morgan had ever seen.

"You are bold. Of course, I expected no less of my own son." When Alec gave no reaction, Harrick's smirk shifted to something even more sinister. "You will come home with me! It is time you take your rightful place by my side!"

"I would rather die."

"Is that so?" Harrick said. The evil smirk returned as four huge Marocks closed in to place their spear tips near their bodies. "How about your lovely companion? Is she willing to die for your convictions?"

Before Morgan could get a response out, Alec squeezed her hand.

"Say nothing," he said to her without looking away from Harrick. *"Keep your mind closed and trust my decisions, please."*

"Let her leave with our dragon, unharmed, and you will have me. I will give up my weapon and accompany you without resistance," he said to Harrick. She squeezed his arm in protest but did not say a word.

"Very noble of you, my son," Harrick said as he backed many feet away. "Agreed." With a quick wave of his hand, the soldiers and dragons opened a path for Menkar.

Menkar dashed forward and reached to scoop them into his palm. Alec moved aside and pushed her to him. Menkar growled as he nudged Alec toward his palm.

"I must stay for her to go. Take her home, my friend," Alec said with a stroke along Menkar's snout. Morgan grabbed Alec's hand and passed her feelings with force as she stepped to him.

"I cannot leave you. I ca—"

"You can, and you must," he said as he picked her up and pushed her into Menkar's palm. *"I love you."*

Menkar closed his fist around her and bolted into the air as Alec added those last words. She watched as the sword was taken from him by two Arshek soldiers who then forced him to his knees before a laughing Lord Harrick.

"I DO NOT THINK he intends war; he took Alec alive and released me," Morgan said, eyeing the battle gear when she arrived in the Admiralty chambers.

They fired many questions at her, most of which she could not answer.

"The biggest question is how they knew you were going to be there?" Daniel said.

"We only planned the outing yesterday afternoon," she said as she rubbed her aching head.

"If you were in the meadow for less than an hour before they attacked, then magical connection is not what brought them. They were lying in wait, my Queen. Who knew you were going up there today?" Maric asked.

"I can't say. We were strolling through the garden while discussing it. There were many people who could have over-heard us talking."

"All of our Queen's movements must be kept very private until we identify the spies," Daniel said.

All agreed with him, and they spent a few minutes discussing who it could possibly be, with no real progress.

"Can we please turn our attention to saving my fiancé?" she barked.

"My Queen, we could send our best men to attempt a covert rescue, but I fear that is exactly what Lord Harrick expects," Josef said.

"What is your plan, Admirals?" she asked. Receiving no reply, she nodded and headed for the door. "Then I will leave you to your planning." Daniel moved to catch her arm before she left.

"We want him back too. Give us time, please. Promise me you are not about to go to the dragons to plan a lone rescue attempt," he said in a quiet voice.

She diverted her eyes and calmed herself as she noticed the rest of the Admiralty watching them.

"Fine, I will give you some time. But, I will not wait long, Daniel. Harrick could do much worse than kill him. He means to convince him to stand at his side, as his son. The type of convincing he would use is the issue. We know Harrick has weak Chemerian magic, but we have not experienced the extent of his darker magic. Think of the torture he could be enduring. Make this point clear to everyone in the room as you make your plans."

Daniel nodded and attempted a reassuring smile before she left.

SHE WENT STRAIGHT to her room and bonded with the Book of the Caretaker. She had to focus to relax before she could reach deep bonding. Once there, she thought of how it felt to experience the darkness firsthand.

She began to shiver as her blood ran cold, and a heavy blanket of sorrowful doubt, abandonment, worthlessness, and fear poured over her. She heard faint cries of anguish echoing in her head, as all happiness faded from her heart. It took all her focus to pull her mind back and remove her trembling hands from the Book.

"Father, I need you to lead our young men in this. I have consulted the Book of the Caretaker and felt the effect of the darkness. Even as a memory, it is nearly overwhelming, even for me. Please, urge our men to act soon. I know Alec's heart is true, but the effects of the darkness may be more than he can bear if Harrick means to have his spirit."

"I will take care of it, my dear. I promise you, I will do all in my power to see that you have him back," her father said. She felt the confidence within him as he spoke and was encouraged, for the moment.

DANIEL CONVEYED Morgan's concerns to the Admiralty of the Guard, and they all sat in silence for many minutes. He then asked each man to give his major concerns and ideas.

"If he thinks Alec to be a simple Knight, he will not expect a large-scale attack," Maric said.

"If the informant was so close to hear their conversations, then he knows very well Alec's importance," Josef countered.

"That is the part that baffles me. Why would Harrick have released her if he knew he had the Queen of Chemerie?" Daniel asked.

This brought silence again. Nikolas had been gazing out the window during much of their discussion, but with that question, he turned to meet Daniel's gaze.

"Father, what are your thoughts?"

The deep respect for Nikolas was palpable as he moved to stand beside Daniel.

"Harrick does not mean for the line of Caretakers to stop, he means to control it himself. He intends to turn Alec to his service, then release him back into our castle to marry and produce children. When the gift is passed to an infant daughter, Harrick will have Alec kill Morgan and us. Then they will have control over it all."

"What? What makes you think that is his plan?"

"History, Son. Many attempts have been made to kidnap the infant Caretaker before she leaves for Earth. Thankfully all have failed. The idea is that if they have the Caretaker line under their control, they have the people and dragons of Chemerie at their disposal. I believe Harrick sees having his son within the inner circle will assure him success of having the child, but only if he controls him." Nikolas paused as he let his eyes pass over each Knight around him. "The question is: Can Harrick turn Alec against Chemerie?"

"No!" filled the room at once. Nikolas smiled and gave a slow nod.

"I agree, of course. I do not think he could be broken by any normal means. He would never betray us by choice. However, what I do question is the power of the Arshek magic within Harrick. Morgan has felt its strength via her fore-mothers' experiences and is rightfully worried about the extent to which Harrick will go to have Alec's allegiance," Nikolas said. Many of the Admiralty dropped their eyes or glanced between one another as deep frowns filled their faces.

"Surely Morgan would be able to tell if he had been affected by the darkness through bonding with him," Daniel said.

"Certainly, but then it could be too late for her. If she bonds with someone with the dark magic within them, it could do great harm to her or even kill her. If that person is skilled enough with it, they could take her life by force. I have seen my daughter's skill with our magic and honestly believe she would feel the dark magic well before it posed a threat to her. Nevertheless, our Queen is right, my friends. We cannot let Alec stay in the presence of Harrick any longer." He took a small step back from the table and scanned the room a few seconds. "I am going to the Arshek Castle tonight. Who would like to accompany me?"

All rose at once.

As the Admiralty filed out, Nikolas caught Daniel's arm and held him back. When they were alone, he closed the door.

"I am sorry if I offended you by taking charge on this, Son. I want you to know that I do not question your ability to lead in any way."

Daniel smiled and shook his head.

"Father, you are a King of Chemerie. Yet, you've allowed me to lead the Guard, and the Admiralty, without interference. You offer advice only in private, and with respect even then. I love you, and I'm grateful beyond words for your support. I will never question you wanting to lead our country."

"Thank you for those words," Nikolas said as he hugged him. "Now, let us tell Morgan our plans."

MORGAN STOOD with her arms wrapped tight around herself as her father and Daniel explained the decision to go after Alec at once.

"You tremble with the desire to go fight to free him your-self. I am proud you have not let your love for him supersede your responsibilities to your country. Put your trust in us, my dear. We will return him to you," her father said before kissing her forehead.

"I do trust you. I know you will both do all you…" She stopped and looked at Daniel. "You are torn once again. So I will ask that you go fight at Father's side. I believe that freeing Alec is the best way you can serve as my protector tonight."

"I agree, but you will have a heavy guard while we are all away."

"I will speak with the dragons and request volunteers to carry you. I love you. May the magic keep you and return you safely home." She hugged both and kissed their cheeks before they left.

THE KNIGHTS of the Admiralty were dressed in black, lightweight battle gear, which would allow them both quick travels across ground and moderate protection during sword conflict. Morgan and GranMay stood at the edge of the lawn, watching as they mounted the major dragons that had volunteered for the mission.

Menkar stood beside Morgan, clawing at the ground and growling deep in his throat. She reached out to comfort him, but he leaned away from her.

"Menkar, have I offended you by asking you to stay? Do you not understand I want you to heal completely before chancing another battle?"

"I understand you asked out of compassion. But you ask

too much in requesting I stay out of a battle I wish to participate in and am fit enough to do so. You know very well Alec is dear to me, my Queen," he said through a growl.

"I am sorry, Menkar. I thought of your physical health and not your heart. Forgive me."

Menkar moved back to her and placed his long head against the side of her body as he crooned deep in his throat.

"I would have gone either way. But thank you for understanding, my Caretaker."

"You are welcome, my friend. Go, bring him home."

Menkar moved to the group being loaded with supplies where he was harnessed and loaded.

A moment later, a minor dragon landed and approached Morgan with a very low bow. It was Manook, Balia's youngling who had been abducted by Harrick.

"May I fight with the others to save my friend Alec, my Queen?" Manook asked.

She knelt and lifted his head from the bow he still held.

"I have no doubt you would fight well, Manook. However, I would ask that you stay by my side. Sir Daniel is joining the rescue party, which leaves me without a personal protector while they are away."

"I very much want to fight, but guarding you would be an honor, my Queen." He moved to stand by her side, looking very proud. Menkar had been listening and bowed his head to the young Manook, who returned the bow and puffed his chest out impressively.

MORGAN WATCHED the squadron fly into the darkening sky with a heavy heart. She had embraced each of her family members before they left and felt very worried as she watched them disappear. GranMay pulled her close and urged her toward the castle.

"Come, we have work to do. I think we need to test your advanced skills. You need to learn to resist an intentional connection by another, with and without physical contact," GranMay said.

"I agree that being able to block my mind to forced connection is important. But, do you think I am strong enough to resist him, GranMay?"

"You are the strongest of our line in many generations, my dear. Let us use our time productively and help you learn to focus your power," GranMay said. Morgan was again impressed at her grandmother's ability to avoid the actual question asked.

They worked for many hours. Though it took many frustrating attempts, she was successful in learning to block connection, break one already formed, and prevent bonding under the full force of GranMay's magic. It was the force of the dark magic that remained a question.

She snuggled under a blanket in her favorite lounge chair on the terrace. She put her palms together, closed her eyes, and shut out all noise to think of nothing other than her need to understand the Arshek magic. Initially, she received only images of different decedents of the Arshek line, so she tightened her focus.

She soon found herself looking into the eyes of one of her foremothers. The pale and trembling woman was lying in the arms of a handsome man as she spoke in a raspy whisper.

"For every ounce of warmth in our magic, the Arshek

magic is utterly vacant. I have never imagined such empty sadness. It was suffocating. I felt as though I did not care to breathe. My power was useless. He pushed into my mind and showed me such horrible things. Truth blended with lies until I could no longer tell them apart. It consumed me, Brother. I am broken, I am empty," the woman said.

Morgan watched her die in her brother's arms. She released the connection and sat sweating and shaking from the cold despair the woman had felt. The effect was profound even though she had only experienced it through a memory.

After a long break, she searched the Book again. She received a few comments from her ancestors that described the overwhelming nature of the darkness. Each was accompanied by an image of a traumatized woman. All spoke of severe pain and many spoke of how the lies told by the wielder of the dark magic started to seem like truth the longer they were in contact with it.

She was surprised a moment later when she heard a much deeper voice. It was the voice of a dragon. There was no image accompanying the voice, but her entire body tingled as she listened to the words.

"To block the darkness, one must hold great strength and skill of magic. To ultimately defeat the darkness, one must have the truest element of the Chemerian magic within you, and its symbol upon you. If you have uncertainty in your heart, the darkness will take you. Under its veil, lies will seem truth, and even the most heinous act will seem just. This is from what Arshek magic was born," said the ethereal voice.

She felt her chair shift and opened her eyes to find Manook cowling at her feet with wide eyes. When she moved to caress him, he avoided her touch.

"What's wrong, my friend?"

He relaxed as soon as he heard her words and pushed his head into her arms.

"My Caretaker, you spoke the words of the ancients. Your voice was that of The Purest."

"I was speaking aloud in a voice not my own?"

He nodded, careful to not interrupt her stroking of his head.

"You recognized the voice from your ancient knowledge?"

"Yes, my Queen, there is no mistaking its resonance. It was surely that of The Purest."

"I am embarrassed to say I have no idea who that is, Manook. Can you tell me?"

He tensed and dropped his head.

"I will speak to the Elder dragons about it later. It is late and I need to rest."

When she stood and turned toward her bed, she noticed Manook looking around as if unsure where to place himself.

"Sirzi is far too large to come in here with me, but you could lie right next to my bed to be sure no one approaches," she said as she settled into bed. The dragon leapt toward her and settled with his head on the mattress to watch her.

She stroked him for a few moments, unable to doze. Thoughts of Alec, the men of her family on their way to rescue him, and the words of The Purest kept her from sleep.

"Manook, do you know your Mother's songs?"

He nodded and began to sing one of her favorites. She drifted into sleep, thinking of how much she missed her dear Balia.

MORGAN FOUND both Falin and Lirpa lying on her terrace the next morning. She wondered to herself how the structure could handle the weight of the dragons. These two were indeed getting large. While Lirpa was younger than Falin by almost a year, her girth had caught up to his already. She knew the females of the Chemerian dragons advanced in maturity faster than the males. She now understood that they grew at a faster rate as well.

She stopped short before disturbing them as she noticed that their tails were wrapped together. The possibility they were to be mates made her heart lift as she moved to stand between them. As she caressed them, she felt the warmth of their love for her, and for each other.

"Hello, my friends. Thank you for watching over me. Are you both well?"

"Yes, my Caretaker, we are quite well," Lirpa said. "We came to relieve Manook a few hours ago. We knew he would fall tired given his youth."

"I thank you for being so thoughtful of him, and of me. You are both wonderful friends, and very special to me. I am very happy to learn of your partnership. It is wonderful news that warms my heart."

Lirpa unwrapped her tail and shifted away from Falin as he gave a little snort. They both looked out across the sky without comment. If she did not know better, she would say they were both blushing.

"Has there been any news of the rescue party?"

"No, my Queen. We would have woken you had we learned anything," Lirpa said.

She nodded and left them to shower and dress. When

she finished dressing, she peeked through the window to see Falin reach out and nudge Lirpa's snout with his own. Soon, their tails intertwined again. The smile she wore was short-lived as her ache of worry for Alec filled her again.

DANIEL, NIKOLAS, JOSEF, AND MARIC lay in wait near the north entrance to the Arshek Castle. The remaining three Knights of their group were to set up near the opposite side of the castle as a back-up group.

The plan was to subdue the next guard patrol as soon as they came on duty, to allow them the most time possible before being discovered. With luck, they could locate and free Alec in that time.

They meant to move about the castle unnoticed, searching for Alec and becoming familiar with the layout of the massive structure. They would not kill if they could remain unseen but were ready to do so if discovered.

As the new guard patrol exited the castle and began to converse with those they were replacing, the stealthy group of Knights readied themselves. Five minutes later, they rushed the guards from both sides, leaving all of the Arshek guards knocked unconscious, bound, and pulled into the woods.

The Knights slipped through the massive doors then moved along the sidewalls, two on each side. With nods of agreement, each pair turned down the first hall they came to.

Daniel and Josef searched many rooms before they had to duck behind some moldy old window curtains to avoid an Arshek Guard patrolling the corridors.

As they moved from behind the curtains, both froze, startled by a loud agonized scream. They gave each other a hard look then headed toward the sound.

They crept through a side corridor and crouched behind a sideboard table when the hallway opened up into a large throne room. Two more pained roars ripped through the air as they scurried from one hiding place to another to reach the far end of the room.

Once hidden behind a short wall, Daniel chanced a glance toward the group at the head of the room. He was pale when he dropped back down and met Josef's eyes. Josef took a glance and swallowed hard at the scene before him.

Alec was on his knees with his ankles and hands bound behind him. His back was covered in long deep cuts and blood covered his torso. Lying on the floor behind him were the lifeless bodies of three Chemerian Knights, their back-up unit.

As Josef watched, Harrick placed his hand on Alec's forehead. Alec let out a guttural groan. After a few seconds, Harrick gestured to a pair of huge Marocks standing to either side of Alec. The two huge beasts raised their arms and brought down thin leather lashes across Alec's bare back.

Josef dropped back down and met Daniel's eye as Alec's screams cut through them. Both had their hands on the hilt of their swords and trembled with rage.

They knew it would be suicide to attack. There were six human and four Marock Militiamen around Alec, not to mention Lord Harrick himself. But, Alec was being tortured less than twenty feet from them. They had to act.

They stared hard at each other as each drew his sword. Both took a few deep breaths to calm themselves Rage would only get them killed faster. A second before they were about to jump, they froze again as the deep chilling voice of Lord

Harrick filled the room.

"My son, you have been lied to your entire life. Open your mind, my boy. See the truth of who you are. Open yourself to our magic, let its power fill you, and follow me!"

Alec's moan of pain became a roar of rage as he jerked back from Harrick's hand.

"NO! Your black blood does not define me. I am a Son of Chemerie! You can take my life, but you will never have my allegiance!" He held Harrick's black eyes through three straight courses of lashings, buckling only with the last set.

"You will pledge yourself to Arshek, or I will end you! I have no use for an insolent, traitorous child," Harrick said as he made a slow circle around him. "However, let me assure you, Sir Alec, that death will not come quickly. I will get you quite close, then heal your wounds just enough to begin again. You will break, my son. You are brave and strong of will, yet, every man has his weakness. And yours … well, yours is your delicious young mate, The Caretaker, Morgan, I believe."

Alec laughed and spat blood at Harrick's boots as he fought to sit up straight and meet his eyes.

"She is not my weakness, you fool! She is the reason you will never break me!"

Harrick ordered another set of lashings. This time Alec did not buckle. He took every blow with his eyes locked on Harrick's.

"If you do not pledge yourself to me soon, I will have your precious Queen killed in her sleep. Though your sister was born with no useful magic, she is at least loyal. She has kept me well informed of your life and will kill at my order."

He stepped closer and grabbed Alec's head with both hands. Alec's body shuddered as Harrick connected and bonded to him by force.

"Look deep in your mind and see for yourself how your precious Queen questions everything about you. She knows you are of Arshek blood, she has always known, and she will never trust you. She fears you. She keeps you close only to control you. Look deep within and see, my son, see the truth!"

Harrick continued his magical attack on Alec for many minutes only to pull back with his own angry howl of rage.

"Lock him away!"

Daniel and Josef moved behind a nearby stack of baskets when they heard the Militiamen dragging Alec toward them. They followed at a distance but could go no further when two Marocks stopped to stand guard at the entrance to the dungeons.

The two debated then decided to join up with the others before mounting an attack. They had backtracked a bit and were headed for the entrance hall when they were grabbed. Maric and Nikolas pulled them behind some crates just in time to avoid a housemaid hurrying along the hallway.

The four Knights moved into a storage room near the entrance to the dungeons. Daniel and Josef told Nikolas and Maric everything they witnessed, and the four decided to wait an hour to act. Nikolas and Maric had been below in the dungeon area searching for Alec and informed the others of the basic layout and the number of guards. Of course, they could not be sure how many guards were there now with Alec present.

To overtake the two Marocks guarding the entrance without getting the attention of the entire castle required a diversion to pull them down the hall and around the corner. As Marocks are not very bright, that was quite easy. Maric took a spool of string from the storage room. Two Knights waited around each corner, and Maric rolled the spool of thread across to Daniel on the other side. Daniel waited a couple of seconds and rolled it back. The big idiots responded just as a child would and came to investigate the odd sight. They were subdued and bound in the storage room without alerting any others.

The Knights moved with stealth down the steps of the dungeon. As they approached the bottom, they heard snoring from a Marock stationed at the foot of the stairs. The stupid creature was stretched across the stairs. Beyond him, they could just see the feet of another guard who was wide awake.

Nikolas patted them each and mimed his idea. Two would leap over the sleeping guard and attack the next one, the remaining two would take out the sleepyhead.

That plan went well, but their luck ended around the next corner. Nearly all of the Militiamen and Marocks that had been around Alec in the throne room were still guarding him. Daniel mimed to the others the number he counted, and all of their faces dropped a little.

The odds were way off in the enemies' favor, but they would not turn back now. Josef gave the others a gesture to wait and disappeared around the corner behind them. Ten seconds later, he returned with a torch and a large straw mat from an empty cell.

The others watched him mime his intentions and all nodded agreement. The plan would take advantage of the Marocks being afraid of fire. It was a simple diversion to give the Chemerian Knights an advantage in their attack.

Nikolas and Josef held the mat and Maric lit it. Once it was burning well, the group rushed forward. They threw the flaming mat into the group of guards and followed the flames with their swords.

Two Marocks had flaming clothing and jumped around franticly while ignoring the striking Knights. The Chemerian Knights wielded their swords with practiced accuracy, and every Arshek Militiaman was down within one minute. The fire, however, was getting a bit out of hand.

Daniel was fumbling with door keys he took off of a guard when Josef pulled him away for Maric to swing a heavy ax-hammer at the lock. When Nikolas and Daniel moved in to get Alec, both went still.

"There are not many men who could take such without breaking," Nikolas said as he dropped to one knee beside Alec.

"I hope I never understand how a man could do this to his own son," Daniel said as he knelt to help lift Alec.

Alec was delirious and mumbling, so Nikolas spoke in a calm soothing voice to comfort him as they moved out of the cell and toward the stairs.

They were running along a corridor toward the north gate of the castle when they were met by a group of guards who, given their ready swords, had just discovered the missing guards outside.

Daniel and Nikolas set Alec down and stepped forward to fight alongside Josef and Maric. Josef dropped to one knee as a sword skewered his leg, and Maric shifted to protect him. Maric was caught across the arm by an ax-hammer, and left fighting one-handed as two massive beasts rained down heavy blows.

As Maric stumbled back from the forceful blows, Daniel moved in. He struck one Marock across the neck as Josef skewered the other with the sword he had pulled from his leg.

Once all the Arshek guards were down, Maric and Josef picked up Alec so the healthier Daniel and Nikolas could lead the way. As they neared the castle gate, they heard a great roar of men and Marocks moving toward them from deep within the castle.

Daniel replaced the struggling Josef to carry Alec faster. The attacking Arshek Guard came into sight just as he and Maric carried Alec through the outer doors.

The sound of the rushing feet made Daniel look back, and he froze. He saw his father and Josef looking him straight in the eye from inside the door. Nikolas gave him a quick smile.

"Go, Son! Get Alec back to Morgan!"

"No! Father! No!" Daniel screamed as he watched his father slam the door between them. He knelt to drop Alec, but Maric grabbed his arm and pulled him onward. Daniel wrenched his arm away and moved to turn back.

"Daniel, they made the noble choice. Do not waste their brave deaths!" Maric yelled. "Do your duty as they have just done theirs. Let's go!"

Daniel relented and lifted Alec again as he struggled to breathe. He ran as fast as he could, keeping pace with the longer legs of Maric. As he ran, he could think of nothing but the smile on his father's face as he turned to face death.

DANIEL AND MARIC kept to the trees to avoid any dragon search parties. The sun had risen, and they were easy targets in the light. They had a couple of very close calls as they struggled through the rough countryside.

When they entered the icy river, Alec gasped and jerked with deep groans and mumbles. Daniel hoped the water would do his wounds some good, perhaps slow some of the bleeding.

They continued through the valley toward the mountains where their dragon mounts waited. As they neared the base of the mountains, the sound of movement ahead of them made them drop to the ground and slide into a thick patch of underbrush.

Daniel lifted his head enough to study the large battalion of the Arshek militia blocking their path. He and Maric both cursed.

"I am too tired to be of any use," Maric said in a breathy whisper as they pulled Alec deeper under the brush.

"It's not like we have a freakin' shot against that many anyway," Daniel said as he dropped his head to his arm. "I wish I could talk to dragons right now. We could call for a ride."

"Can he?" Maric said as he looked at Alec.

"We can't wake him. His pain will be insane."

"I see no other option. If we try to double back, we will be walking straight into the battalion behind us. We have only a few minutes before we are discovered."

Daniel nodded and motioned for Maric to hold Alec's mouth to keep him from screaming. He rubbed his knuckles along Alec's sternum as he said his name into his ear.

Alec woke and started to struggle until Daniel shifted to let him see his face as he said his name in a calm tone. Alec stopped fighting, then lay tense and shaking as he breathed ragged small breaths. Daniel whispered their situation and what they hoped he could do.

"I do not … " he said through gritted teeth as his body started to shake. "I … I … will try."

He closed his eyes and was soon muttering. They heard "Menkar" and "find" and "danger".

"Sounds like he got the idea anyway," Daniel said as he lifted to glance around at the forces ahead of them again. He dropped back down and stared at Alec with horror when the man's breathing quickened and he whispered, "Morgan."

They flinched and ducked as thunderous dragon roars filled the air. Daniel lifted his head up and smiled as he found four Chemerian dragons heading their way.

"Yes! He did it! He … Wait!" Daniel popped up to his knees as he tracked the dragons. "Please, tell me my crazy sister is not aboard one of those dragons!"

"Would not put it past her!" Maric said as he sat up too. They both let out the breaths they had been holding when they saw the dragons held no passengers.

Alec whispered as if talking to Morgan a couple of times more, then passed out again. They carried him to a clearing to board Menkar and Broon as they landed. Menkar bolted high into the air and flew hard for the mountains, then made a sharp drop for a high mountain ridge. Daniel was struggling to hold tight to Alec and cursing when he saw the dragon's target.

Morgan was aboard Sirzi, atop the highest ridge. Menkar

rose out of the dive and continued toward the castle as Morgan and Sirzi bolted into the air to follow.

"I lost connection to Alec. Is he still alive?"

"Yes, but his wounds are wicked," Daniel said.

"I know."

She had felt the anguish in her brother the second she connected, and her chest was aching as she searched all of the other dragons and the valley.

As they flew for the castle, Daniel told her all that had happened and all that he had learned. When he got to the moment their father and uncle had given their lives for them, he had to stop. He took a few seconds, then looked over at her with a fierce expression.

"Father and Josef gave their lives so Maric and I could return Alec to you. Make sure he understands that Morgan. They couldn't have shown any more faith in him than that."

They flew the rest of the way in silence, not chancing putting down early so Morgan could tend to Alec. They knew the Arshek battalions were only hours away from the castle if war was what Harrick intended.

DANIEL AND TWO OTHER KNIGHTS carried Alec to her chambers. Daniel arranged for a four-man guard with instructions that no female be permitted into the room, except for Morgan and GranMay.

Morgan had connected to GranMay and asked that she see to Maric's wounds, then join her in her chambers. Daniel was retreating from her chambers when GranMay called him.

"I feel your pain. Tell me what has happened," she said as she moved to him.

The tears he had been fighting the entire way home slid down his face as he told his dear GranMay she had lost both her eldest son and her son-in-magic that night. GranMay placed her hands to his cheeks and pulled his forehead to hers as both cried.

"Show me how they died," she said as she closed her eyes. Daniel relived it so GranMay could see the bravery with which they left this life.

MORGAN STARED at the great wounds on Alec's naked torso. He had endured such agony and still refused to turn away from Chemerie. Her heart was being torn apart by the loss of her father and uncle while being filled with intense pride in Alec's commitment to her and their country.

She was waiting for GranMay to arrive before healing him. GranMay made her promise to let her connect to him first in case the darkness was strong within him.

When GranMay entered the bedroom, her face was covered with tears. Without comment, she grasped Alec's hands and closed her eyes. After a moment, she released one and reached out toward Morgan.

Morgan took her and Alec's hands and focused to let the magic flow to heal him. The connection broke seconds later, as a blast of pure hatred sent an icy chill down her spine. When she opened her eyes she found GranMay gripping her arm and staring toward the terrace doors. Morgan turned to find a crossbow pointed straight at her chest. The woman holding it crept closer with a wicked smile.

"My Lord and Father told me that if my dear brother returned here tonight, I was to kill the both of you. However, thanks to that meddling old fool, I have only one shot left. So, I will have to choose!" the woman said as she glanced between her and Alec.

When GranMay tried to move toward the woman, Morgan moved faster to place herself between them.

"Trust me, GranMay. Hold your place. We've got this."

The murderous woman swung the crossbow back and forth, then stopped with it pointing at her heart once again.

"The choice is easy really. He is at least my own blood. But you, well, you are simply in my way!"

Morgan ducked and dove across GranMay and Alec as Manook leapt. The minor dragon had snuck up behind the woman and pounced at Morgan's call.

He pinned the shrieking woman with his teeth bared as he sunk his claws into her shoulders and back. The Knights standing guard outside the bedroom door rushed in at the sound and took her away at once.

Alec moaned, and Morgan shifted off him as she caressed his face. She kissed his forehead as she pushed healing magic.

"Alec, wake up and talk to me. You have not been giving me nearly enough attention for days, and I am getting very annoyed."

He tried to smile, but winced instead. She took his hands and continued to let the healing magic flow until she grew weak. It was enough to get him to a more tolerable level of pain and close most of his wounds.

She raised her head to see GranMay waiting patiently as blood soaked her sleeve.

"I am so sorry, GranMay. Here, let me help you," she

said. She gave all she had left to GranMay, then laid down to sleep beside Alec.

SHE WOKE HOURS LATER to find herself alone on her bed. Alec was sitting on her terrace.

"How are you?"

He did not answer, but came to her and lifted her into a crushing embrace.

"I am so sorry. If I could change it, I would give them back to you."

She pushed him back a little and looked at him as tears slid down her face.

"They offered their lives so that I could have you. They would never have done so if they had any doubts that you are my magical partner and the perfect father for my children. They believed in you. Don't ever forget that."

Alec pulled her forehead to his as he fought tears of his own, "I will never forget, I promise you. It was the faith of your family that held me together in the face of Harrick's torture. I kept hearing their words of encouragement. I think that is what kept me from losing all when he entered my mind the last time. He told me horrible lies. Each time they would start to seem real, I would hear you or one of your family giving me words of support. I owe them my life many times over, and I am very grateful."

They held each other possessively. She was careful not to touch his back. He kissed her forehead and took her hands.

"Shall we go find the rest of our family, and make plans to say farewell to King Nikolas and Sir Josef?"

She nodded as she wiped her tears and gathered herself

a bit. As she walked through the castle with him, her heart lifted a bit as she realized he had said "our family" and meant it.

When the family was gathered in the great room, Alec left her and moved to Daniel.

"I will be forever grateful for your father and uncle's sacrifice on my behalf. I promise I will spend every moment of my life trying to live up to that honor."

He put out a hand to shake Daniel's. As soon as their hands touched, he pulled Daniel into a strong embrace and held him tight for a long moment. Daniel had held his face rigid while Alec spoke, but the sentiment of the embrace drew silent tears.

Alec then moved to Maric, thanking him for his bravery, and acknowledging his loss in the same way he did to Daniel. Daniel and Morgan held each other as they watched Alec move to each and every family member in the room to offer his sincere appreciation for the sacrifice, and condolences for their loss.

When Alec moved to where GranMay sat, he knelt before her and kissed her hands. He spoke of the same devotion to live up to the faith the men showed in him. He shifted to kiss her cheek, then lifted her into an embrace. She cried openly as he held her in his arms for many moments.

No one had witnessed the actual death of Nikolas and Josef. They could not say for sure that they were gone. But the idea that Harrick allowed them to live in his rage at losing Alec, was unbelievable. Therefore, they went with the realistic assumption that they had been killed, and held a private ceremony in the great room late that evening. It was a wake in which each person spoke of the lost, and their positive impact on the lives of those around them. The focus was on the quality of their lives, and their accomplishments, not on the grief of those still living.

When the ceremony was over, Morgan and GranMay held each other and cried for a long time. An intense wave of pain from Alec made Morgan look up. He was standing a few feet behind the other men, with his head bowed, and hands clasped behind him.

She flew from the sofa to grab him as he swayed.

"What's wrong?" Daniel asked as he moved to help her carry him toward the sofa.

"Pain. Help me with his coat," she said as they laid him down on his stomach. They eased the coat off, and everyone groaned as they saw his blood-soaked shirt beneath.

"What's going on? I thought you healed these?" Daniel said as he used his knife to cut Alec's shirt away and ease it back.

"What is that?" Burke asked as everyone moved in to look at the black liquid oozing from the many gashes reopened on his red, inflamed back.

"That is Harrick assuring he either serves him, or dies. I felt it as soon as I touched him just now. The darkness is growing stronger, and poisoning him," Morgan said as she took a cloth offered by Neesa to wipe away some of the mess. She laid her hands beside the worst of the wounds and focused to push healing. His body shuddered and tensed even more as her magic fought the darkness inside of him. The wounds closed very slowly.

"Can you fight it? Can you save him?" Emma asked as

she knelt beside her.

"I … I don't know. I just pushed as hard as I could to close that one, and it hurt him every step of the way. I can block his pain if I do not fight against the darkness causing the wounds to fester. But as soon as I act against it, his pain shoots up fast. I will search my memories and try to find another way."

The Purest

MORGAN SAT beside Alec and stroked his hair as she tried to comfort him through their link. Three days had passed since his return, and they had healed his wounds four times. After each healing, the poison of the dark magic had reopened them in less time than before.

"How is he?" Daniel asked as he moved to sit on the bed beside her.

"I've spent hours searching his mind and spirit. I can feel darkness within his mind, pinpoint the locations it is most concentrated, but I can do nothing to remove it. With every healing, and every attempt to fight it, I make him suffer even more pain. I am useless to him, and he won't survive this much longer. I can barely reach his mind to get a response now. There is a bone-chilling wall of negative emotions filled with horrible thoughts all around his consciousness.

Breaching it hurts us both."

"I am watching you get weaker as you try to heal him, and I see your hope fading so fast. Tell me it is just the natural effect of his suffering and not the result of the darkness getting inside of you too."

She glanced at him then looked back at Alec as she wiped away a tear.

"I've been careful to protect myself, not bonding deep enough for anything to pass to me. He made me promise not to the last time he was lucid enough to speak."

"I hope to be as strong as him, and to love someone that deeply, one day," Daniel said as he hugged her tight before leaving.

She needed help. Her bonding with the Book of the Caretaker had given her no useful information to free him from the darkness. In truth, the Book had left her aching, because everyone who had been tortured with the darkness at the hand of a Son of Arshek had died a painful death from the damage done.

As she sat watching him grimace in his sleep, she heard the words of The Purest echo in her head. Since first hearing those words, she had searched her ancient knowledge and the Book of the Caretaker. She learned that The Purest was a great Elder female dragon who bonded to Queen Chemerie, and first established the magical link between the dragons' race and that of man on Erion. The Chemerian magic was created from the bonding of these two magical friends. This was the only piece of information she had left to examine.

"GranMay, have you ever heard of The Purest Dragon?" she said as she joined her on the terrace.

"Yes, I have heard the story of The Purest. She was the first of the Dragons of Chemerie. But that is all I know."

"I heard her voice during my last search of my ancient memories and …" she stopped as GranMay grabbed her arm and looked all around them.

"My dear, are you quite sure? It is my understanding that no human has ever had such information. The dragons hold that knowledge very close to their hearts. The words of The Purest are sacred to them."

"Manook explained that I was speaking her words aloud as I heard them. He said the voice was unmistakable, and was that of The Purest. He did clam-up when I questioned further."

"And with good reason. I am sure the Elder dragons would bite his tail off if they knew he had discussed it with anyone, even you, I expect."

"I intend to question the Council of Elders about what I heard because it seems the key to healing Alec and defeating Lord Harrick. I will have to risk offending them. I am out of options, and he is dying."

"We are foolish to worry," GranMay said with a small smile as she patted her arm. *"I do not expect the Elders would be offended or at all surprised by your coming to them with these questions. For it was by their gift you have the knowledge at all, my dear."*

Morgan felt worry from Menkar as he flew overhead and connected to him.

"He is quiet right now, but I need to find a way to help him soon. How am I to request a meeting with the Council of Elders?"

"I will be glad to make the request for you, my Queen. I will return with their reply when they give it."

She paced for over an hour as she reviewed the words of The Purest to make sure she would speak well when she went before the Council. The instant she felt Menkar approach, she went out to meet him. She felt his anger well before he landed.

"Have they refused to speak to me?"

Menkar shook his head as he landed and grumbled as he answered.

"I would not accept that answer and had to challenge my father to ask that the Eldest Female consider my request. I will pay for that later, I am certain. But they have agreed to speak with you tonight, my Queen. Shall we go?"

She leapt to his back and nodded to GranMay as they lifted off.

THEY FLEW to the top of the mountain cliffs behind the castle. When they cleared the highest peak, Menkar flew out over the roughest and most dangerous of rock formations, then suddenly tucked his wings and shot straight down into a great crevice.

The small squeal she let out as she lifted from the saddle brought a deep chuckle from Menkar, a rare occurrence indeed.

"Sweet mercy, you could have at least warned me!" She gave him a playful smack on the neck, and his chuckle only deepened as he swooped around in circles to slow their descent.

As he settled on the floor of the great rocky abyss, she looked up to see the opening high above. She guessed they had to be standing near the same elevation the castle sat on. The only light was the natural light from the top of the cavern, so her view was limited to the few feet around Menkar. The dragons needed no extra light, given their gifts of sight.

"What do I do?"

"Wait. They will speak when they are ready to hear from you, my Queen."

"Shall I use the magic to connect to them, or speak aloud?"

"As you are the first in many decades to be able to connect to us without touch, I am not sure. However, I am sure you should let them initiate the conversation either way they choose."

She was startled by a booming voice in her head as she felt Menkar crouch low to the ground.

"You are quite right, young one. I suppose I should be grateful my son can give the right advice concerning propriety to the Council, even if the skill to follow such ideals eludes him altogether!"

She had heard the comment through her connection. Menkar's father was speaking to Menkar, not to her. She chose to stay silent, just in case she had eavesdropped without intention.

"You did nothing wrong, young Caretaker," said a new voice. "We know your skill with the magic better than you yourself, as yet. Drieden allowed you to hear his words, or you would not have."

The deep melodic voice came from her right. She heard a great sliding and stepping, then the massive head of an enormous female dragon came out of the darkness.

The slight tension she held within her faded when she recognized the beautiful green dragon. The dragon was silent for many seconds while inspecting her from many angles.

She flinched, then froze as she felt a great gust of air on her back. The large male, Drieden, had approached from behind her, and was sniffing at her. A deep rumbling growl from the great female made him back away.

"The rest of our conversation is not for young Menkar's ears. Please show us your skill with the connection, and open to all of us here, except Menkar," the great female Elder said.

Morgan patted Menkar with a push of apology, and he nodded his head. She closed her eyes and opened her connection. Once she had connected to all she felt within the cavern, she focused to block Menkar.

"I have connected to six nearby. Have I reached all I should include, my Lady?"

"You have found the six who wish to be found, young one. Now for introductions. I am Nulian, Eldest Female and chair of the Council of Elders. You have met Drieden. He is Eldest Male and, as you have seen, rather prone to suspicion. The others will introduce themselves later if they wish."

"Thank you for granting me an audience at such short notice. It is an honor to meet all of the council, and you in particular, Lady Nulian. You were my mother's friend. I remember feeling your love for her."

Nulian hummed and returned the head bow she offered.

"What are your questions, my Queen?" Nulian said.

She spoke with as much confidence as she could muster under the circumstances.

"I would be very grateful if you could help me interpret some of the knowledge you have given me. In particular, I would like to better understand a verse from The Purest."

She jumped, and tucked closer to Menkar, as the cavern was filled with loud angry hissing. Nulian hushed them with a growl that rattled Morgan to the bone. Her own anxiety grew as she felt Menkar lean away from Nulian and tense.

"Hold your tongues. The Caretaker would not know the words of The Purest, had I not given them to her," Nulian said.

Morgan was breathing fast with the tension in the room, and concentrated on calming herself as she waited for Nulian to meet her gaze again.

"My Lady, I realize you have given me this knowledge for the same reason the magic is so strong within me. I must face and defeat the dark magic that has poisoned my partner, and perhaps defeat Lord Harrick of Arshek himself. I am sure you meant for me to find the path on my own, but I am faced with the task with no time to learn at a natural pace. Alec will not survive much longer. Will you advise me, Lady Nulian, so that I may save him?"

Nulian stared at her for a long moment in silence before speaking again.

"What, specifically, do you ask, my Queen?"

"The Purest spoke of needing the truest element of the Chemerian magic within you, and its symbol upon you, to defeat the darkness. I need to better understand those words."

Nulian had given Drieden a nasty look as he grumbled again, then returned her gaze to her.

"My Caretaker, do tell me what you think it could mean," Nulian said in a soft tone.

"I know the Chemerian magic to be born of the essential elements of love, kindness, and respect. The amulet I wear is the only symbol of Chemerie I have seen. But that does not seem sufficient to explain her meaning. I need more understanding, my Lady."

Nulian nodded and was again silent for a moment before continuing.

"Your interpretation of the words is rudimentary, and a bit naïve.

I expect nothing more of people however, for the verses of The Purest have heavy underpinnings of much more than the people have known for many years. But I know you to be capable of much more, because I have seen it in you. Can you not think of anything else that may explain those words?"

Morgan bit her lip. She had agonized over these words since she first heard them. She focused her mind and thought about all the possible meanings of the words. The words "truest element" were her first focus. She thought of the magic itself, of the Caretaker, of the bonding between dragon and human, then …

"You. The truest element of the Chemerian magic is the dragon. Lady Chemerie carried some magic herself, but the rich lives of the Chemerian people and the magic they feel are but a gift of the dragon. In particular, a gift from The Purest herself."

This brought a rich low hum from the dragons of the Council. It sent a wonderful warm flood of love and respect over her, and she shivered at the intensity of it. Nulian bowed her head, as did Drieden.

"That is an understanding we did not give you. Few before you could have been selfless and humble enough to find the truth in the words, and show such loyalty to their dragon kindred. You honor us, and we thank you," Nulian said.

Morgan nodded but her face was wrinkled with confusion.

"Now, what of the symbol?" Nulian said. *"Can you also make that connection on your own? It is a bit harder, I think. For this has not been shared with people since the days of The Purest herself."*

Morgan focused on "symbol" alone and got nowhere. She felt the amulet was too simple. As she considered the combination "the symbol of the truest element upon you", she thought of the dragon markings on her hands. They were a symbol of the Caretaker bloodline within her, not a symbol of the dragon within her … she was not a dragon.

She looked into Nulian's eyes as the answer came to her.

"Can I truly have dragon within me and a symbol of its presence upon me? Nulian, is there perhaps a gift you have yet to give that I could prove myself worthy of? Is it a special way of bonding in which a dragon can physically mark a human and share their essence with them? Is that how The Purest bonded with Lady Chemerie?"

"It is indeed, my noble Caretaker," Nulian said as she bowed her head and started a low rumbling hum from deep in her chest. As Nulian gazed around the chamber, each of the other Elders joined her. The volume of the hum rose to a great roar as their voices added to one another. Morgan cringed at the intensity of the sound and covered her ears as she bent forward against Menkar's neck.

"They honor you, my Queen. Stand proud and trust them," Menkar said.

She sat up tall and tried to relax as her head pounded and her body vibrated with the song of the great dragons. The resonance of the sound bouncing off the cavern walls became rhythmic, and her hands began to prickle and sting. The sensations were much like her Quickening, but the song was different, and the effect far more intense.

As the Elder dragons continued to sing, her markings glowed their brightest ever, and the burning pain in her hands moved up her arms and over her shoulders. She tensed and braced just before the two paths met in the middle of her chest to send shocks of fiery pain all through her.

When she lifted her hands to the most painful spot on her chest, she found her amulet. Her fingers burned against it as she tried to move it with no success. For many minutes, she focused on controlling her breathing and not raising her guard. Her body trembled, sweat soaked her clothes, and her head spun wildly, but still, she did not fight them.

"Lay back, my Caretaker, and trust your brethren," Nulian said.

She looked up into the dark eyes of Nulian as the dragon's head moved to hover above her. They held each other's gaze as the dragons' song shifted to an even more complex cadence and Nulian's snout moved closer.

She felt Nulian's magical request to form a stronger private connection and reached up to lay her hands against her snout. Nulian dropped her snout closer as she connected, then paused just inches above the painful center of her chest. As the great dragon took a deep breath, she did the same.

The instant Nulian touched her chest their connection moved into full bonding. Unlike any bonding she had experienced thus far, an explosion of pain accompanied the initial formation. She screamed, and arched off of the saddle, as she dug her nails into Nulian's scales.

A few seconds later, the pain was gone, and she was left in the most profound magical bonding she had ever felt. The feeling was all-encompassing. She could feel no detectable separation between their spirits, they were one.

The depth of the connection did not change as Nulian lifted her snout away, and raised a huge front foot above her. A rush of loving devotion filled Morgan as a sharp claw pricked her chest where the pain had been most intense.

She shuddered and tensed at the pain of the cut, but made no move of resistance. When Nulian dropped her snout to lie against the wound, another penetrating storm of pain rocked her. She could not help crying out again. She clung to the scales of Nulian's snout and gasped for breath as her body exploded in fiery flashes of the most intense magic she could imagine.

One very long moment later, the dragons' song dropped in volume, and Nulian raised her head again.

Morgan flinched as something struck her chest, then took a sharp deep breath as a warm soothing rush of magic cut her pain by half. The sensation struck again every few seconds, and she grew stronger with each one. As her body calmed, she forced her eyes open and watched as another drop of Nulian's blood fell onto her chest.

When her pain was gone, she lifted a trembling hand to Nulian.

"Nulian, have you given me your gift?"

"Yes, my Caretaker. You now carry my blood within you, and the Heraldic Crest of our dragon line upon you. You have proven yourself worthy of this gift many times since you answered our call at such a young age. Your words to us today confirmed your worthiness beyond question. You are the strongest of your kind we have seen since the very first Caretaker, Queen Chemerie herself.

"We are entrusting you with the abilities the Crest has given you. Your power will now be far greater, and you must respect the responsibility that carries. You must study with us so we may teach you how to use your new power wisely," Nulian said. She crooned as Morgan stroked her and shifted to a more gentle tone. *"It is an honor to welcome you into my family, my Sister."*

All of the dragons hummed together again, and Morgan felt her hands and chest begin to warm and tingle. The more complex the dragons' song became, the more her chest tingled. The tingle was soon accompanied by a faint glow. She smiled, and tears flowed down her cheeks as she saw the beautiful new markings now visible on her chest.

A gorgeous set of major dragons were becoming more detailed each second. They were facing each other with their snouts touching and their tails wrapped together. The colors were rich, and their scales reflected all the colors of the rainbow as they shimmered iridescent in the glowing light.

With a deep croon, Nulian touched her stomach. Her touch caused the center of the markings to warm and glow with brilliant intensity. When Morgan raised a hand to touch the spot, she gasped, and tears flowed even faster.

She looked up with amazement at Nulian as she let her fingers play over the small, velvety, transparent scales. They felt much like the belly scales of a new hatchling, and the edges blended into her skin naturally.

She closed her eyes and let hot tears fall down her face, as she sent her most heartfelt thanks and appreciation to all of the Council, especially to Nulian.

"You have given me more than I could ever repay. Thank you so much, Lady Nulian. It is an honor beyond words to be considered part of your family."

Nulian crooned again, then stepped back as Drieden moved in and eased his snout under Morgan's shoulders. The instant his snout touched her, she felt her chest prickle, almost a tickling effect. She twitched and shivered at the sensation, and heard Drieden chuckle, much like his son. She smiled at the sound, but the thought of their familial connection brought her worry back with a jolt.

"Will you please teach me enough tonight to help Alec?" she said, including all of the Elders again.

"All you need to help him was already within you. My gift will amplify and focus your power beyond any your family has witnessed. To defeat the darkness holding your mate's mind, you need only focus on your love for him, and deny all suggestion to the contrary the darkness provides.

"Trust the magic, my Caretaker, as we have trusted you. Let it lead you, as you have thus far, and you will not fail."

"Thank you so very much for your trust. I will cherish this precious gift and give all I am to wielding it honorably."

The dragons sang in unison to send an intense surge of energy all through her. Within seconds, she felt stronger and healthier than she had ever been in her life.

HER THOUGHTS went to saving Alec. Two seconds later, she grabbed for the saddle bolster as Menkar leapt into the air. As he climbed higher and higher, swirling in tight circles to keep off the walls of the great cavern, she considered the possibility that he had heard her thoughts as she formed them, rather than when she offered the idea to him on purpose.

To test this idea, she thought of Drieden's chuckle, and how it sounded like his. Menkar chuckled deep in his chest at the instant she considered her observation.

"Please hurry, my friend."

Menkar shot from the abyss and stroked hard for the castle. Her mind raced through many thoughts before she flinched as GranMay's voice shouted in her mind.

"I am perfectly fine, dear. But I am glad you are returning. He has worsened, and I believe my efforts hurt him more than they help."

"I am still a few miles away, GranMay, but we will be back soon. Tell him I am coming, please."

A brush of pain was followed by a wave of icy negativity that made her shiver before familiar warmth filled her.

"I…missed you, m…my Lady. You sh…should be ashamed …leaving me ssss…so long."

"I am wholly ashamed, my dear. I will find a way to repay you, I promise," she said with a laugh. She smiled as she felt his interest rise, then cringed as she shared his horrible pain. Her fingers touched the Crest tingling on her chest as she realized she had moved beyond the magical barrier that had kept her at bay. She had felt his pain more clearly than she ever had, despite being a mile away.

Menkar soon landed and lifted her over the railing. She headed toward the bed with a shudder as Alec's pain washed over her again. The cuts were a festering mess, and he was struggling to breathe as his heart beat at a slow, uneven pace.

She leaned across him to lay a hand on GranMay's head and wake her. She felt how weak the dear woman was the instant she touched her, and considered healing her some before starting on Alec.

"No, you will not! Give him your best. I will be fine," Gran-May said as she lifted her head from her folded arms. She froze and stared at Morgan's Crest.

"I will explain it all later," Morgan said.

She shifted to kneel beside Alec and thought only of healing him and fighting the evil darkness torturing him. Letting the instincts the magic imparted lead her, she stacked her palms over the scales at the center of her Heraldic Crest. As her hands and Crest grew warm and tingled madly, she closed her eyes and called for the knowledge she needed from the depths of ancient memories within her. The magic provided the answer she sought within seconds.

"I must eliminate the scars the darkness has left on his mind before healing the physical wounds on his body," she said to herself and GranMay, who was watching with wide eyes. Laying her hands to his head, she deepened her connection to him and felt herself pass into full bonding with no effort beyond the thought of wanting to.

She located memories of his father's mental torture and tensed as the darkness hit her. Her magic responded to the sensation at once; the scales on her chest prickled and warmed, and her guard increased ten-fold above what she had ever known it to be.

Her understanding of what made magic dark or pure was all she needed. She knew that the one and only weapon against the evil that is Arshek is the purity of the love that is Chemerie. As she listened to each awful idea Harrick had placed in his mind, she replied with a strong force of her pure magic guided by a spirit filled with love and trust.

Soon the darkness faded, and she was left with only the loving feelings she knew to be Alec's pure and wholesome spirit around her. With care not to shock his system, she eased out of the intense bonding.

She moved to his back while stroking the scales of her Crest to relieve the sharp prickling sensation. Again, she sought instruction from the dragon knowledge within her.

With her hands stacked over her Crest and her eyes closed, she focused her thoughts, and therefore her magic, on the wounds to be healed. A strong tingle began to radiate outward from her Crest through her body, and her hands grew hot. The heat building between her hands and her Crest increased, as did their glow. The tingle was soon accompanied by the familiar feeling of healing magic.

She used a cloth to wipe the black, bloody mess away, then reached her glowing hands out to let her fingertips touch his skin. As she thought only of healing the wounds, she drew her fingers across them. His body knitted to leave flawless skin behind. With only a few passes of her fingers, his body was fully healed.

As she worked, he relaxed his muscles, took deep breaths, and began to hum as the pain left him. He tried to speak but was far too weak to make any sense. She did not need to hear his words, however. With the new level of magic within her, she could feel his emotions as if they were her own.

"I love you too, you handsome beast," she said as she kissed his cheek and moved locks of sweaty hair from his brow. "Sleep now." He took a deep shaky breath, sighed as his body fully relaxed, and sleep took him.

Training

ALEC HAD FALLEN into a deep exhausted sleep as Morgan completed the healing of his back and arms. Before that day, a healing of that magnitude would have left her near unconsciousness. Now, she was only a little drained. She watched him sleep until GranMay's bewilderment and fatigue washed over her.

She moved to sit down beside her, kissing her cheek. GranMay never met her eyes, she could only stare at the Heraldic Crest of the dragon.

"It is a most precious gift I have been entrusted with by the Elders. Nulian has made me part of her blood family. Her blood will make me far stronger with the magic than we have ever imagined possible."

"It is amazing and beautiful, my dear. May I?" GranMay asked as she raised her fingers to touch the Crest.

"Of course."

She shivered as GranMay's fingers touched her new scales, then giggled at her startled reaction to their texture.

GranMay stroked the scales and traced the beautiful dragons with her fingers as her eyes filled with tears. The dragons wiggled under her touch, and Morgan smiled from the tickle it gave her. GranMay's smile slipped, and Morgan heard her thoughts as they came to her.

If only I had received this gift, perhaps I could have saved my dear Christina.

Morgan was sure she was not supposed to have heard that, so she held back her emotions. She took GranMay's hands in hers, holding them palm-to-palm, so her dear grandmother would feel her emotions with her words.

"I am blessed by this gift, and believe I am deserving of it, and strong enough to have received it, because of all the progress made by my Caretaker Mothers before me. I think our line has been preparing to fight back, and conquer the darkness of Arshek, for many generations. That preparation has culminated within my time to serve. I owe all my Mothers for their strength, and am honored to represent you all in this way."

GranMay had tears rolling by the time she had gotten halfway through those words, and embraced her as she finished. While embraced, Morgan healed her, and passed a strong bolster of magic. They sat on the small sofa and cuddled for a while, before GranMay fell asleep in her arms.

She stroked her hair and hummed a dragon tune while contemplating their reversal of roles. A few moments later, she blushed and smiled as she heard Alec's private thoughts.

"I love that amazing woman with every atom of my being. I

want nothing more in my life than to be with her every moment."

"And this woman wants nothing more than to be with you, my love."

Alec's head turned at the surprise of having his thoughts heard. His puzzlement turned to a broad smile as her sweet words struck him. He had no concern for privacy as he rolled up onto his side and patted the bed beside him.

"Excuse me?" she said with an attempt at a scowl that made him blush.

"I just want to talk, and thank you. Please, come and sit with me."

She laid GranMay over onto the pillows of the sofa and covered her with a blanket. As she walked toward Alec, he flew off the bed in a flash to meet her halfway.

"I lied, I want a little bit more," he said as he kissed her and lifted her into his arms.

She returned the passion of the kiss and did not break it until he pulled away himself. He looked into her eyes with a broad smile.

"We marry in one week, my love. Any last-minute concerns?" he said.

"One: how do you feel about a woman with scales?"

His face made her laugh as she leaned back in his arms. He stared at her new gift for a few seconds and let her slide back to the floor.

"The Council of Elders has shared a very special gift with me, so I could save you. I will be different in many ways now, I imagine."

Alec nodded as he used his finger to trace the dragons, then touched the scales as GranMay had done. She flinched and gasped as she gripped him harder.

"Did I hurt you?"

"No, your touch causes a great deal of sensation under normal conditions, but touching me there seems to amplify things greatly."

She tried to sound unaffected, but her bright red cheeks revealed the true nature of the effect. He smiled, and lifted her in his arms again so he need only lean his head forward to place a gentle kiss to her scales. She shivered and took in a sharp breath. Intense tingles moved over her like lightning, to leave her trembling a bit and breathing much faster.

"I must thank the Council personally for such a wonderful wedding gift," he said in his deep voice.

"You will not be doing that again until I am your wife, my dear," she said as she wriggled to drop back to her feet. Alec chuckled, and pulled her into a strong hug, before letting go.

"Shall I move GranMay to the bed?" he asked. She nodded and watched as he did so. He lifted GranMay with little strain and kissed her forehead before leaving her.

"Are you tired?" she asked.

"Not at all."

"Good, I want you to help me try out my new skill level."

Alec smirked and said, "Gladly!" which earned him a slap on the arm.

She spent a few minutes telling him about her experiences with the Council of Elders, without the details she knew would be breaking their confidences.

"I can actually feel that I am different, it is strange. My biggest concern right now is that I have overheard thoughts from GranMay and you that were not intended for me. It feels wrong, but I can't stop it. I'm also able to send messages without conscious connection. The instant the thought forms in my mind of telling you something, it's sent. So, I am worried about sending information I do not intend to be sharing. Can we do some exercises to see how I can control this until I start my training with the Council?"

"I am glad to help in any way I can. But, I must make one rule first. If you hear some of my personal thoughts, those that are not altogether wholesome, you cannot hold them against me. I am only accountable for what I intend to share aloud or through connection. Agreed?"

"Maybe this is a bad idea. We should wait until I can better control my own sharing as well."

"Why? Are you having unwholesome thoughts, my Queen?" Alec asked with a chuckle as he kissed her flush cheek.

AFTER ALEC had left for the night, she lay in bed tracing her new gift while seeking information about the Crest from her ancient memories. She received an image of a gorgeous woman sitting atop an enormous dragon with deep purple iridescent scales.

Her eyes found the Crest on her ancestor's chest and knew at once she was seeing Lady Chemerie and The Purest. Lady Chemerie smiled and both figures bowed their heads.

"Use it well, our Daughter," The Purest dragon said. Morgan felt her Crest warm and tingle as she spoke.

"Thank you for this gift, my Mothers."

Sleep eluded her most of the night as she considered all the Crest could mean for the future.

THE NEXT MORNING, Morgan woke to find her room filled with younglings while many older dragons looked on from her terrace and windows. She smiled as she sat up and the group around her all gave a long deep hum together. Their hum made her Crest glow and tingle, which made her shiver and giggle.

"Thank you, my friends. I am also very excited about this amazing gift. It will make me a better Caretaker for you all."

"Not possible, my Queen. You were already a wonderful Caretaker. But we are all grateful to the Council, as this will make our bond to you much stronger as we grow. We feel it is we who have received a gift, and we thank you for showing the strength of character necessary to have been entrusted with the Crest of the Dragon. We are both proud and grateful, my Queen," Falin said.

All of the dragons around her bowed and hummed again to give her a rush of great respect and love. The impact was very intense due to the new sensitivity her Crest imparted. She had tears filling her eyes in seconds.

She moved off the bed and knelt to hug and caress those nearest to her. The younglings shuffled around each other as all wanted to see the Crest up close. She moved among them and let each inspect it as she caressed them, then stepped onto the terrace to caress the larger Lirpa and Falin, before turning to Menkar.

"I feel your need to say something. What is it, my friend?"

"My Queen, the Council wishes you to join them. I am told to tell you to let your family know it could be a very long visit," Menkar said. She nodded to him and smiled back at the younglings around her.

"I must begin my training today, it seems. Thank you all for greeting me this morning. I will see you when I return, and we will all celebrate my union with Sir Alec." They all crooned or hummed as they filed out and flew off.

"So, how long is 'very long' would you expect, my friends?" she said as she headed to dress.

Menkar and Sirzi both chuckled at the question, making her move back to them with a raised eyebrow.

"The Elders take their time with most everything, my Queen. I would expect it to be a matter of hours. However, if there is a decision to be made, and they fail to agree on something, days could pass," Sirzi said. Morgan laughed as she stroked them both and leaned into Sirzi to hug her.

"Seriously though, my wedding is in six days, and I have done nothing to prepare for it. Should I assume I can return in time?"

"We really could not guess as we do not know what you will be doing, my Lady," Menkar said.

She nodded then felt silly for not asking Nulian herself to begin with. She dropped her guard a bit and thought of Nulian. To be respectful, she did not attempt to form a connection herself.

"Good day, my Queen. We ask that you begin your training today. We feel this is of the utmost importance," Nulian said.

"I am honored and will postpone my wedding as need be. I would ask if you believe a week delay is appropriate?" She hoped Nulian would see her willingness to change as a respectful gesture, and not be offended she was asking the length of time she would be gone.

"I do not think any delay would be necessary. We will make

sure you return in no more than five days, my Queen."

"Thank you. I will be with you soon, my Lady."

She thought of Alec, and connected to his sleeping mind with a gentle push of magic to wake him.

"I have to go away for a few days, my dear. I am sorry, but the Council has summoned me."

"A few days? What will you be doing that could take a few days?"

"I am not sure. I dare not question the Council, however," she said as she dressed.

"I will miss you. Can I perhaps get a small kiss of farewell before you leave?"

"If you make it to my chambers before Menkar and I depart, you might."

She smiled and giggled as she heard the sound of his bare feet slapping against the stone hallway. He came running into her chambers less than a minute later, panting and grinning.

"I made it. Any chance I get bonus points for speed?" he said as he reached for her waist.

"Yes, you may help me pack," she said as she stopped him with two stiff arms and a smile. "Could you find me a small bag, please?" She laughed and jumped out of his reach as he grabbed at her when she passed again.

He looked around her closets and came back with a shoulder pack large enough for a couple changes of clothes and some light food items. When she was ready to go, she turned to him with a sigh.

"On Earth, women spend months planning their wedding as they tend to every little detail. And the men usually have little to do with it. I have had no time to do any planning; should we postpone?"

Alec looked at her with a sweet smile and shook his head.

"Morgan, you are a Queen. You are not supposed to worry about details like that. I will handle anything that comes up. However, the matters of a royal wedding are far out of our hands, my dear. Traditions must be upheld after all."

Morgan saw that wicked grin creeping up his face again and did not think to raise her guard to avoid hearing his next thought.

"And finally, I will be able to touch and kiss and ..."

"Alec!" she said as she blushed. He blushed a bit, then scowled.

"I thought we agreed you would not hold my private thoughts against me, my dear."

"Yes, well, that does not mean I have to hear them out," she said as she picked up her bag and left the room.

He walked just behind her toward the garden lawn where Menkar was waiting. When she let him catch up, he slid his hand into hers. Both smiled but stayed quiet as they walked.

He loaded her bag onto Menkar's harness and patted his friend hard, for which he received a playful shove in return. His laugh quieted as he moved to her and took her hands. When he remained quiet, she dropped her guard to let him connect.

"I cannot apologize for my thoughts of wanting to be closer to you physically. I love you in every way of the heart, and very much want to love you in that way as well. Does that worry you? You must know I would never push you. I promised you that a long time ago, and marriage will not change my respect for you."

She shook her head and smiled as she answered him.

"I'm not worried, just embarrassed. I trust you to go at whatever

pace we find comfortable together. And I am also looking forward to not having any guidelines to follow when we are alone together."

She lifted to her tiptoes to kiss him and felt the familiar heat of their link rise very fast. They pushed back at the same time and found they were both breathing faster. They laughed at their flushed faces, and she again heard his thoughts by accident.

"Have mercy, if that much heat comes with just a kiss … "

She turned and raised her guard as she vaulted into the saddle, but still had a bright red face as Menkar lifted off.

"I will see you soon. I love you, handsome," she called as they took off. She waved and blew him a kiss as Menkar turned a fast swooping dive over his head before heading to the top of the mountains.

SHE WAS READY THIS TIME when Menkar tucked his wings to drop into the great crevice of the Council of Elders chambers. He landed and let her off, then nudged her with a deep croon before taking off again.

"You love me, yet you abandon me. Heartbreaker!"

She smiled and laughed as she felt his amusement and heard his chuckle echo around her.

"Come to me, my Queen," Nulian said.

With focus on Nulian's spirit, she let the magic direct her. She traveled through half a mile of dark tunnels before entering a huge cavern to find Nulian curled up in the middle of the room.

She noticed the shimmering lights dancing on the ceiling, but saw only a small inlet of natural light high above. Realizing the shimmering was due to reflection, she looked down to see the majority of the floor of this great cavern was a dark purple liquid.

"Are we taking a trip, Lady Nulian?"

"Yes. Come and sit near me, my Caretaker."

Morgan moved across the portal surface and sat down near her belly so she could see her face without having to wrench her neck too much.

"Tell me what you have noticed since receiving the power of our line."

"My ability to communicate through the magic is amazing. I ask that you help me control it, however. I am sending and receiving far more than I am comfortable with at the moment," she said. Nulian chuckled a lovely deep sound as she continued, "When I entered Alec's mind, I felt no resistance to reach full bonding, and was able to find the targeted experiences with ease. The darkness was disturbing at first, but then your gift responded. My strength multiplied, and I was able to overcome all I found within him."

"Do you understand that what you faced were mere memories, mental scarring, and not the true darkness that you will see in Harrick?"

She nodded, and Nulian urged her to continue.

"My ability to focus the healing was incredible. Before, I could not focus on the actual injury. With the magic being dissipated throughout the entire body, the effect was inefficient, and I was left completely spent. With your gift, I healed each specific wound with great efficiency, and was barely tired."

"Have you noticed nothing else, my Queen?" Nulian said. She dropped her head and hummed low in her throat, which made the scales of Morgan's Crest prickle. Morgan laughed and stroked them as she smiled at their glow.

"Oh, yes, I am amazed at the sensations I feel through them. And I definitely noticed their particular sensitivity to Alec's touch."

"Your mate is the reason I wanted you to come to me this week, my Queen. If you are to marry and consummate that marriage in six days, you must gain a great deal of control over your new gift. Without control, it will surely overwhelm you and ruin your week of isolation."

"Week of isolation? Like a honeymoon?"

"It is a tradition in Chemerie that the married couple be taken to a remote location where they are left alone together for one week, without any interruption. I am sure this is so they can perform their mating rituals in privacy, and with the utmost focus."

Morgan winced at the word "mating" and thought, *"What an awful term for something so beautiful."*

Nulian chuckled. Morgan winced again as her cheeks heated.

"My Lady, I am thankful for your training under any circumstances. I am especially thankful for your thoughtfulness for my marriage and honeymoon."

"If you are ready, my Queen, we shall begin," Nulian said as she started to sing a beautiful song. *"Close your eyes and think only of the song. Join in when you are ready."*

Morgan closed her eyes and listened until she found the beginning and end, then memorized the words. She began to sing along, repeating the song as an endless lullaby. The familiar feeling of the liquid level rising up her body began.

She had to concentrate hard to not stop humming when it neared her mouth and nose.

A second later, she smiled and took in a deep breath as a warm breeze brushed her face. When she opened her eyes, she found herself sitting on a large ledge cut into a rocky ridge. Her surroundings were completely foreign. They had traveled to another world, not Earth nor Erion, but a very different planet indeed.

She walked to the edge of the ledge to look down a great sheer rock face, then let her eyes slide up and over the striking landscape before her. The rivers flowed in great eroded canyons with high sheer cliffs around them. The plateaus of the highest ridges were smooth and bald from the wind whipping across them. And the majority of the land was covered with lush vegetation containing the largest trees she had ever seen.

As she looked across the landscape, she saw several huge dragons flying together far away over the forest.

"What is this place? It seems very old and has a very different feel to it."

"This is Berios, an ancestral home of dragons. It has been a sanctuary of the Elder dragons of Chemerie for centuries. Look at those dragons, and focus on them, please."

Morgan did so and recoiled, then shifted to look into Nulian's eyes.

"I feel your anger and understand it, young one," Nulian said. "You fear them because the dragons of their breed you have met are wicked due to their contact with the darkness of Arshek. But these dragons have never been to Erion. None except our Council of Elders has crossed over for hundreds of years."

Morgan's head filled with images of the many Arshek dragons attacking and killing her dragon brethren. She fought them back and tried to calm as she turned away.

"Why have you brought me here?"

"You need to feel the capability of our magic, which you now have full use of. It is easier to do that in a world that is not packed with thousands of human minds. Now, come and sit beside me again, please."

Morgan moved to her and sat down.

"Get comfortable, feel free to lean on me if you wish, my Queen."

Morgan put her hand on Nulian to support herself, and her heart raced as images flew through her mind. She lifted her hand with a jerk as one image grabbed her heart.

"Balia!" She turned to Nulian as tears filled her eyes. "I knew you were my mother's friend. Now, I learn you are the mother of my dearest friend as well. I loved Balia very much, she was precious to me."

"And you to her, my Queen. She shared much about you with me," Nulian said with a deep hum. She dropped her head to the ground beside Morgan and continued, "We may as well work on this now, or it will interrupt us all day. Place your hand back on my side, and do not pull back when you feel the rush of information."

Morgan did so and received the full lineage of Nulian, her parents, and before them as well as all her children and theirs.

"I get the most information about Balia. Is this because of my relationship with her, because I was just thinking of her, or for a reason having to do with you?"

"Because my heart was dwelling on her at the moment, I believe. But if you focus on another, you will see all of their lineage as far as it is related to me as well."

Morgan tried it and learned Sirzi's family connections, but no other details.

"Thank you for sharing that with me. I realize it is very personal."

"You saw a great deal very fast, did you not?"

"Yes."

"That is because of our blood connection. With others, you will have to know what you seek to get past two or three generations each way." She paused as she looked over the valley around them, then added, "You will also develop unique dragon abilities as our blood matures within you."

"Dragon abilities? Seriously?"

"Yes, you received my blood into your body, and that connected you to me and all dragons in a very different way than any before you. You will unquestionably have some of the unique abilities of the dragon develop as you grow stronger. Your eyesight is already changing. Did you not just focus on dragons flying more than five miles away well enough to discern their breed?"

Morgan glanced back toward the flying group and smiled.

"Awesome! What other abilities might I have?"

"We will have to wait and see, my Queen. It is for the magic to decide, not us," Nulian said with a chuckle. "Now, let us get to our main task for the next few days. You can not learn everything before your wedding, and this is essential." She laid her head on the ground in front of Morgan again and said, "Close your eyes and reach out with your magic.

You are capable of reaching further than your eyes can see, even now. Stretch out and seek all the dragons of this world."

"World? Surely she can't mean th——"

"She means exactly what she says, young Caretaker." Morgan's neck and cheeks flushed, but she held her tongue as she focused. "No, not their minds. Seek their spirit, their magical essence."

She redirected her magic that way. Pushing outward, she found nearly fifty dragons. Another push found only ten more. As she tried to push further, she felt Nulian's body shift beside her and received a rush of annoyance. She was afraid she had done something wrong, but opened her eyes to see Nulian glaring at two large Chemerian dragons landing near them on the ridge.

She reached out to their spirits and found them to be males and older than any she had met, even Drieden. They also had curiously similar spirits, nearly identical in every way. As they approached she realized they were larger than Nulian and were identical.

"Twins?"

"Indeed. And double the trouble for me."

"We felt a touch and thought we should introduce ourselves to our little sister's special new friend," the twins said. They alternated who spoke with each few words, but the cadence was perfect. Morgan's new knowledge of Nulian's lineage came forward and identified the two at once.

"I am Caretaker Morgan, and you must be Panish and Palish. I am honored to meet you both."

They exchanged a surprised look and broke into a raucous laughing fit. She had never seen or heard such a noise.

"They seem to be likable fellows at least," she said to Nulian, who had just snorted.

Nulian gave a grunt that Morgan took to be like, "Huh!" The twins stopped laughing as if slapped and looked to Nulian. Clearly, they were being reprimanded and Morgan was not part of the conversation.

They then turned to Morgan and bowed their heads.

"We apologize for the interruption, our Queen," they said in perfect unison. The twin dragons took to the air and disappeared into the dangerous looking cliffs below.

Morgan patted Nulian as she felt her emotions move from anger to regret. She must have been harsher than the moment warranted and now felt guilty for it.

"I will talk with the silly creatures later. Let's continue, please," Nulian said as she settled again. "How many did you find?"

"About sixty."

"About is not a number. Exactly how many spirits do you feel?"

She opened herself again and focused on the spirits of the dragons around her. As she found each unique spirit she counted it. This was difficult as many were in motion.

"I have found fifty-seven unique dragons, including you. How was that?"

"There are only fifty-six dragons, my Queen. But that was close," Nulian said with a note of disappointment.

Morgan frowned and closed her eyes to count again.

"Nulian, I do not mean to argue, but I counted fifty-seven again. What am I doing wrong?"

"Nothing at all, I was testing your willingness to accept

someone's word over your own perceptions. There are indeed fifty-seven dragon spirits around this world."

"It feels disrespectful to question my mentor."

"No, you must have the confidence to speak if you feel you are right. You were perfectly respectful in your manner. By the way, do you know how far you reached to find the last eleven in your count?"

"Forty or fifty miles perhaps? It was much further than I have ever reached before for certain."

"They are several days of flight from here on the opposite side of this small planet. You located every dragon on this world, my Queen."

"Are you serious? It took so little effort … that is amazing," she said as she jumped to her feet and started pacing. "Can I actually send and receive thoughts that far away? Will it work with people too?"

"Yes."

Morgan continued to pace as her mind raced through the possibilities, but soon stopped and her smile slipped.

"I see, I found all of them, every dragon, of every breed. So I can detect and communicate with the dragons of Arshek too."

"I could not let you open yourself there and feel them without warning. That is part of the reason we are training on Berios. The dragons of the Perian breed on Erion have been enslaved and forced to serve for fear of death or torture of their young. They are full of hatred, both for the people who enslave them and the dragons and people they are told will kill them given the chance."

"I felt no darkness in any I found here," Morgan said as she stopped and faced Nulian. "I know now is not the time, but please tell me, would it be possible to show the Perians of Erion the truth about us, and free them from that tortured life?"

Nulian took a deep breath and made a quiet rumbling hum as she gazed over the valley.

"That would be a wonderful thing. But, as you said, not a conversation for today," Nulian said as they both settled back down. "If you do this exercise on our planet, you will find every spirit, all dragons, and all people. You must be very careful. Without proper control, you will form a connection. Forming a connection to Harrick, or another strong in the dark magic, would be a dangerous mistake until you are ready. Right now, you have great ability, but not the knowledge to use it. I need you to understand how dangerous that is for you, my Caretaker."

"I respect the danger and will do whatever it takes to learn."

"Of that, I have little doubt," Nulian said as she pushed a warm rush of pride. "Let us begin. Find my twin brothers and listen to their thoughts, but do not let them detect you. Tell me what they are thinking at the moment."

Morgan found them and strengthened her focus on Panish.

"I feel you, my Queen. Sorry," Panish said. She tried again on Palish and failed, then sighed and dropped her head to rub her temples.

"Are you quitting?"

Morgan's head snapped up, and her eyes blazed the two seconds she looked at Nulian before closing them to focus again. She observed the twins' spirits for a long time from afar and approached carefully.

She considered how she had overheard others before. Realizing she had only been opening herself to hear rather than to speak, she listened to the twins with no thought of giving information. As she approached their spirits again, she started to hear a mumbled whisper, their voices grew louder as she eased ever closer to their spirits. At last, their words were clear. She listened a moment, then backed away from their conversation as if tiptoeing.

"I heard them and do not believe they detected me," she said with a smile.

"Tell me their words," Nulian said. The smile slipped from Morgan's face at once.

"Nulian, I really do not thi—" She stopped as annoyance and a loud snort rushed over her, then diverted her eyes. "One asked if the other thought you would mate again. The other said you were too grumpy for your mate to attempt it."

Nulian raised her head with a deep growl. *"They have no place discussing my mating habits. Meddlesome old wildlings,"* Nulian thought.

"That was never meant for you to hear, Nulian. Will you truly hold it against them?" She felt Nulian release some of her anger, then felt a fresh wave of annoyance.

"I did not intend for you to hear that. We must work on your manners."

Morgan frowned but did not speak while Nulian was so mad. The angry Elder looked out over the valley for a long moment before dropping her head with a soft croon.

"Forgive me, please. That was unkind and unfair. I am sorry, my Queen."

Morgan nodded and rubbed Nulian's snout to pass forgiveness. Through the contact she felt her sincere remorse.

"Shall we continue?" Nulian said.

Morgan's stomach was growling as she nodded again.

"Please try to hear my thoughts again. I will start out blocking very little then increase the resistance. Let us see where you are to start with."

"With or without contact?"

"We will do both. Start with no contact."

Morgan connected to Nulian with ease and heard her thoughts as she recited poetry in her mind. After a few seconds, she heard the volume fade, so she pushed harder.

They went through this for a long time, forcing Morgan to tap the new strength of her magic. They reached a point that even after five minutes of struggling she could not break through.

"Well done, my Queen," Nulian said as she pushed calming. "Ready to try it with contact?"

She held out her hands as Nulian scooted her head closer. The instant they touched she heard the poetry. Nulian progressed faster this time, blocking more quickly and with greater strength. She had no trouble until the last two increases and was surprised when Nulian lifted her head with a deep hum of approval.

"I can block no harder, my Queen. With contact, you will be able to take the thoughts from anyone. And your skill without contact is very near that level already. A surprise I admit."

Morgan smiled and glanced toward her bag.

"Eat when you are hungry, my Queen. I apologize for

forgetting the frequency with which you feed."

"Will you tell me more of what you will teach me while I eat?"

"First, I will take a moment for personal business. I will not go far. Connect if you need me," Nulian said as she walked to the edge of the cliff where she let her front claws and long neck hang over the edge. As she leapt into the air, Morgan heard, *"Now, where are my dear brothers?"*

Morgan smiled as she watched Nulian soar around in circles before shooting down. Unable to resist the urge, she found Panish again and approached his thoughts. She jumped when she heard him yell in panic at the approaching Nulian.

"What has you all excited, little sister? Hey careful, you almost bit me," Panish said. Morgan saw the three shoot up from the valley below and laughed aloud as she saw the more nimble Nulian giving a great chase after both of her older brothers for over five minutes. She nipped at their tails a couple of times each before pulling up and soaring above them.

"Keep your thoughts out of my affairs, Brothers, or next time the bites will be higher and deeper!"

Morgan raised her eyebrows at the threat and was a little worried until the twins rose to soar beneath her with light-hearted chuckles. Nulian joined their laughter as each of them nudged her neck and crooned before swooping off.

Nulian then disappeared behind a tall ridge. Morgan assumed she needed to use the forest's bathroom facilities. A few moments later, it was time to focus once more.

"My Queen, try to hear my thoughts again from a distance. Begin."

They went through the exercise a few minutes and found she was not affected by the distance much at all. Just as she had thought she could go no further, she heard Nulian say, *"Hello, my mate."*

She pulled her thoughts back and looked to the sky to find Nulian flying in close formation with a huge red and black dragon. They flew beside each other for a long time then began to dive at each other as if trying to knock the other out of the air.

She was about to connect and ask if Nulian was in trouble, but stopped when strong waves of desire emanated from her mentor.

After raising her guard to ensure she did not accidentally overhear them again, she watched the two dragons fly together. As the emotions of the dragons washed over her, she realized the swooping at each other was flirting. They did this for many minutes, then shot straight up and flew to the limits of her sight. At the top of their climb, the two dragons came together belly-to-belly with a harsh jolt, then wrapped their wings and tails around each other.

They began to free fall back toward the ground entangled together. Morgan took in a great breath and held it as she crawled to the cliff's edge to watch as they plunged toward the ground. She was about to scream as the two broke apart just in time to keep from crashing into the ground. Releasing the great breath with a rush, she watched the two soar together and felt the intense love between them as they approached her.

The reality of what she had just witnessed hit her, so she turned away and closed her mind as tight as she could with her back to the cavern.

At the sound of wings and a rush of air behind her, she turned and jumped as Nulian's booming voice vibrated the air around her.

"Do not shut me out, my Queen. I must be able to communicate with you to keep you safe!" Nulian said as she landed with a loud crash.

"I was trying to … " she tried to explain. She stopped when Nulian's mate landed beside her. She looked between them, hoping Nulian would get the point. Not only did she not get it, having her mate there did not keep her from continuing the scolding. Morgan took it in silence and held her face as placid as possible until the Elder finished.

"I was trying to respect your privacy, my Elder," she said before turning back around to search her bag for her water. She soon felt hot breath on her head and looked up to find the great head of Nulian's mate hovering above her.

"I am Gerzin, and I thank you for the gesture of respect, my Queen. Please, forgive my dear Nulian's temper. She was excited after the mating and grew very anxious when she could not reach you."

"Gerzin, I can speak for myself, thank you," Nulian said as she nipped at his neck and nudged him aside. He pushed her back hard with his broad chest and knocked her off her feet. They stared at each other with low growls a few seconds before Gerzin's growl turned to a deep hum. He rubbed his snout to Nulian's before taking to the air with a flourish. Nulian watched him go until he was completely out of sight.

She then turned to Morgan with a drooping head.

"I find myself asking for your forgiveness again, my

Queen, I ..." Morgan raised her hand to stop Nulian's apology and was a little surprised when it worked.

"Nulian, I still have much to learn about the habits of dragons. This was a result of my ignorance, so please do not worry about it. I am grateful for your concern and I did not mean to upset you." She walked to where Nulian still lay from being pushed by Gerzin and stroked her snout as she added, "And I do apologize for watching your time with him. I had no idea what I was intruding on until it was too late."

When Nulian chuckled, she backed up with a scowl.

"I am sorry to laugh. But please understand that dragons are not private with regard to our mating rituals. After all, we do it outside in plain sight of any who wish to observe. To us it is beautiful and natural and we are proud of our love for one another. You did not intrude and have nothing to apologize for, my Queen."

Morgan nodded then downed half of her bottle of water as she gazed over the valley again. They were both quiet as she finished her bread and cheese.

"Do you wish to continue with your training now, or would you like a break? Perhaps a swim?"

"I would love a swim. But, I brought no swimsuit."

"You are the only human on this world at the moment, my Queen. And the dragons do not care in the least if you are clothed or not," Nulian said as she rose and offered a palm.

She rode aboard the beautiful Elder dragon for the first time as she took in the ancient world of Berios. They landed beside a great clear water lake fed by a huge waterfall. After a moment of hesitation, she dove into the water and commenced with skinny-dipping for the first time in her life. The water was cool, but not too cold. She swam at a lazy pace for a while to warm her muscles, then put her head in and started to take hard, even strokes.

A great current of water pushed her to the side. When she opened her eyes she found Nulian swimming upside down beneath her, just like Balia had done. She smiled as she pushed friendship and gratitude.

After her long swim, she dressed and sat gazing at the huge waterfall.

"How does it feel?" Nulian asked.

Morgan did not understand the question until she realized she had been stroking her scales again.

"Wonderful. It calms me," she said. "Which is surprising when you consider the explosion of sensations Alec's kiss to them caused."

"I understand that sensation well. I have always been amazed at the difference in sensation at the touch of any other versus that of your true mate," Nulian said with a deep hum.

"So, the magic makes your partnerships special as well?"

"Yes, indeed. You know the first time you connect mentally, and when you finally do touch, it is wonderful. Was it not the same for you, my Queen?"

Morgan blushed a bit, but less than usual.

"Yes. The very first connection we had was before we laid eyes on each other. I had been taken hostage by a Marock and was calling out to the Knights of the Guard for help. He answered my call within connection, and it was like fireworks went off in my head. I was dizzy and grew warm all over. Anytime we are near one another it requires a conscious effort to keep the warm tingling sensations from getting out-of-hand and, like you said, when we touch it is something altogether different. I have had far less trouble controlling the sensations since receiving your gift. Well, the non-contact sensations that is. When he kissed me before I left, things went a little crazy in jus—" She stopped as she felt Nulian's surprise and looked up at her.

Nulian wore a confused expression, much like GranMay had.

"I realize my and Alec's connection is more intense than normal because of his magic. But which parts are not typical, exactly?"

"Most of what you described is far from expected. Normally, all physical sensation is limited to actual physical contact. When I said my mate and I knew from the first connection of minds, I was referring to the ease with which we connected and communicated. It is near impossible to keep my thoughts from Gerzin. I feel physical sensation only when he touches me. You are very fortunate, my Queen. Your bond to Sir Alec is quite unique indeed," Nulian said with a hint of jealousy behind her words. "I have a great deal of control to teach you, but it sounds like I may not be able to handle all of what you will face."

"I'm not so sure I can handle it either. But, I am definitely ready to try."

"Then let us get to it, my Queen," Nulian said with a chuckle as she moved closer and laid her head down again. "Put your palms to my hide. I am going to transfer strong emotions to you. You must suppress them as they climb higher in intensity. Begin."

Nulian did not start gently. She poured the sensations on hard and heavy.

Morgan was able to handle a great deal before becoming uncomfortable. She was sweating and trembling, but held her focus. Nulian soon held the intensity constant and varied the type of emotion. As she turned only to feelings of sadness and hatred, Morgan's guard broke.

She woke to Nulian's healing song and her snout against her stomach.

"Sorry," she said as she righted herself.

"No, you did very well. I was near my limit already, and you showed weakness only when the emotions were negative," Nulian said. Morgan looked shocked at this and moved to place her palms to Nulian again.

"Will you start near that point this time, please?"

The rush hit her and she was ready for it. She focused on deflecting the sensation away as if using an umbrella against rain. She pushed against it as hard as she could, concentrating on calming herself all the while. A moment later, Nulian pulled back her pressure and looked at her with intense eyes.

"I have never known any human to resist the effects of such powerful transfer. The magic is very strong within you and you wield it well, my Queen. Your experiences of suppressing the sensations you receive from Sir Alec have undoubtedly helped you develop such a strong skill."

"Then, is there no more you can teach me about controlling those sensations?"

"I cannot push any harder with the positive emotions, but we will address your weakness in resisting the harsh emotions. The practice itself will be valuable, I believe."

"What about hearing the private thoughts of others when I do not wish to? Can I learn to prevent that, or will I just have to learn not to react to it?"

"I will teach you to keep your guard up for self-protection most all the time. This will prevent much from getting to you without your seeking it. However, the thoughts of others that pertain to you or are associated with strong emotion will always be heard. That is a special part of your enhanced abilities. With that skill, you will rarely be deceived, my Queen."

Morgan sat quiet, looking at the ground in front of her. Nulian nudged her with a quiet hum.

"Not being deceived with lies or secrets will be great, but others may not see it that way. It is an intrusion, is it not?"

"Yes, it may feel that way. But remember that it is the way in which you use the information that is important. They need never know you heard if you do not wish it, my Lady."

"For that to work, I must learn to keep my emotions from showing on my face. That's not exactly a skill I've mastered."

"I agree, my Queen." Nulian looked at her expression with a chuckle. "My point exemplified."

Morgan laughed with her then failed to stifle a yawn.

"Are you ready to sleep, my Queen?"

She nodded and moved to her back.

"Will we go home for the night?"

"No, my Queen. I have a special surprise for you."

Morgan dozed during the long flight, then woke with a start as Nulian nudged her and almost pushed her off. She climbed into her waiting palm, then stood beside her.

She blinked to gain her focus and found she was standing on the terrace of a gorgeous stone gazebo built into the side of a rocky ridge. It was the size of her main chamber room, had a bed, a small table, and a small fountain fed by a natural spring.

"If there are no people here, then who built this and who uses it, Nulian?"

Nulian hummed, sending strong waves of pride as she answered.

"It was carved by dragons for Lady Chemerie herself, long ago. You are the first human to be brought here since that time, my Queen. I brought the new furnishings and linens this morning. Queen May helped to gather the materials. I am certain I baffled her with the requests, but she was kind enough to provide without a great deal of argument. Does it please you, my Caretaker?"

"Nulian, it is wonderful. You have honored me so deeply with the Crest and by bringing me here. How can I ever thank you enough?"

"Just use your skills well and continue to serve with the heart you have thus far, my Queen. Is there anything you need?"

"No, I'm fine. But are you not hungry yourself, my friend? Please, go and feed yourself. I am fine here."

While Nulian was gone, she put the fine linens on the bed and slipped into the beautiful nightshirt she found. She was brushing out her long hair when her Crest warmed, and she heard voices through the magic.

"Gracious! It is quite small, is it not? Is it a hatchling? Is it a male or a female? How can you tell anyway?"

"I do not know, but it is very pale. It looks sick. Maybe it is dying."

Morgan giggled to herself as she listened to the young-lings discuss their first human sighting. A few seconds later, she froze and raised her guard.

"Nulian, I am sorry to disturb you, my friend. But I seem to have company and am not sure I welcome it while alone."

"I am coming."

Morgan kept stroking the brush through her hair as she opened her reception with care to hear the Perian young-lings again.

"We should go, Brit! Mother will nip our tails off if she finds we are gone, and Father would probably kill us if he knew we were here."

"But Hirk, I would like to know what it smells like, wouldn't you? They say they smell sweet and their touch is like the belly of a new hatchling."

Morgan felt Nulian's anger as she approached.

"They are just curious younglings, do not terrify them ple——"

Nulian landed with a resounding crash and a vicious growl as she hung her head over the two younglings with her teeth bared. Morgan felt the fear from the younglings, and it made her heart ache.

"Nulian, please, they are terrified. I do not want them to fear me or my kind. Let me speak with them, please."

"I do not terrify them out of meanness. I do it to make sure they know just how wrong this was. They were told to stay away. If you wish to speak with them, then do so, my Lady," Nulian said as she stopped growling and lifted her head a few feet.

Morgan moved to the back of the gazebo and looked up at the two cowering younglings.

"Hello, young ones, I am Caretaker Morgan of Chemerie.

Please join me. I would love to meet you."

They looked up at Nulian to ask permission and Nulian nodded with a quiet warning growl. They did not fly. They climbed down the rocks in hops, staying close to the ground with care to give no hint of aggression as they glanced at Nulian every few feet.

When they reached the ledge of the gazebo, Morgan was waiting for them. As they moved closer, Nulian put her head right beside Morgan with her teeth pointing toward the younglings. They stopped in their tracks, then flinched back as Morgan took a step forward. She stopped and backed up two steps before speaking.

"I do not wish to scare you. If you want to go home, then please, go ahead. I only wanted to meet you. I have never known a dragon of your kind and have no idea how you smell."

"*What?*" Nulian said. Morgan struggled not to laugh.

The two younglings exchanged nervous glances. While one was ready to leave, the other one was too interested in her. She heard them bickering in thought and cut into their conversation.

"I will ask Nulian to be understanding, maybe even convince her not to tell your parents you came when you were not supposed to. I think if you were very nice and apologized for breaking the rules, she might listen to you. And if we were friends, and I asked her, she would surely do it for me."

"*That is a bold assumption indeed,*" Nulian said. Morgan suppressed another giggle and kept her face placid.

"May I approach you and see how you smell and perhaps how you feel?" she asked the Perian younglings. One of them turned as if to bolt off the cliff, but the other nipped at his wing and pulled him back. The bold one stepped toward her and bowed.

She bowed in return and heard Nulian grumble saying, *"Oh mercy!"*

"Be nice. They have no idea what I am. Their curiosity is as genuine as mine was the first time I saw a dragon."

She walked forward to the small dragon and reached out a hand to touch his head. He held very still with one eye on Nulian. As she drew her hand down his head with a light touch, he shivered all over.

"Hirk, it is softer than anything, even a new hatchling. Come here, you great coward," Brit said.

"Now Brit, that was not nice. If Hirk is afraid of me, then he should not approach. It is a smart thing to follow your instincts."

Both young dragons looked stunned that she knew their names. Whether it was this suggestion of familiarity or the goading of his brother, she wasn't sure, but the smaller Hirk stepped up to her and stuck out his head as if to a guillotine.

She smiled and stroked his head. He also shivered, then both raised their snouts toward her hand only to pull back at Nulian's low growl.

"I feel no malice in them, do you?" Morgan asked her. When Nulian did not answer, she reached out to them and let each sniff her hands.

"So, what do I smell like to you? How will you describe it to your friends?"

One said, "flowers" and the other said, "fruit." She was glad they did not say something bad or Nulian would have lost it for sure. Both nudged her hand with their heads and she stroked each of them across the bridge of their snouts with a laugh as they shivered and crooned.

"It was very nice to meet you, young ones. I hope I will see you again while I am here. But before you go … " she knelt and dropped her voice, "you should address Lady Nulian very respectfully and beg forgiveness."

She stepped back and watched the two young dragons practically crawl toward Nulian then stop short and bow their heads.

"Please, Lady Nulian, will you forgive us and not tell our parents we intruded. We only wanted to see a human and see what it smelled like and felt like," they said in a nervous babble of trading words. Morgan stood behind them and made a very pitiful face to tease Nulian.

Nulian stood and held her head over them for a long time, then hummed as she dropped her snout to them. They raised their heads and rubbed their snouts to hers before running and launching off the cliff to head for home.

Morgan felt her heart lift as she watched the great Chemerian dragon caress the little Perians. She felt the love Nulian had for them and knew that image would never leave her.

"I am sorry for giving you advice on how to deal with a youngling. It was wrong and rude," she said.

"I was not offended. I trust you with my own children, so why would I not respect your opinion? I was only afraid they would hurt you accidentally. They have never been around so fragile a species before, my Queen."

I am not fragile!

She smiled as she found she had blocked Nulian from hearing her at last.

Nulian crooned and pushed trust and friendship as she nudged her back toward the gazebo. She snuggled under the heavy comforter and breathed in the crisp cool air.

This is perfect . . . well, not quite . . .

"Not without your mate beside you, it is not quite perfect," Nulian finished for her. She smiled and did not argue since that was exactly what she had been thinking. Of course, she had believed she was speaking to only herself as usual.

A FORMAL DISCUSSION between Nulian and another female dragon woke Morgan early the next morning. The female was the mother of Hirk and Brit. She had smelled Morgan on them when she woke them.

"The Caretaker was not troubled, my friend. She has a great love of dragons and is quite gifted with interacting with young-lings. She enjoyed meeting your sons a great deal. She has never interacted with Perian dragons before, having only seen the horrible representation of your species on our world."

The other female dragon growled. Morgan felt her anger, but knew it was not directed at Nulian.

"I ask to meet your Caretaker, Lady Nulian. I would like to show her that my breed is much more than she has seen thus far," the female Perian said.

"I would like the opportunity if you think it appropriate," Morgan said to Nulian alone.

"My Queen, you may speak to whomever you wish. But I appreciate the gesture of respect. And by the way, that was very good listening. I did not feel your presence at all," Nulian said.

Morgan sat up and saw the two dragons were sitting to her right on a large rock shelf. She found the female Perian dragon to present a very different mystique than those on Erion.

This regal female was beautiful. The horns did give a more aggressive front at first, but her eyes were gentle. She could still picture the eyes of the Arshek dragons that attacked the Ancestral Lair and saw none of their hatred and rage in this gorgeous dragon.

When she removed her nightshirt to dress in her day clothes, she heard the Perian female gasp.

"Goodness, she is quite pale. Is she ill, Lady Nulian?" the Perian female asked.

Morgan heard Nulian's chuckle and joined in as she finished dressing. She grabbed some bread, cheese, and water and headed to where the two lovely females were waiting. Nulian held her palm out, but Morgan did not climb in.

Instead, she laid her food in Nulian's palm and walked closer to the head of the Perian dragon where she bowed politely.

"Good morning, my Lady. I am Caretaker Morgan of Chemerie. It is a pleasure to meet you."

"It is an honor to meet you as well," the Perian said with a bow. "Allow me to formally apologize for my sons' impropriety in visiting you, my Lady. It will not happen again, I assure you."

"I would consider it a great loss if you were to keep them from visiting me again, my Lady. I understand your annoyance that they broke rules, but please consider allowing me the opportunity to spend more time with them. I am interested in knowing dragons of your magnificent breed."

"My Lady, I expected you to feel animosity or perhaps rage toward my breed, given the awful representation Nulian tells me you have witnessed. I do not understand your kindness, but am honored to have received it."

Morgan felt her surprise, and something else.

"When I touched your children last night, I felt no malice in them. They have beautiful spirits full of kindness and respect for others. That is how I am able to trust you. I chose to believe their mother was of like spirit, my Lady."

The Perian female bowed her head again and hummed. Her hum was different from Nulian's and sent a distinctly different sensation. It was very pleasant, and she smiled at the rush of respect and thanks she felt.

"May I ask your name, my new friend?"

"I am Asira, my Lady. And may I ask to approach closer to you?"

Morgan stepped forward and raised her hand toward the great dragon. Asira dropped her head and moved forward.

"Do be careful, my friend. They are quite fragile," Nulian said.

"I really do not like the sound of that. I am not fragile," Morgan said to Nulian.

"You are indeed a strong woman, my Queen, but still far more fragile than a youngling dragon your same size. I mean no disrespect, my Caretaker."

Morgan held her face passive even through that comment, a feat she was quite proud of.

Asira stopped a few feet from her and went still, so she closed the gap herself. She stepped to the head of the massive dragon and stroked her cheek. Asira trembled much like her sons had.

"I am thankful to have met you, Asira. I hope we will

become strong friends," she said.

"It is I who am honored by your trust. I am ashamed to think of the opinion you had of my honorable breed," Asira said with a hum.

Morgan held her hand still against Asira and sent her a feeling of trust and friendship as answer. The dragon flinched back at the sensation.

"I apologize if I offended you," Morgan said as she stepped back.

"No, my Lady, I just … I have never felt such a sensation before. It is unlike anything I have experienced."

"I too could feel a distinct difference between your emotional transfers and those of the Chemerian dragons."

"Asira has never touched a human before, much less a Caretaker with the gifts you now have," Nulian explained.

When Asira dropped her head again, Morgan placed both of her hands on her head and connected to her. A distinct difference in their magic was clear, yet it flowed together smoothly. She shared the strongest feelings of friendship she could and received the same in return.

Asira gave a great tremble through her whole body and hummed as they broke the connection. Nulian chuckled, and they all shared a warm smile as the magic flowed between them.

"Now you see why The Purest initiated our partnership with our human brethren. The magic is magnified in wonderful ways through the connection of our spirits," Nulian said.

"It is truly remarkable. I am grateful to have experienced even a hint of it, my Lady. Thank you very much," Asira said.

ASIRA STAYED WITH THEM for much of the day. She assisted in Morgan's training by trying to enter her thoughts as she carried on a conversation with Nulian.

At first, she was not helpful because she was hesitant. But Nulian chided her for being weak-minded, and Asira held back no more. Morgan found the trials very difficult, but was proud of the progress she had made by lunchtime.

Nulian suggested a midday swim while the sun was warm, and flew to the beautiful lake again. Morgan entered the water in grand fashion by leaping from Nulian's back as she flew low over the lake.

Predictably, she was reprimanded at length for scaring the Elder to near death. Once she was allowed to reenter the water, she swam with enthusiasm. As she swam toward the waterfall, she felt Brit and Hirk hiding atop a nearby ridge watching her.

After a bit of persuasion, Asira agreed to let them join her. But not before making the younglings land before Nulian to ask permission and receive another lecture about how fragile she was.

The two younglings shot into the water as soon as they were allowed. She played tag with them for a bit and marveled at their acrobatics as they shot up out of the water.

Their stunts gave her an idea. She huddled close to them to make a daring plan. Soon she was being catapulted up out of the water while she clung to their hind legs, then released to splash back into the water. It was great fun. She turned flips in the air or dove from high above to cut smoothly back into the water. She loved the freedom of it but stopped after only a few moments when she felt Nulian's tension rising to a dangerous level.

"I am fine. I am not too fragile to have fun, my friend," she said with a smile to Nulian.

Nulian leaned down and nudged her with a little snort.

"I respect your bravery, my Queen. But I am troubled with the way you risk yourself playing such foolish games. One wrong move by the younglings, and you could have been injured or killed. It is an irresponsible risk to take, my Caretaker."

"Nulian, I do not mean to worry you. However, I must live my life and not hide in fear of losing it all the time, or I will go mad. I have spent so much time since coming to Chemerie worrying about staying alive long enough to have a daughter, that I have barely taken time to live my own life with joy." She stopped herself as Nulian frowned and realized her voice had risen. "I'm sorry. That was very disrespectful. Excuse me, please."

She turned around and walked alone beside the lake's edge as she raised her guard to keep her thoughts to herself. As she walked and forced herself to calm, she realized she was being childish and selfish. She had a duty. While she had not had a few years to just be herself as an adult, she could not ignore her responsibilities. Nulian was right. She should not risk herself when her life meant so much to so many. She turned to speak to Nulian and found she was alone.

She looked all through the sky and reached out with her magic to find Nulian miles away. Nulian had her guard up, so Morgan closed her eyes and focused hard. She pushed against Nulian's guard with all her might and finally heard Nulian's voice. Her heart ached as she heard her words to Asira.

"Drieden calls me. The castle of Chemerie has been attacked by the forces of Lord Harrick. I ask that you protect my Queen while I am gone. Do not let her return until you hear from one of our Council. I must return and fight to protect our castle and the Queen's family. Tell her I am very sorry for leaving without a word. But I have no time to explain, and did not wish to argue with her. She is very brave and will not appreciate staying here away from the battle. She must live, Asira, for all our sakes. She is the key to our future."

When she heard Nulian begin singing to activate the portal she pushed hard to breach her guard enough to speak.

"Fight well, Nulian. And return to me safely, my friend."

"I fight for you, my Queen, with all I have. I will return."

Morgan dropped to her knees and slammed her fists into the ground. She felt the ground shudder as Asira landed and shuffled forward.

"Are you hurt, my Lady? Has something happened to you?"

"I heard Nulian's words. I know she has gone to fight and has chosen to leave me here. I cry from worry for my brethren and anger for my own uselessness."

Expectations

"MY LADY, I must tell you something at the risk of angering my friend Nulian. Do you understand everything she means when she says you are the key to our future?" Asira said to Morgan, who was still pacing the lawn beside the lake an hour after Nulian had left.

"I believe so. I have great skill with the magic and have been given the Crest of the Dragon to fight the dark magic of Arshek. Which is exactly why I should be there fighting along with my brethren right now!"

"It is much more than that, my Lady. You are our only hope for a new world in which Perian and Chemerian live together alongside humans. You are the first to be strong enough to handle the Crest and its power since Lady Chemerie herself. Through you, we hope to see the magic restored to that seen in the days of The Purest.

"Since that time, the magic has weakened so much among humans that only the Caretaker line still has the ability to use it. The Chemerian dragons' magic has also weakened over the years. It has suffered without the deep bond to people.

"The Perian dragons who have lived here have survived without the link to people, and our magic is far weaker than it could be if we had that connection. We hope to feel that connection ourselves one day. We also hope you will be able to reach out to the tortured Perian dragons on your world and guide them out of the darkness and into freedom.

"It is through the strength of magic within you that all these things become possible again. You will help all humans feel the connection to the dragons again. My Lady, our protection of you is protection of our own future."

Morgan stared with no expression for a long moment before looking away and swallowing hard as she gazed over the water.

"I am not only responsible for continuing the Caretaker line and using my personal gifts to defeat Lord Harrick. I am also meant to turn the murderous and tortured Perian dragons of Erion to serve alongside the Chemerian dragons, and…I must revitalize the magic of Lady Chemerie and The Purest throughout all humans and all dragons of all breeds. Does that about sum it up?"

"In a broad and general sense, yes. I believe so, my Lady," Asira said. She then added, "Your children will all carry the Crest as well, my friend. Their power will reinforce yours and make all of your tasks easier."

Morgan dropped her head to her hands and focused to stay calm as the weight of this hit her. She sat in silence, staring at the lake and falls for almost an hour as her mind raced over all Asira had said. Her thoughts returned to the war going on at home, and the dragon battle likely occurring.

"Why have the Perian dragons of Berios not gone to Erion to fight alongside the Chemerian dragons? Surely, with all the numbers, you would be guaranteed victory."

"We have been asked to stay away from your world because we are so susceptible to the dark magic. It was born of a bonding of one of our breed with Arshek. My brethren who have lived here do not have that hate within them. However, we fear it will consume us if we are near it. I am ashamed to have to give you this answer. It makes us seem like great cowards, I am sure."

Morgan stood and went to stroke her neck.

"No, I do not think you are a coward. You are acting to protect the integrity of your breed. I understand your worry. I am quite familiar with the result of your breed being influenced by the dark magic," she said as she thought of Balia and all the others they lost that year.

MORGAN PACED the lakeshore for hours more before asking Asira to carry her to the gazebo. Asira was in no way fond of the idea. She was terrified she would drop her or crush her in her hand. Morgan suggested that she could hold on tightly to the spikes along her back. Asira only consented when Brit volunteered to cover Morgan with his wings while clinging tightly to his mother's hide with his talons.

Once back in the Gazebo, Morgan ate a little to relieve the pain in her stomach, then curled up against the headboard wrapped in the comforter. There was no expectation to sleep. She sat thinking for hours. Though thankful to know, she understood why Nulian had not told her all Asira had. It literally felt like a heavy weight on her chest.

To calm her mind, she closed her eyes and hummed a favorite song she had learned from Balia. She thought of her friend and wondered how much of this she had known. Did only the Elders understand this, or was it known to all Chemerian dragons? She thought of how the Council had asked her to exclude Menkar and reasoned that it was only fully understood by the Council of Elders themselves.

"Shall I sing to you, my Lady? I would like to help you relax if possible," Asira said.

"Thank you, that would be nice," she said as she settled a bit deeper into the comforter.

Asira's songs were different from those of the Chemerian dragons as well. They had a tendency to change tempo from time to time. As she focused on the words and harmony of the song, she felt as though she were the dragon of the song flying over the fields and lakes below them. The songs were wonderful, and she did relax, but sleep was impossible.

"COME TO ME, my Queen, I need you!"

Morgan shot from the bed as she felt Nulian connect and flinched as the dragon's pain hit her. She leapt down the steps and ran toward Asira.

"To the portal, please! Nulian is injured and needs me."

Asira did not argue as she vaulted from her palm to her back.

"I am coming, my friend. Try to relax. You gave me great power, and I will have you feeling better very soon," she said to

Nulian. She felt her anxiety and then sensed what she was so upset about.

Not only was she hurt badly herself, she also had Sirzi and another younger female with her. The two younger dragons were very near death, which is why she had not sensed them sooner.

She shared the urgency with Asira through contact and the dragon put on a great burst of speed. Lying down low to her hide, she wrapped her arms around the large spike in front of her and closed her eyes to the ripping wind.

As they flew, she concentrated on the younger dragons and sent them the strongest rush of loving support she could. Sirzi was far too weak to answer in words, but did send a sweet brush of gratitude.

When they landed, Nulian moved aside so she could get to Sirzi. She dropped to her knees in front of the huge gashes along Sirzi's neck and chest. After examining them a few seconds, she closed her eyes and placed her hands together to let her magic build and focus. She did not rush because she knew she must be frugal with her energy to heal the horrible wounds on all three dragons.

She placed her hands on Sirzi's chest across one of the largest gouges and let the magic flow through her. Her Crest tingled and grew warm as her hands, eyes, and Crest glowed. Pulsating waves of energy began to move from the Crest outward through her as she worked.

She moved over Sirzi's neck and chest as quickly as she could, yet still be thorough. Her friend's breathing deepened and became regular as she finished knitting the wounds together. She stopped there, leaving Sirzi to regain her strength through rest.

Next, she turned to the minor female who had a very deep gash along her back, revealing many broken ribs. She focused to mend the bones and close the wound. When she felt the minor female was also stable, she turned to Nulian.

The great dragon's head was hanging over the back of Asira who had lain down beside her and was now humming a healing tune to help as she could. Morgan smiled at Asira as she moved to inspect Nulian's wounds.

"Please keep going, Asira. I can use your energy to do this faster," she said as she moved to the largest wound on the lowest extreme of Nulian's belly.

She was shaken by what she found. The wound had cut through Nulian's egg sack and exposed four small, barely developed eggs. The damage was severe and the eggs could not be saved. She gathered herself as she removed and placed them on the ground with care, then focused on healing the great wounds. She found them very difficult to mend, as there was a great deal of ripping and tearing as well as missing tissue.

She worked for many minutes without stopping. When she finished, she moved to Nulian's head and sat beside her. Though very tired, she was not exhausted as she had become before receiving the Crest. She closed her eyes to rest for a moment, then felt a surge of energy. Brit and Hirk had come to sit beside their mother. Morgan smiled as they nuzzled her and hummed their healing song.

The younglings were worried, so she sent back feelings of assurance to them. She laid her hand on Nulian's snout and gave the dragon her energy until she woke and opened her eyes. As Nulian shifted to a more comfortable position, Morgan leaned back against Asira's side with a smile.

"Hello, my Queen. I told you I would come back to you," Nulian said. They all shared a relieved laugh together.

MORGAN LEARNED that the fighting still continued, but was encouraged to know that the Chemerian forces had driven the Arshek militia back beyond their borders and expected their retreat anytime.

Nulian told her of how bravely Daniel, Maric, and Alec were leading the Guard and the volunteer army of citizens. She viewed scenes from Nulian's memory of the battle's progress, flinching at the images of Sirzi and Nulian crashing into the enraged Arshek dragons.

After a moment of viewing, she opened her eyes and stared at Nulian as she let her anger pass through their touch.

"You risk yourself to give mercy where it is not deserved. They are Arshek's servants, not the noble Perian dragons of this world. They want nothing more than to kill you! Why do you risk yourself to only wound and force withdrawal?"

Nulian lifted her head and turned away. Morgan cursed under her breath as she crawled over Nulian's legs and climbed up onto her back to look her in the eye.

"Asira explained the hope that I can one day bring those dragons back to an honorable path. I could understand your hesitance if that hope were actually within our reach at the moment, but it is not. Nulian, you lectured me on the importance of keeping myself safe. Well I would say the same to you. I need you! If you die, who will teach me? Who will guide me?" she said as her eyes brimmed with tears.

Nulian put her snout against her chest and hummed a deep croon. Morgan felt the rush of love as she laid her head against hers. Tears soaked her face as she shared magic with her friend.

"I need you to promise not to risk yourself so. I will make the same promise to you, my friend. I do not want to lose you as I lost Balia. My heart could not take it, my Sister."

She and Nulian sat quiet for many minutes, each resting and sharing loving feelings.

"Nulian, I trust you to keep me away while it is too dangerous to risk returning. But I ask that you please let me go back as soon as possible so I may care for the injured. My heart is breaking at the thought of their suffering when I could take their pain away."

"I have asked Drieden to send word as soon as the castle is secure. I will take you back then, my Queen. I understand your pain and frustration at being held back, and promise to never hold you back longer than is necessary to assure your safety. This place will be your sanctuary from now on. When danger comes to our country, you will be brought here," Nulian said.

With a nod she moved to Sirzi and placed her hands on her hide again. She passed energy, but was too weak to wake her.

"Come, my Caretaker, let me take you to rest. You will need your strength to help our brethren back home," Nulian said. "Asira will stay and watch over them."

Morgan did not rise. She looked to Asira and then to Sirzi.

"Does Sirzi know of the gentleness of the Perian dragons here? Will she attack Asira when she wakes?"

"Share your feelings of Asira with both of the young ones. They will trust you and not harm her," Nulian said. Morgan did so before rising to climb aboard Nulian's palm.

She flew with Nulian the long way back to the gazebo, thinking of all she had learned in the past two days.

"Asira said all of my children could bear the Crest and its power as well. She said that they would help me bring the magic back to its original strength. If I interpret her words correctly, my children are meant to stay with me now. Is that true, Nulian?"

"Yes, my Queen. You will not be separated from your husband or children. This will be their sanctuary as well and they will be safe here," Nulian said.

Morgan felt all the tension leave her body as she took a deep breath. She relished the knowledge that she would never have to let Alec go and they would raise their children together in Chemerie and here on this beautiful world.

Nulian grumbled, and her disappointment washed over Morgan.

"What troubles you about that? Are you not pleased for me?"

"I am very pleased for you, my Queen. I am just quite disappointed in not being able to tell you myself. I had been saving the news for when you became pregnant the first time. I had looked forward to giving you that knowledge with great joy."

"Do not be angry with Asira, she did what she felt was right to help."

"I know. I am just disappointed, my Queen."

"Besides, I still have hundreds of questions. I imagine you will not feel so disappointed after answering the first few dozen."

Nulian chuckled as they landed beside the gazebo and Morgan slid to the ground.

"You should return to Sirzi to comfort her. We can ask Asira to come sleep near me."

"No, Gerzin has just returned and will sit with her. Besides, she is healed and will come when she wakes. I wish to be with you," Nulian said as she settled down next to the gazebo.

"And I am very glad that is the case, my friend. Thank you."

Nulian noticed her begin rubbing her Crest as it glowed and felt her heartache rising as a tear slid down her cheek.

"Tell me what pains you, my friend," Nulian said.

"I was able to heal three great dragons of horrible wounds and had more to give. I only wish I could have had the Crest earlier so…"

Nulian crooned to send love and understanding as she nudged her gently toward the bed. She fell atop the bed without undressing and was asleep in seconds.

SHE WOKE hours later to find Nulian curled around Sirzi near the gazebo. She watched the two for many moments and felt something very new stir within her. It was a longing for the bond the two dragons shared, the bond of mother and child.

After bathing off a bit and changing clothes, she headed toward them.

"Thank you for healing my precious mate and our daughter, my Queen. I am very grateful," Gerzin said. *"May I help you in any way while they continue to sleep?"* She found him standing

tall at the top of a ridge about four miles away. He bowed when she spotted him.

"I am a bit hungry and have run out of food. Do you know where any fruit trees are by chance?"

Gerzin dove for the forest and returned with an entire limb of an apple tree grasped in his talons. He set the limb beside her and flew back to his perch atop the ridge.

She sat on the gazebo wall, looking across the valley and her dragon friends, while eating two wonderful apples. To practice her new skills, she opened herself and located all of the dragons of this world. She followed their movements while eavesdropping a bit.

While checking the health of the minor Chemerian female, she felt a new spirit appear. It was Drieden. He was on the portal and very weak. She felt no major injury, but many minor wounds. His weakness was pure exhaustion.

"I will come to you, my Elder. Please rest there," she told Drieden. Changing connection to Gerzin she asked, *"Gerzin, will you carry me to the portal so I may help Drieden?"*

"I mean no disrespect in refusing but would not dare take you from Nulian's side. She will not mind your waking her, my Caretaker," Gerzin said.

"Nulian, wake, my friend. I need your help," she said as she stroked Nulian's cheek with a push of love and devotion.

"How may I help you, my Queen?" Nulian said with a yawn.

She explained about Drieden and Nulian eased away from Sirzi to stand. They traveled to Drieden at a quick pace. Nulian reached out to him as they approached the ledge.

"We are here, my friend. The Caretaker will return your strength

very soon," Nulian said. Drieden responded with the bravery and determined spirit Morgan had seen in his son.

"I am fine. There are others that need her at home."

When they landed Morgan moved to him and laid her hands over the largest wound. She focused the magic on the wound and closed her eyes as she healed it and the worst of the rest. Before removing her hands she sent the Elder a burst of strength as well.

"I would never leave you to suffer like that. There are none more deserving than you, Drieden." She turned to Nulian and said, "Shall we go then?"

Nulian looked to Drieden and he nodded saying, "The castle is secure."

Drieden moved out of the circle of purple liquid and stood looking out over the valley as Nulian settled herself beside Morgan.

"Rest, my friend. Then return to us at home," Nulian said to Drieden as she nudged him.

Nulian and Morgan sang the melody to activate the portal and soon found themselves in the cave of the Council Chambers. The instant they emerged, Morgan gasped and grabbed her stomach. She was hit by a great deal of pain and lost her breakfast at once.

"Close yourself off, my Queen. Quickly now," Nulian said.

Morgan concentrated to do so and the nausea subsided as her guard rose. She forced deep breaths as Nulian placed her on her back to move through the caves toward the main cavern.

"I am sorry, I should have anticipated that. Your perception of emotions is strong, and there is a great deal more emotion flowing here than on the ancient planet, especially now. Are you feeling better?"

"I'm fine. I need to drop it enough to assess the injured. I will be careful."

She focused herself and reached out to find the dragons and people of Chemerie. She found most of the wounded had been brought to the main courtyard of the castle. She told Nulian as they flew up the steep chamber and out the top of the great crevice.

As they cleared the crevice and soared over the craggy cliffs, she found a dragon many miles to the east that was suffering great pain as it lie dying alone. As she approached its mind she felt rage and found it to be a Perian dragon of Arshek.

Using the new skills Nulian had taught her, she listened to the Perian's thoughts without being detected. The dragon was cursing Harrick for leaving her to die, and reaching out to her children to say goodbye. Morgan could not stand the anguish and backed away from her. After surveying the wounded at the castle she found none so injured as the lone Arshek dragon.

"Please turn to the east, my friend, and drop low to the ground. There is a badly injured dragon that needs me more than those at the castle," she said. Morgan knew Nulian was searching for the dragon she spoke of and was not surprised when her mentor made no change of course.

"I cannot do that, my Queen. It is far too dangerous for you."

"Nulian, I believe in the purity of the spirit within that Perian dragon, as do you. She is dying and is in great pain. I am the only hope she has for life, or at least a painless death. We may gain her

trust as a result of a merciful act. Please Nulian, you can hold her down while I heal her. We can take another to help you."

Nulian grumbled loudly and rattled Morgan to the bone. She took that as a "No" until she saw Menkar rise to fall in with Nulian as she banked to the east.

"You will stay away from the wounded female until I call you to approach. Agree to this or we turn back now," Nulian said.

"I will follow your orders, my friend, I promise you."

Nulian landed about a mile from the Arshek female, and Menkar settled beside them. Morgan jumped to his back then watched Nulian take to the air again as she listened to the thoughts of both the females and tried to relax herself.

She heard the Arshek dragon roar at the sight of Nulian and felt its fear rise when she landed. The female Arshek tried to stand but could not. She snarled and hissed as Nulian moved closer.

"You great coward! Have you come to finish me off?"

"No. I come to offer you mercy."

The Arshek dragon laughed through blood-filled lungs and said, "Mercy? How, by killing me quickly?"

"It is not my mercy I offer, it is that of my Queen and Caretaker. She wishes to heal your wounds." The Arshek dragon continued to growl low. "Will you allow my Caretaker to heal you without fight?"

The Arshek dragon still did not answer beyond a growl. The wounded dragon coughed hoarsely and dropped its head a few feet as it weakened further.

"I do not think you have a better option, do you? Would you rather die and leave your children in the hands of Harrick without you there to protect them?"

This brought a great roar and lurch from the Arshek dragon. The exertion and pain of her attempt to stand were too much, and she fell unconscious, landing hard on the ground. Nulian moved to place her front feet across the Perian's neck and called Menkar to bring Morgan.

Menkar came to assist Nulian in securing the female, while Morgan stood at its back and looked to Nulian before starting her work. Nulian was squeezing the Perians neck, and Morgan felt a great surge of rage within her.

"What about the darkness poisoning her? Will it be a factor during healing?" she asked.

"You must focus to give only. Allow no reception from her," Nulian said as she loosened her grip a bit and glanced her way.

Morgan walked around the dragon's body and eyed the worst of the wounds. The worst were along her sides. She had been grabbed from above and the Chemerian had sunk in its talons. She approached the dragon from its back rather than its belly to avoid the reach of its hind claws.

She placed her hands together and focused her healing energy, thinking of the specific wounds she wished to heal before placing her palms to the wounded dragon.

When she finished with the side she could see, she asked Nulian and Menkar to turn her over. When they did so, the female woke and began to thrash against Nulian and Menkar. They held her still, but Morgan stayed back.

"Do you not feel better from the healing thus far?" she yelled aloud. The Arshek dragon stopped her thrashing while still holding herself very tense. "I am going to finish the healing of your largest wounds. My friends will not let you harm me, but I would appreciate it if you did not try. It will take more energy for me to focus if you are fighting me." She did not expect or wait for a reply and stepped up to place her hands beside the great wounds of the dragon's exposed side.

She pushed hard and felt the dragon relax a little as she finished the healing of her worst wounds. Before lifting her hands away she pushed a burst of magic and information. Keeping herself well out of reach, she circled around to her head.

"I have healed you simply because I cannot stand to see a dragon suffer if I can help them. I do this knowing you would kill me if my friends allowed it. I hope that you give that some consideration in the days to come." She had noticed the dragon looked from her to Nulian with a different scowl as she spoke.

"Yes, I said friend, and I meant it. I serve my dragon kindred, and they serve me. There is no imposing of wills by either side. We work together because we love one another. If you doubt my genuine affection for my friends, look within yourself at the feeling I have given you concerning this dragon," she said as she gestured to Nulian. She then turned to walk further away from the female.

Menkar released the female and flew to pick her up in a fluid movement. Their movements were well choreographed as their thoughts were transferred with no delay now.

As they flew above Nulian and the Arshek female, she heard Nulian's warning.

"My Caretaker has shown you great mercy and saved your life. If you choose to dishonor her by attacking when I release, I will show you no mercy, I promise you." She let go of the Perian's neck and backed away in a defensive posture before bowing her head a little and taking to the air again.

The Arshek female did not attempt to get up or make any aggressive move of any kind. That alone was a victory in Morgan's opinion.

As they flew back to the castle, Nulian rose to fly well above Morgan and Menkar. Morgan was concerned as she felt the anguish and sorrowful guilt building within her mentor.

"I do not understand how Nulian could have shown such mercy to that Arshek dragon knowing it had taken the life of one of her young," Menkar said.

"Which of her young did it kill today?"

"None today, my Lady. That was the one who struck the last blows to Balia before I and the other males arrived to drive them away."

Morgan felt instantly sick again and slumped forward onto Menkar as she fought the nausea and the guilt causing it. She did not know what to say to Nulian. She had asked so much of her friend unknowingly. Nulian was truly an honorable spirit. She gave mercy to the one she was least likely to ever forgive.

AS SOON AS SHE LANDED Morgan started to heal all she could. She kept her focus and acted in a conservative manner, healing all the major wounds first, before going back through and finishing the healing of the remaining smaller wounds. She spoke with no one as she worked.

As she finished healing the last dragon in need, she turned, smiling as Alec came to hug her. She felt his pain from the wound on his arm and healed it as she held him. He squeezed her tighter as the pain left him.

"That was amazing, my dear. You saved so many in such a short time. Are you very tired?"

"A little, but I will be fine," she said as she turned her gaze to Nulian. She saw her lying in a tight ball, alone, near the far wall. Alec gave her a light kiss and a nudge toward Nulian. She went straight to Nulian's head and leaned into her.

"I am so sorry. I would not have asked had I known. Thank you, my dear," she said.

"You would have done the same thing because it was the right thing to do. I did not realize it was the one who took Balia until I overheard Menkar's thoughts when he saw her. It was very difficult not to take her life in return. But your words resounded in my head. You were right. One act of mercy could make the difference in changing the perception of those enslaved by Arshek. It just feels as though I have failed Balia somehow, and it hurts, my Queen," Nulian said as she stood and took to the air. Nulian's pain made Morgan cry as she watched her fly back toward the high mountains and the Council's chambers.

She thought that perhaps she was going back to the ancient world to be with Sirzi and Gerzin for comfort.

"I will never be there when you are here again, my Queen. I just need some time alone. Please forget this pain and go enjoy your time with your mate."

MORGAN WALKED toward the garden and called to Alec to join her. He came at a jog and fell into step beside her, taking her hand without pushing her to talk.

She did not feel like sharing. There was too much churning inside her and she wanted nothing more than to put it all out of her mind.

"Will you join me for a swim?" she said.

"Without hesitation," he said with a wink.

When they reached the deserted lake, she stripped to her t-shirt and under-shorts and dove into the water. She looked back to see Alec standing on the bank with his back to her, still fully dressed.

"What's wrong? Are you not coming in?" She opened herself to him and felt his embarrassment. Only then did she realize he had barely seen her in anything other than her full attire of formal dress or uniform. Even all the hours he had spent in her chambers had been in urgent conditions where they had fallen asleep fully dressed from fatigue.

An initial brush of shame was swept away quickly as she felt conviction to no longer be embarrassed of what she shared with him. They were magical "mates" after all.

"My, you are a big coward, aren't you? One woman in a huge lake and your knees grow too weak to carry you in."

Alec turned to face her and stared for a few seconds before stripping to his own under-shorts and diving in to swim straight for her. She turned and put on a great burst of speed toward the waterfall.

"If you promise not to be angry anymore, I will slow and let you catch me."

"I do not need you to let me do anything, my dear. I was simply driving you to the other end of this lake, away from prying eyes," he said as he caught up to her and grabbed her feet to stop her. He pulled her to him and held her to his chest hard as he scowled and panted. "I very much want to see more of you, but I am not alright with anyone else doing so. My

embarrassment was for that and not for my own eyes, my dear!"

"Sorry, I di—" Her words were lost as she was dunked under the water. She came up sputtering and heard his loud laughter as he swam away.

She caught up to dunk him only to be flipped over his shoulders instead. They continued this wrestling match for many minutes before finding themselves breathing hard and laughing, having called an unspoken truce.

"I missed you very much. But I was so glad you were safe within the mountain with the Elders," he said. She failed to keep a smirk from her face before turning away. "What did I say funny?"

"Nothing. I just think it's sweet you missed me while also being glad I was away."

She cringed with guilt the second that was out of her mouth and felt even worse when Alec backed away.

"Why are you lying to me?"

"I'm sorry, but I am not allowed to tell you all that occurred during my time with the Elders. Not yet," she said as she swam to him.

"I respect that you cannot tell me, but do not lie to me as a replacement. It hurts, Morgan," he said with genuine distress in his eyes.

"I am very sorry. It was stupid and I will not do it again." He was still scowling, so she slipped her arms around his neck and moved very close to him with a smile nearly as wicked as his best.

She kissed him lightly and drew in a deep breath as he deepened the kiss. After a moment, she leaned back a little to look into his eyes. "Four days and we will be husband and wife. I am ready, are you?"

"I have been ready since the first time I laid eyes on you in the forest above the Ancestral Lair. I have been yours since that moment," he said. As her face warmed, she smirked and started a splashing battle.

When they tired of it, she shifted back a bit and held his eyes.

"Before we marry, I need to know something," she said. "Had you dated many women before meeting me?"

He glanced away as his thoughts came to her without his intention. She raised an eyebrow.

"Others? What others exactly?" She felt monstrous jealousy rise in her chest and continued, "Alec, tell me of the other women you have cared for."

"Morgan, I am considerably older than you. And yes, over the years, I have courted other girls. But, please do not hold my actions in the years before I met you against my devotion to you now. I love you completely and am completely yours. I will never seek another because you are all I could ever want." His deep voice was soothing, but it did little to quench the fire in her belly.

She swam around him to the rocks at the base of the waterfall as she tried to keep her face placid. He followed her but stayed a few feet away. She had not realized he was a lot older than her. If she had known she would have been even more anxious about her lack of dating experience as compared to his likely ample experience. She sat on the rock brooding over this for a moment before calming enough to be rational.

"So, how old are you?"

"Twenty-five years in two months."

She rubbed her face as she took a few more deep breaths, fighting to calm the fire in her belly fueled by the idea of him holding another woman.

"That warms my heart."

"What?" she asked, her face still flush.

"I can feel that you are jealous. You are possessive of me. That makes me feel wonderful," he said as he moved to her and kissed her cheek. "But you needn't be worried, my dear. I am yours forever now that I have finally found you."

"Yes, you are," she said as she slid her arms around his neck again and hugged him tight. "I pity the woman who tries to come between us."

"As do I!" he said with a chuckle.

15

Wedding Gifts

THE NEXT THREE DAYS passed quickly as Alec, Daniel and the other Knights oversaw the rebuilding and repair of the city. Morgan and GranMay spent that time organizing the last-minute decisions concerning the wedding.

Morgan soon found herself standing in front of the large mirrors in her room, stunned by the beauty of the pure white dress she wore. The bodice was contoured to match her figure and embroidered with corded silver and white thread in the designs of dragons. The fabric from her waist down was the same light-as-the-wind material she had worn before on formal occasions. The dress was neither too fitted nor too puffy, it hung naturally and flowed as she moved.

When her stomach started quivering, she closed her eyes to concentrate on calming herself. It took great effort to push the emotions back before her heart rate returned to normal.

"You are so beautiful, my girl. Alec may faint before he can reach you," GranMay said.

"Not likely. He's too mature and confident for that."

"Really? Well, why don't you take a peek into his emotions right now and see what you find?" GranMay said.

"I will not!"

"Well, I did, and I can tell you he is just as nervous as you are," GranMay said as she kissed her on the cheek.

"GranMay, you really have no shame," she said as she laughed and shook her head.

"Are you ready, my Queen? Your fiancé and your country are waiting," GranMay said as she held up her crown.

GranMay placed her crown on her head and her robe over her shoulders before they walked out onto the terrace.

"You look very nice, my Queen. You also look very happy. Are you ready to go?" Nulian said with a head bow.

"I think so. But, I am going to be riding side-saddle, so watch the banking, please."

Nulian chuckled as she moved into her palm and said, "I will be very careful, my Queen."

"Sorry, I am so stupid nervous."

"Do you love him and believe he loves you in return?"

"Yes, of that I am actually confident."

"Then what can you be nervous about? This is but a formality. Your love was established long ago, my friend."

Morgan patted her and relaxed as she considered that simple view of the whole thing.

ALEC STOOD in his chambers fidgeting with his uniform as Kisik, Burke, and Emma waited with smiles.

"You look very handsome, little brother, but you must stop scowling. You look angry," Emma said as she stepped forward to straighten him a bit.

Alec concentrated on relaxing his face and Emma giggled.

"Now you look nauseous," she whispered. "Just calm down. Think only of Morgan."

"Do not worry, my boy," Kisik said as he stepped forward. "Focus on your love for her, and the words will come. Ignore everything else, and you will be fine. I am proud of you, Son, and I love you."

When they stepped back, Alec saw tears in his father's eyes.

"I am so thankful for the life you have given me, Father. Never did I question my place in your arms or your home. I only wish Mother were here to give me one of her special hugs as well."

Emma bounced forward and latched on to his neck to kiss his cheek many times very fast, mimicking their mother's habit. Alec lifted her off her feet and kissed her cheek back and everyone laughed.

Burke grabbed him and pulled him into a tight embrace.

"I am proud of you, little brother," Burke said as he leaned back enough to spin him around and give him a shove toward the door. "Go on then. Your Queen awaits, as does your week of isolation."

Alec smiled and chuckled as he stepped into Menkar's waiting palm.

NULIAN RECEIVED word from Menkar that he and Alec were ready, and she took off. The wedding was set to take place on the great lawn of the gardens behind the castle. Morgan and Alec had laughed at this, given their history on that particular lawn.

They were flown around the lawn as a formal gesture of the dragons' support to their union. The two dragons stayed in perfect unison opposite one another as they circled lower and lower to the ground.

"Last chance. Menkar is a very fast dragon, and you could probably make it away if you flee now."

"Not a chance, my love. And if you flee, I will give chase until I die."

The two dragons landed in front of the marble gazebo in the middle of the lawn. They placed Morgan and Alec within ten feet of one another before lying down as to not block more view than necessary. Morgan had requested that they remain close, much to the dismay of the wedding planners.

Morgan and Alec stared into each other's eyes as the dragons settled.

"Ready?"

"Absolutely."

They stepped forward together, and she took the hand he offered as he bowed. The shock wave of sensation at touching when they were so nervous made both of them take in a quick breath.

"As if I needed convincing," he said with a smirk as he gripped her hand. She struggled to not laugh out loud as they walked up the steps of the gazebo to stand in the middle facing each other.

"Now behave. I am going to open to everyone here so all of our brethren will hear our vows."

"That is a wonderful gesture, my dear."

She smiled and closed her eyes as she searched to find and touch every spirit within her country. When she had reached the borders of their land, she opened her eyes and nodded for him to begin.

"I, Sir Alec, Knight of Chemerie, do pledge my love for you openly and with great pride, my Caretaker. I offer my spirit to be joined with yours forever."

He smiled at GranMay as she offered a small silk pillow bearing their rings. Once he had untied her ring, she slipped her finger into it and squeezed his hand, letting him feel every ounce of pride coursing through her.

"I, Caretaker Morgan, Queen of Chemerie, am honored to accept your pledge and offer my love and spirit to you in return. May our spirits become one and support one another from this day forward."

She offered his ring and slid it onto his finger. They held each other's eyes as both raised their hands in unison to lay their palms together.

Her eyes, markings, and Crest were very bright as the magic flowed through them. She let everyone present share a bit of the wonderful feeling as they let their magic seal their vows.

They looked into each other's eyes as they entered bonding and their spirits touched one another. Together and in perfect unison they said, "Together we become Husband and Wife, and forever we are One."

There were great gasps from the crowd as they saw the intensity of the glow emanating from her hands and Crest increase dramatically and felt the tremendous surge of energy that came with those words.

Alec tensed a bit as his palms burned like fire against hers. He did not flinch or make any attempt to move them. He held his place and looked into the beautiful glowing eyes of his bride.

She had to raise her guard a bit to keep the sensations in check, then slowly broke the bonding. They lowered their hands but did not let go of each other as they took deeper more controlled breaths.

"Your pledge to me must be accompanied by a pledge to your country. Do you now pledge to stand by my side, as King of Chemerie, in service to all of your brethren, both human and dragon?"

"I pledge my service and loyalty to you as my wife and to all my brethren as their King and humble servant of their Queen," Alec said as he beamed at her.

She was barely conscious of her efforts to suppress the sensations traveling between them or of the hundreds watching and listening.

"Kneel and receive their blessing and your rightful crown, my Husband." She smiled as he dropped to one knee and bowed his head slightly.

Daniel walked forward, bowed with a wink, and offered a pillow bearing the magnificent crown.

She lifted the crown to shoulder height and stepped closer to position it over Alec's head.

"What say you, my brethren? Do you accept this man's pledge to serve as your King by my side?"

"As brethren of Chemerie, we acknowledge and welcome our new King, servant to our Caretaker and Queen. Hail,

King Alec," said all the men and women present. Every person present dropped to one knee and all of the dragons bowed their heads. She placed the crown on Alec's head, and Maric stepped forward to place a striking robe, much like hers, around his shoulders.

"Rise, my love. Rise and stand with me as my Husband and King."

Alec rose to his feet amid raucous cheering, then stepped forward to cradle her face and draw her to him. She dropped the connection to all but him as she lifted to her toes to take his kiss, unwilling to wait a second longer.

The crowd's cheers amplified as they kissed, and yet again as he lifted her off her feet to spin her in a circle.

THEY TURNED TO WAVE to their cheering brethren before boarding Nulian. Morgan soon settled in Alec's arms with a great sigh.

Nulian soared in great circles over the crowd of humans and dragons below and was swarmed by younglings flying in intricate patterns, making dramatic and dangerous maneuvers look graceful. Nulian broke off toward the lake and shot up with her belly skimming the waterfall.

"I have a surprise for you, my King," Morgan said with a sly smile as she let her head fall back on his shoulder.

"That sounds very promi— Whoa!"

She laughed as Nulian folded her wings and shot straight down into the great crevice of the Chamber of Elders.

She soon stepped out of Nulian's palm beside the great purple pool deep within the council chambers and giggled as he stumbled a bit when he followed.

"What do you think?"

"Of what, my dear? It is too dark in here to see anything," he said with a smirk.

"Is it? It seems fine to me," she said as she looked up at Nulian.

"Yet another dragon trait for you, my Sister," Nulian said with a hum that passed pride.

"Your gift just gets better and better, my friend," she said as she reached out to take Alec's hands. "Oh, Alec, look!" she said as she stared at the glowing patterns just visible in his palms.

"They now mirror yours when your magic touches me. How wonderful. I thought I felt something happen but never dreamed I would carry a marking."

"His magic made it possible, my friend. The magic within the average Chemerian male allows them to only feel the sensation," Nulian explained. Morgan translated as she drew her fingertips over his palms.

"That tickles like mad," he said as he shivered and rubbed his palms together.

"Feel this," she said as she knelt to direct him. She drew his hand across the carved metal ring and then over the dense undulating purple liquid it held.

"A portal? Are we going to Earth?"

"No, somewhere much better. Come," she said as she led him to stand near Nulian. "Stand behind me, then reach around me to take my hands, palms touching. Take hold and do not let go, no matter what you feel."

"Never, my Bride," he said as he kissed her neck and gripped her hands.

She and Nulian sang to activate the portal, and Alec hummed along when he identified the melody. As the sensation of the rising liquid began, he only tightened his hold on her.

The instant they emerged on the ancient world of Berios, Alec made a fast move to push her behind him and drew his sword.

"Alec! No! They are my friends!" She leapt around him to kneel in front of Brit and Hirk, taking their heads in her arms to cradle the terrified younglings. He hesitated only a second before sheathing his sword.

"I am sorry they scared you. I would have explained earlier, but I wanted it to be part of the surprise."

Nulian chuckled loudly and said, "It worked. He is definitely surprised." Morgan translated for Alec and they all laughed as Alec knelt beside her and the younglings.

"So, they are the same breed as the Arshek dragons? I am not mistaken?"

"They are the same breed, but the Perian dragons here have never been to Erion, and have never come into contact with the dark magic. They are as pure of spirit as our Chemerian brethren, and I consider them as precious to me as any," she said as she stroked the younglings. Both crooned and shivered as they relished her touch.

"Perian dragons that are gentle and loving toward the Queen of Chemerie. Amazing, and something I never expected to see for certain. Will you introduce me to your young friends, my dear?"

"Hirk, Brit, this is King Alec, my Husband. He is as gentle as I am when not protecting me, I promise. I would very much like it if you would give him your trust, as you have given it to me."

Brave little Brit was the first to step forward and bow to Alec. He put his head forward to allow Alec to touch him. Alec returned the bow and stroked the youngling with an amazed smile. Brit shivered and glanced back at his shy brother.

"Are you coming, or do I have to call you names again?"

Hirk moved forward and sniffed at Alec a little while he stroked Brit, then nudged his hand off of Brit and onto his own snout. Alec laughed as they scuffled, then used both hands to stroke them.

"Nulian, do you see that?" Morgan said in dragon-tongue as she saw the blue light beneath Alec's palms. "Why are his markings glowing with their touch?"

"It is likely his magic responding to theirs. I doubt he can see it in the daylight," Nulian said. Morgan nodded and moved to stand beside him.

"What do you think, boys? How does your second human touch compare to your first?"

"It is very nice, my Lady. But not as soft or as sweet-smelling as you. He makes me tingle less than you and he smells like wood," said Hirk. Morgan burst out into laughter and Alec joined her once she translated.

"My Lady, what is 'husband'?" Brit asked.

"It means he is my mate," Morgan said with as straight a face as she could muster.

"I thought you hated that term, my Queen?" Nulian said with a great chuckle.

"It was the easiest answer, and it is true after all. I think it's time I start getting used to it."

Morgan walked to Alec's side where he now stood by the edge of the cliff looking out over the valley below.

"Welcome to Berios," she said as she moved into his arms. She explained all she knew about the place then moved toward Nulian.

"Would you like to go for a swim, my Husband?"

"Absolutely, my Bride."

Nulian took them to the lake and left them alone while she went to spend time with Gerzin. They helped each other out of their robes and placed them and their crowns on the ground neatly then proceeded to undress. Both stopped when they were still wearing their undergarments. The sun had set, and it was getting dark.

"Are you sure it is not too cool?" he asked.

"I think we will be fine," she said with a wink.

They swam lazily and enjoyed the complete solitude a great deal after the busy days of the weeks before.

"Hirk and Brit are wanting to play. Would you like that?"

"Not this time. I prefer to keep you to myself for a few days."

He moved in to kiss her and was dunked instead. When he came up, she backed away from the mischievous look in his eyes. A vicious game of dunking and wrestling ensued until they were both out of breath.

"Are you ready to see our honeymoon suite?"

He raised an eyebrow and she smiled.

They returned to the bank and wrung the excess water from their hair and clothes. As she looked up at Alec, she spotted Nulian and Gerzin soaring up together again and pointed them out to him. He had of course seen a dragon mating before, but still watched with awe just as she did.

The dragons clashed together right in front of the moon and wrapped each other as they began to fall. Alec pulled Morgan into his arms as they watched them fall. Both let out a small breath when the dragons finally separated.

"Glorious, but far too quick," Alec thought.

"Agreed."

Nulian and Gerzin landed beside them breathing heavily from the exertion of their chasing of each other.

"That was glorious, my friends. We were honored to witness such a magnificent show of love," Morgan said. She noticed Alec looked at her and felt his surprise.

Nulian and Gerzin both hummed as Nulian leaned over to nudge her mate's chest with her head. Gerzin wrapped her neck with his, then gave a low rumbling growl before releasing her and taking off.

"What was the growl all about, Nulian?" Morgan asked as they flew toward the gazebo.

"He does not like being told to wait."

"Well you should drop us off and get back to him then, my friend."

"I certainly will, but I will make him wait a bit first. It is good for males to have to wait sometimes, my Queen," Nulian said.

"I will remember that. Something tells me it will apply sooner than later," she said as she patted her friend.

MORGAN LED ALEC up the stairs through the darkness then laid his hand to one of the bedposts.

"Here, let me get you some light," she said as she knelt by the trunk she had packed and sent ahead.

"I would like to see you and this place you have brought me to a bit better."

She placed candles around the edges of the gazebo on the railings. Alec turned to take in the great stone structure.

"This is magnificent. It is a larger and perfect replica of the one we exchanged vows in this afternoon. It is beautiful, my Bride." She had not even made the connection and thought it sweet that he did.

As she rummaged in the trunk, taking out some food and toiletries, he took her hand and pulled her to him.

"We can unpack later, my love," he said as he held her close and caressed her face and neck.

"I love you, Alec. I am so happy to be here with you."

"I could imagine no more perfect place to start our life as husband and wife, my dear."

She leaned back in his arms and gazed at him for many seconds.

"I think it time we discussed advancing our level of familiarity, my Husband."

"A conversation I am eager to have, my Bride, I assure you," he said as he gave her a wicked smile.

"Just one request," she said, feeling her face and neck flush.

"Anything."

"No more chivalry. No more propriety. No more hiding what we feel. From now on, we make our own rules."

He lifted her off her feet to kiss her with everything he felt as he never had before.

"I see no need for rules at all, my Bride," he said without interrupting the kiss.

"Nor do I, my Husband."

THEY SPENT the bulk of the next two days at the gazebo relishing the complete solitude and lack of limitations. They talked for hours on end. Nulian had told Morgan she could share everything with him from now on, and she did just that.

The second day they performed a long bonding ceremony.

With her new level of control over the magic, it was a wonderful experience that left them so close in spirit their thoughts were shared with no delay. They practically stopped speaking aloud at all.

As they were swimming one day, Morgan felt an intense feeling of sorrow and longing coming from a ridge behind her. She focused on the area and found Hytha, the minor female Chemerian dragon she had healed along with Sirzi. The dragon was lying alone and gazing out over the valley to the north.

"Hello, my friend, can I help you in any way?"

"No, my Queen. I simply have to accept something I do not like. It is not something anyone can help me do. But thank you for your concern, my Lady."

A moment later, she felt Hytha's heart race as a handsome Perian male circled the ridge near her then turned to head off to the east. Hytha felt another huge rush of grief as he flew away.

"What is wrong with our dragon friend up there?"

"I think we may be witnessing a very new and possibly huge step in our dragons' lives, my love."

"What are you talking about?"

"Our female Chemerian friend up there has profound love for a Perian male. And from the intensity of their exchange a moment ago, I would guess the feeling is mutual, and the magic has actually mated them."

She swam toward the bank and called to Nulian, leaving him to play with Hirk and Brit. A few moments later, she sat on Nulian's outstretched front leg and connected to her through touch to avoid any chance of being overheard.

"Nulian, has there ever been a mating between Chemerian and Perian dragons?"

"Not that I am aware of, my Queen."

"How would such an idea be perceived by each breed's Council of Elders?"

"I have no idea as the issue has never come up before."

"Well, how would you feel if Sirzi had wished to mate with a Perian male?"

"Sirzi is already mated to Menkar, my Queen." Morgan let her face speak her annoyance. *"Hypothetically speaking, I suppose it would make me uneasy, my Queen."*

"But I know you consider them as precious to you as our Chemerian brethren. Why would it matter to you?"

"It has simply never been done, my Queen. The magic has never mated two dragons of different breeds. I suppose that in itself is the reason for my hesitance. It is unprecedented and therefore seems wrong."

"So, if the pairing was the result of the magic mating them, it would be accepted by the Elders?"

"It is not our place to ever question the partnerships made by the magic. You know that very well by your own experience, my Queen. Why do you ask these questions?"

"Because I suspect the precedent has now been set, my friend. Hytha has fallen in love with a Perian male. I worry for them

fighting against their natural mating instincts out of fear of going against custom. I felt their love and truly believe they have been mated by the magic. As you and Balia have both told me, the magic has never failed to make a proper match. So I am asking you, as chair of the Chemerian Council of Elders, to consider the matter before it becomes a problem. I think we should discuss it with the Council soon so the couple can live happily again."

ALEC WATCHED as Morgan paced the floor of the gazebo. She had been doing so ever since Nulian dropped them off and headed to the Council meeting alone.

He drained his glass of wine, then grabbed her and spun her to pin her to the bedpost as he lifted one finger to touch her lips and another to caress her scales. Her initial fight turned to a series of shivers and she calmed under his gentle touch.

"Nulian's powerful gift of her blood has given you a much stronger connection to her and all dragons. It is a precious part of who you are, yet only part. You are the Caretaker, and they respect and love you. But this issue is the integrity of their breed. Nulian is not being disrespectful, she is trying to handle it among her kind as best she can."

"You are wise, my Husband," she said as she kissed him then smirked as she started to slip away. "It must be all those added years."

He tickled her savagely for a moment before she got free of him and caught her breath. She leaned on a column and gazed over the valley as she sighed. He moved to slide in behind her and kissed her head.

"You are right, of course," she said as she rested back

against him. "My annoyance was childish, and arrogant. Nulian's blood is changing me more each day, making me stronger in magic and body. But as different as I am from before, I am not a dragon, and I do need to remember my place."

"Please do not say that, my Queen," Nulian interrupted. *"You share my blood, and I consider you as much a part of my family as any of my children. I will be at your haven soon and will explain my actions, my Sister."*

She translated for Alec, and he kissed her cheek to give her a little push toward Nulian when she landed.

"I don't want you to explain anything about not taking me. I understand it was not my place, my friend," she said as she moved to lean into her snout. "Just tell me what you have learned, please." Nulian hummed and passed love and devotion before answering.

"It took some time, but in the end your words made them see the matter for what it is. If the magic has truly mated them, we can not deny them that joy. It did not sit well with some of the Elders that the magic would have truly mated them, so, they asked for you to confirm that they are indeed connected by magic."

"Nulian, you know very well that in order for me to determine that I will have to be included in full bonding with both of them, and share in their most private thoughts and feelings. Gracious, that is asking quite a lot of all three of us."

"I know it is a profound request. But I told them you would do it because I knew you felt that the magic had mated them."

"What happens if they are only in love and the magic has

not mated them in any way I can tell?"

"Their partnering will never be accepted if it is not designed by the magic. That has nothing to do with the crossing of breeds. No partnering is accepted if it is not a design of the magic."

"Not that anyone has admitted you mean. Every partnering is not exactly confirmed by an outsider," she pointed out. Nulian only nodded. "If I feel a strong love between them, but cannot say I can identify a magical bond, am I to then condemn them to separation? Nulian, you are asking me to rely on a skill I do not even know how to use. What if I fail to recognize the magical link and condemn them falsely?"

She heard wings and turned to see Gerzin land behind Nulian. He moved to lie beside his mate, nudging her on the neck before bowing to her and Alec.

"Am I to join in your bonding to learn this new skill?"

"I thought it an odd request as well, but my mate is quite convincing when she wants something," Gerzin said as he crooned and rubbed Nulian again.

Morgan had included Alec in all of this. He could only understand her English words, but that was enough for him to follow most of the conversation.

He was currently trying to control his face as he watched her neck flush.

"I think you should join me in this wonderful and intimate experience, my Husband," she said as she gave him a strong push of annoyance.

"Actually, my Queen, we were going to suggest that ourselves," Nulian said. "It would give you both a unique perspective of your dragon kindred. As Queen and King with the Crest between you, it could prove a valuable understanding over the years."

Alec stepped closer and took Morgan's hand as she translated, then bowed to the dragons with a smile.

"Are you sure you want to do this? It is sure to be quite intense."

"Why would I not want to do this if it means another opportunity to better know your gifts, and an amazing opportunity to better understand my dragon brethren?"

"And that, Sir, is why I love you," she said as she gripped his hand and pulled him closer to lift to her toes and kiss him.

She knelt between the dragons and he knelt behind her to let her rest back against him as she reached out to lay a hand to each of their friends.

"Lay a hand over the scales of my Crest," she said to him as she focused to calm herself. Once they were ready, the dragons laid their heads against one another and started to hum deep in their throats.

Their tones mingled into a beautiful harmony. As their humming intensified, she felt the scales of her Crest begin to tingle and burn. As she focused on the spirits of the two dragons, she connected.

She gasped and shuddered as their powerful magic swept over her. The dragons were sharing at a profound level, and she struggled to keep control of it as it passed through her. Sweat slid down her neck as she fought to direct the magical current through her, without driving her own level too high.

As the pain climbed, she acted to push her and Alec into bonding. When it took hold the pain faded, and the dragons' magic flowed through her much more easily. Once calm and in control, she pushed to full bonding with each of the dragons.

It was amazing. There was no question of a magical link between them. She could feel it as if it were electricity flowing over them in great waves. It took many minutes before she was able to discern their shared deep emotional connection from the powerful magical link between their spirits.

Nulian and Gerzin changed the cadence of their humming, shifting their focus to examine the link between their human friends. She did not resist, nor did Alec. The feelings of shared love, respect, and trust were intoxicating. It was so precious that she held them there until she was completely spent.

MORGAN WOKE AN HOUR LATER, snuggled in Alec's arms in their bed. He was stroking her hair and humming a beautiful tune she had never heard. She focused on the tune and realized he was not just humming, he was singing.

"Did you receive more than a memorable experience today, my love?" she asked

"What do you mean?"

She smiled as Nulian and Gerzin raised their heads to hum a deep tone that conveyed profound trust.

"My King, my dear Gerzin has given you a wedding gift. He saw the purity of your spirit and felt the love you have for our Caretaker and for your dragon kindred. He found you more than deserving of the gift of our language."

Alec's face was one of absolute shock and confusion at first, then turned to one of deep gratitude.

"Gerzin, I thank you for trusting me with this gift. I am

deeply honored. It will help me to serve our country far more effectively. And thank you both for allowing me to participate in your bonding, it was truly amazing."

The two dragons bowed with deep hums again before Gerzin nudged Nulian toward the cliff edge with a light growl. She offered no argument and both dropped off the ledge to soar over the valley.

Alec pulled Morgan closer to kiss her, then shifted back to smile as he caressed her face.

"What was that for?"

"For being my mate, my Queen, and my Bride. You make me a ridiculously happy man."

"You are welcome, of course. But if I am honest, I have to say that I do not think a quick kiss on the lips is proper reward for such an exhausting job."

He gave her his best wicked smile as he shifted above her.

"Do you feel it a matter of duration or conviction, my Bride?"

"I think both qualities to be very important, my Husband."

He smiled and laughed a little as he caressed her cheek.

"I love that you still blush when trying to be wicked."

She drew him closer and lifted to kiss his neck, jaw, then lips.

"And I love that you still think I am blushing, when I am actually flush from my efforts to behave with you so very close, my Husband."

LAUGHTER AND WHISPERS woke her the next morning. Alec was sitting on the ground surrounded by Perian younglings. One was even curled up in his lap.

She eavesdropped and found they were asking him about the habits of people and he was fielding each question with grace. An odd feeling rose inside her again. It was the longing to feel the love of a child. But this time the focus was different; she wanted to see him with their child.

She thought of him as a father, and then of herself as a mother while watching him caress the younglings. The first idea brought waves of confidence, the second waves of uncertainty.

He glanced back at her with a smile as he whispered something to one youngling who hurried toward her. The little one hopped onto the bed and lay next to her.

"What did my sneaky husband say to you, little one?"

"He said to tell you that you will be a wonderful mother," the youngling said with a gentle touch of his snout to her arm.

"Really? Well tell him that I think he will be a wonderful father as well," she said as she caressed his head.

The youngling shot from the bed like a dart and flew to Alec. He chuckled at the little one's enthusiasm and hugged him to his chest as he looked back at her.

"I too have thought of it recently and would never have mentioned it had I not heard you first. But I can now admit that I am looking forward to the day I see you holding our child in your arms. I imagine that to be the most glorious sight I could behold."

She had tears running down her face and was in no hurry to wipe them. He started to play a wild game of tag with the younglings. It was hardly a surprise when he hissed and grabbed his arm.

"Come here, please."

He met her at the fountain and released the wound. A bad gash across his forearm was bleeding a great deal. She rinsed it then laid her hand over the wound and healed it as she blocked his pain.

"Thank you, my dear," he said as he kissed her hands, then turned and went right back to the game. She laughed as she realized that any child they had would need healing on a daily basis if they learned from their father.

NULIAN TOOK THEM to seek the young couple to be tested. They found Hytha near the lake, sunning herself at the base of the waterfall, with her head drooped over the side of a rock.

"Hello again, Hytha. I would like to speak with you in person. Do you mind if I join you there?"

"I would love for you to join me, my Queen."

Morgan dove from Nulian's back as she swept low over the lake and swam over to the rocks to sit beside Hytha.

"It is lovely to see you again, my Queen. I thank you for saving my life."

"You are welcome. I would like to help you again," she said as she stroked her snout to pass feelings of loving understanding. "I felt your love for him yesterday, and I have been asked to confirm that the magic has mated you, as I believe it has."

Hytha raised her head and gave her a harsh glare. She did not flinch or look away as she laid her hand to Hytha's side to let her feel her honesty. "I acted to serve you, my friend. I am sorry if you feel I intruded on your privacy. I only wanted to see you and your intended mate together and happy." Hytha dropped her head as her anger turned to anguish again.

"I had no idea anyone knew of my feelings. I have told no one because I realize it is against tradition. But I do love him very much, my Queen."

"I know. I felt the love between you when he soared over you yesterday. And I want to help you be with him. To do this, I will have to be connected to both of you as you enter full bonding. Are you willing to allow that?"

"I am fine with the notion, but it is Tagien I am not certain of. We have never even spoken of our love openly to each other. We have never entered into bonding alone, so asking him to do so with you included is a large request."

"Tell him that if he loves you, and believes you to be his intended mate, then he must agree to this or the Council will consider the union against the magic and will fight against it."

"I will go speak with him. Shall we come to you here, my Queen?"

Morgan nodded and gave her a loving pat before she took off.

She swam to the other end of the lake where she joined Alec to lie quietly in the warm sun. They were almost asleep when roars and screeches from the north startled them.

"Oh no!" she said.

"Tagien's mother does not approve, my Queen," Hytha said as she and Tagien flashed overhead, followed closely by a roaring Perian female.

"I will try to help," she said to Hytha. She focused on the major female Perian and pushed against her guard to connect. *"I am not your Queen, but I ask that you hear me out, Lady Tevish."*

"This is not of your concern, Queen of Chemerie."

"Indeed, it is. I believe the magic has mated these two. If that is the case, it is not our place to question it. I only ask that you allow me to confirm their magical link, my Lady."

She had watched the pursuit as she spoke, flinching as Tagien slammed into his own mother to protect Hytha from her rage. Alec gripped her hand as he glanced at her. They both expected that act to anger Tagien's mother to the point she would not yield.

Once again, she found herself surprised by the dragons' methods. The great major dragon broke off and landed atop a ridge overlooking the lake.

"I will not interfere with your search for the truth. My son obviously believes in this female. If you find a link between them, I will accept her, but if you do not, I ask that you take her back to Erion at once, my Lady."

"I will ask on your behalf, but I would never make any dragon do anything, even if I could, my Lady," Morgan said. The great Perian nodded.

Hytha and Tagien were flying together above the lake, well away from the ridge where Tevish waited. A moment later, they landed near Morgan, panting and jostling around.

"I do not want to do this while you are both so anxious. May I connect with each of you alone and help you calm before the bonding ritual?"

Hytha nodded and looked to Tagien, who eyed Morgan a few seconds then nodded as well. She connected to each in turn to push contentment and encouraged them to focus on their love for one another. They were far calmer as they moved closer together to settle down.

"I need to know that both of you believe your connection to be a magical pairing, and that you enter into this bonding willingly."

The dragons turned to each other, touched snouts while humming, and looked back to her with a nod. She smiled at them as she felt their love washing over her.

"Then let us get started."

She asked that they scoot closer then sat down between their shoulders. With a quick wink to Alec, she placed a palm to each of them and closed her eyes. She opened a connection to each, then deepened both very close to bonding.

"Now, please enter into bonding with each other, my friends. I will join you as it forms."

With initial nervous twitches, the dragons brought their snouts together while making sweet short crooning sounds then began to hum together.

Morgan felt their connection forming as her Crest tingled. They were each tentative and dropped their guard in small steps. The rush of sensation she received from them was similar to that she received from Nulian and Gerzin, but unique to itself. She felt them sharing their spirits with each other and could feel the very intense passion they shared, but did not feel the distinct magical link she had found so easy to identify in the Elder dragons.

Again and again, she acted to delve deeper into the bonding. She soon gasped and tensed as the dragons quivered and changed the cadence of their song. They were all trembling a bit with the intense pulses of magic that accompanied initial formation of their magical link. It was not the soothing sensation of the Elders long-established link, theirs was a sharp, energetic shock. Their magical link now mingled with the love between them. Both let their guards drop away altogether to allow a very deep bonding to their mate.

Morgan let them share the time in private and released the bonding to both dragons. With a sharp gasp and groan, she leaned forward, holding her head on trembling hands. She sat quietly, breathing through the lingering pain of her abrupt drop from bonding.

Alec moved to her, crawling under the heads of the dragons, to wipe her flushed face with a cold, wet cloth.

"You are amazing, my Bride. I felt your emotions through all of it and could tell the exact moment when you detected their link. I felt it so clearly, even that far away."

He lifted her into his arms like a baby while he waited for the dragons to complete their bonding.

She woke later to his kiss on her forehead and his deep voice in her ear.

"Wake up, my love. There are a few friends here who wish to speak with you."

She opened her eyes to see the area around, in, and above the lake filled with dragons. Nulian was lying in the shallow water near them.

"We are quite curious as to the verdict. Please share what you discovered with us all, my Queen," Nulian said.

Morgan turned to see Tagien and Hytha lying next to one another, both tense and anxious. Hytha was shooting quick glances at Tevish, who now loomed over him.

"Do they not know the answer themselves?" she asked Nulian.

"That was their first bonding of any kind, so they do not know what to recognize. They only know they love each other.

And I believe Tagien will react very badly if you have the wrong news for him," Nulian said as she eyed the Perian male who was currently shifting away from his overprotective mother toward Hytha.

Morgan stood and looked around at all of the dragons. She connected to every mind around her, including Alec.

"I would never ask that you simply take my word on this very important question. I will give you a sample of what they share. If you have felt the magical link with a mate, you will recognize its presence."

She smiled as she heard the deep hum coming from most everyone present. Tagien's mother stepped forward and touched her snout first to Hytha and then to Tagien. The two minor dragons then touched their snouts together and the crowd of dragons erupted in roars of celebration.

Morgan flopped down on the ground with a huge sigh and lay back in Alec's lap to watch as the two minor dragons flew high in the air to perform their first mating ritual to the raucous roaring of the crowd below.

Birth

MORGAN LAY IN BED with Alec staring at the stars above them.

"I can't wait to see what Hytha and Tagien's hatchlings look like," he said. "They are sure to be beautiful. I am imagining all the possible combinations of their features."

"I wonder if their children will have all the skills of the two breeds, only some, or even more as a result of the pairing."

They lay quiet for a long time before she gasped and grabbed her belly.

"What is wrong? What hurts you?" Alec said as he sat up and pulled the covers back to see her torso. She was silent, tears filling her eyes, as he stroked her face and asked again what was wrong.

Tears slid down her cheeks as she laid his hand over her

Crest to bond and share the sensation she had just felt. He gasped then dropped his head to kiss her belly. Tears slid down his cheeks as he moved to kiss her lips.

"Thank you, my love. That was a wonderful way to tell me our child is coming," he said as he wiped her tears away.

"No, not child. Children ... twins, my love. One boy and one girl." He kissed her with all he had as they shared their profound joy at those words.

After a long time holding one another and relishing this news, she felt his heart begin to ache as he shifted to turn his face away. She touched his cheek to turn his face to hers and saw the pain in his eyes as well.

"I have more news, my love, and I think this the perfect time to share it," she said as she moved above him to look into his eyes. "Our children will bear the Crest as well. Both of them will share in its great power. They will help me restore the magic of Chemerie to its original state among our people." She paused to let him take that in and watched his eyes as he saw the hope within her words. More tears flowed as she smiled. "I will never have to say goodbye to you. We will all live together in Chemerie."

He shot up into her arms to wrap her in a crushing embrace.

"I have never been so happy in my life. Bond to me now so we may share this joy properly, my love."

THE NEXT MORNING they rose late to pack their things and wait for Nulian while eating some breakfast. He was staring at her with a silly grin.

"What is it?"

"You are glowing?"

"Right! I have heard that saying before back on Earth, but never expected you to use it," she said with a dismissive laugh.

"Morgan, look down at your Crest."

She found that both her scales and the dragons around them were indeed putting off a glow that was visible even in the sunlight. She brushed them gently with her fingers and found they were also warm. The tingling sensation from the touch radiated down toward her navel.

When she felt Nulian approaching, they picked up their bags, closed the trunk of supplies they would leave there, and moved to meet her. When they drew close, Nulian hummed and touched her snout to Morgan's belly.

"Welcome, little ones. I look forward to touching your spirits," Nulian said. She nudged Alec as well before raising her head.

"Congratulations, my friends. I had hoped the magic would bless you this day," Nulian said with a deep croon.

"Nulian, are my scales glowing because of my pregnancy or because it is the Day of Light? I realize this is the actual calendar day that The Purest and Lady Chemerie bonded for the first time. But the way the tingling is radiating down toward my belly, I thought it to be connected to the children's presence." Nulian hummed again sending more tingles through her as well as lighting her Crest to glow even brighter.

"Both of those factors are involved, my Queen. Your children will have a great connection to the magic as you do. It is not a surprise that their awakening has coincided with the Day of Light," Nulian said.

Morgan raised one eyebrow and said, "Well that was cryptic. I will be asking for a more thorough explanation later, my friend."

Nulian flew them back to the ledge bearing the portal and they found friends waiting to say farewell. Asira and her sons, Hirk and Brit, as well as Tagien and Hytha were there. They went around to all of them and said their goodbyes.

Hytha asked Nulian permission to stay with Tagien for a while before returning to Erion. Nulian said it was her choice when she comes and goes.

"Just as well she is far away while I deal with more of her father's annoyance at being asked to keep his temperament out of their testing," Nulian grumbled as she curled around Morgan and Alec on the portal.

"Who is her father?" Alec asked.

"Drieden!"

Morgan and Alec laughed as they took hands and started to sing along with Nulian. This time Alec understood the words and joined in as well. He did not choose to release Morgan's hands, however.

ONCE BACK in the main hall of the Council chambers, Nulian said farewell as Menkar was waiting to take them to the castle. Alec stepped to Menkar and stroked his head with a wide grin.

"I missed you, my friend," Alec said in dragon-tongue. He laughed openly at Menkar's shocked expression as he and Morgan stepped into his waiting palm.

"You feel different, my Caretaker. Your magic is making me tingle more than usual," Menkar said.

Morgan smiled and connected to him, then nodded to Alec so he could share their news. As he finished, Menkar hummed loudly, and they both received a rush of love through the connection.

They landed in the garden where they were greeted by a large group of younglings led by the now quite large Falin and Lirpa. The instant they stepped from his palm, Menkar crooned and wrapped his neck to nudge them against his side.

"I am very happy for you, my friends. My heart has not been so full since Sirzi and I discovered our first clutch," Menkar said. He held them in place against his side for a few more seconds before leaving with haste.

"That was wonderful," Alec said as he watched his dear friend fly away.

"He hides it most of the time, but there is a great depth of passion within him," she said. *"He is going to Sirzi and their clutch now."*

The younglings moved up once Menkar was away, and Alec relished his new gift as he spoke with every one of them. Morgan noticed Lirpa lurking behind the group.

"What troubles you, my dear?"

Lirpa gave Falin a long look before saying, *"He comes of age soon and is being courted by a much larger female, my Queen."*

Morgan moved to her and caressed her as she said, *"If your mating is meant to be, the magic will make it so. Do you believe it to be a magical partnership?"* The young dragon nodded. *"Then have faith in him and the magic, my dear."*

She stood back and looked at the size of Lirpa with amazement.

"It is hard to believe you were riding on my shoulder a year ago, my friend. You have grown magnificently and seem large enough to carry me on your shoulders already," she said with pride.

"I would be most honored if you would allow me to carry you now as my first rider, my Queen. I am more than capable, and would not ask had I any reservation," Lirpa said.

"That sounds wonderful, our first flight together. Your mother would be so proud of you, Lirpa. You are a wonderful friend to me and are among my most loyal, just as she predicted. You are very special to me, my dear, and I would be more than honored to be your first rider." Lirpa crooned and placed the length of her head against her body.

Morgan called for a harness and saddle from a keeper nearby and beamed as he fitted Lirpa. The excited dragon offered her foreleg for her to do her customary vault into the saddle.

"As this is your first flight, I think formality is in order, my dear," she said with a smile and a curtsy. Lirpa offered her palm, lifted her to the saddle with grace, then waited while she strapped in.

Falin came toward them at a trot and snorted at Lirpa.

"Lirpa, you have not practiced with others. You should not risk our Queen so!"

"Falin, hold your tongue!" Morgan said matching his tone. "Lirpa is honoring me by allowing me to be her first rider."

Lirpa glared at Falin as she moved past, while holding herself as tall over him as possible, then moved away from the crowd and took to the air. Morgan praised her for the exceptional smoothness of the lift-off and stroked her to ease her tension as they flew.

"My Husband, will you please question Falin on his coming of age soon and his possibilities of mates. I would like to hear his answer."

Alec patted Falin and stepped close to his head to speak to him.

"You are near the age of taking a mate, are you not, Falin?" Falin nodded and stood a little taller. "Have you felt the magic with anyone yet, my friend?"

Falin lifted his head to follow Lirpa's movement across the sky.

"I believe it to be Lirpa, my King. I will wait for her to come of age in the winter, and we shall see," Falin said as he continued to watch Lirpa soar above them.

"I think that would be a splendid pairing, my friend. You are right to wait for the one the magic has set for you. Trust me, it is truly worth it," Alec said as he watched Lirpa and Morgan soar high overhead.

"I agree, my love," Morgan said. Alec smiled and winked, knowing she could see him clearly.

Lirpa landed a few minutes later, breathing a bit hard. Morgan sent her love and pride as she dismounted, then a little healing energy while stroking her head.

"Let's tell them. We are about to tell the family anyway," she said to Alec. He smiled as he nodded, then asked Falin to join them.

She took Alec's hand, and they each laid a hand on one of the young dragons. She deepened her connection to all three. Tears slid down her face as the dragons felt the presence of the two new spirits and moved to touch her belly while singing the Song of Connection together.

ALEC AND MORGAN walked toward the castle and were met on the terrace by their family. Daniel, GranMay, Maric with his wife Halen, Kisik, Emma, and Burke with his wife, Mira, were all there to welcome them back with hugs and smiles.

Morgan stayed behind Alec until she could step out in front of GranMay, who beamed as she saw her glowing markings. GranMay stepped close and touched the glowing scales with a light laugh.

"They are warm and glowing on The Day of Light. How wonderful, my dear," GranMay said.

"That is part of it, but not quite everything," Morgan said as she placed one of GranMay's hands over her Crest to push them toward bonding. GranMay closed her eyes and tears slid down her cheeks. Daniel moved forward and put his arm around GranMay.

"What happened? What's wrong?" he asked.

Alec placed a hand on his shoulder and gave him a smile.

"She cries from joy, Daniel, not sorrow. Morgan has shared the joyful news of our children's awakening this morning. She is pregnant, with twins."

Everyone around them gasped and cheered as Daniel stared at Morgan. She felt his growing disappointment, then shook her head as she explained.

"The magic allowed me to feel my children's presence shortly after conception. It is much quicker than the methods we are used to on Earth," she said. His face relaxed into a broad smile and he hugged her.

"This is wonderful news. I am very happy for you, little sister," he said as they held each other. He stepped back to shake

Alec's hand and broke into a jovial laugh.

"Mercy, you two don't believe in wasting any time, do you? At this rate, we should expect these babies next month." Everyone laughed along with him, but GranMay, Kisik, and Maric laughed the hardest as they exchanged glances.

Alec looked at Morgan and she shrugged.

"Something we should know, GranMay?"

GranMay got her laughing under control and took Morgan's hand.

"Well, he is not too far off, my dear. The average gestational period for a Caretaker is six months. But given everything you have showed me about your magic thus far, I would not be shocked to find us meeting your children well before then."

Daniel burst out laughing again as Morgan's face blanched. Everyone joined in the laughing and hugged the couple in congratulations.

THE FAMILY GATHERED in the private dining room on the second floor and ate a fabulous lunch. It was a very welcome hot meal for the newlyweds who had eaten simple cold meals all week.

They were questioned about their week, but had to be vague or dodge some questions altogether. They could not discuss the ancestral world or the existence of the Perian dragons there. They did, however, share the news of Alec's markings. They illustrated how they revealed themselves when touching and faded when she moved away.

Kisik was most interested and stroked Alec's hands as he said, "Tomas and Nikolas often spoke of feeling the sensation in their palms, but neither had a marking reveal itself."

Morgan felt a rush of love and sorrow from GranMay as she reacted to the name of her dear mate lost so long ago.

Alec revealed his gift of dragon-tongue by asking Gran-May to pass the salt in that language. It wasn't until he said, "Thank you" in that tongue that her eyes went wide, and her fork slipped from her hand.

They talked of their enjoyment of having the time to just be together and relax. The family laughed as the two finished each other's sentences, or forgot to speak aloud at all, due to their strong connection.

As they sat talking, Morgan felt a strong sense of excitement coming from the small terrace off the dining hall. She excused herself and found Manook, pacing back and forth on the railing.

"What has happened, Manook. Why are you so agitated?" she asked as she stroked his head.

"My mother's last clutch is hatching, my Queen. Lady Sirzi and Lady Nulian thought you would want to know, as we all know your bond to Mother was very strong," Manook said as he fidgeted. "Lady Nulian asked that I come tell you." He gave a little flourish of his wings as excitement and pride filled him.

"Thank you so much for letting me know. I will go there right now."

Alec had already risen from the table and told the family where they were going, so no one questioned her haste when she flew through the room.

MORGAN SAT BESIDE SIRZI AND ALEC watching the eggs wobble and jerk. This was the first clutch she had been present for from laying to hatching. Her connection to these dragon hatchlings was profound given her love of their mother. Since Balia's death, she had kept close tabs on them along with Sirzi.

They all fell silent as the first hatchling forced the sharp egg tooth on the tip of his snout through the shell and poked his little head out. Morgan was brought to tears when the little hatchling crawled into her lap and rested against her glowing hands. She stroked his back with her fingers and felt her Crest burn hot as it lit the room.

Nulian could not fit into the egg room. She was lying just outside in the largest room of the dragon chambers. Morgan had stayed connected to her and now shared the joy she felt.

"He recognized his family blood and is perceptive of your magic as well. My Queen, will you honor us by naming this hatchling in Balia's absence?" Nulian said.

"I would love to." She closed her eyes and focused on her memories of Nulian's family heritage. She opened her eyes and said, "I will honor your traditions and name him after his father, Zirak. Let us call this little gentleman Zirath. Welcome to our family, little one." The hatchling hummed a sweet sound as it snuggled against her.

They watched as the remaining four eggs hatched over the next few minutes. To her absolute bliss, they all piled into her lap and fell asleep atop one another. There were three males and two females, and all were gorgeous and healthy.

Morgan and Alec caressed them for a long time while humming one of Balia's favorite songs with Sirzi.

"The hatchlings must be fed, my Lady. Sirzi and I will

take care of it. Thank you very much for welcoming Balia's last children into this world, my friends," Nulian said.

Morgan placed each hatchling against Sirzi's side, then headed upstairs with Alec.

WHEN MORGAN AND ALEC entered their chambers, they found it to be filled with flowers and redecorated in less feminine, yet gorgeous materials. After much-needed baths, they climbed into the plush bed and snuggled in.

"This has been a most wonderful day, my Bride. We learn we are to be parents in a few short months and are blessed with witnessing the birth of five new dragon brethren. I am exhausted and exhilarated at the same time."

"I feel so blessed right now. Things have happened so fast the last few months. With little time to stop and take it all in, I was feeling a little overwhelmed. But now, with you fully bound to me, I feel nothing but blessed by it all. I know there is nothing I can not handle with you with me."

"I feel the same way. I was worried about my responsibilities to you and our country as well. But now I welcome those challenges, especially the challenges of parenting two exceptional children."

"I wonder how difficult it will be raising two children who carry great skill of magic from birth. We may be in trouble, my dear," she said with a smile as they drifted off to sleep.

"CARETAKER OF CHEMERIE, will you talk to me? I would like to thank you," a voice called again and again.

Morgan sat up in bed and focused on locating the spirit of the one calling to her. She was surprised to find the spirit to be the female Arshek dragon she had healed. The dragon was currently within the dragon hold of the Arshek castle and focusing hard to reach her from so far.

She woke Alec and told him what she was hearing and who it was.

"No, my love, the darkness could harm you or the children," he said as he jerked upright. "What if this is a trap by Harrick? What if he realized she had been healed, has forced his way into her mind, and is lying in wait for you? Please, at least consult Nulian before you do this. It is so dangerous for you."

"I just did, my dear. You should have more faith in my good sense," she said with a smile before kissing his head.

Nulian landed beside her terrace moments later and dropped her head over the railing to rest on Morgan's lounge chair. Morgan connected to her, then, with the protection of the great dragon's defenses reinforcing her own, she sought the Arshek dragon.

"Hello friend, it is Caretaker Morgan. I heard your call and welcome your words." She waited for many seconds before hearing the female again.

"I would like to thank you for your kindness, my Lady. I owe you my life, though I did not deserve your mercy."

Morgan felt no hint of Harrick's presence. She asked Nulian if she felt anything before responding.

"You are welcome. May I ask your name, my friend?"

"I am Valen."

"Have you thought of my words and the feelings I shared with you, Lady Valen?"

"I find it difficult to understand the feelings you shared with

me, my Lady. I have never received love from a human nor felt it for one."

"I hope to change that, my friend. I believe in the purity of spirit of all dragons of all breeds. I consider your Perian breed as precious and noble as the Chemerian dragons I serve. I would like to help you see what life could be like for you and your children, if only I can defeat the darkness of the Arshek line."

"I can believe no such life is possible for us who have been bound by Arshek. Our spirits are tainted by the darkness. When he uses his magic it takes over and we fight without thought. The oldest among us carry that hatred at all times. How could we ever be free of something that has affected us so?"

Nulian spoke to Morgan only saying, "Tell her it is not impossible, but will take a great commitment. If she wishes it, you can fight the darkness and keep it from taking her will. Perhaps then she can free herself." Morgan said those words to Valen and waited for her reply.

"You believe we could learn to fight against his magic and free ourselves from his rule, my Lady. I am not sure why you would want us to. We are responsible for the deaths of many Chemerians. You say you forgive, but I question if your dragon brethren could ever forgive and accept us into their world as equals."

"You will never know until you decide the possibility is worth the effort to try, my friend. I want very much to help you. I offer the possibility of a free life to you, your brethren, and all your children. It may come at a great price during the battle to free you, so you must decide if the risk is worth the possible gain. I ask that you think of your children."

"I will consider your words, my Lady. Thank you for speaking with me," Valen said before raising her guard again.

Morgan broke the connection and looked to Nulian.

"Nulian, do you believe the Chemerian dragons will be able to forgive and welcome these dragons into our family. I must admit, it seems very unlikely."

"If we find their spirit to be pure and carrying no malice, forgiveness will come easily. But if they have embraced the darkness such that it is embedded within them, we will consider them enemies forever."

"So, not only do we need to free them from Harrick's castle, we need to enter the mind of each and judge the purity of their spirit. And, I must remove any traces of the darkness left within them."

"And do so without getting maimed or killed in the process," Alec added.

They all discussed the likelihood of this happening for a long while before Morgan stood to say goodnight to Nulian.

"My Queen, I need to ask a favor of you," Nulian said.

"Anything, Nulian, how can I help you?"

"Zirath has refused food and is growing weak. If he does not take food tonight, he will die. Will you attempt to feed him? He may have taken you as his mother figure, and that is the only thing we have not tried."

"Of course, my friend, I will dress and go now," Morgan said as she turned for the doors.

"No need, my Lady. I will bring him and fresh food to you here momentarily," Nulian said as she launched toward the dragon chambers.

"Fresh food?" Morgan said as she watched Nulian disappear around the castle.

"As a dragon will only eat freshly killed meat, this may be

quite gory, my dear. You should put on something you do not care for very much," Alec said.

She put on a very dark smock and collected some linen with a bowl of water to clean up with, then headed back out to the terrace just in time. Nulian landed in the garden with a squirming goat in her jaws, and the hatchling held within one of her front feet.

Morgan took Zirath and he latched onto her smock to lie flat against her chest. Her Crest warmed and prickled at his touch. She caressed him as she swayed and hummed one of Balia's songs. The little one began to hum along with her and relaxed against the support of her arms.

"Explain what I need to do to make the best effort at this, no matter how gross I may find it," she said without breaking her hum. Nulian chuckled before she explained.

"First, we need to get him to take blood from your hand. I mean, off of your hand, of course. I will bleed the goat and pour some into your hand when you are ready. If he accepts it, we will try the meat. If he takes some blood, it will at least keep him alive for a bit longer. If he will not, no healing will save him."

She nodded to Nulian then squinted at the sound the goat made when Nulian dropped her head. With focus on the weakness in the little one, she continued to sing and wandered to the railing to hold her hand out for Nulian.

She sat down and began to stroke her bloody fingers over Zirath's mouth with pressure against his jawline. After offering the blood for many minutes, he had not reacted or opened his mouth.

"Is there nothing more a mother dragon would do to

convince him? A certain song or a certain force?"

"No, this is not often a problem. While it may seem cruel, if the hatchling is too weak to fight for survival, it usually dies. I just wanted to give him the best chance. I am sorry, I will take hi—"

"I am not quitting!"

She uncovered her Crest and laid the weak hatchling over it with his head on her shoulder and his chest contacting her scales. When their scales touched she gasped a bit and shivered.

With her heart and mind focused on Balia, she pushed them into bonding. She shared memories of Balia, focusing on her fierce love of her children and willingness to die for them.

With Zirath held tight against her, and his spirit bathed in the essence of his mother's love and devotion, she reached her blood-covered hand around to his mouth and forced it open with her fingers. She rubbed the blood against the inside of his mouth and his tongue.

He rolled his tongue over her hand with increasing interest for a moment, then began to bite down. She opened her eyes and nodded to Nulian.

Nulian's eyes widened a bit as she dropped her head to the goat. Morgan did not react to the goat's death. She was eager to have the warm flesh in her hand so Zirath did not have to wait. Alec took the meat from Nulian and cut it into small pieces.

Morgan put a small piece of warm flesh into the little dragon's mouth and rubbed it against his gums, squeezing blood onto his tongue. After many tense seconds, the little dragon began to chew. He was lazy at first, but with each piece he became more energetic.

Soon, he had swallowed enough to make his belly bulge. Once he was satisfied, he hummed and tucked himself deep into her arms and went to sleep. Nulian leaned over and smelt of them.

"I smell your blood, my Queen. Show me your injury, please." Alec moved in and grimaced as he inspected the deep cuts on her hands.

"They do not hurt. My hands and chest are tingling so much I can barely feel it," she explained.

Nulian hummed and sent her healing energy while she held the cut hand against her snout. The bleeding stopped, and the cuts began to close from the inside out as Nulian hummed. It was not as efficient, or as complete, as when Morgan healed someone, but it was enough.

Alec knelt beside her to clean and dress her hand with the linen cloths she had gathered earlier. He kissed it and her cheek when he finished. Next, he helped her get more comfortable in the lounge chair. He brought her a blanket, knowing she had no intention of putting the hatchling down before it woke.

"How did you convince him, my Queen?" Nulian asked.

"I let his mother tell him he should fight to live," she muttered with a smile as she dropped off to sleep.

"She is truly a wonderful Caretaker of dragons, my King, and a wonderful friend," Nulian said. Alec nodded and stroked Nulian as they watched her sleep with the hatchling wrapped tight in her arms.

MORGAN WOKE the next morning as Zirath stirred on her chest. She looked over to see Manook sleeping next to them and Nulian gone. The hatchling began to screech and nudge her hands.

"He is hungry, my Lady," Manook said as he bolted into the air and stroked hard for the dragon chambers. Morgan stroked Zirath to comfort him as much as she could, but he was not settling.

"You may want to hurry, my dear, he is getting very anxious," she said to Nulian.

"Manook is returning now with Zirath's breakfast, my Queen. I will come get him after he has fed, so you may have some time to yourself."

"Alright, but I would like to feed him each meal for a while until he is stable and sure to be fine."

"I am glad to hear it. Thank you, my friend."

Manook landed beside her, placed the large bit of meat on the ground, then used his teeth and claws to tear small bits off and place them in her hand. She took each piece and fed little Zirath on her chest. He held her hand with his front feet and only accepted the meat from her. He would not pick it up off of her chest or anything else. If she moved her hand away while he was chewing up a piece, he would stop and move to her hand.

She did not understand but did not care. He was eating and would live if he kept eating. That was all she cared about. She would feed him every meal if she needed to.

Over the next week, she got good use out of the specially designed cloaks she had requested the year before. Zirath hid in the pockets when napping or feeling shy of others and climbed all over her when excited or hungry.

He had let Alec hold him on the third day, but only if she was nearby. He was a bit messy, and the chambermaids were being wonderful by not moaning when they found another surprise hiding somewhere for them.

He slept on her chest each night. On the fourth night, Alec tried to roust the little one off so he could cuddle with her, only to get growled at in return.

"I am getting quite jealous, little one. You better watch it," he said as he rolled over. "Ouch!"

Zirath had snuck over and poked him in the back with his sharp little egg tooth, then dashed back atop Morgan's belly. She laughed at both of them without intervening.

The next morning, she gave Zirath to Nulian when he was hungry in hopes that he would eat with her. She then returned to the bed and snuggled up to Alec.

"My dear, you smell like a dragon," he grumbled.

"Fine, I will go bathe," she said as she rolled back over and started to get up. He jumped up and grabbed her around the waist to pull her back under the warm covers.

Less than twenty minutes later she heard Nulian call.

"Zirath will not eat, my Queen. And he is quite irritable. May I return him to you?"

"Alec is also irritable, but as you once told me, it does a man good to have to wait."

"I have waited, my dear," Alec whispered. She told Nulian to bring Zirath, and Alec dropped his face into the pillow.

"He sleeps for at least an hour after he eats, my love. I will send him with Nulian after I get him to sleep, and then you will have my full attention, I promise," she said as she kissed his shoulder.

BY THE NEXT WEEK Morgan was feeding Zirath only his breakfast and sending him to play with his siblings the rest of the day. He had started taking food from Nulian after Morgan refused to feed him except for in Nulian's company and with her help.

She went to the egg room often to visit with the other new hatchlings as well. Two weeks after they were hatched, she bonded to each of them for the first time, a process essential for their development. Nulian crooned with pride as she told her of the intensity of the bonding due to the blood link they shared.

Nulian felt it was time to have Zirath spend a night away from her, so she did not bring him back after dinner as usual. She and Alec had a private dinner alone in their room and were just settling into bed when she climbed back out and put on a robe.

"What is it?"

"Valen calls," Morgan said as she headed for the terrace and connected to Nulian. *"My dear, has our special hatchling settled down?"*

"Not in the least. But he is not being given the option of coming to you. He is currently pacing the egg room. He is a headstrong little tyrant this evening."

"I need to speak with Valen. I am sorry to ask, but I will not do so without you involved."

"I will join you momentarily. I will have to bring the tyrant or the others will be kept awake all night. He will think he is getting his way and that will not work well for us in the end."

"Alec can watch him inside and keep him away from me perhaps."

"Not likely!" Alec and Nulian said at the same time.

"My dear, there is no way he will stand for seeing you and not touching you," Alec said as he sat beside her on the terrace and covered them both with a blanket.

"I do not want to risk his being affected if we encounter the darkness."

"I see your point, my Caretaker. I will arrange for other care of the little beast and join you soon," Nulian said.

Alec laughed out loud when they saw Menkar fly over toward the entrance to the dragon chambers.

"Menkar is about to get a very bitter first taste of fatherhood, I expect," he said as he continued to chuckle.

"I am not sure who will win in that battle of wills. Menkar may squish him before the night is out," Morgan said as she joined his laughter. They were still chuckling when Nulian landed looking harassed.

"I am sorry to make such a bad night of it, my friend," Morgan said as she stroked her snout.

"You are not the one squawking like a crow and ramming your head into the chest of a growling male major dragon, my Queen. I fully expect a night with a dominant male will do our tyrant some good."

She settled herself down as comfortably as she could and nodded for Morgan to begin. Morgan did not waste time. She connected to Nulian and they raised their guards together.

"I am here, Valen. Do you wish to talk?"

"I do, my Lady, but Lord Harrick is coming, so I may break off at any moment."

"I understand. If he approaches I will back away, but stay near enough to hear. I would like to learn from his interactions with you."

"I would fear danger to you and his wrath on my younglings if he found out, my Lady. Can you do so and not be detected?"

"If I am careful, you yourself will not detect me. The only way he will detect me is if he bonds to you while I am connected to you."

"Very well," Valen said. She then hesitated a few seconds before saying, *"I have decided that I would rather risk death at the hands of your dragons, which have every right to hate me, than condemn my younglings to the life I have led. If you are willing to help me escape with my younglings, I am eager to try. I have not mentioned this to any others here as yet. I did not know if you wanted me to."*

Morgan spoke only to Nulian and Alec saying, *"Do we try to rescue only one and her young, or encourage her to convince her brethren?"*

"Ask Valen if she believes they will be convinced before you worry over it," Nulian said. Morgan did so and waited for her reply.

"I believe the females could be convinced, but I am not sure of the males, as they are kept from us except during the scheduled mating flights."

"Valen, do you mean that you are told when to mate and who to mate with?" Morgan asked for Nulian, who was growling.

"Yes. The Sons of Arshek have always controlled the pairings."

"Do you feel the magical link with a true mate at all?"

"I have heard of it happening. I myself have had no such feeling."

"Do you believe you can trust your brethren to keep your secret, even if they do not wish to try to escape themselves? I would rather save only you before risking their betrayal of your connection to me."

"I trust my brethren with my life, my Lady. They will not betray

me. I will call on you again when I have spo— You must go now, Lord Harrick approaches. Goodnight, my Lady,"

Morgan backed away, yet stayed close enough to see and hear what was said. She, Nulian, and Alec listened as Harrick addressed his enslaved dragons.

"Well, how are the females of my dragon army?" Harrick said as he strolled in front of the dragons. "I am glad to see that most of you value the lives of your young and continue to serve me loyally. I come to you with two orders of business. First, given our depleted forces, all of you will fight in all battles, no matter your brooding status. The second matter is related to this, I believe. One among you decided not to fight with the proper ferocity in the sparring matches. I felt a great resistance to my … encouragement. I, of course, forced her service in the end, but am gravely disappointed in having to do so." As he finished his speech he stopped right in front of Valen and turned to face her. "Valen, you disappoint me. Do tell us why you chose to not serve your master?"

Morgan had felt Valen's tension climb during that speech, and now it doubled. Her body tensed as she felt the deceit in Valen's reply to Harrick.

"I thought to protect the many eggs I carry so my young can grow to serve you, my Lord," Valen said.

"It is not your place to think!" Harrick barked. "You will do as you are told, or you will not see those eggs hatch. Perhaps a bit of a reminder is warranted."

Morgan had to raise her guard a bit more to block Valen's terror over the next moment. With a wave of Harrick's hand, a youngling was drug out in front of the females and struck with many brutal blows by a huge Marock. Valen roared and lurched against the great chains binding her. Harrick stared at her hard, then waved his hand for another round of strikes as a punishment for her attempt to fight. She dropped her body low and bowed her head. The only sound for many seconds was the pained cries of the youngling. Harrick wore a sinister smile as he slowly turned to meet the eyes of each of the females in the hold.

"You will all serve me without question and without hesitation, or you will watch your young pay for your failure!" He turned to glare at Valen once more, then marched out of the hold.

Morgan released the connection and leaned back against Alec's chest. She took a moment to calm her anger as she thought.

"It's time. We must start considering how we are going to free them. I will work to master my new skill level so I can fight Harrick effectively. We can not hope to free them without having him weakened at least."

Alec tightened his grip on her shoulders so much she flinched.

"Sorry, excuse me for a moment," he said before heading inside.

"He is torn, my Queen. He wants to support you, but is distressed over your fighting Harrick, especially now," Nulian said.

"I know his feelings, and he knows that I will face Harrick. He will support me despite his fears."

"I will try to ease them a bit, my friend," Nulian said. She leaned closer to the doorway and spoke louder to say, "My King, will you join us again, please?"

When Alec returned his face was red and stern, but he sat back down and looked up to Nulian without a word.

"Having your children awakened within Morgan has understandably made you more worried, my King. But I want you to know that she is actually stronger with their spirits reinforcing hers. The fact that she felt their awakening on the Day of Light is a reflection of their individual power and that of their link to her. She will also have the ability to block and protect them completely if she is in danger while they remain inside her. I can not take your worry away, but I can swear that I will guard her with my life, and so will every dragon within her service, my King. She must do her duty because that is who she is. We will do ours for the same reason."

"It is very kind of you to offer such words, Nulian. I do respect your devotion to protect her and understand her duty well. But tell me, am I wrong in assuming that when she eventually enters into a magical battle with Harrick, you will not be able to intercede to protect her from the darkness?"

"You are not wrong. She will have to fight him alone."

"I have felt his power and the pain he can inflict. I am fully aware that our Caretaker is strong with our magic, but I do fear for her and my children," he said as his emotions rose. "I am sorry, but I do not feel the risk is worth the gain in this situation, my friend. You ask me to accept the possibility of losing her, and our children, to save the lives of dragons who may never serve her willingly and with pure spirit. How am I to do that, Nulian? How can I do that and live with myself?" He stopped and moved to the terrace doors to look first at Morgan and then at Nulian as his anger spiked, "I know what killed Cora. It was no blade!"

Morgan felt Nulian's sorrow before the Elder raised her guard.

"I know that Cora died while with my mother nearly a year before my Quickening. Tell me what happened, please," she said while controlling her temper with difficulty.

Nulian dropped her head a bit and crooned a long, sad sound before looking at her.

"Lord Harrick's forces captured Queen Christina and Lady Cora when they were out riding one day. In hindsight, I believe Alec's sister was involved. Harrick tortured and eventually killed Cora in an effort to convince your mother to give him her mind. He then tortured her to near death with the darkness as he tried to extract knowledge from her by force.

"She had called to us, and a large force of dragons went to her aid as quickly as possible. The other Elders and I worked to heal her for hours, and then periodically for days. We were able to heal her physical wounds and remove most of the magical scarring, but … severe damage was done, which we could not undo.

"She slowly lost the ability to use her magic, and her health followed that decline. We Elders saw the end of her life approaching. That is when we initiated your Quickening."

Tears were escaping Nulian's eyes as she continued, "She is not the first Caretaker to suffer such a death. I gave you the memory of one of your foremothers as she lay dying from an attack by Harrick's great grandfather. She was much older, and her daughter already crowned Queen, when she died."

Morgan had turned away to face the gardens. Nulian shifted to make her look at her again.

"From this, you see that the danger the darkness poses to the Caretaker is very real indeed. However, you must also appreciate the difference between their experiences and your own, my friend. Your magical power is many times greater than your mother's or any before her for many generations. And you now have the best advantage I could give with my blood within you."

Morgan could not speak. Her entire body trembled as she fought to contain the storm of emotions within her.

"I know you can do this, my Queen. I know you have the magic, the skill, and most importantly, the will. You will do it because you could never rest if you did not. It is that reason alone that makes it certain you will succeed."

Morgan remained silent as she stared over the garden for a long moment. She turned and moved to the door where she paused and shifted to glance back over her shoulder without meeting Nulian's eyes.

"Did Balia know of this?"

"Yes."

"And all who were close to my mother as well?"

"Yes."

She had to pause to check herself again, then turned to hold Nulian's gaze.

"You are my mentor, my blood-giver, and now, my dearest friend. Yet … you held this from me each and every time we bonded. That truth hurts far more than the facts you shared."

She raised her guard to its highest and blocked everyone

as she left Nulian and her chambers. Cold emptiness grew within her as her trust in all around her was questioned. She knew the dragons had knowledge she would not likely ever understand. But to know so many around her, both dragon and human, had hidden something so profound from her was agonizing.

She found Alec on the terrace of his old quarters, with his head in his hands. He had felt her coming and stood as she entered. They embraced each other without a word. Morgan placed her hand to his neck to deepen their connection. She shared Nulian's words and all of her feelings as they came to her.

"I have to do this, it is my duty. I am not reacting with rage to learning he killed my mother. And it is not only to free the dragons Harrick enslaves. I do this to free our people, their children, and ours from the threat the darkness of Arshek imposes. You know I must do this, and I know you will help me no matter the risk, because it is the right thing to do, my love."

"Of course, I will. I will always support you in whatever you do, my dear. I would gladly give my life to prevent your ever having to face him. Since I can not prevent it, I will do everything possible to help you prepare, and fight at your side with all I am."

"Did you know how she died? Did you hide this from me as well?"

"I only guessed from things I saw and overheard while growing up around Kisik and your other family. I did not know anything for fact. I would never have hidden that from you. I hide nothing from you."

SHE WENT BACK to her chambers and settled down on the terrace. She sat quietly for a long time as she struggled to deal with all she had heard.

"I feel not only your anger, but also your disappointment in me. Will you talk with me?" Nulian said.

"Give me time, please."

Her heart ached as she considered how her mother must have suffered during her last year. She imagined how difficult it was for those who loved her to watch her suffer and not be able to help her at all.

Her ignorance and naivety in it all made her insides burn. She had accepted that her mother died of an untreatable illness and felt like a fool for not considering this as a possibility.

A nauseating chill ran through her as she considered how many had hidden this from her. A moment later, she felt someone unexpected approaching her chambers. She did not rise to meet him as her chambermaid showed him in.

"I understand you have now been told of the reason for your mother's early death," Kisik said. "I imagine there is a great deal of anger within you toward those of us who knew the reason and withheld it from you."

She responded with a slow nod.

"I would be angry as well, but you must know our reason, my dear. We were keeping a promise. Christina made me, Josef, Maric, and the Elder dragons swear to keep it from you until you were strong and confident with your magic and your role here," he said as he strolled closer to her. He sat in the chair beside her and held her gaze with his soft, confident eyes as he continued.

"Morgan, she felt your great magic when you were within

her. She spoke often of her belief you would grow to be our strongest Caretaker and worried over all that would mean for you. When she found herself weakening and realized you would be called so young, she was distraught. She feared you would act rashly and seek a battle with Harrick if you knew this. Her choice to keep her suffering a secret was meant to serve and to protect you. We love you, my niece, and wanted only to keep you safe as you grew stronger. We trusted that the Eldest Female of the dragon Council would tell you when the time was right."

Morgan sat up and kissed his cheek.

"Thank you for coming to tell me this. Please know that I hold no ill will toward you or Maric. Have a good night, Uncle."

"I pray you will not continue to question our love and loyalty, my Queen. Neither could be stronger, I assure you," he said as he stood and bent over to kiss her head before leaving.

She focused on the high ridge over the lake and found Nulian sitting there staring at her. She had told Kisik she held no anger for him or Maric, but she could not say the same for her dear friend.

"Nulian, I respect your role as Eldest Female, and I understand you were bound by the Council's pledge to my mother. I also respect my family's duty to keep her confidence. But, there is one truth in all of this that cuts very deep.

"I have made a mistake every time I have bonded deeply to those I love. You see, I assumed our bonding to be fully open and complete. Though I have more than enough skill to do so, I did not assure that was the case directly. For me to have not felt this within you…to know you hid this consciously every time we…"

She stopped as her temper rose and waited until she was calm again to continue. *"This is a mistake I will never make again, with you or anyone else. I will seek all and be aware of purposeful exclusions from now on, in all bonding with everyone. This is a powerful lesson and a painful one."*

"I love you, my Sister. I am sorry for giving you this pain."

"Do not apologize for doing your duty. You put your duty and the safety of our country before your love of me. You have nothing to apologize for."

"You are wrong. It was my love for you that made me continue to hide it, even after I should have told you. I convinced myself that holding it from you was right simply because it meant saving you from the pain of the truth for a bit longer."

"I understa—"

"I have hidden nothing else like this from you. Please let me show you. Bond to me now and seek all you wish, my Sister."

"No, I will not bond to you only to seek a lack of deceit. It is late. Let us both get some rest. Goodnight," she said as she stood and moved toward the terrace doors. She felt annoyance rise in Nulian and turned just in time to catch Zirath against her chest.

He was breathing very hard from the long flight from the dragon chambers and had a triumphant expression as he nuzzled her with sweet croons. She could not help but smile. The love from the little hatchling was the perfect comfort for her aching heart.

She smiled when she felt anger rise in Menkar as he woke and discovered Zirath had escaped his company. She caressed Zirath as he settled down against her and hummed a lullaby to him. Alec soon joined her and wrapped her and

Zirath with his arms as he stood behind her to sway along to the tune.

"Did you speak with Nulian, my dear?"

"Yes."

"Did you truly forgive her?"

"I am not sure. I believe she did what she had to. And I believe her when she says not telling me was easier because it spared me the pain of the truth."

"What keeps you from forgiving then?"

"Knowing she purposely deceived me. I simply have to get over it before I can fully forgive."

"There is much she will always keep from you, Morgan. She is an Elder dragon and keeper of many secrets of the dragon race. She loves you, and that is what matters," he said as he kissed her neck. "Do not make her sleep like this." He shifted to ease the sleeping Zirath from her chest and slipped back inside to leave her alone. Zirath started to protest, but fell quiet as Alec spoke to him.

"Please come to me, my Sister," Morgan called to Nulian. She smiled when she saw Nulian take to the air and stroke hard toward her.

When Nulian landed and moved her head over the railing, Morgan moved to lean against the length of her head and rested her forehead to hers. She said nothing as she let Nulian push them into bonding, then sighed as her tension eased. They stayed within that blissful place for a long time before Nulian spoke.

"I love you, my Caretaker," Nulian said as she pushed an intense rush of that precious emotion.

"I love you too, my Sister."

OVER THE NEXT FEW WEEKS, Morgan spent most of her time training and studying her gifts' capabilities with Nulian on the ancient world. Alec spent most of his time training with the Guard and planning strategies for the assault on the Arshek castle.

It would be a great strike, and all would be involved except for a small force that would stay to protect the castle of Chemerie. Alec poured himself into his work to keep from thinking about the possible outcomes of her facing Harrick. It was not that he did not believe in her skills. He was simply aware of just how evil his father was and knew that while she was likely to show mercy, his father was not.

They both marveled at the rate of her advancing pregnancy. After only one month, she was showing noticeably and could feel the babies moving a little. GranMay and the midwives believed the children would arrive within three more months if the rate of development held.

This was a huge issue for the planning of the assault. They could wait until the children were born and have them safely away on the ancient world. Or, they could move quickly to allow her the opportunity to fight before she becomes too large and her mobility is hampered. Alec was torn, of course. Nulian had said Morgan would be stronger with the children within her, yet, if she were lost they would die as well.

MORGAN FOCUSED on her ability to detect the darkness and used Alec's imprisoned half-sister, Irika, as the source of the dark magic.

After being injured by Manook during her murderous attempt, Irika had refused healing. She had suffered through great infection and heavy scarring as the deep dragon gouges healed. Her time was spent within the dungeon of the castle except when allowed outside in the company of many guards.

Morgan began to sit outside her cell and connect with her. At first, the experiences were very challenging. She had to learn to fight the darkness while focusing to break through her defenses.

Harrick had said Irika had been born with no appreciable magical skill. He was wrong. She did indeed have skill, but it was all focused on hiding her feelings and closing her mind.

Morgan delved into her mind by force in order to fight the darkness. She was able to reach far within her mind and was sickened to find the level of hatred she carried. Her spirit itself was dark. She had no kindness or love of any great amount.

However, after many hours of combing through her mind and killing the darkness as she discovered it, she felt a brush of sorrow. It originated from a small glimmer of loving feelings buried deep within her mind.

She worked for over an hour, clearing the area of the darkness until she heard the woman begin to sob. Irika had softened her face, relaxing all of the heavy scowling.

"What is this sorrow you carry, Irika?"

The woman pulled herself into a tight ball and buried her face in her arms to cry hard.

"I ache for my son. Father took him from me when he was born and then sent me here. He told me that if I failed to bring him Alec, he would serve his wrath to my boy in my place."

"If only I could trust you, I would try to help you. But

even now, I feel the deceit in your words. You are so full of hate, and you hold onto the darkness so tightly, that I can not believe in you. I have seen only a desire to kill me and my family and a loyalty to the dark magic of your father within you. Your words do not outweigh what your spirit says to me."

Irika glared at her as deep scowling lines and a macabre sneer twisted her face again.

"My father will kill you, the creatures you carry, and my dear brother. And then, my son will rule this land by his side. You can delve into my mind all you wish, but you will never take my loyalty to my father from my heart!" She had rushed at the bars of the cell and reached out at Morgan as she screamed.

Morgan didn't flinch. She held her eyes through the vicious threat, then took a deep sigh as she slowly stood.

"It is your choice, Irika. You may stay loyal to him and live out your days here, or you can open yourself to the love of the people around you and allow us to free your heart of the darkness." She bowed to the snarling woman trying to grab her legs and left the dungeon.

MANY WEEKS LATER, Morgan leaned against Nulian's broad chest as she watched Alec finishing a long sword fight with Daniel and Maric. They and the many other groups of sparring Knights fought with such force they came near injuring each other many times, but their control left not a scratch behind.

"Is it possible to use the magic as a defense against a physical attack? Can you touch the mind of the attacker and use suggestion to break their will?"

"I am not sure if it has been tried, my Queen," Nulian said.

"Hmm."

She walked forward into the circle of fighting Knights with a small smile to those around her. When she stopped, everyone quieted and looked to her.

"My King, please have a Knight with a very strong will come at me with the intention of taking hold of me. I wish to try something."

Alec looked at a powerfully built young Knight and nodded. The Knight glanced between them without moving.

"Do your duty, Sir Ruik! Your task is to take me into your grasp. Now act!"

As Sir Ruik rushed forward, she connected to him and pushed a simple order.

"Stop and kneel!" With the words, she pushed feelings of uncertainty and confusion.

Sir Ruik stumbled, his feet stopped moving forward, and his knees buckled, dropping him to the ground. He righted himself with great effort, looked away from her eyes as he shook his head, then struggled to step toward her again.

"Stop!" With that order she sent images of bright blinding light. The young man gasped and grabbed at his eyes. While he was weakened, she sent great waves of sadness and despair deeper into his mind.

Sir Ruik fell to the ground and grabbed his head as he moaned in pain. She stopped her assault and went to him while pushing feelings of love and kindness. As her hand touched his shoulder, she shared healing energy to relieve any true pain. He relaxed and met her eyes with his wide.

"Thank you, Sir Ruik. I am sorry if I hurt you," she said. The Knight righted himself and showed no lingering damage except for a bit of confusion.

Alec came up to her side and kissed her cheek with a smirk. *"Remind me never to make you angry, my dear."*

She elbowed him as they turned to walk away.

"My Queen, is that what we are to expect from Harrick when we face him?" a female Knight called out in a nervous voice.

Morgan asked Nulian's thoughts as she turned to face the Knights gathered around her.

"Nulian and I can not say for certain, as there has been no precedent set. But we believe it is a good idea to assume he can. We all know he is an evil man without mercy, who governs his people by force. I am sure he uses his magic to control them by fear of pain, but it may be by more direct control as I just used. I am certain that if he has the capability he will use it. I would like to work with each of you alone and then in larger numbers to help you learn to combat it and to improve my skill at using it. As with Sir Ruik, I may hurt you. If so, I will remove the pain quickly, I promise," she said. All of the Knights bowed in unison to agree to the offer.

"Your Knights welcome the experience, my Queen," Daniel said in a formal tone as he bumped the shoulder of a young Squire who was staring at her Crest a bit too hard. The young man blushed like mad as his friends snickered. They hushed at Daniel's glare as he continued. "What time tomorrow would you like to begin?"

"First light would suit me, my Admiral," she said, matching his formality with a smirk as she moved to kiss his cheek. She then moved to the blushing Squire and touched his cheek to push understanding, and allow him and the rest of the curious ones to see the beautiful marking without embarrassment for the deep cut of her dress.

"My Queen, my first clutch is hatching, and you are welcome to visit if you would like. Menkar asks if King Alec would like to join him as well." Sirzi said.

"We are honored and will join you as fast as your mother can deliver us," Morgan said as she and Alec moved into Nulian's waiting palm. They spent the evening welcoming the new hatchlings and visiting with their dear friends.

TIME PASSED QUICKLY as Morgan continued to hone her skills with Nulian and with the Knights. She worked for four to five hours a day before having to rest, and then a few more in the evenings. Alec doted over her, and she often had to tell him to back off.

She had begun to meditate in the mornings to focus and clear her mind. In the middle of her third month of pregnancy, she was able to bond to the spirits of her growing children. It was a light awareness of them that felt like a warm wash of water flowing over her. It was a very special sensation for her, and she shared it with Alec the next morning as a surprise.

She let him enter bonding with her and then opened her connection to bond with the little ones. He fell unconscious the instant she connected to the children. She woke him, and he bent over to kiss her belly as he chuckled.

"That was wonderful and powerful, my dear. I think that was the most intense thing I have ever felt," he said.

"I find the sensation very comforting. I did not know to

warn you."

"Thank you for sharing it with me. I would have done it even if you told me I would fall unconscious like a swooning fool."

She jumped and put a hand to her swollen belly.

"Mercy, one of our children is working out," she said as she squinted at the sharp pain in her side. She placed his hand to her belly and smiled as he felt his children moving under his hand for the first time.

MORGAN'S WORK with the Knights progressed a great deal during the next three weeks. She had managed to control ten at the same time while Nulian tried to break her focus by forming an unwanted connection.

One morning while engaged with a large group of Knights, she felt a rush of warmth accompanied by intense tingling radiating from her Crest down to her children. She dropped her attack on the Knights and raised her guard as she eased down to one knee with her head spinning.

Within seconds many strong hands lifted her, and Daniel slid an arm around her middle.

"What's wrong?"

"Well, I'm not injured," she said with a reassuring smile. "However, I am going to have to excuse myself from the training, my friends. It seems my children are ready to say hello," she said as she let him support her. The group cheered as she connected to Alec, who was fighting a group of five men in open-hand combat. As she connected, he punched a bit too hard, and almost knocked out one of the men before turning to smile at her.

"It is time, my dear," she said as he helped the dazed man to his feet. He took off toward her and slid into Nulian's palm with her.

"I am not in pain. Relax, my love," she said as she hugged him and passed calming feelings.

"Nulian, we want to have our children on the ancestral world. May we bring GranMay to be with us there?"

"Of course, my Queen. But you will have many here who will be very upset not to be part of this happy occasion. Are you certain?"

"Yes, we want it to be a private experience in the safety of the ancestral world. Having them born where they were conceived will be special to us."

"Daniel," Alec said. "We are going to the safety of the sanctuary where the children were conceived. You will be in charge of things around here for a couple of days, my friend. We hope to take Queen May along. Do you mind delivering the news to the rest of the family in person?"

"Not at all. Just take good care of my little sister, then bring her and the twins back so we can all spoil them properly," Daniel said. When Morgan gave him a conflicted look, he smiled and offered a hand. "I'm not insulted to stay. Really," he said as he squeezed her hand. "I'll breathe easier knowing you'll be well out of Harrick's reach as you welcome the munchkins." He gave her a long hug, then shook Alec's hand before stepping back to join the rest of the crowd in cheering as they took off for the castle.

"GranMay, we would like for you to take a quick trip with us. Please pack an overnight bag and meet us in the garden."

"It may be a bit, my dear. Kisik and I were about to..."

"Well, if you want to witness your great-grandchildren enter-ing this world, you better hurry." Her tone matched the urgency she was beginning to feel. She shared the emotion with Gran-May and heard no more argument.

When they reached their chambers, they found the cham-bermaids had already prepared their luggage, including a bag full of baby items and a large trunk full of foodstuffs.

"Mercy, Neesa, you ladies are more prepared for this than I am. Thank you all," she said as she and Alec added a few more things to their clothes bags. The ladies curtsied and wished her well as they carried the bags out for them.

"Is there anything else I can get that will make you more comfortable there, my love?" Alec asked as he knelt beside where he had insisted she sit.

"Yes, but it would be inappropriate," she said. She looked to the terrace as she felt a great rush of sadness and longing from the very 'something' she was referring to.

Falin, Lirpa, Manook, and little Zirath had just landed around the terrace with sad faces all around. She went to them and knelt in the middle of the group. Zirath jumped to her shoulder and clung to her chest while she stroked each of them and fought tears.

"I am going to a very safe place to have my children, my friends. I will return to introduce them to you soon, I prom-ise. I can not take you with me. I'm sorry."

"But we will protect you here, my Queen. Why must you go away?" Manook asked.

"It is what the magic tells me I should do. It is a special place and is where they were conceived. I trust that you will all care for our brethren while I am away. I will be back soon."

She kissed each of their snouts and placed the pouting Zirath on his big brother's back before turning to leave with Alec.

Streams of tears ran down her cheeks as she walked away. Three feet out into the hallway, she stopped and looked at Alec. He kissed her cheek and cradled her face as he wiped her tears away.

"Do what your heart and the magic tell you, my dear. Be where you feel the safest and happiest."

"Those are not the same place," she said through her sobs as she dropped her head to his chest.

"My Sister, I feel your pain and understand it. You love the younglings as your own children and want to share this with them. Therefore, I am granting that they come along with us. The other Elders will simply have to deal with it," Nulian said.

They thanked her many times over as they turned and hurried back to their special friends. Zirath flew to her, and all crooned at the news.

"You must be quiet about this and go straight to Nulian at once. She will guide you from there," she said. Zirath stayed with her and Alec as the rest launched from the terrace.

Morgan, Alec, and GranMay flew to the Chamber of Elders with Drieden and Nulian. Once all of the party was gathered in the portal chamber, Morgan knelt in front of her friends and held a serious face.

"We are going to a very special place, my friends. Lady Nulian has graciously granted you permission to join me, and I expect you to be respectful of her instructions. Do you understand?" She looked at Zirath pointedly and he nodded with a chirp. "You will see many wondrous things in this new place, and I am going to tell you about one of them before we go. You will meet dragons of a different breed there. They are as kind and gentle as you are and they are also very precious to me. I tell you this because you may be shocked when you see that they are the same breed as those enslaved by Lord Harrick."

All of the younglings crouched into a defensive pose except Zirath, who hissed loudly. She waited until they read her expression and quieted.

"I trust them completely, and I expect you to trust me. Do you?" They all nodded and hummed. "Then off we go. Be sure to have contact with me or Nulian until you learn the song."

GranMay was struggling with Morgan's news, but held her questions as she laid a hand to Nulian and joined in as she learned the new song. Everyone was soon carried across to the ancestral world.

The younglings and GranMay looked around in amazement to find themselves on a whole different planet.

"Ahh ... " Morgan squinted and grabbed her belly. "That was ... impressive." Alec picked her up into his arms and climbed into Nulian's palm. Gerzin landed next to Nulian and offered a palm to GranMay and Manook.

Lirpa and Falin worked hard to stay with the two Elders during the long flight to the gazebo. When they arrived, GranMay prepared the bed as Morgan changed to a light gown and braided her hair. Alec unpacked while eyeing Morgan's every move. When she hissed and doubled over, he lifted her onto the bed and moved to help GranMay ready the supplies.

The younglings were crowded around the gazebo with

Manook resting on the sidewall and Zirath on the headboard. They all hummed their healing song to help control her pain.

When the pain got quite bad, Zirath looked to Nulian then moved to lie across her Crest. Her scales prickled, and the tingling sensation spread all over her. The rest of the dragons strengthened their healing song and her pain faded away. As she relaxed, GranMay moved to check the position and health of the babies.

Morgan squeezed Alec's hand and smiled.

"Our friends have taken most of the pain away. I can focus on the children now, and feel their magic flowing through me along with that of the dragons. It is amazing, my love," she said as she connected to him deeply. She sent him a sample of the elation she felt and he nearly fell over.

"Too much, my dear! I do not want to pass out and miss this," he said, grabbing the bed post. She laughed as she backed off on the transfer to him, then grimaced as a massive contraction hit her again.

"Alright, my dear, you can push when you are ready," GranMay said as she took a seat on the foot of the bed and slid the sheets aside while pushing additional healing magic with every touch.

Morgan took in a great breath and pushed with all her might. She repeated this process several times before a great rush of hot tingles filled her abdomen. She pushed once more, then let out the breath when she heard the beautiful cry of her daughter. Two more great pushes and her son joined in with his sister.

She lay back, breathing hard as Zirath moved off of her

chest with a soft croon. Alec and GranMay laid her children in her arms against her chest and settled down beside her.

The children quieted when they touched her, and her Crest began to glow much brighter as the dragons around it stirred. Morgan and Alec both thought the same thing and rolled the children over to see their chests. Both had a small patch of scales on their little chests, and both were glowing like their mother's.

GranMay was crying as she beamed at the new family. The dragons crowded around the bed as Nulian lowered her head to take a closer look. Zirath dropped down onto Morgan's pillow and inched his head forward to sniff at the babies. He touched his snout to their daughter's head as he hummed.

"It is time to find names for these special ones, my friends," Nulian said. "Enter into bonding as a family and let the magic guide you."

Alec lay down and wrapped his arm over his family, then snuggled up to kiss Morgan and touch his head to hers. He joined her in their first bonding with their children with a gasp and fierce shiver. Together, the parents explored the spirits of their children and found them beautiful and gentle.

As they let their spirits mingle, they heard two voices calling out the names of their children. Morgan backed away from the bonding and opened her teary eyes to see Alec looking at her with a tear rolling down his cheek. They kissed their children and watched them sleep for a few seconds before GranMay interrupted in a harsh whisper.

"Well, are you going to share or make us guess?" she said, making everyone laugh.

"Our daughter is Brya, after the first daughter of Lady Chemerie, and our son is Kyan, after the first son of The Purest."

GranMay cried even harder as she leaned over to kiss the children's heads and Morgan's. All of the dragons hummed the children's names and began to sing the beautiful Song of Connection. Everyone joined them in the song to welcome the children.

Morgan fed the babies, then Alec took one at a time to bathe and swaddle them. She watched with amazement how natural handling the children seemed for such a strong man. His face expressed the deep happiness she felt within him as he swayed with the children in his arms. She knew that was an image she would hold forever. He lay back down with her and she soon fell asleep with the children nestled between them.

THE SOUND OF QUIET GROWLS and fear from the younglings woke Morgan. She and Alec both covered the babies as they lifted up from the bed. Zirath was on the headboard staring toward the back of the gazebo, trembling and growling. Lirpa, Falin, and Manook had taken tense postures as they stared in the same direction.

"Settle down little ones, they are friends of your Queen and therefore friends of yours as well," Nulian said.

Morgan sat up and spoke aloud to all of the younglings around her.

"My friends, may I introduce Brit, Hirk, and their mother, Asira. They have been wonderful friends to me, and I know you will find them to be pure spirits and true friends of yours as well. Falin, please show your younger friends how to be polite to our guests."

Falin backed down the Gazebo stairs and bowed to the Perian dragons.

"It is very nice to meet new friends of my Queen. Welcome. I am Falin. The others are my beautiful friend Lirpa, young Manook, and little Zirath," he said as he indicated each of his brethren. Each of them nodded or bowed in reply, except Zirath who dropped to the bed to hide behind Morgan.

"Hirk, Brit, please come up and meet our children. I would be honored for you to be among the first to call them friends," Morgan said.

Falin and Lirpa moved aside so the Perian younglings could approach the bed. Manook mounted the footboard to stand watch, but made no aggressive move.

Brave little Brit was the timid one today. It was Hirk whose curiosity pushed him forward to touch Kyan's foot with his snout. Morgan felt anger boil inside Zirath and caught him as he lunged for Hirk, snapping his teeth just shy of his snout. She held him firm and turned him to face her.

"Zirath, I will not accept your company if you disgrace me by attacking my friends. Go to Nulian. Now!" She pushed him off the bed and watched with an aching heart as he walked to Nulian, looking back over his shoulder at her every few steps.

"Please take him away for a while and speak with him, my dear. Make him see that I love him dearly but must have his trust," she said to Nulian. Nulian nodded and flew off with Zirath in her front foot.

Morgan stroked Hirk to calm him, as Alec hummed to the children to calm them. They had started to cry when the anxiety level within their mother shot up.

"He is very young and knows only to fear Perian dragons. Please give him time to understand, my friends. He has a beautiful spirit, and I know he will prove to be a valuable friend to you," she said to Hirk and Brit.

The two Perian younglings and Manook laid their heads on the bed near the feet of the babies. Their breath on the children's feet brought giggles from the newborns. The dragons soon started tickling their feet with their tongues, which made them and everyone present laugh and relax.

MANY MORE FRIENDS came to visit, but none made more of a ruckus than Nulian's older twin brothers. They were babbling over one another at the sight of a new set of twins. The duo gave advice of every kind imaginable. Morgan and Alec thanked them for their advice, and said they would certainly be calling on them for more.

"They could not possibly be any more different than Nulian. They are a bit crazy, yes?" Alec said. She nodded but wore a weak smile. It was difficult to be happy while being very aware of the great feelings of abandonment within Zirath.

She slid from the bed and flinched as she stood. The younglings all moved to touch their snouts to her. Together, they all began to hum, both Chemerian and Perian. She closed her eyes and focused to let her magic flow with theirs. She felt the aches and pains begin to leave her as the loving healing song washed over her.

"Thank you, my friends, you are all so good to me and I

love you all," she said as she stroked each of them. She took a deeper, easier breath as GranMay gripped her hand to take the rest of her pain. "I will be back shortly. I need to talk to Zirath," she said to Alec as she kissed the children and him. He nodded and turned back to the babies with a huge smile.

"I get you all to myself, my children," he said as he kissed each of their bellies. He raised his head with a crinkled nose and GranMay burst out laughing.

"And, lucky for you, it is time to change diapers, my dear King," GranMay said. Alec looked a bit queasy as he turned to Morgan. She laughed out loud and waved at his pleading gaze as she slid into Asira's palm.

"I am coming to talk with him myself. I need to spend some time with him, my dear," she said to Nulian.

Both adult dragons left her alone with Zirath. The hatchling was lying on the ground and did not turn to look at her as she sat near him.

"Do you love me, Zirath?"

"Like my own mother, my Queen," he said as his head snapped up. She opened her hand to him, and he scurried to her to push his head into her palm.

"Do you trust me?"

Zirath looked up and nodded his head.

"Do you think I would ever betray your mother, who was my precious friend?"

"Never, my Lady."

"I believe you think I have done just that by befriending these Perian dragons."

Zirath dropped his head again and scratched at the grass as he answered.

"I know you loved my mother, my Queen. I just do not understand how you can trust them after what they did to her and so many others."

"They did nothing, Zirath. They have never been to our world. The Perian dragons here have nothing to do with what has occurred on Erion." Zirath sat up and gave her an attentive gaze. "They are as pure of spirit as you, my little one. The darkness has never touched them. I trust them and I love them. If you are my friend, and you truly trust me, you will show them kindness and allow them to show you who they truly are."

Zirath nodded and rubbed his head to her hand again. She picked him up and placed him to her chest before continuing on to the more difficult part of the conversation.

"I am going to need your help, my friend. I am going to ask that you be very brave and very mature. Can you do that?"

He held himself out from her chest and looked into her eyes as he gave a slow strong nod.

"I am going to ask you to forgive the one who killed your mother." Zirath pulled his head back a bit, but did not move away from her. "I have been in contact with the Perian female who is responsible for the death of Balia and perhaps many others. I need you to listen and consider the horrible conditions in which they live. Once you understand their torment, you will see why I am asking you to forgive."

Zirath nodded but looked very uneasy.

"Do you understand that your mother would have killed to protect you or any of her young?"

Zirath nodded with a furrowed brow.

"Exactly, you would expect that of any mother. Well, that

is part of what has caused the Perian dragons on Erion to fight for the Sons of Arshek. He threatens to kill their children if they do not fight for him. He is cruel and often hurts their young to keep control over them. He also uses the dark magic to control their minds and enrage them to make them fight so fiercely. Once he has control of their minds, they are driven only by the evil that feeds the darkness."

Zirath looked down at her chest for many seconds before returning his gaze to her eyes.

"They have no choice, do they, my Queen? They can not just refuse to fight and watch their own younglings get killed. They are forced to choose the life of their own young over the life of our dragons. But does the dark magic not make them evil forever?"

"I have seen a great amount of love and respect within the female I have been speaking with. I believe I can rid her mind of the traces of darkness that linger, and free her from it forever. She has asked that we help her and her brethren to be free of him, and I want to try. But I need the support of our Chemerian dragons, and that is where I need you. Can you find it in your heart to forgive her, Zirath? Can you help me show the others why we can not hold the dragons enslaved by the Arshek line responsible for their deeds, and why we must show mercy to them?"

Zirath looked across the valley below for a long time then said, "If I could not forgive, I would be no better than Harrick, would I, my Queen? I must see the goodness in others before I can hope to have goodness in myself."

"You are wise little one, just like your mother and grandmother, I see," she said. He tucked his head under her chin and hummed. "I love you too, little one. Now, would you like to go back and visit with Brya and Kyan?" He rustled his wings with excitement, and she called to Nulian for a lift back to the gazebo.

As they landed back by the gazebo, she laughed out loud as she heard Zirath say, "Thank you, GranNulian," and heard Nulian snort in response.

"I imagine my children will be calling you that as well, my Sister," Morgan said. Nulian hummed at the idea as she lifted off to visit with Gerzin.

Zirath flew to land behind Hirk and tapped his tail to get his attention. He bowed low to the Perian youngling when he turned to face him.

"I apologize for my ignorance. I should not have judged you based only on your appearance. I hope to prove myself worthy of your friendship."

Hirk bowed to him in return and said, "You just did, my friend," before lifting the little one to the bed with his snout.

GRANMAY RETURNED to the castle with the older younglings the next morning, but Morgan and Alec spent one more night in the gazebo with their new babies. Zirath stayed with them, of course.

Morgan was overjoyed with her healthy little ones and was amazed at the power of the sensations she felt from them. Their thought patterns were not complex yet, so she did not actually receive full ideas, but their emotions were clear. Alec's connection to them was not as strong, but it was still considerable. The new parents knew when their children were hungry or needed changing before they had to cry for it.

Alec doted over her, and they both saw to the feeding, changing, and cleaning of their little ones. They marveled at the children's excitement over new sensations or sights. Morgan had done some baby-sitting while growing up, and she was sure these two were much more aware of their environment than any Earth-born baby.

She nearly cried as she felt their joy when they touched one of the dragons with their hands. She and Alec both took great pleasure in watching the children laugh and wiggle as Zirath played hide-n-seek with them. The loving hatchling let them grab him and pull whatever they wanted. He never complained and was very gentle. They knew the three would have a very special bond as they grew together.

One Family

MORGAN AND ALEC stood beside Nulian in the portal room of the Chamber of Elders, holding their children and listening to the disturbing news being delivered by Drieden. Overnight, a small militia of Arshek guards had stormed the castle and managed to free Irika by threatening to kill the children of many citizens.

As Alec's anger rose, Brya began to cry. Morgan explained the connection and he calmed himself while humming to her. Brya calmed as he did and was soon asleep.

WHEN THEY EXITED the Chamber of Elders aboard Nulian, they were met and accompanied by a large fleet of dragons with Knights. Once at the castle, they were escorted the rest of the way into the main structure by another large group of Knights. GranMay and Emma met them in Kindred

Hall with two of Morgan's chambermaids and offered to take the children upstairs. Morgan and Alec kissed their little ones then joined the Admiralty.

"Irika must have been giving them details of the castle's layout for years. They knew exactly where to find her and how to make the most efficient strike," Daniel explained. "The Arshek Knights and Marocks covered their scent with cakes of wet mud and snuck past the outer dragon lines. Once to the city proper, they took small children hostage and used them as human shields when cornered in the dungeon later. We did not feel the life of Irika was worth the life of any of those children, so we let them go in exchange for the children's release."

"This is more motivation to move forward with breaking the Sons of Arshek for good. Let us discuss the assault on Arshek castle. Have a seat, everyone," Alec said. He waited for all to settle then continued, "Until this moment we have told no one of the more difficult aspect of our plans. It is our intent to free the Arshek dragons, as they wish to align themselves with us." He paused a moment for the shock to lessen. "I can see no way Irika would know about this. It is surely a perfect way to surprise Harrick. He will send his dragons to fight against us. We could have a guard unit come at the castle from the back and remove the younglings from the hold. Once their young are safe, the Arshek dragons will turn and fight at our side against Harrick's forces."

Most of the faces in the room still wore blank stares, and all remained silent.

"Morgan, will you tell us how you have come to believe these dragons will turn on Harrick, please?" Daniel said.

"I have been in contact with a major female Perian dragon enslaved by Harrick. I healed her after the last major assault here. That act allowed her to see the truth of our nature. I ask that you trust in me. I believe in her and trust her word that her brethren want a free life for their children. They do this knowing many of them will likely die in the effort."

"I don't think anyone here would question your reasoning," Daniel said. Everyone nodded, and he looked to Alec. "So what is the basic plan, my King?"

The group discussed options for hours. Morgan left after the plan was in place, and went upstairs to feed the babies. She told GranMay of the plan and saw her face darken.

"Speak your mind, GranMay."

"My dear, I have to say that you are putting a lot of trust in the Arshek dragons when they have done nothing as yet to deserve it."

"Our dragons will be present in full force, and there will be more than enough of them to defeat the Arshek dragon force if it does not turn its allegiance."

"And you will be alright with that, my dear?"

"I will put trust in them and give them their chance to show their pure hearts. If they can not break free from the darkness after I have Harrick occupied, or if they choose not to, then we will be left with no choice. Because there is no choice. Chemerie will be triumphant, and Harrick will fall."

SHE FINISHED feeding the babies, then dressed in a black riding suit with light armament. When she rejoined the Admiralty, she stood beside Alec to listen as he went through the final plan again, interrupting him to correct a crucial point.

"No, I will not be waiting until the dragon army of Arshek turns to our side. They will have no hope of turning to our side if I have not broken Harrick's hold on them. I must have his focus for them to fight against it. After we know the Perian younglings are safe, Nulian and I will focus on Harrick from above his castle to begin breaking his hold on them. Until then, our Chemerian dragons will try to wound, but not kill, the Perian dragons unless given no choice in order to protect themselves or us."

Not one person spoke against her, but every face moved between her and Alec, waiting for him to speak. He was looking at her with intense eyes.

"It is the proper plan. Support me in it, my King."

"You need not ask, my Queen. Of course, I will." He nodded then looked around the table. "In light of this change, are there any other modifications we need to make, Admirals?"

"Would it be best to draw the Arshek forces further away from their castle? Will the distance make it easier for the Perian dragons to fight Harrick's influence?" Daniel asked.

"Possibly, we do not have enough information to know for sure, but it could only help, I would think," Morgan said.

"Drawing their forces away means less risk to the Queen as she initiates her interference in Harrick's control," Maric said.

"Not to mention making it easier to secure the safety of the Perian younglings to begin with," Burke added. "I am concerned Harrick will be cautious with them after losing so many this year."

After a bit more debate, they agreed, and Alec went through it once more using the great contour map spread over the table.

"We will place a large and visible force of dragons and men at the base of the mountains near the river. Harrick is sure to send equal forces out to engage them. With that battalion engaged, we bring another Guard unit into sight to the south, to which Harrick will commit the bulk of his remaining troops. This will leave the Arshek castle weak and signal the time to move to secure the hatchlings.

"Morgan's attack against Harrick's control over the fighting Perians will begin as soon as the younglings are secure. The Chemerian dragons will give her twenty minutes before advancing their level of aggression against the Perian dragons.

"Morgan and Nulian will direct any alterations necessary from overhead until she is engaged in the fight against Harrick. I will speak with the dragons, and they to one another. This will enable communication between battalions and make coordination of the Guards' efforts very efficient. Any questions? Alright then, to your duties Admirals, we act in one hour." The Knights of the Admiralty all bowed to him and Morgan before they left to organize their units.

Daniel moved to Morgan as the group broke up and hugged her fiercely.

"I am so relieved to see you back whole and healthy. Can I meet my niece and nephew before we go?"

When they reached the babies' room off of Morgan and Alec's chambers, they found the babies asleep. GranMay sat quietly as she watched them.

Morgan and Alec each lifted one of their children and kissed their little heads as they turned to Daniel.

"May we introduce your niece, Brya," she said, then Alec finished, "And your nephew, Kyan."

Daniel beamed as his arms were filled with both of the little ones. He studied them a few seconds then looked up at Morgan with a lifted eyebrow.

"They both bear the dragon Crest as well. So will they have magic as fierce as yours?"

"Yes, similar at least. They already have a considerable amount, which amplifies mine. Our connection is very strong, and the magic connects them to Alec uniquely as well."

"Yes, well, I plan to be an amazing uncle and have a special little connection of my own as I spoil the boogers out of these little cuties."

Morgan and Alec laughed as he kept talking to the babies about all he planned to do to spoil them.

When she felt the great anxiety building within her grandmother, she took her hand and pulled her out onto the terrace. She bonded with her and shared the confidence she had gained through her experiences with Valen and training with Nulian. GranMay was a little calmer with all that knowledge but still had a stern expression as she moved to lay her hand over Morgan's Crest.

"You do not need this encouragement anymore, but I promised to share this with you when I believed the time was right."

Morgan slid back into bonding with GranMay and followed her focus to a well-hidden memory. Her heart ached as she saw the face of her mother as she lay dying in her father's arms. She had used the last of her ebbing strength to encourage him.

"Do not worry, my mate. I know her power is great enough

and her spirit pure enough. Our family will help her find her way to the confidence she needs before she faces him. Oh, my love…I wish you could see how great she will be once she truly believes."

Morgan opened her eyes as her markings all burned on her skin, and her glow lit the terrace around them. GranMay smiled and nodded.

"That is exactly what your father hoped he would see in your eyes when you heard and felt your mother's confidence. Use it, my girl. Face this evil without hesitation and without an ounce of doubt in your heart. Give him no opportunity to hurt you by striking with all you are."

"I will not hesitate, and I will not hold back. He will feel the full brunt of everything the magic has entrusted me with. Thank you for sharing this. It was the perfect time."

THE TEAM which was to secure the release of the younglings was flown by minor dragons to the far end of the mountain range that curved around the back of the Arshek castle. Each minor dragon who carried a man also wore a harness fitted with egg bags and baskets for the hatchlings. There were three extra minor dragons to carry only the rescued cargo.

The men dismounted far from the castle and carried the sacks and some baskets with them through dense woods. The minor dragons held to await a signal to swoop into a field behind the castle and pick up the men and the younglings.

MORGAN SAT IN THE GAZEBO in the middle of the garden lawn with her legs crossed and her eyes closed as she reached out to Valen.

"*Are you free to talk, my friend?*"

"*Yes, my Lord celebrates his victory in recovering his daughter, my Lady,*" Valen answered.

"*Good for him, his distraction is to our advantage. We will come for you tonight, my friend. I need your final word. If I can release you from the hold of the darkness, will you and your brethren turn and fight against Harrick once we have freed your younglings?*"

"*I am very confident that all of the females will indeed turn if they can break free of the hold Harrick imposes on us with his magic. But I am afraid I can not speak for the males, my Lady. I have been unable to address them as I am holding a clutch and have not been taken to breed. I dare not use thought for fear of being overheard by Harrick.*"

"*That gives me great concern for the safety of the Chemerian dragons. I have asked that they use non-lethal force against your brethren as long as possible to give you the opportunity to fight against Harrick's hold as I fight against him. But if you feel the males will not turn, then I dare not ask them to hold their force against them. What do you think, Valen? Can you speak to them in flight, perhaps?*"

"*I ask that you give me that opportunity at least, my Lady. If they are not convinced, I will tell you immediately, and you can warn your brethren to give them no mercy and to protect themselves. I fear my breed will not survive this day if many of our males are lost.*"

"*Worry not, I know your breed will survive, my friend, I have no doubt.*"

She gave Valen a second to contemplate this and smiled as she felt the dragon's query.

"*How can you have no doubt, my Lady?*"

"There are others, Valen, many others, my friend. Now, ready yourselves and fight against his hold on you as hard as you can. I will see you soon. Good Luck!"

She rose and turned as Alec stepped forward to take her into a fierce embrace. As they held each other, she sent him love and calming feelings. He relaxed against her and gave a light laugh.

"How is it you are the one who is going to fight Harrick, yet you are comforting me?"

"It is a wife's job to keep her husband happy," she answered with mocking sincerity. He smiled and held her close to him with his face growing serious again.

"Promise me again that you will not take too much risk tonight. Say that you will not let yourself get so weakened that you can not escape if he is stronger than you anticipate. Just say you will come back to me, my love. I could not live without you."

"I promise that I will do my duty. If I fall, you will live for our children, my King. You will be a wonderful father and raise them to be strong with the magic so they can serve and protect our brethren. You promise me that."

Alec nodded, and they kissed before heading to board Menkar and Nulian. A few feet from Nulian, Morgan stopped and turned as she felt her children. GranMay and Emma had brought them down to the garden so she and Alec could see them once more before going.

She took Brya and Kyan into her arms and felt their love flow over her.

"I asked Queen May to bring them, my friend. Their power will strengthen you tonight. Bond with each of their spirits for a moment before you leave," Nulian said.

Morgan did so with pleasure. She let her spirit mingle with theirs and felt her Crest grow hot and tingle like mad. In the fading light of the day, she could see that all three of their Crests were glowing again, and she felt a wonderful surge of magic flowing within her.

It was as if someone had turned up her power level with a push of a button. She felt the tingle radiate through her and intensify. It centered in her scales which remained very hot and tingled even after she released her children.

"You will wield a great deal of power tonight, my Queen," Nulian said as she boarded.

MORGAN SAT WITH NULIAN atop a mountain about five miles from the Arshek castle. Her enhanced eyesight allowed her to watch the progression of the attack in the valley below.

She watched as the large battalion of the Arshek army headed east to meet the first wave of the Chemerian forces led by Alec and Daniel. She informed Alec as she realized the male Perian dragons were among that force.

She watched as Valen flew in between the males, trying her best to save them. Within a few minutes, the second wave of Chemerian forces, led by Maric and Burke, appeared far to the south and held in plain sight of the Arshek castle. As expected, another large battalion of Marocks and dragons filed out from the Arshek castle to meet this force.

Next, she reached out to Sir Urick, leader of the youngling rescue party waiting near the back of the castle, and told him to act. Less than four minutes later, she heard Urick's screams of terror just before his spirit went silent, he was dead.

"Let's go, Nulian. Urick's unit was attacked."

Nulian took off and flew just above the treetops.

"Tighten your defenses, my Sister. Keep him out of your mind as long as possible," Nulian said.

When they reached the castle, both saw the battle being fought within the dragon hold. Nulian made a quick move and dropped onto the metal cage covering the hold with a mighty crash. The noise startled the group of Marocks below her.

Morgan reached out with her magic and sent thoughts of confusion and orders of "Stop!" to the Marocks. It did not seem to hamper them much. Then she remembered how simple-minded they were and thought of what they feared. She sent images of great snakes of all sizes and colors and pushed hard against their minds.

Every one of them started roaring with terror as they slapped their bodies to remove the invisible snakes they felt all over them. She then sent an image of a wall of flames between them and the Chemerian Knights.

The Knights hurriedly removed the last of the eggs and the younglings small enough to handle. The larger younglings were refusing to go with them.

"If you want to be free with your mothers, then you must trust us. We will never force you to serve us, as Harrick does. Valen trusts me, and I offer you my friendship as well," she said as she sent them feelings of loving trust and samples of her love for Nulian and her special younglings. Nulian sent them her feelings as well. Given the choice of the Marocks or trusting them, they joined their younger brethren in the arms of the Chemerian Knights.

Morgan kept up the imaginary snake and fire assault on the Marocks until the Chemerian Knights overpowered them all. As the group of Knights moved into the woods, she felt fear from a youngling hidden under a table in the corner of the hold.

"Please come out and let us take you away, little one."

It hopped forward, and she saw it had a badly injured leg. It was Valen's youngling she had witnessed being beaten at Harrick's order. As she started to dismount, Nulian shifted to prevent it with a growl.

"We cannot leave him," Morgan said.

Nulian did not reply. She was looking toward the castle base. Morgan turned her head to see Harrick emerge from the castle just as the pain of his assault hit her. A hot searing pain in her head lasted only a second before she raised her guard.

Harrick moved forward to stand beneath them. She looked into his black eyes and smiled as she blocked almost all of the terrible force pushing on her. She pushed back into his mind and was overcoming his defenses as Nulian crouched in preparation to take off.

The same instant Nulian jumped, she clenched and let out a loud roar of agony. A long lance had just been plunged into her underbelly. She shuddered and fell limp under Morgan as they crashed back onto the cage, crushing it to a few feet above the hold floor. Harrick had been knocked to the ground and away from them.

Morgan peered into the evil face of Irika, who had wielded the lance. The wicked sneer of triumph on the woman's face turned to one of terror as Morgan sent her mind the strongest feelings of suffocation and emptiness she could. Irika dropped as she clutched at her throat and shook violently.

Morgan kept up the assault on Irika as she climbed down Nulian's side to her wing and then moved along it to the cage surface.

Harrick offered a weak counter to her attack on Irika. She split her efforts between the two of them while dropping to the hold floor under Nulian to inspect the wound.

The lance had gone very deep, puncturing a lung and piercing her heart. Morgan pulled the lance free, then shifted her focus to heal the wound. Seconds later, she was forced to stop healing and raise her guard against another strong attack from Harrick.

As she turned to face him, she lowered her guard in small steps while pushing with all her might. The strong surge of magic made her scales prickle and sent a fierce tingle over her body. Her magic grew stronger as her focus and conviction to end him sharpened.

The instant she formed a connection to him, the force of the cold darkness buckled her knees. He moved toward her as he murmured something and lifted his hands toward her head.

Sweat soaked her body as she reached for more from her magic. She soon felt it lead her again. Closing her eyes, she stacked her palms over her Crest and redirected a portion of her magic to let it build within her.

She let it build to the point her skin was numb with the searing tingle. Then, in one move, she dropped her guard away and pushed every ounce of her magic into Harrick's mind. She let out a roar of rage and got to her feet just as he staggered and stumbled to the ground.

She stood in front of him as she pushed further into his mind, focusing on the source of the darkness. At first, he glared and cursed her, but soon howled in pain and clutched his head. His power was fading fast, and he was trying to retreat further back into his mind.

As she stepped closer to him, she was knocked to the ground with white-hot pain searing through her shoulder.

DANIEL AND ALEC were positioned to the rear of the Knights' lines focused on the oncoming Arshek brigade. The dragon forces were fighting without riders to allow more aggressive maneuvering. As the Arshek Knights entered the river valley, Alec and Daniel called for full assault.

Chemerian dragons shot over their Knights to meet the Arshek dragons. The night was filled with the roars and screeches of dragons as the two forces collided. The Chemerian dragons were doing as their Queen had asked, injuring the Arshek dragons as little as possible to subdue them and protect their Knights.

"Yes! Look, Daniel! The Arshek dragons are holding," Alec called as he leapt atop a huge boulder.

"Not all! Get down!" Daniel yelled.

Alec looked up to see a huge Arshek male flying straight down at them. Daniel tackled him just as another dragon slammed into the Arshek male to knock it off course. Both dragons hit the ground with great speed. The vicious fight that ensued between the two made both Alec and Daniel stare in shock.

It had been an Arshek female who had saved them, and

she now faced a male twice her size. She fought with all she had but was no match for the huge Elder male. The male killed her, then spun with a roar at the Chemerian Guard. Alec told his unit to hold and looked into the Perian's rage-filled eyes as it lunged. He smiled as Gerzin and Menkar slammed into the Perian with a coordinated effort to kill him with precision.

"You must see this. It is a triumphant moment, my King," Menkar said as he proffered his leg.

The sight Alec took in was both gruesome and righteous. The Perian dragons had turned on the Arshek militia with intent to leave no man or Marock standing in their path. The Chemerian forces withdrew to stand as reserve while the Perian dragons served their just revenge for decades of torture.

Alec shivered from a profound chill that passed through him just as Menkar banked and put on a great burst of speed for home. He saw all of the Elder Chemerian and Perian dragons pulling away ahead of them and closed his eyes as his chest tightened.

MORGAN ROLLED OVER to find the lifeless face of Irika inches from her own. Nulian's head fell hard against the cage as a gurgling breath rushed from her lungs. The dragon had woken to act just as Irika approached Morgan with a dagger. The blow had slashed Irika's throat and broken her neck.

Nulian now lay near death with blood streaming from the wound in her chest. Morgan ran and hung from the bars by one arm and her feet to reach Nulian's underbelly near the wound. She pushed healing energy fast and furious as she disconnected from Harrick's mind.

The rate of dripping blood hitting the floor slowed as the healing progressed, and Nulian finally took a breath. Her dear dragon sister's breathing became steady just as her own body went ice cold.

She screamed as the darkness cut through her like a thousand knives. Harrick gripped her by the neck and shoulder to pull her off the bars, then slammed her into the ground. He roared with rage as he dropped on top of her and gripped her throat with both hands.

Her magic surged, allowing her mind to calm and focus. She refocused all of her power to her center as she thought of her children and her mate. Harrick hissed and trembled as his hands burned against her skin.

A sudden rush of physical strength allowed her to buck and throw the larger man off her. She quickly focused on the darkness in his mind again, then flooded him with the pure magic surging through her. He gasped for air and clutched his head again as he crawled away from her.

She moved fast and grabbed his head in her hands to initiate a connection. He let out a deep guttural roar as he grabbed her wrists and met her eyes. She attacked his spirit and felt it begin to crumble as his fight faded and his grip weakened.

Searing pain suddenly filled her entire body and ended her attack. She gasped and arched back with a piercing scream. Her vision darkened, her mind quieted, the cold of the darkness filled her, and she fell.

NULIAN SCREECHED and reached down to swipe at the boy holding the lance buried in Morgan's back, then picked up her Queen's limp body. She took to the air and flew with all her might toward the Chemerian castle. As she flew, she hummed the healing song to her precious friend while ignoring the severe pain she felt from her own injuries.

She called to the dragon Elders and requested they retreat to meet her back at the castle at once. A call went to Menkar to bring the King, and another to her dear mate to convey her deeper fear as she cradled Morgan to her chest and wept. As she tired and began to slow, Panish and Palish reached her.

Her brothers lifted her from underneath and carried her on their backs. She trembled against them as they all hummed their healing song.

As the twin dragons tired, they were replaced by two great Perian females, one of which was Valen. When they neared the castle, the Perians dropped away and let Nulian glide into a gentle landing.

Nulian dropped to the ground and laid Morgan beside her. Her brothers and the two Perian females were joined by Gerzin, Drieden, and four other Elders. All gathered into a tight circle and began to hum the song of healing together. The song grew loud and the overlay of the Chemerian and Perian versions mingled fluidly to create a complex melody that increased the rate of magical transfer for them all.

After a moment, Morgan's Crest began to emit a faint intermittent glow, but she had not taken a breath, and her heart was silent.

Menkar landed, and Alec ran full speed to the crowd of dragons. He crawled over and under the dragon's legs to reach Morgan, then froze. He could not breathe as he took in her white face and unfocused eyes. Feeling no pulse or breath, he looked to Nulian.

"Bring her children," Nulian said.

Alec hesitated then bolted to sprint into the castle and up to the babies' room as fast as his feet would take him. He scooped up the screaming children, put both in a smaller bassinet, and turned to head back with GranMay and Emma right on his heels. They did not ask any questions; his panic was explanation enough.

When Alec reached the garden, Drieden shifted to let him reach Morgan easily. GranMay followed and started to push healing energy.

"Lay them against the bare skin of her chest, on either side of her Crest," Nulian said.

Alec and Emma quickly undressed them, then he tore Morgan's jacket and shirt away. He placed each baby on its stomach, against her chest so their Crests were touching her skin.

He held his breath as he watched her Crest glow brighter and waited for her to breathe. One minute, two minutes. He was unable to keep the hot tears from falling down his face as he watched her lying there still and ashen.

"NO! You can not leave us!"

He took both of her hands and folded them to have his lying directly against her Crest and hers between his. He focused on her with all he had, and she gave a single small gasp. GranMay jumped back, shaking and holding her hands as they burned.

"Keep going, Alec. Your link with her and the children is the only way to help her," GranMay said with a sharp glance at Nulian as she laid back against Emma.

Nulian and the other Elders shifted to lay their snouts to Alec, and he joined their song. He felt the magic flow through him like a constant lightning bolt. It hurt everywhere, but he did not let go. He held on and focused on his love for her, willing his magic to help her. Her Crest began to glow more brightly. A few seconds later, she took a great gasp. His heart leapt as he felt hers beat in an uneven pattern beneath their hands.

Shallow, irregular breaths and erratic heartbeats continued for many minutes before she coughed and gurgled. He and GranMay supported the babies and rolled her to her side. Both cringed as blood poured from her mouth with each weak cough.

The amount of blood on the ground beneath her made the severity of her injury clear. Tears filled Alec's eyes as he took her hands again.

"Can I give her my life force, Nulian? Can you help me?"

When Nulian shook her head without breaking the humming, he focused on pushing his magic to Morgan as the dragons laid their snouts to him again. He gritted his teeth and growled as the painful transfer returned. It helped. Her breathing became more regular, and her color improved a bit as her heart rhythm stabilized.

Only a moment later, his pain vanished as Nulian and the others stopped humming.

"What are you doing?"

"We have healed the wound as best we can. There is no more we can do for her now. Her spirit is strong, and with the help of her children, she should pull through, my King," Nulian said through labored pants. GranMay moved to her to take her pain.

"What do you mean that is all you can do?" Alec shouted as he looked to the Elders around him. "Keep going! Make her strong again!"

Gerzin hummed as he nudged Nulian to quiet her response, then touched his snout to Alec with a deep hum to push respect with his magic.

"Like you, my King, we would give her all of our life force if we could. But our power to heal is limited. We will give her more energy later when it will help her, I promise you. For now, her body must regenerate the blood she has lost. Her greater struggle we can not help with at all. She alone must fight the darkness that holds her mind."

Alec scooped the children off of Morgan and glared at Gerzin and Nulian.

"Will it harm them?"

"Not unless they are connected," Nulian said. "The children cannot initiate a connection on their own yet. But, their magic will help her heal faster when they are in contact with her. Please, place them back against her, my King."

With the children removed, Morgan had stopped breathing. Alec laid them back on her chest and watched as her Crest glowed and her shallow breathing returned. Her glow was still weak as compared to her normal radiance when touching them.

Alec wrapped her and the children with a blanket, then carried his family in his arms through the castle to their chambers. He, GranMay, and Emma worked together to remove her clothes and wash her down. As the others to steadied the babies, he rolled her to clean her back.

When he pulled her clothes away, he swallowed hard. There was still a substantial flesh wound where the lance had entered her. Queen May and the dragons had healed the inside and stopped the bleeding, but their healing power was not that of hers, for certain.

"Queen May, can you heal this any further?"

GranMay shifted and looked at the wound with a deep scowl. She passed healing energy until she fell weak again. The wound was better, but still open and painful.

"The dark magic blocks me. I will try again when my strength returns."

Alec nodded as he cleaned her back and cringed when she tightened or flinched. He dressed the remainder of the jagged puncture wound and the gash to her shoulder, then laid her back over so the babies could lie against her.

He, GranMay, and Emma paced for hours, taking the babies from her chest only to feed them a bottle of goat's milk or to change them.

When Morgan began to mutter in her sleep and toss her head, they worried she would jerk suddenly. They took turns sitting to her sides and keeping a hand on the babies.

The rest of the family had gathered in the large receiving room off their chambers. Daniel and Maric relieved Gran-May and Emma against their protests. Burke tried to relieve Alec, but he would not leave. Burke stayed to help anyway.

Alec saw tears rolling down Daniel's face and pulled him into a strong embrace.

"She prepared so much for this … I should have been with her … what happened?" Daniel asked.

Alec shared all he had learned from Nulian.

MORGAN DEVELOPED A HIGH FEVER in the night, and her muttering worsened. They watched as she struggled through the next day and night. She would mutter and toss her head while grimacing and scowling. The wound in her back was still painful, making her arch off the bed and moan often. She was drenched with sweat, though her skin remained cold to the touch.

Alec and Daniel carried her to the terrace so the dragons could share their magic with her every few hours. After several days, her overall state had not improved.

On the fifth day, Alec awoke to GranMay patting his arm. She insisted he go speak with Nulian and the other Elders to get more information about what happened and what they might do to help her.

He kissed Morgan and the children, then walked with Daniel out to the garden where all the Elder dragons still waited, standing vigil.

"Is there anything more we can do for her, Nulian? She does not seem to be improving. Morgan told me once that it was possible for someone to take your life force during bonding. Is it possible to give life force that way as well?"

"As Queen May well knows, only magic as strong as a Caretaker's can enter into bonding deep enough to give or take life force, my King. Others can only share through a Caretaker."

"Oh, No!" Daniel yelled as he bolted back toward the castle. Alec quickly realized what he was thinking and followed.

They entered the room to find GranMay holding Morgan's hands palm-to-palm with her eyes closed. Emma and Maric stood near the window, unaware of her intentions.

GranMay had moved the babies to the bassinets and was now slumped over Morgan's chest. Daniel grabbed her hands to wrench them free, then carried her to a sofa to check her.

"She is still alive, but her breathing is very shallow."

Alec laid Brya on Morgan, then laid Kyan onto Gran-May's chest. He hoped the magic of the child would help her. Once GranMay's breathing had improved, he moved his son to Morgan's chest to lie by his sister and sat with them.

GranMay woke and stood to face Daniel with tears flowing from angry eyes.

"Morgan would never have forgiven us for letting you do that, GranMay," Daniel said.

GranMay stepped forward and grabbed him by the shirt as she trembled.

"Her life is far more important than mine! If she is not well by tonight, I will do it. And you will not interfere! I am a former Queen, and do not take orders from an Admiral!"

GranMay shoved him away from her and left the room. Daniel watched her go, then rubbed his face and sighed as he moved to sit beside Alec.

"I have never seen her mad, much less had her be physical like that. She truly intends to give her life to Morgan, having no idea if it will help. Alec, we must find another answer."

Alec nodded then went to Nulian when she called from the terrace.

"My King, Valen tells me there is a special skill the Perian dragons have in healing that may help and offers herself as martyr," Nulian said.

"As martyr?"

Nulian looked to Valen, who bowed to him before speaking.

"The strongest among us can take the suffering of others into themselves. If it is too great, they will die. I ask to do this for the Caretaker. I owe her my life and the lives of all my young," Valen said. Alec looked at her and Nulian as he shook his head.

"Do you honestly think Morgan would ever allow a dragon to give its life for hers? How can you ask such a thing?"

Nulian growled and swung her head away as she snorted in frustration.

"I am worried there may be no other way, my King. If I had the skill, I would do it and would not ask! They are asking to give their life for the Queen they now consider their own. It is an honorable thing they do, and I do not think they should be denied."

"She would never forgive us, my friend. You know her heart. If we allowed a dragon to give its life to save hers, she would never be able to live with it," Alec said as his eyes filled with tears.

"But she may not live without it, my King. I will take the blame and let her place her hate on me. I would rather her hate me than lose her," Nulian said as she laid her snout to him.

Daniel had come up behind Alec and now cleared his throat to interrupt.

"I think you need to come in here."

Alec hurried inside to find his infant children humming to their mother along with Zirath. The hatchling had laid himself over the scales of her Crest and wrapped his wings over the twins.

He and the rest of the family gathered around the bed

and watched Morgan's body relax as her breaths became slow and steady. After only a few minutes, her Crest began to glow brighter under Zirath.

An hour later, Zirath stopped humming, nuzzled both twins, and shifted to Alec's lap, exhausted.

"She has defeated the darkness holding her and is strong enough to wake, my King."

Alec caressed Zirath and cradled him close as he reached over to slide a finger over the scales of Morgan's Crest. She shivered and drew a deep breath, then smiled and hummed a bit as she turned her head toward him.

"All of our children are precious," she muttered, before falling back to sleep.

Alec rose and went out to the terrace to give Nulian the news. Everyone jumped as Nulian and all of the dragons around the castle roared in celebration.

"That is a sight I will never forget," Alec said to Maric as he watched the silhouettes of both Chemerian and Perian dragons celebrating their Queen together.

"DO YOU REMEMBER the struggle, or breaking free of the darkness, my Sister?" Nulian asked Morgan late that night as Alec and the children slept.

"Yes, I will share it all with you later." She stared into Nulian's eyes as she deepened their connection. "My escape from the darkness was possible because the boy chose the wrong weapon. The lance was covered in your blood. It gave me the strength to act when Zirath and the children reached me. Zirath pushed his love along with thoughts of you and Balia. Your gift responded to crush the remaining darkness holding me. I owe you my life, my Sister."

She caressed and kissed Nulian's snout then gave her a push.

"Please go sleep, my dear. I promise not to get in trouble until you wake. After that, all bets are off, of course."

She laughed as Nulian nudged her with a little snort, then pushed love and devotion as she flew away.

An hour later, she was still staring into the dark night as Alec woke and headed her way.

"What is keeping you awake, my love?" Alec asked as he wrapped her from behind and kissed her cheek.

"I can't find him."

"Perhaps you did succeed after all and he is dead."

"No. I destroyed most of the darkness within him, but not all. The boy struck just as I was at the point of ending him. He is alive."

"So, he now carries so little magic that you can not feel it from this distance. That is a fabulous victory, my dear." He turned her to face him and smiled. "The tyranny of the Sons of Arshek is broken. The dragons enslaved for centuries are free. Our country is safe and filled with joy. It is time you let yourself feel the tremendous pride you deserve, my Queen."

She blushed and patted his chest, then smiled as she headed inside just before both children woke and started to fuss. They gathered up the little ones and returned to the terrace to snuggle together on a lounge.

"As difficult as getting to this moment has been at times, I feel nothing but grateful for all the magic has given us. We are so blessed," she said.

"I am, for certain," he said as he shifted to kiss her and

smile as he caressed her face. She laughed as she looked down at Kyan who was clapping his hands.

"Let us hope we are both blessed with parenting skills because our children are already using their magic to make demands." She switched to take Kyan from him and sat up to feed him. "Our boy has been badgering me with nudges since you picked him up."

A minute later, she lifted an eyebrow and looked over at Brya.

"What is it?" Alec asked before jumping with the sudden arrival of Zirath and his siblings, who piled onto the lounge around him to croon and tickle Brya. "Did she just call them?"

"Yes, she did."

"I was going to ask if you thought they were growing rather fast. Their magic clearly is."

"I was hoping I was wrong, but I think we are past denial. Our babies will not be babies for very long, my dear."

"Which could mean you are meant to face something profound far sooner than my heart wants to consider."

They were both quiet as she fed both of the children and laid them on the lounge to play with the hatchlings. Alec leaned over to kiss her shoulder and nudged her with his magic. She sighed, then quickly forced a smile as the children went still and looked at her. She blocked them from her emotions and tickled them until they returned to playing, then pulled her hands back.

"The hard truth is that I now understand my destiny is to face many far more difficult tasks than bringing an end to the tyranny of Arshek. The magic I carry, and the skills

I now have to wield it, have a purpose. I am not meant to sit back and be safe. I am meant to fight the darkness, to serve and protect by bringing all I have been blessed with to bear against what awaits us. I understand and accept that. Now, it is time for you and the rest of our brethren to accept that too."

He took a slow deep breath and shifted to look into her eyes as he pushed to deepen their connection.

"I did not argue when you insisted on going so near Harrick because I do understand that truth, my love. While I will never accept standing back when I can help, I am well aware that my skills with a sword will be useless against those that wield darkness as their weapon. It is very difficult to accept that you and our children are meant to face such evil, but you will not find doubt lingering within me, my dear. I am both confident and proud of all you are today, and all you will be.

"All of your human and dragon brethren know that they serve a truly powerful Queen. None will balk at learning a new way to serve you. We will clear your path, we will fight at your side, and then, when we can offer no more, we will hold to our faith in the wisdom of the magic you carry and in your remarkable skill in wielding it. Your Chemerian family loves you dearly, my Caretaker. Trust in us, as we trust in you." ⬡

Continue the adventures of the Caretaker in

THE BOOK OF THE CARETAKER
BOOK 2

One Magic

BOOK 2
EXCERPT

Kalias

MORGAN AND TARU both flinched at the roaring of dragons the instant they appeared on Kalias. Both women pushed against Panish's side as they used their magic to take in their surroundings.

"Well, it could not have been too much worse than this. We are trapped with a large angry group of dragons who will likely wish to kill us on sight. Lovely," Morgan said as they all moved off the portal.

They now stood in a pitch-black cavern in the bowels of the Ceruk castle dragon hold. Even with their dragon-sight, the cavern had barely enough light to see each other.

"We must hide our dragon markings. To get out, we must wait until the dragons are needed for battle," Taru said.

"You two can surely get out through the bars of a gate, my Queen," Panish said.

"No, we will not leave you here," Morgan said.

"You will save yourself, my Queen!" Panish said as he gave her a sharp glare. *"You must return to Chemerie to care for our brethren. I am of no consequence in that matter."*

Morgan nodded as she felt his anger, conviction, and the grief driving both. She pushed love and devotion as he moved to the opening of the cavern to peer down the tunnel in both directions.

"I feel over a dozen dragons nearby. Can you tell the number within the hold, my Queen?"

"Oh yes, I feel them alright. I have found thirty-one dragons filled with hate for humans of all kinds. We will need patience and a great deal of luck to reach the gates." She looked over the great Elder dragon and patted his shoulder. *"Can you hide us under your wings?"*

Panish raised his wings a bit to let them climb up and lie along the main bone of his wing. He looked odd with the extra bulk, but given his size, it was not too noticeable.

He moved at a slow pace through the tunnels as Morgan guided him to miss the other dragons for as long as possible. When they could avoid them no longer, Panish tucked his wings a bit tighter and took a deep breath. He growled low in his chest as he approached a small group of females.

The female dragons moved to the side and crouched lower to the ground as they watched him. He growled constantly to let them know he was in no mood to be tested as he moved past.

His successful intimidation ended as he rounded a corner to face a massive battle-scarred male near his own size. Panish side-stepped to flank the Elder male and dropped his head to show submissiveness in hopes of moving by unchallenged.

The Elder ignored him until he side-stepped into another male who emerged from a small tunnel. The smaller male growled and reared to strike. Panish made a quick shift back to protect the women under his wings. That move encouraged the Elder male to advance on him.

"Fight, Panish! We will hold on," Morgan said.

Panish reared and struck the attacking Elder with a great roar and pushed him hard with his chest. He knocked the male over and stepped on his neck while growling. The Elder went still as he felt Panish's teeth against the tender underside of his neck.

Morgan's heart ached as she felt fear and pain from the trapped dragon. That compassion turned to fear as his roar brought more males into the cavern to surround them.

"When I engage them, run, my Queen," Panish said as he held off their attackers.

"Wait!" Morgan said. *"If you try to fight, they discover us while enraged, and we are all dead."*

"That feels inevitable at the moment," Taru said as growls rattled their bones.

Morgan blocked Panish and slid to the edge of his wing with a hard look at Taru.

"Hold, but be ready to bolt, my Sister."

Morgan dodged Taru's attempt to grab her and dropped to the cavern floor. There were many hisses as the crowd spotted her.

Panish crouched low next to her. She focused her gaze on the injured Elder snarling at her.

"I want only to heal your wounds. I will not hurt you, I pr—"

The dragon lurched to bite her, but went limp as Panish struck to end him. Morgan backed up to Panish and climbed to his back. Taru followed, and another round of hisses broke out. Panish turned as he swung his tail and snarled with bared teeth.

"Bold attempt, but hardly helpful, my Queen," Panish said.

"Agreed!" Taru said.

"Either of you have a better idea?" Morgan snapped.

"Daniel spoke of you using suggestion to control the minds of others. Can you do that to dragons?" Taru asked.

"Doubt it. They are far too intelligent. But I'll try," Morgan said as she connected to the minds of all the dragons around them. *"Rest, you are very tired. Lie down and rest."*

The cavern went silent, but the dragons around them did not lie down. They looked at each other, and her, with obvious shock.

"I am a friend," she said aloud in dragon-tongue. "We are not the cruel people of Ceruk. We do not wish to hurt you. My friend only killed to protect me. He loves me, as I do him."

"Hold your lies, Human! We will hear none of it. The lies of humans have led us to evil deeds too many times," the largest male present said.

"Have you ever known a human you could trust?" Morgan asked.

"No, not one! They use us for our ability to fight and control us with their power of mind. They feel nothing for us. We are only animals to them."

"Then I feel very sorry for you," Panish said. "You have known only the lowest form of human possible. I have been blessed to live among kind and loving humans who mean as much to me as my dragon brethren. I will die for this woman because I love her, not because she controls me. She would never ask me to do anything that I did not wish to. You may choose not to believe me, but you can let her show you and judge for yourself. Or, are you so afraid of the magic that you would not allow it?"

Many growled at his accusation of fear and advanced toward him. A second later, they all quieted and moved back. A great Elder female moved into the chamber and to the body of the slain male dragon. All of the males moved further back and bowed their heads to their Eldest Female.

The enraged female raised her head slowly and moved toward Panish with her body low in an attack position as she growled and snarled.

"I do not know you, dragon. You are not of this family. You have slain my brother. I will now take your life in return. If you wish your humans to have any chance of survival, I suggest you put them aside," the Eldest Female said as she circled Panish, and he moved to keep his head between her and Morgan.

"My Elder, he only killed to protect me," Morgan said. "Please, consider his reasoning. Your brother was injured. I wanted to heal his wounds, but he chose to strike at me before hearing my words." After many seconds of being ignored, she took a bolder tone. "I would expect the Eldest Female to have more self-control and use her intellect before her brawn."

The Eldest Female stopped and glared at her before raising her head and sitting down.

"You ask for thoughtful consideration and trust when you have drawn first blood. Why would we trust the word of an outsider who has just slain our kin?" the Eldest Female asked as she turned her glare on Panish. "You say you love this human, and claim she loves you. I have heard of this only in ancient fables of the old world. I do not believe it possible given what I have seen. But, I admit that I hear sincerity in your words."

The Eldest Female stared at Panish for a long moment in silence, then looked to Morgan again.

"Show me what you will, Human. However, do not touch me!"

Morgan focused on the Eldest Female's spirit to connect to her.

"If I push through your defenses by force, I will cause you pain. You must allow me to connect with you by choice, or I cannot share with you. Will you drop your defenses, please?" Morgan said. The dragon hesitated then gave a small nod.

Morgan focused again and found she had dropped them halfway. It was enough for her to share information, but nothing more.

First, she sent all she felt for Panish as she worked to save his life, then shared his loving response. She sent her love for Nulian, the last words they shared, and the intense rush of love she received from her just before falling through the portal. When she opened her eyes, she saw a look of complete bewilderment on the Eldest Female's face.

"You traveled to our world from another through the great portal below? From where did you come?"

"An ancient home of the dragon. We are trying to get to a second portal on this world, so we may go to our homeworld."

"What is the name of your homeworld?"

"I do not think you should be honest, my Queen," Taru said only to Morgan. *"These dragons are not to be trusted."*

Morgan shifted to look at Taru and shook her head as she spoke aloud.

"We must think of the future, not the past. If they are to be our friends in the end, we cannot start with lies," she said as she gripped Taru's hand to push reassurance. She turned back to the Eldest Female, who was studying Taru.

"My blood-sister does not wish for me to tell you the truth because she grew up here, on Kalias, fearing you. She has great love for dragons, but also has profound memories of the carnage your breed has done to humans here. I wish to look to the future, and the hope that we can become friends. Feel the truth in my words through our connection as I say that we are from Erion, home of the children of Puria."

The room filled with growls. The Eldest Female quieted them with an angry roar, then stepped closer to Panish. He turned to protect Morgan from a quick lunge. The Eldest Female gave him another harsh look, then addressed Morgan again.

"I have heard that name in old fables, but know very little of its significance. How can we possibly believe you human? What proof do you have of this great love for the dragon? How do we know you are not controlling your mount as the Ceruk control us when they wish us to kill for them?"

"Do you believe a dragon can be forced to share magic with a human?" Morgan asked.

"Never!" the Eldest Female said among many hisses and growls from those around them. "Forceful sharing would never be possible! No dragon would give magic to a human.

No human is worthy of that trust or power."

"What would it mean to you if a dragon did share magic with a human?"

The Eldest Female did not answer at first. She looked to many of the Elder males and females in the crowd as she conferred with them in thought.

"It would mean there are pure-spirited humans, and we have never met one. We are not likely to believe that. Humans have never proven themselves worthy of trust so deep, nor love so profound."

"I have shown you the love I have for this dragon and for his sister. In fact, his sister is my dearest friend. It was she who gave me her blood and her Heraldic Crest," Morgan said as she untied her wrap and allowed it to fall open to reveal the scales and markings on her chest.

The entire chamber went silent. The Eldest Female shimmied forward to see it, but Panish stopped her with a low growl. Morgan placed her hand to Panish, which made her Crest glow brightly.

The Eldest Female stepped back and arched her neck at the sight of the glowing Crest while many around her dropped low to the ground.

"I have never seen such a marking. I believe I have just met a race of humans unlike any on this planet," the Eldest Female said in a respectful tone.

"No, you have not!" Taru shouted as her entire body trembled. "There are many humans of pure spirit on this planet. They are my people, and we are also capable of profound love for a dragon." She was sweating, and her entire body was very hot as her magic surged. Despite her fury, she thought to freeze the water on her skin, cooling herself as she continued. "I was raised among dragons here. They were my family, and I loved them dearly. I too was given the gift of blood by my dragon father before he died." She opened her cloak and let them see the scale lines along her clavicle and sternum. She was fighting tears as she spoke but held herself together.

"Your Dragon Markings do not glow as does the other. Why is that?"

Taru tensed and stayed silent for a moment. Morgan was proud she chose to give an honest answer despite the possible response.

"I received blood from a Perian dragon, not an Alerian."

The cave filled with growls again. The Eldest Female did not hush them as her face darkened.

"I should kill you where you sit! Perians have taken the lives of too many of our kind to forgive. If you carry their blood, then you carry that burden," the Eldest Female said as she took an aggressive stance.

"You will have to kill me first," Panish said as he matched her fighting posture. "I will die for her because I have felt her spirit and know it to be pure and beautiful. I do not care what the dragons have done to each other on this world. I know all dragons are pure of spirit, and I know that both of the women on my back have love for all dragons of all breeds." He growled and moved sideways away from the female as she stepped forward. "You will be surprised to know that the woman you just threatened to kill has intentions of saving your brethren from the Ceruk, for no reason beyond her faith in the purity of your spirits." The female growled in return and swung her head in frustration.

"This talk of love for humans makes me think you are indeed controlled by them. Clearly, their control is great if they forced an Elder to give them the gift of blo—"

Panish cut her off as he rose up to his full height and roared with rage before speaking in a booming voice that rattled Morgan and Taru to the bone.

"You should be ashamed for being so narrow-minded and ignorant of your heritage! Have you no ancient knowledge that shows you the true nature of the bond between humans and dragons? Do you know nothing of the day of Puria, when all humans wore the Heraldic Crest of their dragon family?"

The Elder Female dropped her head and backed up a few paces as her anger faded.

"Most of our knowledge has been lost through many decades of magical torture and control. Our knowledge of the old days and the old ways is limited, existing only as untrustworthy fables," she said. Panish calmed and softened his tone as he stepped closer to her.

"My Queen can share much with you, if only you will let her. What is there to lose in the gain of knowledge?"

"Do you know of our ancestors here on Kalias? Do you actually know of our lineage?" the female asked Morgan.

"I have a great deal of knowledge of your lineage because your line is the same as the blood within us," Morgan said as she caressed Panish's neck. "Puria was of Kalias. She traveled to Erion with a few others. Their blood is within both an Alerian and a Perian line on Erion. I will gladly share the details I carry. Perhaps that information will convince you that we are worthy of your trust. However, you will have to show some trust in order to receive the information. I will need to touch you to bond deep enough for such a transfer."

The Elder Female nodded as she settled to the floor. Morgan started to dismount, but stopped halfway and remounted.

"I feel the distrust within you, and a bit of deceit as well," Morgan said. "You intend to take me away from Panish to question me in private. That is not acceptable."

Looks of shock were exchanged between the dragons around them.

"I had no idea you could hear my thoughts. It is true, I do not feel trust for you as yet, and your mount makes me … uncomfortable," the Eldest Female said as she shot Panish another sharp glance.

"She makes me anxious as well. She is quite … large, my Queen," Panish said only to Morgan. She lifted an eyebrow and fought to not smirk as she felt Panish's profound attraction for the fierce female. ◆